ANACHRONIST

INFINITY ENGINES BOOK I

ANDREW HASTIE

To my beautiful wife and daughters, thanks for putting up with my obsession.

To Steve and all the things you never got to do.

A x

1

GO FASTER

[London, UK. Date: 2011]

They were racing at over a one hundred miles per hour, weaving through the traffic like it was standing still. Everything was a blur except for the car in front. He focused on nothing else but overtaking it. In the passenger seat next to him, someone was shouting, 'FASTER! GO FASTER. YOU CAN TAKE HIM!' and he knew that he could. He cranked up the volume on the stereo.

> *You won't see it coming*
> *The power builds inside*
> *Motion taking over*

Josh felt his pulse racing to the beat as he dropped down into fourth gear and pressed the accelerator to the floor. The steering wheel juddered slightly as he veered too close to the central reservation; he fed the wheel back through his hands and knifed between a car and a lorry that were going so slowly they might as well have been parked.

Gossy was in a Porsche in front, driving like a demon. Josh watched him swerve round another slow driver and had to brake and dodge just to avoid slamming into the back of him.

'PUSH IT! HE'S GOING TO BEAT US!' screamed the passenger.

Moving out into the night
Taking on the world
At the speed of light

Up ahead Josh knew the road would narrow into two lanes. He had one chance to overtake his friend before the traffic became too congested to race.

Then Gossy took the next bend too wide, and Josh saw his opportunity and took it. His friend anticipated the move and pulled across to block him, but Josh wasn't about to back off, and their bumpers connected.

Time slowed as he watched his friend's car swerve into the central reservation. The speed of the impact caused the car to take off and spin end over end into the oncoming traffic. Glass and metal cascaded across the tarmac as it collided with other vehicles, reducing it to a battered metal shell.

'Josh!' screamed his passenger.

He looked back at the road ahead to see the rear end of a lorry rushing towards them. His feet pumped the brakes, but the car was moving too fast. It skidded, and Josh felt the seat belt bite into his shoulder as he lost control. The last thing he saw was the time on the dashboard — 12:24.

'I've got you,' said a voice somewhere beyond the darkness and the pain.

COMMUNITY SERVICE

[London, UK. Date: 2016]

Two schoolboys sat on a bench watching the brightly coloured 'Community Payback' team cutting down the overgrown bushes on the other side of the park. The boys should have been well on their way to school by now, but had taken a detour so they could have a quick smoke and watch the local gangsters being punished.

Matt, who was the younger of the two at twelve, was fascinated by the older boys, some of whom had stripped off their jackets and T-shirts to show off their muscles and gang tattoos: each had a different collection of designs, but all of them had a black skull over their heart.

'So are they really dangerous?' he asked James, his older brother.

'Yeah. They're part of Ghost Squad — see the tattoo over the heart?' answered James, taking a quick drag on the cigarette. He coughed as the smoke hit the back of his throat. Fighting back the urge to throw up, he passed the butt to Matt.

'One of them's a killer.'

'Which one?' whispered Matt, carefully studying each of the gang in turn as he took a drag on the cigarette.

James nodded towards a tall boy with blond hair who was working slightly apart from the others. He was hacking away at a bush with a machete as if it were his worst enemy.

'The loner. His name's Josh, but they call him "Crash" because he killed a kid with a car he stole.'

'Did he go to prison?'

'No. Lenin sorted it.' James tried to sound as if he knew the leader of the Ghost Squad personally. 'They're both from the Bevin estate. They've known each other all their lives.'

Matt threw the cigarette on the ground and stamped it out under the sole of his shoe.

'I don't want to end up like that,' he said, standing up.

'It's all about choices, bro.' James stood too, picking up his school bag. 'Just remember that next time you're thinking of bunking off.'

The loner had got his machete stuck in the trunk of the bush. He left it there while he took a drink. Wiping his mouth with his sleeve, he looked around the park.

'I think we should go,' said Matt nervously.

'Yeah.'

Time was running out for Joshua Jones.

He'd had five days to pay back Lenin, his mum's dealer, and had wasted four of them cutting back bushes in Churchill Park. There was nothing left to sell other than the TV, which was the only thing that kept his housebound mother from going insane.

Josh tried to free the machete from the trunk of the stupid bush, but it wouldn't budge. It was like that with his life right now — nothing was going right for him. He just needed a break, for fate or destiny or whatever it was that kept giving him the shitty end of the stick — to just look the other way and deal out some good luck. He'd spent the last few days trying to think of a scheme that would make him a quick £3,000, but his options were limited: cars, bikes, phones — they were all risky, and he couldn't afford to get caught again. This was his 'last life', as his offender manager had pointed out: the next offence would end up with him getting locked up for real — prison time — and he couldn't bear the thought of leaving his mum on her own, not in her condition.

A month ago he had been caught in someone's shed. It was supposed to have been a quick job, a couple of mountain bikes worth at least £2,000 each. It had been a stupid, spur-of-the-moment thing, which his mate Billy had said they could split fifty-fifty. But Josh should have known better than to trust Billy; he wasn't the sharpest tool in the box and hadn't scoped it out properly. There'd been a dog, a big one, and it had taken a chunk of Billy's backside and trapped Josh inside the shed until the police arrived.

He could tell the owners weren't that impressed when they discovered he was on first-name terms with the cops who showed up.

At least they knew not to call his mum.

The blade refused to budge.

The morning sun had reached his end of the park, and it was getting warm — sweat had begun to trickle down his back. The kit they issued for community work was too cold in winter and too hot in summer, but he wasn't about to take his top off like the others — he had his reasons, and the lack of tattoos was only one of them.

Josh gave up and stood back to review his work. The bush was definitely winning. It showed little evidence of his attempts to tame it while he was covered in scratches. Turning round, he saw that the other members of the crew were all sitting on the grass, smoking and playing with their phones. There was a mixture of newbies and old-timers — mostly from Lenin's gang — all paying for some stupid mistake. Josh had been here many times; he didn't try to make friends or swap stories any more — he just kept his head down and let his reputation do the work for him.

Their supervisor, Mr Bell, or 'Bell-end' as they all liked to call him, was talking to one of the yummy mummies over by the kids' playground. It was a beautiful autumn morning, and Churchill Park was filling up with young families enjoying the last of the good weather. The Salvation Army was out tidying up the flowerbeds around the war memorial in preparation for VE Day, which seemed a bit pointless. After seventy years he doubted there would be many actual veterans left to turn out for it.

It was an old Victorian square; a park surrounded on three sides by large houses, the kind of homes his mother dreamed of — beautiful old three-storey townhouses with big bay windows, spacious rooms and long gardens. A far cry from the fifth-floor flat the council had given them.

Still, he knew this park well — it had been one of his favourite routes to school. He'd explored every part of it: where the gaps in the railings were for a quick exit, the hidden places where the junkies left their stashes of used needles and the dense shrubberies that made perfect hide-outs for when you wanted to bunk off lessons, which was ironically the main reason the council had ordered them to be chopped back.

It also happened to overlook the road where the local crazy man lived.

'The Colonel', as the kids had nicknamed him, lived at no. 42. It was an easy house to spot as the unkempt jungle of a front garden stood out like a festering thumb compared to all the other neatly manicured hedges along the rest of the street. The man was something of a hoarder — his house and gardens were packed with all manner of junk. No one really knew if he was ex-military, but the nickname came from the dark green army greatcoats he would wear in all weathers. He was something of a local legend and his house, an eyesore for his long-suffering neighbours, was an inevitable draw for the local kids when it came to dares.

Suddenly, as if he'd summoned the old man, the colonel appeared at his front door, his long coat catching on a stack of metal pots and pans and sending them clattering down the steps. His appearance was as disorganised as his house, his hair its usual matted mess and his beard looked like things were living in it. If you met him on the street, you'd think he was homeless, not the owner of a house on one of the most expensive streets in town.

The colonel muttered to himself as he consulted an old fob watch, shook it and looked up at the sky, like a ship's navigator checking the position of the sun. He put the watch away, pulled out a tatty old notebook and took a pencil from behind his ear. Licking his finger, he flicked through the book until he found the relevant page and hastily scribbled something onto it. As he closed the book, it seemed to disappear, like a magic trick. Flicking his long scarf over his shoulder, he marched down the steps to the front gate, took a moment to decide which way to go and then marched off down the street with an old lady's wheeled shopping bag clattering along behind him.

The front door swung back on its hinges unnoticed by the old man as he disappeared round the corner.

Josh knew he'd never get a better opportunity; it was too good a chance to pass up. He whistled to the gang sitting on the grass and one of them, the most junior by the look of his tattoos, eventually got up and sauntered over.

'Whatsup, Crash?'

Josh put his foot against the tree, yanked the blade out and handed it to the kid.

'I need to disappear for five minutes. You need to be me.' He took off his hi-vis jacket and threw it at the younger boy. 'Put this on and go work in the bush. Bell-end won't notice you're missing.'

Thirty seconds later, Josh was through the nearest gap in the railings and out onto the street.

As a kid, he had sat and watched the colonel's house for hours. It had always fascinated him — not because of the usual playground nonsense about how the old man kept children in the basement or ate the local cats, but because there was something different about it. He couldn't put his finger on what it was exactly, a kind of feeling that it was special — like a mystery or a secret. The hairs stood up on the back of his neck whenever he walked past it. Other kids had dared to go into the house (the colonel was notorious for forgetting to lock his doors) and reported that it was full of newspapers and smelt of urine; Josh doubted anyone had ever had the guts to venture further than a few steps into the hall.

Sixty seconds later he was through the front door of No. 42. He closed it gently and let his eyes adjust to the dim light of the hall. The others were wrong about the smell; it was a mixture of mildew, dust and decaying things, like a house that had never been cleaned, or the inside of a tomb.

His body tingled all over with pins and needles, as if the house were electrified.

The pale light of the sun failed against the gloom of the hall, turned away like an unwelcome guest. Josh paused to listen for sounds of anyone else in the house, but there were none.

The hallway was narrower than he expected, stacks of old newspapers were piled up to the ceiling along both sides. As he moved along, he spotted the remnants of old pieces of furniture poking out through the paper. Small manila envelopes with long numbers scrawled on them were tucked in random points along the stacks. There was no doubt that the old man had a problem with throwing stuff away — he was a first-class hoarder. Josh estimated there were literally thousands of editions of *The Times* crammed along the walls.

The stairs had received a similar treatment; each step had become another shelf brimming with old books, leaving only the smallest of pathways up through the stacks. He had considered trying upstairs — small valuable stuff tended to be kept in bedrooms — but the cluttered staircase would make it slow going and time wasn't on his side. So instead he continued down the hall towards the back of the house, scanning the cluttered shelves for anything that would fit in his pocket.

There was something weird about the way old people collected so much stuff. His grandfather used to have a shed at the bottom of his garden packed with jam jars full of various-sized nuts, bolts and bits from old TVs. Josh had never understood what the point of keeping it was — Grandad never used any of them, but he would spend every spare moment in that shed taking something apart and storing the various components in their relevant jars. His nan used to call them his 'dust collectors'.

A Welsh dresser had been squeezed into the space under the stairs. Its shelves had been reinforced with large metal nails to hold the weight of all the battered old tins that sat precariously on them. There were square metal boxes with faded images of tea plantations or Bisto gravy logos; each was crammed full of random things. His eye caught the unmistakable glint of gold from the top of one marked 'Valkyrie 44'. Josh tentatively lifted the golden object, careful not to disturb any of the surrounding clutter. It was a medal from World War II; the writing round the edges looked like German, and it was heavy, the kind of heavy that spoke of quality. It probably wouldn't pay off the whole debt, but it would definitely be enough to get Lenin off his back for a few more weeks.

He looked closer at the other tins and realised that each had its own yellowing label with a year scratched on it in pencil. There was no logic to the collection; some were stuffed with an assortment of old pens, others looked like spare parts for watches, one even had what seemed to be human hair.

The chance of finding more treasure was ended by a noise from the front garden — like a bear wrestling with a dustbin, the colonel had come back. As the front door creaked, Josh moved stealthily along the hallway and into the kitchen. The door to the back garden was wide open, and he bolted through it, hardly noticing the spotless, orderly table laid with a china tea service before he was taking the back steps two at a time down towards the garden.

Time seemed to slow as he descended and somewhere off in the distance he could hear music, an old-fashioned tinny gramophone sound. As his foot left the bottom step, the medal began to tingle in his hand. Ribbons of light were beginning to unravel from it, draining the colour from the world around him. The music grew louder, and he felt himself being pulled in many directions at once. He lost his balance and his grip tightened reflexively on the medal.

Closing his eyes, he felt the floor drop away from him and he instinctively put his free hand out to brace for the impact, but there was none. Instead, his fingers found a cold tiled wall.

3

1944

[Wolf's Lair, Eastern Prussia. Date: 1944-07-20]

There'd been a few times in Josh's life when he'd blanked out, lost moments or even entire evenings — usually due to alcohol. Worst case would normally involve waking in someone's front garden or their shed, not in an underground washroom of the Third Reich.

The walls were covered with dark green and white tiles. On one side there was a line of white porcelain washbasins with gold taps and along the other was a series of wooden cubicles. The hand towels were neatly folded to ensure the embossed swastikas were prominently displayed.

The music he had heard was playing through a metal grilled speaker on the wall above his head. It too had the familiar symbol of the Nazi war machine.

Josh's stomach lurched. He felt disorientated, off balance, the way you got from reading in the car. The overpowering smell of the toilets finally caught up with his other senses and he felt the clammy cold sweat that told him he had seconds to get to the toilet.

He pushed open the nearest stall to find himself staring into the face of a Nazi officer in full dress uniform. The man was staring at him in amazement, which was when Josh realised that he was totally naked.

The officer was every inch a classic German villain, including eye patch and leather-gloved hand. The gun he pulled out of his holster looked every bit the real thing.

There was a briefcase at the officer's feet that Josh had knocked out of his hand with the door, and its contents had spilled onto the floor. It was a mess of wires, waxed paper cylinders and what looked like a timer. Part of Josh thought he should apologise and offer to help collect it up, but he changed his mind when the officer pointed the gun at Josh's head and proceeded to use his gloved hand to scoop everything back into the case. Josh could see from the way he used it that it was artificial.

His nausea was forgotten in an instant, replaced by a cold knot of fear: the kind you experience when a loaded gun is being pointed at you — especially one that was so close that even a one-eyed man had little chance of missing.

Suddenly there was a loud knocking from the door marked 'AUSGANG' at the other end of the room. It was quickly followed by: '*Herr Oberst? Der Führer erwünscht Ihre sofortige Anwesenheit!*'

The officer swore under his breath, holstered the gun and picked up the case with his good hand. He pushed past Josh and walked to the door. Before he opened it, he looked back and shook his head in disbelief.

In his rush to leave, Josh noticed that the officer had left one of the wax cylinders behind.

· · ·

The lights in the washroom flickered and went out and Josh was standing back on the lawn in the garden of No. 42, naked, his clothes a few feet behind him in a crumpled heap. In his hand he was still holding the medal, which glowed ever so faintly.

What the hell just happened?

Adrenalin was coursing through his veins as Josh's mind started searching for a rational explanation, trying to process what he had just experienced, but the smell of toilets and a final wave of disorientation got the better of him and his stomach heaved; he fell to his knees, relieving himself of what remained of his breakfast.

As the nausea receded, he noticed the grass under his palms had been recently mowed — which he found really odd considering the state of the front garden. His eyes slowly adjusted to the brightness of daylight and he wiped his mouth as he sat back on his haunches. He filled his lungs with a deep breath of cool air and waited for the queasiness to subside. Josh realised then that the back garden was immaculately maintained, like something from the Chelsea Flower Show — another one of his mother's favourites. He looked back to check that he hadn't landed in a different garden, but the house behind him was definitely the colonel's.

A shadow passed across one of the upper windows, as if someone was watching him, and Josh instinctively grabbed his clothes and bolted for the back fence.

4

RETURNED

Mr Bell was waiting for Josh when he appeared from the bushes. He was holding Josh's Hi-Vis with an expression that fell somewhere between dismay and disappointment — it was a face Josh had grown accustomed to seeing on every adult he had ever had to deal with.

Josh could see the idiot he'd asked to cover for him, standing behind Mr Bell with a smug grin on his spotty face. Delland had obviously gone to the supervisor the moment Josh had left the park — knowing full well that it would result in him getting extra time. It was a challenge of sorts, a dare to score some respect from the others. Josh had met his type before, the over-ambitious mouthy ones that always got you into trouble.

'Having a little problem with your bladder, Mr Jones?' his supervisor asked sarcastically.

'No, sir,' Josh replied, squaring up to Mr Bell and staring directly into his eyes. Josh was taller than the man and more than capable of taking him down. 'Is there a problem? I told twat-face to let you know,' he added, nodding towards Delland. 'I wasn't gone more than five minutes.'

'Ten actually,' Bell responded, his eyes looking agitatedly from one side to the other. Josh had learned the staring technique from Lenin years ago. It intimidated people, and anyone who couldn't hold it had already lost.

'Ten!' Josh could have sworn he had been away for longer. 'Is there a law against that?'

'Well, legally you're under my supervision during the s-s-service,' Bell started to stutter.

Josh continued to stay in his face. 'So you're going to do what exactly?'

'W-w-well, I should report this.' Josh shifted his weight as if preparing to fight. 'B-but as this is o-obviously Delland's mistake I think we can overlook it this time.'

Josh nodded and walked towards Delland as the others watched carefully, expecting a fight.

'Crash, I didn't mean nothing,' Delland whimpered as Josh approached.

'No, of course you didn't,' Josh said, holding out his hand. 'No hard feelings?'

Delland took the hand nervously and Josh gripped it tightly as he leaned in to whisper: 'Next time, I'll leave the machete in your leg.'

As Josh trudged towards home, he could feel the weight of the medal in his coat pocket — he didn't dare touch it, but the constant thudding against his leg brought back visions of the officer in the washroom. He was trying to convince himself that it was a flashback — a result of smoking too much dope when he was younger. His friends were always talking about the weird experiences they had months afterwards — but he hadn't touched anything in over a year and it felt too real to be a hallucination. Even if it was, why would his subconscious conjure up some Nazi officer in a toilet? And what was he doing with a bomb in his suitcase anyway?

There were too many questions flying around in his head, and no way to answer them. He considered going back to the colonel and asking him about where he got the medal, except that would involve admitting that he'd stolen it in the first place.

Josh tried to focus on the more immediate problems, like offloading the medal and settling up with Lenin for good. He would take it to Eddy, the local fence — who would shaft him on the price, but Josh had little choice. Everyone who went to Eddy was desperate.

The Bevin Estate was a thirty-minute walk from Churchill Park. It had once featured on a Channel 4 documentary as a classic example of sixties inner-city planning gone wrong. Everywhere else in the country they were tearing down tenement blocks like his and replacing them with 'social housing'. Someone had obviously forgotten the Bevin. Fifteen concrete high-rise monoliths glowered over the leafy suburbs of South London like the ugly second cousin that you try to avoid at family parties, but who followed you around silently with that sad look on their face.

He toyed with the idea of going straight over to Eddy's shop and getting rid of the medal, but it was too close to dinner time and Josh had to make sure his mother ate.

Over the years his mother had slowly become a creature of habit. Everything had its place and meals were served at the same time every day. Multiple sclerosis was an unpredictable disease; her diet, and her medication had to be strictly regulated. Through years of trial and error, they had found a routine that had given her some sense of normality. But every so often, for no apparent reason, her MS would flare up, and he would spend weeks stuck in the flat nursing her back to something approaching normal.

He'd been doing this since he was twelve. His teenage years had been nothing like the others in his class. While they all had mountain bikes, Xboxes, iPhones and laptops, he had an agoraphobic mother who hadn't left the flat in the last five years, and a list of debts as long as the opening credits in *Star Wars*.

What he'd discovered during these monotonous weeks of caring was a love of cars, or, more accurately, speed. His only release from the self-imposed prison sentence of his mother's condition were the midnight joyrides around the empty streets of his town. Josh found he had a knack for getting into other people's cars. There was something about his touch that short-circuited their alarm systems, and allowed him to override the ignition. He drove them fast so that the world became a stream of light beyond the window. For a few wonderful minutes, there was no past, no future, just the now.

Josh stopped at Malik's corner shop to get something for dinner and some Rizlas for his mum. He checked the time: it was 5.30pm. The news channel was playing on an old TV that Malik had wedged into a shelf behind the counter. Footage of fireworks going off over Berlin were overlaid by a ticker tape feed running across the bottom stating:

GERMANY CELEBRATES 15 YEARS SINCE REUNI-FICATION.

Josh read the words quietly under his breath. It was the way he had taught himself to conquer the dyslexia, to stop the letters from jumping around.

'Hey, Malik. What's with the party?' he said, nodding at the TV.

'Oh that,' Malik said nonchalantly, looking up from his

paper, 'anniversary of the Brandenburg gate, or the Berlin Wall, or something like that. You know, back in the nineties when East Germany rejoined with West.'

Josh had no idea what Malik was talking about, and he was too tired to ask any more questions.

'Settle up tomorrow. OK?' Josh said as he took the shopping.

'Yeah, no probs,' said Malik, going back to his crossword. 'Say hello to your mum.'

5

THE FLAT

His mum was in the front room as usual; he could hear the sounds of her favourite TV show and caught the scent of the joint she was smoking as soon as he closed the front door.

Cannabis was one of the best remedies for her spasms. She used to be able to restrict her 'medicine' to those times when she was feeling rough, but he had noticed that recently she was smoking every day.

Initially Josh had tried to persuade her to eat rather than smoke the dope, but she was addicted to the nicotine as well, and he couldn't face trying to force her to kick that habit at the same time.

'Hi, love,' she shouted from the other room, 'had a good day?'

'Yeah, Mum. Just putting your dinner on,' he called back as he unpacked the shopping: two pieces of white fish in a boil-in-the-bag sauce — it was hardly a feast, but it was easy, and he was too tired to do anything fancy.

As the pan of water began to bubble, he took the medal carefully out of his pocket. It was cross-shaped, with oak leaves where the ribbon connected. At the centre was a Nazi symbol encircled by letters in a language he couldn't make out — except for the name 'Stauffenberg'. It was a name he had a feeling he should know, but the reason escaped him.

As he held it in the palm of his hand, glowing lines began to rise from its surface. Concerned that he might trigger another flashback, he folded it into a piece of newspaper and hid it under some tea towels in a kitchen drawer. He knew it would be safe in there; his mother hadn't been in the kitchen in years, let alone attempted to help with any washing up.

The name of the German officer was annoying him. The answer was flickering just outside his reach, like a fly buzzing around the back of his head. He would have to ask Mrs B. tomorrow. She lived next door and was the oldest person he knew — she was always banging on about the war. Her surname was Bateman but everyone called her Mrs B. She'd been friends with his mother for what felt like forever, and would sometimes look after her when Josh couldn't. The lady was ancient, her skin so thin that it had a kind of translucent quality, but she still had all her marbles and an uncanny knack for seeing through every lie Josh had ever told her.

'How's Mrs Davies?' his mother asked as Josh placed the tray of steaming white fish onto her lap. This was not the first time she had forgotten about Mrs Davies.

'She's gone, Mum. Left after her husband ran off with that woman from 21A.'

'Tart. She was always after him,' she muttered as she dug around under her leg for the remote control.

Josh laughed at the joke again, but he made a mental note to check his diary later. She usually had memory issues just before a flare up, which was the last thing he needed right now.

They ate together in silence, watching some pointless game show. Josh watched her more than the screen — he loved the way she would snort at all of the lame jokes or shout the answer before the contestant. His mum had watched so many of these programmes that she had become something of an expert on unusual and random facts.

'Did you know that the moon is the second densest object in the solar system?'

'No, Mum. I thought it was made of cheese.'

'Don't be ridiculous, Joshua. That Brian Cox is a very clever man. It's fascinating, astrology and all that.'

'Astronomy,' he corrected her.

'Yeah, that too.' Her concentration lapsed as her eyes returned to the TV screen.

She had told him once that she was studying at university when she had fallen pregnant, but he couldn't remember what subjects she was taking. They never spoke about who was the father. It was a forbidden subject, but Josh knew that she had dropped out and never finished her degree. There were moments when her mind cleared, and he saw the fierce intelligence still burning behind her eyes, but it was buried deep and was surfacing less and less.

'Your friend Lenny came round again today,' she said as she swept up the final remnants of cod and parsley sauce with her fork. She had eaten it all without looking down once, her eyes permanently fixed on the TV screen. Josh never failed to be amazed how she could do that — it was like a superpower — she just seemed to know instinctively where the food was.

'He's a funny bugger. Always acting like he's the big man.

I remember when he filled his wellies with wee in reception.'

Josh had to bite his lip. Only his mother would have the balls to bring up that particular incident. Lenin's family had been very poor when he was younger and used to send him to primary school in wellies and on one particular occasion he couldn't be bothered to ask to go to the toilet and simply pissed down his leg into his boots. Josh could still hear the sound of the squelching as he was marched out of the class.

'Did he say what he wanted?' he asked, trying to sound disinterested, even though the fact that Lenin had turned up at his flat was a serious issue: a personal house call was unheard of. It was usually one of his minions, all of whom Josh knew well and could handle without much of a problem, but for Lenin to come himself and to have him talk to his mum — that was basically like saying, 'You're in deep shit sunshine!'

'Oh, the usual nonsense. Something about you borrowing something that he needs back by tomorrow. He was quite nasty about it. The sooner we get out of this dump and find you some better friends the better. He's not good for you.'

'One day, Mum,' he said as he lifted the tray off her lap.

'Maybe my numbers will come up this week?' she said, holding up the tattered old lottery ticket that spent most of its life down the side of her chair. 'Then we can get that house with a garden, and you can go back to college, like I promised.'

She was looking directly at him — her hand stroked his face. 'You deserve a better life than this, Joshua.' There were tears welling in her eyes.

'This time next week, Mum. Yeah?' He gave her one of his reassuring smiles and took her tray back to the kitchen.

'Yeah,' she echoed as her attention returned to her programme. 'Did you get me some Rizzies?'

'In your pot on the coffee table,' he shouted as he dropped their plates into a sink of greasy, lukewarm water. The gas had been cut off two weeks ago and he had to boil the kettle to wash up. He checked the electricity meter. It was running low and in a couple of days they would be out of credit — which was bad news as it was another two weeks until her next disability cheque. He was going to have to sort something out — something that would get them through the winter.

He went into his bedroom and closed the door. It was just thick enough to block out the blare of the game show. The room hadn't been redecorated since she'd got sick. Old posters of rally cars and Formula 1 trading cards were holding back the peeling wallpaper with drawing pins. There was hardly any furniture apart from a bed and you couldn't see the carpet for his clothes that lay scattered across the floor, as if someone had detonated a sack full of charity-shop rejects. Next to the bed was a very badly assembled cabinet that he had rescued from a skip, it was barely holding together, and he knew how it felt.

Josh had never really been one to think about the future; he could just about manage to make it through the next twenty-four hours: 'Makes more sense to live in the present tense.' He knew that it couldn't go on much longer, that there would have to be some big changes soon. Mum wasn't getting any better and the frequency of her relapses was increasing.

He sat down on his bed and took out his journal from under the pillow. It had been his faithful companion during the long nights of watching over her, his only record of the nightmare that had been the last five years. Now held together with Sellotape and football stickers, he had kept track of every one of her episodes — documenting every day, every symptom, every drug until she recovered — he knew her condition better than any doctor.

As Josh flicked back through the pages, he realised that his handwriting had changed little since he had started all those years ago. To anybody else, it would look like the scrapbook of an eight-year-old, but he understood every misspelling, every reversed character — it was like his own secret language.

A Polaroid fell out from between the pages. It was an old photograph of the two of them on a beach. His mother looked so young and so well in the faded image. His younger-self was beaming as he held up an ice cream that was nearly as big as his face. There were hazy, fragmented memories of that day, it was Brighton or Bournemouth, somewhere with a beach, on one of those long hot summer days that seemed to go on forever. It was his sixth birthday, and she had taken him on an adventure to the coast by train. He could still remember the moment he saw the sea, it was quite a revelation to a kid who had grown up in the city — a wide curving horizon of blue that stretched beyond the edges of his vision. It made him wonder how big the world really was, and from that day he was determined to see what was over the 'edge of the world'.

Those were the days when he used to dream of being a pilot, of flying all over the world, the last few golden years of his childhood before his mother's illness forced him to forget such fantasies.

He used to convince himself that his father had taken the Polaroid, that the mysterious man whom his mother refused to talk about was standing on the other side of the lens. He would imagine what it would be like to go back through the image and speak to him — ask him why he had left.

He put the photo on the cabinet and lay down on the bed. It had been a crazy, messed-up day. His arms ached from the chopping and his stomach was undecided about keeping the meal he had just eaten.

He closed his eyes and tried to relax, letting his mind wander. He called it 'drifting'. It was a trick he had discovered back in the classroom when he got tired of trying to read the books they gave him. It was like having a TV inside his head; he found he could replay old memories like they were DVDs or just make up new ones. The teachers called it 'daydreaming' and usually sent him to the headmaster.

The memory of the Nazi officer resurfaced, and Josh allowed it to run back and forth, looking for clues as to what was going on. He focused his attention on the things that had fallen out of his suitcase, the strange wax packages, the wires and the timer. He switched his focus to the expression on the man's face as he went into the stall. The man had looked guilty — as if he had been caught red-handed. The more he went over the scene, the more convinced Josh was that the contents of the suitcase had looked like the parts of a bomb.

His eyes snapped back open.

That made no sense, he thought to himself. There was no way he had gone back in time and met an actual Nazi officer. It was more likely the colonel had some kind of fetish cosplay going on in the basement and he had fallen through a trapdoor. There would be a rational explanation for what had happened. Although it still didn't explain how he had lost all of his clothes.

The possibilities were beginning to make his head ache, so he tried to think about something else.

He would take the medal down to Eddy in the morning. It should be worth enough to keep Lenin happy and get the electric topped up for another couple of weeks, giving him some breathing space to focus on getting a regular job — although there weren't many he could apply for with his police record.

He closed his eyes and let out a long, slow sigh. Something would come up, as Mrs B used to say.

6

NO TELLY EDDY

E ddy had one of those trustworthy faces: his brown eyes were large, doe-like and sat on either side of one of the biggest noses Josh had ever seen. His hair was receding over his head in direct contrast to the beard that was sprouting from his chin. These features tended to give someone the impression of a kindly old gentleman, which was the one thing he was not.

Josh had sold Eddy a few things over the years, mostly old stuff his gran had left him when she died, and every single time he had come away feeling cheated. Eddy had an innate ability to know the value of a thing and then offer you less than half of what it was worth.

To the casual bystander he was the manager of a launderette — one that had the appearance of being constantly busy without ever having any visible customers. Josh knew this was just a front for the real business that took place out back beyond the beaded curtain, where he ran a very successful trade in buying and selling second-hand goods.

He took them in any condition, although he especially liked to fix electrical appliances: vacuum cleaners, washing machines, toasters, but not TVs. He hated them with a passion and it had earned him the nickname 'No-Telly-Eddy'.

Eddy was a great believer in the free market, which meant he was happy to buy and sell just about anything, no questions asked.

The chill of morning melted away as Josh walked into the warm, tumble-dried air. It was like stepping into another climate. The washing machines were all droning away, each full of the soapy items of someone else's life — he wondered if anyone ever actually turned up to collect them or whether Eddy just washed the same things over and over again.

Eddy was sitting in his usual spot behind the counter, busily disassembling a hair dryer, the component parts of which were laid out in careful order on the desk in front of him. He didn't look up but simply raised a finger to acknowledge Josh's existence and command him to wait.

There was a large pair of spectacles balanced on the end of his nose, which enlarged his eyes even more as he peered over them into the heart of the motor. With the concentration of a master watchmaker he was carefully adjusting something with a long thin screwdriver.

'These are always buggers to put back together,' he muttered. 'Bloody Chinese manufacturer uses cheap brushes in the motor — they wear out in days.'

There was another twist of the screwdriver and something wiry dropped out onto the counter. He looked up at Josh. 'See what I mean? What can I do for you, Mr Jones?'

Josh had always admired Eddy's style; — he spoke like an old-fashioned shopkeeper from *Downton Abbey* — even though Josh knew it was all an act. Eddy had grown up in London's East End and had an evil temper when he didn't get his own way. Some of his more naïve clients fell for it, which meant that they got ripped off even more than the regulars.

Josh pulled the medal from his jacket, still carefully wrapped in the newspaper. Eddy's eyes narrowed as Josh unwrapped the precious object.

'Let's take this to my office, shall we?' he whispered, glancing at the front door and closing Josh's fingers back over the medal. The old man put his hand on Josh's shoulder and guided him through the beaded curtain.

The back of the shop was an Aladdin's cave of broken and part-repaired appliances, dimly lit by a random collection of low energy bulbs. It felt like Josh was entering the workshop of some mad inventor. It smelt of dead machines, of grease and metal, wires and solder.

'So, Mr Jones, if you would be so kind as to let me inspect that lovely piece?' Eddy asked as he put on a pair of thick leather gloves. He motioned towards a workbench with a bright desk lamp and a huge magnifying glass.

Josh unwrapped the paper bundle once more and placed it in the circle of light on the bench.

Eddy moved his spectacles onto his forehead and picked up the medal with a pair of long-nosed pliers. Josh knew Eddy was a little bit weird about germs and bacteria, but these precautions were excessive, even for him.

'Hmm. 1944. Stauffenberg. SS long-service medal with oak cluster. Very rare, very rare indeed,' Eddy noted as he turned the object over under the glass.

Josh congratulated himself; he'd known it had been a good one. The name still escaped him, but he was only interested in what it was worth, not what some dead German had done to earn it all those years ago — that was ancient history.

'How much?' Josh asked directly. He didn't really have

the time for Eddy's Antiques Roadshow act.

'That depends.'

Eddy placed it on some antique scales and began adjusting the weights.

'On what?'

'Just under four ounces of twenty-four-carat gold.' Eddy pretended to do some maths in his head. 'I would say it's worth £500. But it depends on where it came from,' said Eddy, putting the medal back on the newspaper.

'You know better than to ask,' Josh replied, smiling.

Eddy shrugged and placed his glasses back down on his nose.

'Anything strange happen when you acquired it?' he asked, fixing Josh with a piercing glare.

'No. Why? Does it make it more valuable?'

It was Eddy's turn to smile. 'The thing about medals, apart from their base material value, is who they belonged to, the more notorious, the more their worth.'

'I don't care about its history — it's just a lump of metal.'

'Ah, but you should. This Colonel Stauffenberg, for instance, was once a very important man, and he nearly killed the most evil dictator of the twentieth century.'

That was when the memory finally surfaced, like a birthday card that turns up two days late from your aunt with a tenner inside. It was a history lesson on the Second World War and the way Hitler had died in a bomb blast. Stauffenberg was the name of the officer that had taken the suitcase full of explosives into a meeting of the high council and ended the war. He was a hero, and this was his medal. Josh couldn't believe that he had met the man that had killed Hitler.

'So that makes it way more valuable. Yeah?'

'Maybe, to the right people. Would be even more valuable if he had succeeded.'

That wasn't right, Josh thought.

'What do you mean — if? He did kill Hitler. I remember that much from school.'

Eddie looked at him strangely as if unsure of what to say next. Then he shook his head and handed him back the package.

'No, my boy. I don't know what they've been teaching you. But Hitler survived that particular attempt, and the war lasted another terrible year. It wasn't until 1945 that the Allies took Berlin and Hitler committed suicide. The Nazi's surrendered on the 8th of May — it's called "Victory in Europe" or VE day.'

Josh was confused. He remembered the officer in the washroom and the things that had fallen out of the suitcase. It *had* been a bomb, he was sure, but what kind of crazy shit was he dealing with now? It made no sense — VE day was today. The Nazis had surrendered after the death of Hitler in 1944; he could still hear his history teacher Miss Field-house reading it out to the class.

'Eddy. Stop messing around. Do you want to buy this or not?'

The bell chimed from the front door telling them that someone else had come into the shop.

'Too specialist for my clientele, I'm afraid. The gold is worth something, but the medal would be worth £30,000 in the hands of the right dealer,' he said, taking off the gloves as he made his way out of the workshop, 'if it isn't a fake, that is . . . Let yourself out.'

Before Josh could ask Eddy if he knew any dealers, he'd disappeared through the beaded curtain and begun talking to someone about the hair dryer.

Josh let himself out of the back door and stood for a

moment watching the world go by. Nothing seemed any different; people looked just as dumb as they always had, the adverts on the sides of the buses pushed the same old crap — there was no sign that history had changed at all.

He decided Eddy must be pulling his leg — it was just part of a negotiation strategy to get the price down — but Josh didn't have the time to play games. He thought about going back and threatening the old man, getting him to admit it was a wind-up, or at least give him the name of a specialist who might buy the medal from him. They could even negotiate some kind of finder's fee for Eddy.

Except Josh knew better than to threaten Eddy, he was like an endangered species, protected by his clients, most of whom were way more dangerous than Lenin, and that was saying something. He had no choice but to find out for himself. It was Saturday so there was no community service today, and there would be a few more hours before Lenin would surface and come looking for him; time enough to do some digging of his own.

He started walking in the direction of Churchill Gardens. If the past had changed somehow, then VE day would have moved, and there would be nothing going on at the war memorial in the park today.

From a grimy upstairs window of his office, Eddy watched Josh until he disappeared from sight. Then went to his desk, unlocked the bottom drawer and took out a Bakelite telephone with a rotary dial. As the last number clicked back into place, there was burst of static in the earpiece — he took a deep breath and spoke slowly into the mouthpiece.

'This is William Edward Taunton, Antiquarian 7-382. I wish to report a temporal deviation.'

7

CAITLIN

When Josh got to the park, it was full of kids; a school fête had transformed the serene green space into a bouncy-castle showroom with a sideline of stalls selling home-made cakes and offering tombola prizes. There was no sign of the Salvation Army or their band and no WW2 veterans — no poppies and not one Union Jack.

Josh circumvented the ring of parents screaming encouragement at their hobbling children in the sack race and went over to the memorial. The weather-beaten brass statue of a lone soldier stood sentinel above him with the dates of the two world wars: 1914—18 and 1939—45 etched into a brass plaque at his feet. Josh scanned down the names that were listed on each of the sides of the marble base, running his finger over those that died in 1945 as if to check they were real. The metal letters were cold and hard under his fingers, and he could feel the pitted edges where acid rain had eaten into the surface. Nothing was making sense, he thought. Was he the only one that remembered it differently? How do you go about asking someone without sounding like you're going mad?

He felt the medal in his pocket, and knew he had to find out more about it. He needed to find a dealer, but had no idea where to start. They could never afford a PC, broadband or even a smart phone at home. It had never really bothered him that much until now; electrical stuff always used to go wrong when he came near it, which was useful for disabling car alarms but not much else. It was the same with watches — they would just stop working for no apparent reason.

A grumpy parent announced over the PA that the tae-kwon-do demonstration was about to start and a crowd of candy-floss-fuelled kids swarmed to a roped-off square of grass. Josh took one more look at the memorial and walked out of the park in the direction of the local library.

Aside from graphic novels, Josh had never been a big fan of books. At school his reading levels were way lower than those of the other kids. His numeracy was higher than average, and maps were his absolute favourite. So they assigned him a special teaching assistant and that worked well for a year or two, but then his mum got ill and they had to move to a poky little flat and a different school. Without the dedicated teaching, his grades dropped, as did his interest in education. At sixteen, with no real qualifications and very little in the way of job prospects, his offender manager had managed to get him onto a car-mechanics course at college, which, even though it was mostly practical, still had a heavy amount of theory — something he failed miserably at.

Libraries were alien places to Josh. To him they were just drop-in centres for the homeless and old people. He hadn't been inside one since a school trip in year eight to the Bodleian in Oxford. That had been like something out of another century, stacks of books that nobody read, lined up in the vain hope that someone would borrow one. 'Where books go to die,' Mrs B had remarked when he'd told her about it afterwards.

His local library was equally as old. A wealthy merchant's name was elegantly carved into the stone arch above the door — in case anyone ever forgot who forked out the cash to build it. If there was one thing Josh knew about the Victorians, it was that they were not shy about naming things after themselves.

He sat down in front of the PC and keyed in the code the librarian had given him; she had wanted to charge him a pound for an hour, but he had managed to charm his way around that. He had a way with women, especially older ones who apparently spent a lot of time talking to their cats and who obviously knitted their own jumpers. He wasn't a bad-looking bloke or so he had been told, and he was never shy about pushing his luck.

He began with a search, which thanks to Google's correction of his dyslexic spelling, served up over half a million results for 'Assassination' and 'Hitler'.

Scanning down the page he picked a site that he recognised; it was a Wikipedia article about the '20th July plot'. The screen refreshed to display a long and wordy article. He scrolled down until he found an image of a blasted meeting room and clicked on it. The picture enlarged to show what was left of a room with most of the ceiling hanging down and a group of German officers in leather coats standing on the shattered debris. There was a footnote that described how there hadn't been enough dynamite in the briefcase to kill Hitler outright. Stauffenberg had gone to the washroom to prepare the bomb and then placed it under the conference table next to Hitler.

Josh went cold. Eddy had been telling the truth.

The computer made a strange clunking noise, and the screen went black. The librarian behind the desk swore out loud and began hitting random keys on her keyboard and muttering something about 'useless technology'. Josh turned to look around at the rows of books and decided that maybe they were a better option after all.

The boy was wandering along the aisles like a lost child when she saw him. Caitlin was busy pretending to reorganise the military history section: the second most popular subject in the library, beaten only by romance novels, which, considering that her typical customers were mildly inebriated ex-service men of no fixed abode, was slightly disturbing.

The library was not frequently visited by good-looking young men. Miriam on the front desk had tipped her off as though it were going to be the high point of an otherwise dreary day. She and Miriam had an unspoken affinity for games and practical jokes to help the hours pass quickly.

He wore the universal look of someone who needed assistance, and she was only too happy to oblige.

'Can I help you?' she asked as he scanned the spines of a row of books.

Josh took a moment to check her out. He'd not been expecting to meet anyone under the age of forty and especially not such a pretty girl. She couldn't have been that much older than him and although she wasn't his type, she had all the usual trademarks of a goth: piercings, eyeliner, tattoos and a band T-shirt — he was finding it difficult not to smile.

'Yes,' he managed to croak. His voice tended to fail him

when he was nervous. Not that he ever usually got shy around girls. He cleared his throat to make his voice deeper. 'I'm looking for a book on the War.'

'Well, you've come to the right place!' she replied chirpily. 'Which one?'

'Which book? I was hoping you could tell me,' he replied with a cheeky glint in his eye.

She laughed, and it was a clear, pure sound that made her eyes light up. 'No, dummy, which war: First, Second, Boer, Gulf?'

'Didn't realise there were so many,' he admitted as he scratched his two-day-old beard and wished he had remembered to shave.

She gave him a stern look; he could tell she liked a bit of banter.

'Second — anything about Hitler's assassination on July 20th, 1944,' he added.

She nodded and walked off along the stacks. He couldn't help but admire the way her arse swayed under her skirt as she glided down the aisle, and he only just managed to look away before she caught him. She'd stopped at a sign that clearly read World War II, and pulled a rather large book from the shelf.

'So what exactly do you want to know about the July 20th attempt?' she asked, flicking through the book.

They sat down at a reading desk. She was so close that he kept catching the scent of her hair. It smelt of flowers and something more exotic. On her wrist she had a small tattoo; it looked like a snake eating its tail.

'I'm looking for an officer, Stauffenberg,' Josh said, trying not to stare at her breasts.

'Colonel Stauffenberg,' she corrected, turning the book towards him to show a full-page photograph of the officer.

Stauffenberg looked different in the picture, younger, and he didn't have the eye patch or the gloved hand. There was an air of nobility about him, and a sense of hope in his eyes. Seeing the picture of him sent a chill through Josh's spine, as if having it in print made it more real, but he still couldn't believe he'd actually met him. There was no way he could have changed history . . . There was no such thing as time travel.

'What happened to him?' Josh asked, realising she was waiting for some kind of reaction.

'Oh, he was shot for trying to kill the Führer, along with a hundred and eighty other conspirators,' she replied, scanning the text on the opposite page. 'He would have been a hero if there had been more explosives in the case.'

'It wasn't his fault. He only had one good hand, he couldn't hold it properly.'

'Ah,' she said, her eyes narrowing. 'I didn't realise you were an expert.'

Josh knew he might have said too much. She was looking at him differently. He needed to think of something fast, or he would have a load of explaining to do.

'Yeah, you know. In the movie, he was injured, wasn't he?'

She was staring directly at him. 'The film, of course. What's so important about him anyway?'

'My grandad left me a medal and it's got his name on it,' he said, tapping on the picture of Stauffenberg.

'You mean your great-grandfather?' she said with air quotes. 'Wouldn't your grandfather have had to be a hundred and twenty to have fought in the Second World War?'

Josh didn't usually screw up so badly. There was something about her that was putting him off his game.

wasn't in the war. He was a detectorist. You know
ctors?' Josh mimed someone sweeping the floor
ng to imaginary headphones. 'Every Sunday he'd
be out in some field or other. Even went on holiday to
France just to scope the battlefields.'

'So he just happened to find a medal that was awarded
to the German colonel who tried to kill Hitler?' She was
obviously not convinced.

'No. Swapped it for something — a rare Roman coin I
think.'

The trouble with a lie was that it had a tendency to take
on a life of its own; once you started it was very hard to stop.
He would have to stay on his guard — she was very sharp.

'So do you think the war would have ended that day if
he had succeeded?'

'Who knows? Maybe. Doesn't matter now, though, does
it? The past is the past. You can't change it.'

She unconsciously stroked an old pendant she wore
round her neck. It looked like a dragon. 'Twentieth century
isn't really my cup of tea.' There was a tinge of sadness in
her voice.

'So what is?' he asked, relieved to move away from the
subject of the medal.

'Ancient history. The library of Alexandria — the
greatest centre of learning the ancient world had ever seen.
I'm studying it at Uni.' There was a light in her eyes as she
spoke. He liked the way her whole face glowed when she
talked about something she was interested in.

'I'm currently writing a dissertation on Sun Tzu, the
Chinese general that wrote the *Art of War*.'

There had been girls like her at school: smart, geeky
girls, who didn't bother too much with the way they looked
and tended to prefer books to boys. He hadn't paid too much

attention to them; they were too hard to get to first base with and generally made him feel stupid. This one, however, was unusual to the point of making him forget what he was supposed to be doing.

'So, Caitlin . . .' he said, spending too much time looking at her name badge, and it was obvious he was more interested in what was rising and falling beneath, 'do you have anything on ... medals?'

'Do you want to see them?' she asked as he continued to stare.

'What?' he coughed, trying not to blush.

'The band. They're playing tonight in Highgate. They're kind of a fusion of indie and hiphop.' She pointed straight at her breasts. The word INFINITUM was emblazoned across her T-shirt in an old-fashioned script that wound through the gears of a clockwork device.

'Yeah, maybe,' he said, trying not to sound too keen.

'As for the medals. That's known as numismatics — you'll want the coin and medal collectors directory.' She pulled down a thick book from the top shelf and leafed through the pages, turning it towards him and pointing to a section entitled 'Coin & Medal Dealers — W.W.2'.

'I'm assuming you want to sell it,' she sighed as she handed him the book. 'I'll be in The Flask from 8 o' clock,' she added as she walked off.

Josh took Caitlin's advice and used the public phone in the library to call a couple of the local dealers. He could tell from their questions that the medal was worth a lot more than Eddy had quoted. Apparently, a similar one had gone for nearly £200,000 a few years ago.

He dropped the calls each time they started asking

awkward questions about how he had come to own it — that was going to be a difficult thing to explain unless he could invent a better story than his granddad's fictitious metal detector.

He lost track of the next hour looking at the grainy black-and-white photos of World War 2. There was something unreal about the haunted faces of the men that stared back at him. They were like deleted scenes from a movie, one that he had never seen. He was beginning to wonder if he had imagined the version in which Hitler had died in 1944.

When he looked up, it was nearly 1pm. Lenin's deadline and his mother's lunch fought for priority as he ran for the exit.

'No running!' the cat lady screamed as Josh cleared the non-fiction section and vaulted over the 'newly arrived' display. He was out of the door before she could say another word.

8

HOSPITAL

The front door of their flat was ajar when he got home. The wood had splintered around the locks from the force of someone kicking it very hard.

'Mum?' he called as he shoved through the door, and then again louder when there was no response: 'MUM!'

He listened intently, holding his breath. There was no answer. Various scenarios ran through his mind as he ran down the hall: she had been taken ill and the paramedics had to break in, or there had been a gas leak and the firemen had rescued her — but the gas had been cut off weeks ago . . .

When he saw the state of the living room, it all started to make sense. Like a CSI crime scene, each step he took uncovered more signs of mindless destruction: the breaking of a mirror, the scattered pieces of a cheap vase of silk flowers, a photograph of his gran ripped out of its frame. Small things of sentimental value that gave him all the clues he needed. Lenin had been to collect and had brought some of the Ghost Squad along with him. Mum must have tried to bar the door, but they had kicked it in and then swept the flat for anything of value.

He searched the other rooms, but it was much the same. The television was gone, and so was his mother.

On the mirror above the gas fire they could never afford to put on was a message scribbled in thick black marker. He recognised Lenin's handwriting.

DON'T DO ANYTHING STUPID!

Which was exactly what Josh wanted to do. Very badly.

He clenched his fists, angry with himself for spending so long at the library. He couldn't think of anything other than what Lenin had done to his mum, how scared she would have been when they broke the door down and went through her things. How he should have been there to protect her.

He lashed out, kicking the coffee table over — where the hell was she now?

Mrs B will know.

Heart hammering, he sprinted across the hall and pounded on Mrs B's door.

'Oh, I'm so glad you're back,' she said as soon as she had managed to undo all of the various locks on her front door. 'There was a terrible commotion earlier, and then the ambulance came. They've taken her to Bart's.' She had that concerned look of someone who actually cared.

'Bart's? Are you sure?'

'Yes, one of the nice young men said to tell the next of kin.'

'Thanks, Mrs B.' He turned to leave and then thought of something else. 'Will you look after something for me?'

'Of course, dear.'

He handed her the medal still wrapped in newspaper.

'It's all we have left, and I think your place is safer than ours.' He nodded to the door opposite and the footprint-sized hole in the middle of it.

'Ooh. Is it precious?' she asked, starting to unwrap it.

He placed his hand over hers. 'It's just one of Great-grandad's old medals.'

She looked a little disappointed and put it into one of the pockets of her apron.

A thought flew into his mind. 'Mrs B, do you remember much about the war?' he asked.

'Cheeky boy, I'm not that old. I was only twelve when it broke out.' She smiled, remembering something. 'It was a very exciting time for a child.'

'So you remember the day it ended?'

'Oh yes,' she said, her eyes glazing over, 'VE Day. 8th May, 1945. We had so much fun that afternoon. The whole street came out for the party. It was the best day of all. That was the first time I met my Sydney. God rest his soul.' Her eyes were full of tears, and Josh wished he had time to hang around for one of her stories.

'OK, thanks. I'll give Mum your best.'

'You do that, love,' she replied, squeezing his hand.

St Bartholomew's, or 'Bart's' as it was more affectionately known, was one of the oldest hospitals in Britain. Based in the heart of London, its gothic architecture made it feel more like an asylum than a place for healing the sick. Josh hated all hospitals; the smell of sickness, and the chemicals they used for cleaning, always reminded him of death.

It reminded him of Gossy.

He'd gone in to visit his friend after the crash. The surgeons and their machines had managed to keep him alive for little more than a week. Josh had sneaked in to see him when his parents had stepped out. Gossy was lying in the bed with tubes and wires attached to various parts of his body, but it still looked like him, if a little beaten up. His head was wrapped in bandages, but his face was unscathed. The machines beeped and pinged while the respirator next to the bed breathed for him, and Josh sat there, trying hard to think of something to say. When he moved closer to the bed, the monitors registered a slight change in Gossy's heart rate.

'I'm sorry,' he whispered to his friend.

For a second Gossy had opened his eyes, the bright blue irises staring right into his. He would never forget that look, the way his pupils were nothing more than tiny black dots. It was a haunting, vacant look of seeing but not seeing — and he knew his friend had gone.

Josh had been so scared he'd run out of the ward.

Gossy died two days later.

Josh made his way along the corridors full of people looking dazed and confused. Hospitals were strange places; they were so massive, so imposing that you felt immediately lost the moment you stepped inside one. They were places of beginnings and endings, but for Josh they were where you learned some awful truth about one of your own.

Instinctively, he found his way through the maze of corridors to his mother's neuro ward and there he paused at the door. There was always a moment, just before he saw her, when he would convince himself it wouldn't be too bad this time, that she had just had a mild relapse. Her MS had been slowly worsening, and the doctors had started making noises about something called 'secondary progressive', which was another way of saying she was never going to get any better.

She was asleep when he walked in to the ward, her arms and hands drawn up onto her chest where the muscles were locked in spasm. An IV drip ran into her thin arm. He inspected the label — intravenous steroids — they would be trying to help her body back from the edge. The skin was pale and waxy: a sure sign she had suffered terribly. He knew the signs so well now, probably better than most of the doctors. There were no visible cuts or bruises, so he had to assume that Lenin hadn't harmed her in any physical way. He wouldn't have — he wouldn't dare.

A nurse walked over to check the monitor on the other side of the bed. She smiled at him in that way that said, 'Sorry about your mum,' and then wrote on her chart.

When she spoke, he could hear the trace of an Eastern European accent.

'Your mother will be sleeping for most of the day. I would come back later. We will look after her.'

He checked the time on the clock at the nurse's station. It was 1.40pm and visiting finished in twenty minutes.

'I'll stay if that's OK?'

'Sure. You're a good boy,' she said sincerely, and then walked over to help another patient.

No, I'm not, Josh thought. *I'm the one who got her into this.*

If he had gone straight round to Lenin this morning, it would all be different. That bloody medal — all he had to do was give it to Lenin, and this would never have happened. It was Eddy's fault for telling him what it might be worth — that kind of money changes lives.

He had seen a way out, a chance to get a better life for the two of them. Now he would have to sort Lenin — he had gone too far this time.

9

LENIN

As Josh walked out of the hospital, he could hear the bass of a jacked-up sound system in the car park. The sound followed him as he made his way towards the exit. A BMW X5 with tinted windows slowed down to crawl beside him.

'All right, bruv,' said a familiar voice from the half-open passenger window. 'You need a lift?'

It was Billy, the not-so-clever bike thief, his face half-hidden by a scarf. A cloud of dope-scented smoke escaped through the open window.

'Nope,' Josh replied as he continued to walk.

'Wasn't asking.'

Josh knew better than to argue. He got into the back. Lenin was sitting in the rear seat, smoking a large joint. He was wearing sunglasses and a large blue parka as if he were about to go on some polar exploration. The music was so loud that it made talking impossible. As the car pulled out into traffic, Josh noticed that Lenin had a gun resting in his lap.

They went back a long way. Lenin had always been the

bossy kind of kid, the clever one that got the bullies on his side and then told them who to beat up. His actual name was Richard Leonard Belkin, but over the years various versions of nicknames had led him to adopt 'Lenin'. There was some link to the Marxist philosopher and founder of the communist movement, but he certainly didn't follow the teachings of his namesake.

Lenin had got into drugs at a young age. He was selling dope to kids way older than himself and making a tidy profit — enough to afford all the luxuries that Josh had always dreamed of. When his mother had to quit work and move to the Bevin estate, Josh had found he had two choices: be beaten up every day or join a gang and have some protection. It was not much of a choice: he was no boy scout. He managed to stay away from the drugs by being incredibly good at getting into other people's cars — without their permission or their keys.

'So, Crash. Am I going to have to use this?' Lenin broke Josh's reverie, waving the gun at his face like a gangster.

Josh had been so angry when he'd thought his mum was in danger that he would have killed Lenin. But, since seeing his mother, he realised that he was mad at himself. Lenin had no choice but to make an example of him: Josh hadn't played by the rules. He'd never been afraid of Lenin, not in all their years, but the guy was starting to do some serious drugs, and his behaviour was changing. What Josh had decided, sitting beside his mother in the ward, was that he needed to get away from this life altogether. It was not healthy. There was no future in it. He just had to cut all ties and move on, move away. Which meant settling the debt.

'No, Len, we're cool.'

'No, Crash! We! Are! Not! Bloody! Cool!' he said in a loud

voice, punctuating every word by pointing the gun in Josh's face.

The two guys in the front shrank down in their seats a little, as though trying to disappear.

'You disrespected me. You little shit! You owe me!' He was getting more wound up with every word.

Josh could feel his anger rising too. No one spoke to him like that, not in front of others, but he knew he had to control it. One wrong word and Lenin would probably shoot him.

'I have the money, Len.'

'No, you fricking don't! We just went through your flat, remember? You don't have shit!'

Josh remembered the chaos. They had gone through everything, invaded the sanctity of his home.

'Len, seriously, stop waving the gun around. It's going to go off!' Josh said nervously.

Lenin's eyes seemed to clear for a moment. Whatever he was smoking was obviously messing with his brain. Josh couldn't read him at all.

He levelled the gun at Josh's head, and Josh closed his eyes. Could this be it? Had Lenin finally lost it? He could hear Lenin breathing hard, could smell the oiled metal of the gun. There was a long pause when nothing happened, and Josh opened his eyes, realising that his hands were over his head.

Lenin was smiling like a Cheshire cat. He pointed the gun at his own head and pulled the trigger. There was an empty click — the gun wasn't loaded.

Lenin began to giggle and then broke into a bout of hysterical laughing. The others in the front joined in.

'I so had you there, Joshy! You were shitting it!' Lenin said between fits of laughter. He drew in a deep breath and started coughing. 'It's a replica, you dummy. Haven't had it modded yet.' He threw the gun into Josh's lap.

The weapon was heavy, not that he knew what one should feel like, but it certainly seemed real. Josh knew better than to retaliate. He smiled to show he took the joke and placed the gun on the seat between them.

'So how's your mum?' asked Lenin. 'We were real worried when we found her. Collapsed on the floor she was. Billy called the ambulance.'

Billy looked round from his seat and gave Josh a wink. Josh nodded his thanks.

'Bad. The doctor says it's going to be a couple of weeks.'

'Not cool. Do you want some more weed?'

'No, they have her on stronger stuff, steroids and shit like that.'

'Diazepam or some other benzodiazepine.'

One thing you could say in Lenin's favour, Josh thought, was that he had a very extensive knowledge of pharmaceuticals. In another life, he would have made an excellent chemist or maybe even a doctor.

'Did you have to turn the place over?'

'It was overdue. Debts gotta be paid, dude.'

He wanted to complain about them taking the TV and leaving the place in such a state, but Lenin shook his head as if to say that this conversation was over.

'Anyways, Josh-man. I'm going to be needing some of your specialist skills soon — just wanted to make sure you're up for it. Considering what you owe me.'

'How much is it now?'

'Three K still,' Lenin said, flashing a gold-toothed smile — holding up a hand before Josh could protest. 'The TV just paid off the interest.'

Josh was about to tell him about the medal, but something caught his eye out of the window. It was the sight of the colonel sitting down in the middle of the busy street, rummaging through bulky shopping bags, looking for something.

'Hey, look, there's old Colonel Cuckoo!' said the guy next to Billy. 'What's he doing?'

As they crawled past him in the traffic, the old man looked directly at their car and for a second Josh thought he was going to shout something at them, but he went remarkably quiet and took out his book and wrote something in it. A few seconds later he was being helped up by a couple of security guards.

'Damn! The man is a total nutter,' said Billy.

'That's what happens when you don't take your meds,' said Lenin. 'So, Josh, get your shit together. I'll be in touch about the job. Going to need a fast set of wheels for this one, so find me something special. Yeah?'

With that, the car pulled over to the kerb and Josh was left standing on the pavement.

He dug his hands deep into his pockets and walked away. The colonel was shouting at the top of his voice as the guards dragged him off in the other direction. Josh could have sworn he heard the old man call his name, but he'd had his fill of madness for one day. Right now all he wanted was to escape. Right now he needed to drive.

10

CARS

For as long as he could remember Josh had loved everything about cars: the smell of the leather, the sound of the engine and the acceleration were all exhilarating. It was like being on a ride at Disneyland and way better than any video game, or at least it was until that day Gossy died.

It all began when he was eleven. His best friend, Steve Goss, dared him to break into an old Ford Fiesta. Josh discovered that he had a knack for starting cars without a key: he just had to touch the ignition and the engine would kick in. By twelve, he had refined his abilities to a point where he could disable virtually any alarm with a simple touch on the bonnet — Gossy nicknamed him 'the Keymaster'.

Soon they were stealing to order, and between him and Gossy they were bringing in two to three cars a week. Lenin had an older brother who sold them on to a local dealer and started to get requests for certain models. Gossy and Josh turned it into a game and competed against each other to fulfil the orders, which led to more than one race across town as they rushed to be the first to get their stolen vehicle to the drop-off.

Neither ever really thought about the danger, or the consequences. Walking up the darkened, urine-stained stairs of a multi-storey car park, Josh thought back to the last time he'd been here. He could still see the wide grin on Gossy's face as he climbed into the driver's seat of the Porsche Boxster.

They'd stolen from this car park so many times that he knew it was very unlikely he would need to go up more than three levels to find what he was after.

Level 3 was full — it was mid-afternoon, and the locals were at work or shopping. Josh scanned the lines of bonnets and boots looking for a likely candidate — they were all newer models. Anything over a '52 plate was going to be too conspicuous.

The next level down was more promising: a Renault Clio RS16 dwarfed by two larger, gleaming Land Rovers. The Clio would have a simpler security system, without an immobiliser or tracker. As he touched the handle, he felt the usual tingle on his fingertips. Like a static shock, it interfered with the electrical system.

There was always a buzz when Josh sat behind the wheel of someone else's car: not because it was illegal but because it was like stepping into someone else's life. For a moment he wasn't himself; he could imagine what it was like to be them.

Every car had a unique essence, one that gave him a hint of the owner: the salesman with a glove box full of receipts and condoms, the meticulous old lady with potpourri scent sacks hanging from the rear-view mirror, or the student with the three-day-old McDonald's wrappers festering in the footwell.

This one smelt of engine oil and damp; the seals must have gone under the wheel arches. He considered going for another but changed his mind when he touched the ignition and it started up the first time. It was a four-cylinder turbo with a decent 2.0-litre engine and a six-speed gearbox, a powerful rally car that could corner well and squeeze through narrower escape routes. The only thing that would be able to follow it would be a motorbike, and they could be stopped.

He drove the Clio slowly out of the car park, obeying the speed limit so as not to attract attention. He took it out of the town centre, and then made for the nearest A-road so he could test it properly.

Driving helped to clear his head — to focus his mind on something other than the crap life was dealing him.

Speed was his 'obsession' the prosecution had told the court, 'one that could have easily ended his life or, at least, endanger that of others'. He had been twelve years old when the accident had killed Gossy — too young to be locked up. At the time, the words of the judge were nothing more than a series of sounds strung together. He wasn't really paying that much attention to what the adults were saying. He was numb, lost in grief, trying to come to terms with the death of the nearest thing he had to a brother. He didn't realise at the time that they were basically banning him from ever doing the one thing he was any good at.

As the world rushed by at 90mph, Josh felt the left front pulling slightly. The differential was slightly out as he cornered, the brakes were soft and third gear was not particularly happy below 3,000rpm. With a bit of TLC, it would've been a perfect little car, which was all the more saddening as by the end of this job it would be nothing but a burnt-out shell.

The petrol gauge was reading just over half, and he eased back on the accelerator — he didn't want to be forking out for any more fuel. He took the next exit, the plates would need to be changed and Shags would need to give the brakes a once over.

11

FRIENDS

M ost of his friends, those who weren't doing time, would spend their Saturdays hanging out in the abandoned industrial estate at the end of Dickens Lane. Once the home of a caravan factory, it had quickly fallen into ruin and was now nothing more than a dumping ground for random bits of household junk and industrial waste. They'd managed to create their own skate park from the discarded parts of abandoned mobile homes, and there was enough open ground for some decent car stunts, should you wish to burn off a few inches of rubber.

As he turned into the estate, he spotted the usual crowd collected around a pile of burning wooden pallets, at the top of which someone had dumped a badly dressed mannequin.

He swung the Clio into a tight circle, locking the wheel so he could leave a donut skid mark, balancing the clutch perfectly as the car's back wheels drifted around behind him. The crowd stood frozen to the spot, their heads rotating like meerkats as their eyes followed the orbit of the car. He reversed the lock on the steering to weave a series of slick figure 8s that produced clouds of dust and burning rubber until he'd virtually disappeared, then slammed it into reverse and parked it with a handbrake finish between two rusting freight containers.

'Yo, Josh. You still got it, bro,' said Shaggy as he raised a can of Red Bull in salute.

'Shags. Benny. Coz. Lils,' Josh acknowledged each of them with a nod as he approached. 'Where's Dennis?'

'Looking for something else to burn,' said Benny, pointing to a scruffy-looking boy in a tracksuit digging through a pile of recently dumped fly-tippings.

Josh had known them all since they were in primary school, they were wasters with no real ambition, other than to score another high, get hammered or laid — whichever came first. Unlike the Ghost Squad, they were harmless, and they were all he had left of an ever-diminishing set of friends.

'S'up?' Coz asked Josh as he handed Shags a joint and started to roll another.

'Will you give it a once over?' Josh replied, nodding towards the Renault. 'The brakes are soft on the left front, and I'm going to need it running sweet in a couple of days.'

'No probs. You got a job on?' asked Shags, who was one of the best mechanics Josh had ever met.

Josh sat down on what was left of an old car seat and told them about Lenin and what he'd done to the flat.

'Shite. He's out of control, dude!' said Benny.

The rest of the gang nodded in agreement.

'You got to disappear, J,' added Shags, blowing out a copious amount of smoke.

'And go where exactly?' Josh replied. 'It's not like I can just up and leave mum, is it?'

They all agreed glumly.

Benny vocalised what they were all thinking: 'It's proper bollocks.' The joint made its way round the circle until it reached Josh.

Lils, officially a girl, although she'd been treated like one of the boys since anyone could remember, had obviously been giving the matter a lot of thought, because she suddenly jumped up and announced: 'You have to go, Joshy. You're way clever. You could do anything if you put your mind to it. Take your mum and ... and ... go be a racing driver or —' she pointed at the half-hidden Renault — 'or test them or something. I don't know just, like, get out there and be who you were meant to be.' She sat back down again, exhausted by the effort. The others nodded their heads in agreement; they were all a little taken aback by her speech — no one could remember Lils saying that much ever.

'Lils. I'm afraid that only happens in the movies,' Josh replied.

'Well, yeah, maybe, but you know,' she muttered staring down at her trainers.

Dennis returned with a couple of boxes full of toys: discarded and broken Barbie dolls and other random parts of old board games.

'Who wants to play dead-Barbie Monopoly?' asked Dennis with a broad smile. He was obviously as high as a kite.

The others helped him unpack the various items as he described how the game would work. Josh sat and watched them as they each chose a severed Barbie head to act as their game piece, and Dennis handed out the scraps of paper that would serve as money.

'What we gonna do for dice?' asked Benny, taking the whole thing far too seriously.

Dennis looked about for something; then his eyes landed on a dented tin box, and he picked it up with one hand and scratched numbers on each side with a rusty nail. Josh thought the tin looked familiar — it reminded him of the ones in the colonel's house.

'There you go, Benny,' Dennis said, throwing it to him. 'You can go first.'

'I hate going first,' muttered Benny as he caught it.

'Do you ever wonder where this stuff came from?' asked Coz, picking up one of the eyeless heads, 'like who owned it before?'

'Before what?' asked Dennis, rearranging the pieces on the board.

'Before they chucked it away. These things came from somewhere, someone made it, someone played with it — it meant something to someone.'

'Not any more,' replied Dennis with a twisted smile that made everyone feel a little sorry for the toys.

'Yeah, who cares? They chucked it out. Their loss,' said Josh spinning one of the heads round on his finger.

Lils was staring at Josh as she took the joint. He rarely smoked dope — he's seen what it did to his mother.

'You should go, Josh,' repeated Lils.

'Where, Lils? Where can I go?'

Her naive outlook was beginning to annoy him. She approached life in a very childlike way. There were times when he wondered if she wasn't a little autistic.

'I dunno. Do something different, have a night off. Your

mum's not going to need you for a while yet, is she? Go wild. Go be someone else for a night!'

She was right, of course, Josh was sick of his life. No matter how hard he tried, it never went his way. He knew he had to break out of this cycle somehow, start taking some kind of control of his life.

Shags took a large swig from a cheap plastic bottle of cider, the type where the sides caved in as you drank. When he finished, he belched so loudly that everyone laughed. It was contagious — even Josh in his dark mood couldn't help himself. The drink reminded him of Caitlin's invitation and he stood up.

'You going?' asked Benny.

'Just remembered I was supposed to meet someone.'

'What's that? You got a hot date?' said Lils with a wink.

'Yeah. Something like that.'

Josh walked away, but before he reached the gates Shags caught up with him.

'We had a whip round,' he said, emptying a handful of coins into Josh's palm — it was probably all they had. 'Have one on us, yeah?'

Josh grinned his thanks and walked out of the gates, turning north towards the tube station. He needed to get to Highgate.

12

THE GIG

The Flask was in Highgate, which was far outside of his usual territory — Josh tended to stay away from the north side of the Thames. There were rules and borders that needed to be respected between the various gangs; moving outside of Lenin's sphere of influence made him vulnerable. If one of the Kurdish or Albanian gangs caught him out alone, it would end very badly.

The red bricks of the pub were turning orange in the warm evening sun as he walked up the street towards it. He could hear the happy chatter of people standing outside and slowed down, his resolve waning. The street was lined with very expensive cars, and his hand brushed instinctively along their paintwork as he considered his options. He could leave now in one of these fine motors and make it more of a business trip, or he could walk into a pub full of strangers to meet a girl he hardly knew.

The outer courtyard was packed with an eclectic mix of people: drinking, smoking and generally enjoying themselves. There was a bar strung with fairy lights and lined with impatient customers waving twenty-pound notes at the flustered bar staff. Josh tried to count the donated cash in his pocket. It was certainly not going to go very far in this place, but still something made him stay.

This was how the other half lived, he thought to himself, what people did when they wanted to relax while he was usually trying to break into their cars. Josh never bothered with the pubs on the Bevin estate. They had grilles over the windows and were guarded by doormen from the Russian mafia. Here he could be someone else, outside of Lenin's world, at least for one evening. For one night he could forget about all the other shit.

There was no sign of Caitlin, but there were posters for 'Infinitum 12.016' on the side of the bar, and some of the drinkers were wearing T-shirts similar to hers. The more he studied the crowd, the more he realised there was something unusual about some of them.

Mrs B. would have called them 'eccentric', dressed in old-fashioned suits, with long coats and quirky beards. They were older than him, most in their late-twenties. As he admired their different styles, he began to wonder whether he should have made more of an effort with what he was wearing — there wasn't a hoodie in sight.

He was just beginning to wonder if he'd been stood up when he spotted her, or rather she spotted him. Caitlin appeared out of the crush and walked over to him with a pint of Guinness in one hand and a shot glass full of some dark spirit in the other. She looked like something from another age: her velvet coat was so long it nearly touched the floor, and her leather boots stretched halfway up her thighs. She reminded him of a pantomime he'd seen once.

'Hi, medal collector — or was it metal detector?' she said with a half-smile, handing him the shot glass. It smelt like rum.

'Josh,' he replied, realising he hadn't told her his name. He should've given her a fake one, but he hadn't thought through his cover story. He would have made a terrible spy.

'Josh. Cheers,' she said, clinking her glass against his. 'I'm glad you could make it. Come and meet the gang.' She grabbed his empty hand, turned on her heel and ploughed back into the throng. He was dragged along behind, trying to keep up with her as she slid between the revellers towards the main entrance to the pub.

'I love this place,' she said, letting go of his hand. 'But it's getting too bloody popular these days.' She pulled open the door. 'It's nearly four hundred years old — it's like going back in time.'

As he stepped inside, Josh immediately knew what she meant.

The interior of the pub was dimly lit by low-energy bulbs; each one looked as if it had been taken from one of the many old radio sets his grandad used to keep in the shed. The low, sagging ceiling was supported by worm-eaten wooden joists, which separated the space into a random collection of odd-sized rooms.

Caitlin's friends had commandeered a large side room, one that looked more like a Dickensian curiosity shop: two of its walls were made of bullseye glass panes, and the other was taken up entirely by shelves of old-fashioned glass bottles. Even the table that they were sitting round resembled something from a pirate ship that had been cut down to fit into the space.

When they walked in, everyone was deep in conversation. In the centre of the table was a cluster of empty glasses, Josh realised he wasn't going to be able to stand them a round.

'Guys!' bellowed Caitlin over the noise, pushing Josh forward into the room. 'This is Josh.'

Some of them looked up and gave him a nod of acknowledgement; others blatantly ignored him.

'Not another foundling, Cat?' resonated a deep, well-spoken voice from behind them.

For some reason, this seemed to suddenly attract the group's attention. Josh could see from the expectant faces of Catlin's friends that this was the overture to an argument.

'Josh, let me introduce Dalton Eckhart. Possibly the most arrogant, infuriating man in England.'

'Why thank you, my dear,' said Dalton sarcastically, holding his hand out to Josh.

Dalton was a tall, handsome man, immaculately dressed in a dark tweed three-piece suit. He had a well-trimmed beard that made him look older than he was. Josh shook his hand firmly, trying to match the pressure that Dalton was exerting. There was a moment when something seemed to pass between them — he felt a tingling sensation creep along his arm like pins and needles.

'Pleasure,' Dalton added in a voice that was straight out of Eton. 'One rarely ever gets to meet anyone from Caitlin's charity work.'

His expression was hard to read, but his eyes were studying Josh keenly, in a way that made you feel instantly inferior. Dalton let go of Josh's hand.

'Hi, I'm Sim,' said a small voice next to Dalton.

Sim was not much older than Josh and looked like a student, with a mop of shaggy blond hair. 'Don't take any notice of Dalton,' he whispered as he placed a tray of drinks down on the table and shook Josh's hand weakly. It was like holding a wet fish. 'He has an innate ability to get under your skin. Thinks he owns the place.'

'Well, actually, he kind of does,' admitted Caitlin. 'But that's not the point. He's still bloody rude.'

'What did he mean by charity work?' asked Josh.

'Just ignore him. He's a snob, trapped in the old ways. Still believes in a class system. Sim, I think a drink would be in order?'

Sim handed them each a glass. 'Dalton's a total arse.'

He gave Josh a Jack Daniels and Coke, one of his favourites — never having been a big fan of beer. He was about to ask how Sim knew when he remembered the little money he had. Apart from the change rattling around in his pocket, he only had his mum's credit card and there was a high chance that it would be declined — particularly with the size of this group: there were at least eight or nine of them squashed round the table.

'I should pay for this.'

'Not a chance, you're my guest,' Caitlin replied, holding up her hand. 'Anyway, Dalton's buying so I'd make the most of it.'

Caitlin pointed to each one of the group in turn and told Josh their names, but the combination of the dope and the alcohol was making it difficult for him to concentrate. Dalton came back with two helpers carrying trays loaded with more drinks, and before Josh knew it he was feeling rather merry. After they had finished the second round, Caitlin went off to organise a third, leaving him with a table full of strangers.

At first Josh had thought they all must be academics: they had that arrogant, carefree air of students and they all dressed strangely, as if they'd been to a vintage charity shop. He'd assumed it was all part of being a superfan of the band, since the pub seemed to be full of steampunks, but when he looked closer he realised how authentic

Caitlin's friends' clothes appeared to be compared to the others.

'So where did she dig you up from?' asked one of the group, who Josh thought was called 'Lisa' or 'Lyra'. She was very pretty, but had wild eyes that seemed to stare straight into your soul.

'The library,' he answered, still trying to think of a plausible cover story.

'I bet they don't see many of your type in there,' she said with a grin — she was flirting with him.

'Quite enough of that, Lyra,' Sim remonstrated as he sat down between them. 'Ignore my sister — she's a total tart. Do you come from around here?'

'No, South London. Never been this far north.'

Lyra chuckled from behind Sim and said something under her breath that Sim ignored.

'Never been to Highgate? It has the most famous graveyard in London. Karl Marx is buried there.'

'And Milton,' Lyra added.

'And Faraday.'

'Malcolm McLaren.'

'And Rossetti . . .'

The game continued round the table, naming various famous dead people that were interred in the cemetery until it came to Dalton. He took a long sip of his beer before he spoke.

'Something you may be interested to know, Josh: there are actually fifty-nine soldiers of the Second World War lying dead in the cold earth of Highgate.'

The silence was deafening. The game was spoilt, and all eyes had turned on Josh.

'Why would I find that interesting?' asked Josh.

'Oh, I don't know, maybe something to do with —'

'Your interest in military history,' interrupted Caitlin as she put down the tray of drinks. Her expression was difficult to read. Josh thought he saw a glint of a warning to Dalton, but couldn't be sure.

'Just time for one more before the gig starts,' she said, handing out the drinks. Which, to everyone's relief, gave them all an excuse to change the subject.

Caitlin sat down next to Josh and raised her pint.

'Cheers!' she said as she tapped his glass. 'Still glad you came? I know these guys can be a little eccentric so don't take them too seriously.'

'Did you tell him about the medal?' Josh asked, staring at Dalton.

'Of course not. I just said you were interested in the war. Don't pay him any attention.'

Josh couldn't shake off the idea that Dalton knew about what had happened with the medal.

'So what are you into?' asked Caitlin. 'Other than war memorabilia?'

'Cars.' He thought it was wise to stay as close to the truth as possible.

'What, like a mechanic?'

'No. Like designing them.' He couldn't help himself — the lie just created itself instantly, driven by his need to impress her.

'Wow. Which course?'

'CAD at Coventry. It's supposed to be the best in the country.'

She looked impressed. 'Good for you. I would never have taken you for a student.'

'Really? What did you think I was, then?' he asked, taking a drink to calm his nerves.

'Oh, you don't want to know. It was silly really.'

'You can't drop that bomb and walk away.'

She looked down into her lap as if embarrassed. 'Well, I thought that maybe you were a thief and that you had stolen the medal.'

'Yeah I get that a lot. Something about my swarthy complexion.' He screwed up one eye and pulled a face.

'Ignore me,' she giggled, 'and stop that — you look ridiculous!' She hit him on the arm.

'Now tell me something about you,' he said, rubbing his arm as if it hurt.

'Nothing much to say. Studying History at Oxford. I work in the library during the summer, stay with my godparents in Camden. Drink too much, smoke too much, the usual kind of stuff.'

He wanted to ask her about boyfriends, but knew better than to go there. He would have to wait for her to make the first move. She was way out of his usual league, and he needed to play it cool.

'What's Oxford like?'

'Beautiful, and full of brilliant people — they make me look completely stupid.'

'I can't believe that,' he said, making a mental note never to go there. 'I bet you know loads of things.'

'Ha. You think so? Ask me a question.'

He thought for a moment, then the years of having to endure his mother's quiz shows finally came in useful.

'Which English king was the last to die in battle?'

Caitlin nearly spat out her drink. 'Blimey, I was expecting something a little more easy to start!'

'Do you want an easier one?' he asked, apologetically.

'No. No. It's fine. Has to be something in the fifteenth century — give me a second.' She screwed up her eyes and caressed the dragon pendant on her necklace.

'Do you want a clue?'

'Shh!'

'I'm going to have to hurry you.'

'Wait. I know this.' Her hand waved about in the air. 'It was Bosworth, which means...' Her fingers counted out against her thumb. She opened her eyes. 'Richard the Third!'

He clapped his hands together. 'You're good. That was a third-round question. Even my mum had difficulty with that one.'

'Is your mother a historian?' Caitlin asked eagerly.

'No,' he laughed, 'more of a collector of useless facts. An armchair expert.'

She shook her head. 'No such thing as a useless fact. She sounds like a very clever lady.'

She was once, he thought to himself, *and I think she would like you very much.*

Josh wanted to spend more time with Caitlin, but she'd made some lame excuse to go off and argue with Dalton. He managed to glean more about her from Sim, how she was an adopted sister. He wouldn't go into details about what had happened to her parents, but she had lived with his family since she was ten. Sim was obviously a maths genius, who was about to start working at a highly respected institution that Josh had never heard of. He also figured out that Sim really liked the little dark-haired girl in the corner, whose name was Thea, and that he was too shy to ask her out.

From his accent Josh assumed that Sim had been to private school, but in other ways he really wasn't that different from him, and Josh couldn't help but like the guy.

Apparently the band was about to start. Caitlin finished the argument with Dalton and tried ineffectively to get everyone to leave the 'snug' and make their way through to a large room at the back.

Dalton, who looked rather sheepish after Caitlin had finished talking to him, took control and marched them all out in military fashion.

Josh stayed back, but Caitlin caught his arm.

'Ready for some dancing, then, medallion man?' she asked with a slightly inebriated snigger.

'I was going to shoot off actually.'

'Why?' She looked genuinely surprised.

'It's not really my thing.'

'So what is?'

'Not this. You're all public school and loaded — I've got about a fiver in change.' The truth slipped out before his drunken brain had time to filter it.

'It doesn't matter, Josh. They like you.' Then she saw his doubtful expression. 'Well, Dalton doesn't like anyone other than himself so don't take any notice of him.' Her eyes narrowed. 'Stay for a couple of songs — they really are awesome live.'

The sounds of a guitar tuning up rose over the chatter, and the bar began to empty.

'I tell you what.' She held out her hand as if they were making a bet. 'If you make it through the first set, I'll help you find a collector tomorrow. For your grandfather's medal?'

He'd totally forgotten about the damn medal. Somehow it had slipped his mind. He took her soft, delicate hand and shook it gently.

'Deal.'

13

NECROPOLIS

The sound of the last song was still buzzing in his ears as he followed Caitlin and the others out into the cold night air. It was way past midnight; the sky was a clear dark velvet, lit only by a full moon, which painted the landscape in silvery tones.

The pub crowd had emptied out onto the street and were either standing staring into the pale light of their smartphones or heading towards the high street in search of taxis. They were like some strange circus troop singing and dancing their way into the night. Josh watched them go, undecided as to whether he should follow them. But he was still buzzing from the gig, and there was nothing to go back home for — at least, nothing he cared about right now.

Caitlin and her friends had broken away from the main group and disappeared down a side street. When Josh caught up with them, he could see that they were heading for a church. Its silvered steeple stood out against the curtain of stars like a gothic ice sculpture. Josh had no idea where they were going or what they were planning to do, which suited him. He didn't want to think about anything.

As they walked through the churchyard, he caught up with Sim.

'Where are we going?' Josh whispered.

'Another party!' Sim said with a grin. 'A special one.'

'In a graveyard?'

Sim smirked. 'Kind of.'

At the back of the churchyard was a tall brick wall; it was covered with ivy and stretched away in both directions. The group made for a dark, shadowy part of the wall and seemed to vanish into it. As Josh got closer, he saw there was a door, a wooden gate bound with rusted iron, and at its centre was a symbol, a snake devouring its own tail.

Dalton was standing waiting for him on the other side of the gate, his profile a black silhouette against the moonlit marble tombs. The grey walls of a sprawling necropolis stretched out behind him for miles. Josh could see Caitlin was standing next to him, she was protesting about something, but Josh couldn't hear what it was about. The others were climbing down into the stone avenues of the crypts. The gate was another way into Highgate Cemetery, not somewhere he had ever really wanted to spend any time, but it was different and kind of exciting.

'He's not one of us!' he heard Dalton say.

'He is under my jurisdiction. You have to let him try.'

As Josh came through the gate, she turned towards him. 'Josh. There is something I need to explain.' She sounded serious and incredibly sober.

'No need. I know when I'm not welcome.' Josh's head was spinning. The night air was making him feel a little weird.

'See. Even he knows!' said Dalton, slurring his words.

'You can't just go picking up any oik off the street because he shows a little talent.'

'Who are you calling an oik?' asked Josh, his temper flaring. He was finding it hard not to punch the pompous git in the face.

'You really know how to pick them, Cat. I've seen his type before — they're destined to fail.'

Josh had the feeling that there was more to this conversation than he knew. He wanted an explanation, and he felt his fists tightening as he thought about how he was going to get it.

'Josh. Listen to me,' said Caitlin calmly. 'He's just looking to provoke a reaction. Don't give him the satisfaction.'

'Yes, Josh. Be a good boy. Do as you're told. Wouldn't want Mummy to get upset now, would we? Not in her condition.'

That was the final straw, Josh lashed out with his right hand and punched Dalton in the jaw. Dalton went down hard. It was possibly the most satisfying thing he had done in years, suddenly all of the pent up frustration and anger broke free, and he was on top of Dalton hitting him as hard as he could.

'JOSH!'

He could hear Caitlin screaming from somewhere far away. He didn't care. He was focused on destroying everything that was wrong in his life. Dalton was Lenin, MS, the father he had never known, all these things and more. He felt the punches landing one after the other and with each one a door opened to more painful memories.

There were other voices around him. Hands grabbed his arms and dragged him off the ground. Dalton's body was no longer there.

Then the world around him twisted, and he was

standing at the gate once more. Dalton was talking to Caitlin as if there had never been a fight.

'The first test of any gentleman is the ability to control one's temper,' he said, adjusting his tie. He didn't have a mark on his face.

Josh lunged forward, but this time Sim grabbed his arm and shook his head.

'I rest my case. He's a bloody savage.' Dalton added turning to Caitlin.

'You did that on purpose. You read him, didn't you?'

Dalton shrugged. 'Well, it is my job after all!' He took out his watch, which was on a chain like the colonel's. 'Shall we? I believe the Sun King is about to start the ball,' he added as he walked down in the direction the others had taken.

Caitlin turned toward Josh. She looked very disappointed 'Let him go, Sim.'

He felt Sim's hands relax and move away. The guy was stronger than he looked.

'What the hell is going on? One minute he's on the floor and the next he's over there!' Josh shouted at them.

'You wouldn't understand. It's complicated,' Caitlin replied, shaking her head.

'Well, he deserved it,' declared Josh checking his hands for cuts and finding none.

Caitlin's eyes lit up with a fire of her own. 'No! That's not true. I expected you to be better than that! You're my guest, and you punch the first guy who gives you a hard time.'

'You don't own me! I don't need to explain myself to you or anyone else!'

'So that's how it is. Josh against the rest of the world?'

'Yeah. It's done me okay so far.'

'Really? Has it? Can you honestly say you're happy with your life? Based on what I've seen I would say not!'

'He started it!' Josh heard himself say, and knew that he had lost.

'Oh, grow up, Joshua!' Caitlin said as she stormed off.

Sim followed a few steps behind. He shrugged at Josh as if to say, 'Women. What can you do?' and they disappeared down into the crypts.

Josh stood alone in the doorway trying to work out what had just happened — the night wasn't supposed to end this way. He had never really cared about what other people thought of him, but the look of disappointment on Cailtin's face was bothering him. Without her, it was going to be difficult to find a dealer for the medal. If he apologised now, maybe he could salvage something.

He followed her down the steps into the dark street of tombs.

Caitlin and Sim had caught up with the rest of the group, who were easy to spot by the glow of the torches they were using to read the inscriptions on the tombs.

One of them shouted, and the others collected around the voice.

Josh wanted to talk to Caitlin alone, and he slowly worked his way through the shadows of the baroque vaults until he was close enough to see what they were doing.

Dalton inspected the inscription on a large stone sarcophagus and then produced a small book from his jacket, tore a page out and began to recite from the text. From his hiding place, it sounded like poetry to Josh, who was just thinking how weird this was becoming when he saw Dalton hold the page up to the tomb and disappear. Then, as if to confirm his disbelief, the rest of the group followed suit — each one taking a page out of the book and vanishing. Not through some secret trapdoor, but just basically winking out of existence. Caitlin was the last — she looked around as if expecting someone else to turn up, then she too disappeared.

He went over to where they had all been standing and inspected the inscription on the grave. The weather-worn text read:

Here lies what remains of John Milton. Author of Paradise Lost. 1608—1674

The ground was littered with torn pages from the book. Some seemed to be glowing, and as Josh tentatively picked one up a string of light grew between it and the stone. He could hear the faint sounds of laughter and a string quartet, as the line turned into a ribbon that grew out from the page. Spreading like a vine, it twisted and turned round his arm. There were knots of energy with strange symbols floating around them. The motion of the twisting made him feel dizzy, as if he was looking down at it from a great height. He dropped the page, shaking his hand as if it had been burnt; the light died away. It left him feeling weird, a mixture of being on some major high and incredibly drunk at the same time.

Something was tingling on his hand, but he ignored it and ran back to the gate. This night had given him enough surprises — now he just wanted to be in his bed.

14

THE COLONEL

Josh slept through most of Sunday, only waking up once to eat cold baked beans out of a tin. He'd never felt this rough. It was as if man-flu and a hangover were fighting over the rights to his body — something had drained all his energy.

His dreams were full of wild things, strange twisted versions of events that folded in on themselves. In one, his mother was completely cured and happy but one of her eyes was missing. She kept repeating: 'It was a small price to pay,' as she hoovered the flat. Another had him back in his old primary school trying to reach a rope that was just out of reach. He could hear his gym teacher shouting at him and when he turned round he found it was himself screaming at him to make the jump.

He awoke in a cold sweat. It was morning, and the clock showed it was well past 9am, which meant he was already in trouble with Mr Bell. He was lying on top of the duvet, still wearing the clothes from Saturday night. There was a faint aroma of Caitlin about them, from which he took a moment of indulgence. She'd spent most of the gig jumping up and down against him — something she apparently considered to be dancing. Josh remembered the way she'd felt as they had been pressed together in the crowd. He had restrained himself from putting his hands on her, even though she probably wouldn't have noticed; his mother had taught him how to treat women with respect.

There was still a faint ghost of a headache lingering at the back of his head, but it didn't hurt anything like as much as his hand. He pulled off his hoodie and examined his arm. There was a subtle, fractal-like pattern of burns all the way up from his wrist to his elbow — like a henna tattoo from an Indian wedding — except it was etched into his skin like a scar. His right hand was covered in a filigree of intricate symbols and shapes that were not from any language he'd ever seen. Josh tried to remember what had happened on Saturday night, but it was a blur. The last moments in the graveyard were particularly fuzzy; he remembered something about a crypt and some fireworks, but it was vague and shapeless, like a dream. Did he get a tattoo on the way home? He doubted it.

He stumbled out of his bedroom to find the flat was even more trashed than when he'd left it. From the state of the carnage, it was obvious that word had got around — it was now open season on Josh's place. Every thief and their second cousin had been around and helped themselves to anything that wasn't nailed down. There were no taps in the bathroom, no carpet in the hall and the kitchen was lacking a sink. Some inspired genius had even started on the boiler, but had given up and taken the doors off all the cupboards instead. The boiler hung precariously away from the wall, supported only by the pipes, a fitting end to something that should have been condemned years ago.

Based on the smell, Josh decided it was wiser not to go

into the toilet, and simply changed his clothes before going across to No. 52.

'Hello, dear,' said Mrs Bateman once her door was finally unlocked.

'Hi, Mrs B. Can I borrow your loo? Mine's been nicked.'

It took more than an hour to get away from Mrs B. She insisted he finish a full English breakfast and two rounds of toast before she would discuss any other business. She was a cross between a grandmother and a sergeant-major — kind, but with the ability to make you do exactly as you were told. There had been times when she had been more like a second mum — in the early days she would take care of him when his own mother was too ill or hospitalised, before they knew it was MS.

'Now I'm not going to ask how you did this,' she said, as she brought out the first-aid kit and began to bandage his arm. There was a knowing look in her eyes, 'but I do want to talk about that medal you left with me the other day.'

Josh felt a cold chill run down his spine at the thought of having to explain how he came by it; Mrs B had a way of making him feel like a six-year-old. He'd never been able to lie to her, she seemed to see through every one of his excuses, and she was certainly never going to believe what really happened. He was having enough trouble with that himself.

The face of the German officer loomed large in his mind once more. Because of Josh, the assassination of Hitler had failed, and Stauffenberg had been shot, not to mention the many others who had died in the extra year that the war had lasted.

He stopped the thought before it went into overdrive —

could he seriously be considering that he'd travelled back in time and changed the outcome of the Second World War?

'When you get old,' she began, interrupting his train of thought, 'your memories are all that you have.' There was a wistful tone to her voice, the kind that old people used when they reminisced about the 'good old days'.

She finished dressing his arm and carefully pinned it in place.

'The mementoes we've collected throughout our lives become part of us. They help us to remember our past; they connect us to our memories and remind us of those we have lost.' She looked up at him. Her skin was deeply wrinkled, and her hair fine and thin, but behind those bright blue eyes he knew she had a mind as sharp as any twenty-year-old.

'Now I've known you since you moved here, Joshua, and you're not a bad lad, not like some I could mention. You still care about things, but you never consider the consequences of your actions. Young people don't — you've always been a challenge for your poor mother.'

She was possibly the only person who could say this to him, and he would take it.

'So,' she said, producing the medal still wrapped in the newspaper. 'In all that time there's never been a mention of a great-grandfather, and especially not one that could have come by this. It was precious to someone once. It may be all they have left of the person that earned it. No matter how bad the trouble is that you are in, is it worth the cost of someone else's happiness?'

He hated it when she got inside his head. She was like his conscience, a moral compass, the one person he could rely on to tell the truth — something that had otherwise been missing from his life. He assumed it was the role that one of his parents was supposed to play, to keep you on the straight and narrow, but since Mum was always sick and he'd never known his father, it was a hard thing to imagine. He wasn't sure he was missing anything, really, because most of his friends' dads seemed to be utter twats and more than half of his mates' parents were divorced . . .

She was right, of course. He couldn't admit to her that the crazy man whom he'd stolen it from probably hadn't a clue that it was missing, but that wasn't the point. He stole cars because they were easily replaced; taking other people's treasured possessions wasn't his style.

'Put it back.' She patted him on the hand. 'There's a good boy.'

That was when the thought struck him. Maybe he could keep her happy and still get something out of it.

The bandage would be a perfect excuse for his lateness, Josh thought, as he walked into Churchill Park. Bell couldn't punish him any more than he already had, but at least he might score some sympathy for the burn, which he could see from under the wrapping had already begun to fade.

He wracked his memory for any more details of what had happened the night before last. He could have sworn there'd been a fight. He had a vague feeling that he'd punched the posh boy, Dalton, but it was all so fuzzy and muddled. There had been some kind of argument with Caitlin, which would explain why he hadn't woken up in her bed that morning — what the hell had he drunk that had screwed up the evening so badly?

Something was already kicking off when he walked into the park. All the community-service crew were crowded round in a circle shouting at someone. Mr Bell was standing in the centre of them, talking to whoever was sitting on the ground.

As Josh approached, Mr Bell looked up and frantically beckoned him to come through. The circle parted to let Josh pass and he saw the crazy colonel sitting crossed-legged on the grass, rocking back and forth, hugging a large bag of gardening tools that included the machetes. He looked very upset.

'Joshua, this gentleman says that you have stolen something of his and he refuses to move until we summon you.' Mr Bell put air quotes around the word 'summon'.

The colonel looked up through his tangle of wild hair and smiled at Josh with a flash of amazingly clean, white teeth.

'Ah, the thief has finally surfaced!' he said, standing up and handing the bag to one of the bystanders. 'Thank you.'

Mr Bell managed to look both relieved and concerned at the fact that the crazy man had surrendered the bag of very sharp knives. Josh knew the supervisor was only thinking about the mountain of paperwork and inquiries that would result from this.

The colonel grabbed Josh by the arm and frog-marched him back towards the park gates. 'You still have the medal?' he hissed under his breath as they walked. 'Eddy told me you tried to sell it to him.'

'Ye-ah,' Josh stuttered. The old man stank of sour beer and sweat — being so close to him was making Josh gag. 'I was going to give it back.'

'Of course you were,' the old man said sarcastically. 'Couldn't shift it without provenance so you were going to try to sell it back to me no doubt.' His voice was rough, as if he'd gargled with gravel.

'But —'

'But what? You think you're the first light-fingered Johnny I've had in my house? In another age, they would have had your bloody hand off for this! Now, for the sake of our audience, try to look like you're in a whole lot of trouble. Which, by the way, you are.'

Josh looked back to see the dumbfounded Mr Bell staring at them, his mouth flapping like a fish. The rest of the crew were laughing and pointing at Josh — clearly amused by the crazy man's abduction.

'Let go of me!' demanded Josh, struggling to free himself from the iron grip.

'I swear if you don't play your part I'll cut your nuts off and use them to stop that trap of yours from flapping. In twenty seconds your supervisor is going to think about calling the police, and young Delland hasn't gone for the knife yet.'

They were already through the park gates and onto the street when Mr Bell had the sense to reach for his mobile. He was on the verge of dialling 999 when one of the other lads sliced his hand open getting a machete out of the tool bag.

'Brian Delland, where were you when they were handing out brains?' Mr Bell said as he put the phone away and reached for the first-aid kit. The others were hooting with laughter as the blood sprayed out over anyone that got too close.

Once out of sight of the others, the colonel released Josh, or, to be more precise, dropped him. Josh was impressed by the strength of the old man; his feet hadn't really touched the ground the whole way across the park.

'Now,' said the colonel as he walked towards his front door, 'do you have the vestige?'

'The what?'

'The medal,' the colonel growled.

Josh stopped and produced the newspaper bundle from his pocket.

'Ah!' The colonel shook his finger and lowered his voice once more. 'On second thoughts — maybe not out in the open. Wait until we are inside the house.' His head flicked nervously in all directions as if they were being followed. 'You never know who might be watching.'

A minute later they were standing in the hall of the house, which still smelt as badly as it had before. The colonel took off his greatcoat and pulled out a notebook from one of the pockets. He checked his fob watch, which hung from a dirty, dark green waistcoat. 'Eleven fifteen on the dot,' he said, closing the book. 'Now the medal, if you please.'

Josh unwrapped the parcel and offered the open package to the old man who produced a single, garish pink, rubber glove and proceeded to put it on while staring at the medal.

'The Stauffenberg incident. Well, you're nothing if not predictable. How much did Eddy tell you it was worth?'

'Thirty grand.'

'Ha. I don't know who is the bigger thief!' he muttered, picking up the golden cross by the ribbon. 'I take it you checked with an expert?'

The colonel rummaged through one of the drawers in the Welsh dresser and took out an unusual magnifying glass that seemed to have numbers running over the lens.

'Yeah.'

'And?'

'Someone bought one for £200,000 a couple of years ago.'

The colonel nodded. 'Good. You're not as stupid as you

look. Now, let me see, which variation does this hail from? Hmm. Fourth or maybe fifteenth variant.'

He muttered a stream of random numbers and probabilities as he consulted his notebook. Page after page of nonsensical symbols flickered in front of Josh's nose, symbols that looked a lot like the ones on his hand. He pulled his sleeve down a little further.

'Yes. Stauffenberg. Tried to kill Hitler in 11.944, sorry 1944. I sometimes forget the temporal context.' He closed the notebook and placed the medal on the side, taking off his pink glove with a thwack.

'He succeeded.' Josh blurted. The colonel obviously knew his history so he thought that maybe the man might be able to help solve the mystery.

'What?' The colonel's eyes narrowed.

'The past has changed somehow. I was taught that Stauffenberg killed Hitler. The Second World War finished in 1944. But no one seems to remember that any more!' Josh blurted it out quickly before he changed his mind, but it still sounded completely mental.

This disturbed the old man, who became very flustered and went off to rummage through a set of drawers, mumbling to himself about remembering where he put something.

He returned to Josh and held out a handful of old dice.

'Throw these,' he demanded, closing his fist and shaking them.

Josh took the dice and threw them onto the floor. They all came up sixes.

'Six sixes,' the colonel said as he gathered them back up. 'One in 46,656.'

'What does that mean?' asked Josh.

'Highly unlikely,' the colonel mumbled as he pulled out an old pack of playing cards. 'Pick four cards at random.'

Josh did as he was told. They were all aces.

'What are the chances of that?' said Josh.

'One in 265,825,' replied the colonel. 'You're right — something is very definitely out of kilter.'

He consulted something in his notebook and then went to the large stacks of newspapers and began to rifle through them. They appeared to be in chronological order as the old man worked his way over the years, calling them out as he checked a random date from each.

'Well, don't just stand there! Look for 1944,' he barked at Josh as he pulled the papers out.

Josh chose a yellowing edition of *The Times* dated 1812. Its headline read 'American Attack on Kingston Harbour'.

'American War of Independence. Wrong end. Wrong century. You need to start over there.' The colonel, who was halfway up a small ladder, was pointing to a spot a few stacks to his left.

Josh put the newspaper back carefully and moved past the colonel. He climbed the stairs and began searching the upper parts of the stacks.

'What exactly am I looking for?' he asked.

'A date. And, if possible, a time and a bloody location.'

Josh had more luck on his third attempt. It was from the right year. 1944. But too early: the news was mostly of battles and propaganda about the war.

Then he found it: 21 July 1944 edition. It came quickly out of the pile — as if it were waiting to be discovered. Although the edges were a little tattered, the paper itself was still crisp and white, as if it had just been delivered that morning. It was strange to think that it was nearly seventy years old, that it had been printed before his grandparents had been born.

'Got it,' Josh shouted, holding up the paper. The colonel jumped down off the ladder and snatched it out of his hands.

'Good. Now where is it?' he muttered, flicking through the pages without any respect for the age of the document. 'Ah. Richardson. Now he was a real war correspondent. Got to the heart of the matter. None of this celebrity blather we have to put up with these days.'

The colonel folded the paper over so that Josh could see the page. There was a blurry photo, taken from a distance, and some copy about the location. 'Wolf's Lair . . . rings a bell. Think that's in Poland somewhere . . .10.20am. 20 July 1944. So that would be sometime along the lines of 71.3219.'

'71.3219 of what exactly?'

'Years — approximately. I could wait for the clackers at HQ to send me the exact details.' He pointed at the notebook. 'But they're getting awfully slow these days, and we don't need to be to the exact second.'

Josh would have thought the man a complete nutter if it hadn't been for the memory of the washroom.

'I think — I think I've been there.'

'Really? And how do you think you did that?'

'It happened when I touched that,' Josh said, pointing at the medal.

The colonel's face hardened. 'Tell me exactly what you saw.'

So Josh did exactly that. He recounted everything he could remember: the sound, the feel of the cold tiles under his feet, the look on the officer's face when he dropped the suitcase. The colonel listened intently, showing no emotion until Josh stopped talking. Then he shivered as if there had suddenly been a cold draught.

'So it appears you may have changed history,' he said, walking off down the hallway towards the back of the house. He stopped at a door that had been slightly obscured by a stack of papers. 'We'll have to go back and check,' he added nonchalantly, pushing the piles aside and opening the old door. 'Not one of my favourite decades that one.'

Inside the room, there were rows of costumes on rails, like a theatrical wardrobe department. The rails were on rotating racks that stretched up to the ceiling and further back into the room than should have been possible. Each contained a selection of the most authentic-looking pieces of fancy dress Josh had ever seen.

The colonel turned a series of wheels using a large brass crank and the racks reorganised themselves until one with the numbers 11940 appeared at the front. He then began to search through the garments like a Paris couture designer, 'No. No. Hmm, maybe. No. Wrong side.' And then, 'Yes, of course. SS. Who would question a member of the Gestapo?' He handed Josh a black uniform and took one for himself.

'Put this on. I'll be back in a minute,' he said, making for the door.

'What's this for?' asked Josh, holding up the uniform.

'Well, you don't want to turn up naked again, do you?' He smirked and left.

Josh stood staring at the elaborate collection of vintage clothes. There were so many incredibly realistic costumes hanging around him that he felt like a child in a toy shop — except this wasn't kids' stuff — this was like cosplay or re-enactment. Josh had no real idea what the old lunatic was up to, but dressing up like a Nazi was not something he thought he would be doing when he woke up this morning.

He tried the door but it was locked. The mad bugger had bolted the door on the way out. He had little choice but to play along and part of him wanted to see whether he could go back there again. The colonel seemed to think he'd changed history, which meant maybe he could help him change it back again, or at least explain what the hell was going on.

He undressed and put on the uniform. It was a bit big for him, and heavy, the cut of the jacket spoke of fine tailoring, the stitching was so small as to be nearly invisible and he was pretty sure the buttons were made of silver. His knowledge of the SS was patchy, but from what he could remember they were the top dogs in the Third Reich, the badasses that everyone else was scared of.

The colonel came back into the room wearing the uniform of an SS officer. His beard had gone, and his hair was shaved down to a grade two. It had taken years off him; he looked more like a man of forty, and the uniform made him look respectable — even if you could still see the remnants of the shaving foam on his collar. The man had been out of the room for less than five minutes. Josh was amazed by how he could have got a shave and a haircut so quickly.

'So.' He put on his cap and straightened it. 'Are you ready, boy?'

Josh nodded, placing his hat on his head and looking at himself in the full-length mirror. It was amazing how the uniform changed him. The person who stared back at him looked every bit the officer. He could see why some people got a kick out of the whole role-play thing.

The colonel produced the medal and held it out in his palm.

'Place your finger upon the vestige,' he said, opening his

notebook with his free hand. 'Now, nothing you are about to see will make any sense, but, trust me, no matter what you think you know it is very important that you don't change anything.'

Josh wanted to ask about how this worked, but suddenly he heard the music again, and then tendrils of light began to unfurl from the medal.

The colonel began to play with the air around the medal, manipulating the lines of light in a way that made the burns on Josh's arm itch. It was as though he were looking for something specific in a knotted ball of twine.

'There,' he whispered as the room vibrated around them and went dark.

15

WOLF'S LAIR

[Wolf's Lair, Eastern Prussia. Date: 11.944-20-07]

W hen Josh stopped retching, he realised he was kneeling in a thick carpet of pine needles in the middle of a forest. It was dark, and the treacle scent of pine sap filled the air. The moon was half hidden by cloud, but in the weak light he could see that the trees went off for miles in all directions. The colonel stood a few metres away, checking something on his watch. As Josh went to take a step towards him, the ground seemed to shift, and he stumbled.

The colonel helped him back on his feet. 'Takes a bit of getting used to. Time displacement does strange things to the inner ear. Drink this.' He handed him a small hip flask — it tasted like brandy.

'Where are we?' asked Josh, taking a sip. It was good stuff. The nausea dissipated as he handed it back to the colonel, who took a long draught himself.

'Prussia. No . . . Poland. Used to be called "Masuria" once upon a time. It's had a rather tumultuous history. Anyway, we're half a mile south of the Wolfsschanze,' he said, pointing towards a twinkling array of lights in the distance.

Josh stared blankly at him.

'The Wolf's Lair. Hitler's eastern front headquarters — although the accurate translation should be Wolf's Fortress.'

'This is not where I came before.'

'No, well, we didn't want to jump right back into that. The aim of the mission is to stay in the shadows. To observe, not blunder in like an uninvited guest at a banquet. Just follow me.'

The colonel headed off up the hill. Josh tried to keep up, but the big man's strides meant he was nearly running to stay with him. It was then he realised that the heavy holster bouncing off his hip must actually contain a gun.

'How come these clothes didn't disappear when we landed?'

'Actualised,' corrected the colonel, breathing heavily. 'When we *actualised*.' Josh could see sweat beads glinting on his forehead.

'What?'

'The correct term for the completion of a displacement is actualisation.'

Josh preferred his version, but continued anyway. 'So the clothes?' His voice echoed across the forest.

The colonel stopped for a moment to catch his breath. 'I don't suppose you get to go on many secret missions, so I will forgive this constant barrage of questions, but just so you appreciate the seriousness of the situation: there are approximately two thousand Nazi soldiers over the next ridge with excellent eyesight and incredibly powerful weapons. The basic plan is that we don't give them any reason to exercise one with the other. So keep your voice down. Agreed?'

Josh nodded.

'Good. Now, to your point: clothes are complicated. It really depends on when the materials were invented, but, more importantly, it's about not looking out of place. Blending in with the era is not always as easy as it looks.'

Josh thought back to the way people would stare at the colonel's greatcoat and wild hair, but decided this probably wasn't the appropriate time to bring it up.

For the next ten minutes, he followed behind him in silence as they skirted the high, razor-wired perimeter fence. There were various death's head signs about mines, and searchlights that intermittently swept the ground behind the fence. He could hear dogs barking somewhere off in the distance and shuddered at the memory of Billy getting his backside bitten; he guessed these hounds were more likely to tear your throat out. They stopped where the ground rose up and gave them a good view of the compound.

The colonel took out his watch. Josh could see it was no ordinary clock face — there was a complex set of dials and symbols whirring across the front of it, and it shone with a strange blue glow that illuminated the colonel's face.

'So the Allied forces landed on the beaches at Normandy over a month ago.'

'You can see that in there?' asked Josh, pointing at the timepiece.

The colonel snapped the watch lid back and dropped it into his pocket. 'Not really. I read up on the subject while you were getting changed. Wanted to have a better appreciation of the challenge.'

Josh was still mystified as to how he could have done the research, had a shave and a haircut and got changed into his uniform in the time he was out of the room.

'There have been four other assassination attempts in the last two years. Himmler and the Gestapo have been on high alert ever since. They suspect someone within the German High Command.'

The colonel took out some antique-looking binoculars and studied the compound for a few minutes.

'Three rings of defence, each more secure than the previous. The outermost is defended by land mines and the Führer Begleit Brigade, a special armoured security unit, which mans the guard houses, watchtowers and check-points.' He took out his notebook and Josh could see a 3D map of the base rotating around on the page. Lines and data appeared and disappeared at various locations on it as if someone was trying to plot the best way in — but kept changing their minds.

'Inside this is where the barracks are located as well as the quarters of the Reich's ministers.' A smaller shape was drawn inside the first. 'And inside that is a Führer's bunker made from two-metre-thick steel-reinforced concrete and guarded by the Reich Security Service, an elite group of SS officers handpicked to be Hitler's bodyguards.'

'So not much chance of us just busting in, then?' joked Josh.

'None,' the colonel replied gravely before going back to his surveillance, 'but that's not what we're here to do.'

'You're not going to change it back?'

'I haven't been instructed to do so. No.'

'Instructed by who exactly?'

'Whom.'

Josh ignored the correction. 'Whom do you work for?'

There was a noise, the dry crack of a boot snapping a twig. It resonated through the quiet of the forest like a bullet.

The colonel lifted one finger to his lips, his eyes scanning the woods in the direction of the sound. 'Save the questions for later.'

He took out the medal once more. It immediately lit up in his palm, throwing the craggy features of his face into sharp contrast. Josh felt him take his hand, and the world around them began to vibrate, the trees shimmered in and out of phase, then he felt the ground fall away.

It felt like less than a heartbeat before they appeared inside the camp. It was light now and, judging by the position of the sun, close to midday. The inner compound was busy. There were German soldiers and officers going about their usual business, none of whom seemed to notice the sudden appearance of two high-ranking SS officers from behind Bunker 5. Josh assumed that, even if they had, they knew better than to question them — he could see from the fear in the guards' eyes that the insignia on his uniform carried a lot of authority, and he kind of liked it.

The colonel was talking fluently to one of the sentries at the door of a large green bunker. He took a letter out of his notebook and shoved it into the man's hand. Josh strode over to the colonel and nodded at the guard. The hard-faced man finished reading the letter, snapped his heels to attention and handed back the document. The colonel folded it carefully and placed it in the notebook. He saluted the other officer with a 'Heil Hitler' and turned to Josh with an expression that said: 'Follow me and don't say a word.' Then he walked straight into the bunker.

Inside they found themselves in a corridor that tunnelled deep into the rock. It was lit by a small line of electrical lights that illuminated gold-framed oil paintings — some of which Josh recognised.

'The Führer's private art collection, appropriated from museums all over Europe,' whispered the colonel.

Josh heard music once more, and looked up to see a tinny metal speaker. A shiver went through him as he realised that this was definitely the same place as before.

The colonel stopped at a door further along the corridor. The gothic script on it read *Oberkommando der Wehrmacht*. He knocked once and waited for an answer from within. A very long minute went by before he tested the door handle and went inside.

The interior of the office was the opposite of what Josh was expecting. It was a plush, carpeted, executive room with panelled walls and beautifully carved furniture.

The colonel closed the door quietly and locked it. He took off his hat and sat behind the massive gold-inlaid mahogany desk. Behind him stood a sculpture of a giant eagle, its wings spread wide while grasping a swastika with its claws, the Nazi flag was draped behind it.

'Welcome to the office of the Supreme Commander of the Armed Forces,' the colonel said opening his notebook. 'I'm glad to see you managed to keep your mouth shut out there.'

'Languages aren't my strong point. What did you tell them?'

The colonel paused to study something on one of the pages. 'That we'd been sent to investigate a potential conspiracy. The great thing about a well-drilled unit of elite soldiers is that they are trained to accept orders without question — as long as you know whose name to put at the bottom of the document.' He waved a piece of paper at Josh.

Josh examined the order; it was in German so meant

nothing, the name at the bottom of the signature read *Heinrich Himmler*.

'The head of the Gestapo, Minister of the Interior,' the colonel said, as if anticipating Josh's next question. 'Now we only have ten minutes before your appearance so I suggest you tell me exactly what happened and where. I believe the washroom is through here --' He opened another door, and Josh immediately recognised the green tiles and white basins with their golden taps.

'Where exactly do you appear?' the colonel asked.

Josh showed him.

'And the officer comes out of here?' He pointed towards the end cubicle.

Josh nodded.

'OK. Good.' Looking at his watch again. 'Now we have to make ourselves scarce for a few minutes.'

They went back into the main office and through a connecting door into the next room. This second office was smaller and nowhere near as ornately furnished. 'Secretary's out having a sneaky smoke,' the colonel said with a wink. 'We just have to wait for a couple of minutes.'

Josh's pulse was racing. His brain was still having trouble accepting the fact that he was standing in the Führer's bunker in 1944. The colonel, however, was taking everything in his stride, as if he did this everyday. Josh was trying desperately not to look weak or frightened in front of him, but he was having serious difficulty holding his nerve.

The door to the executive office opened, and they could hear Stauffenberg enter and walk through into the washroom. The colonel opened the connecting door slightly to see if the coast was clear and then went through, signalling to Josh to stay where he was.

Josh moved so that he could watch the colonel, who was

checking something in his notebook and counting time with his finger.

Suddenly there was a loud crash from the washroom. Stauffenberg had dropped his suitcase. Josh held his breath, he could picture the scene vividly: the man's gloved hand scrabbling to push everything back in, the explosives scattered over the floor, the second charge rolling too far away.

'Herr Oberst,' barked the colonel. He was standing at the door to the washroom knocking on the glass. '*Herr Oberst? Der Führer erwünscht Ihre sofortige Anwesenheit!*'

There was a noise from inside, and Stauffenberg opened the door. He looked back once before leaving; Josh knew the look well, and then Stauffenberg cooly nodded to the colonel and walked straight out of the room into the corridor.

The colonel went into the washroom and reappeared a moment later tucking something inside his jacket.

'Right, we'd better leave now!' His eyes were burning with an intensity that Josh had never seen before.

He placed his hand on Josh's shoulder and took out his watch.

The room twisted away.

By the time Josh had got changed back into his own clothes, the colonel had made a large pot of tea and a plate of small round pancakes. The kitchen was something he would have expected from Mrs B instead of a crazy old man who lived alone. In contrast to the rest of the house, it was spotlessly clean and had the delicate looking china cups and plates displayed on an ornate Welsh dresser. The table was covered with a white linen cloth, and the silver cutlery looked antique and expensive.

There was no sign of the colonel and Josh was famished. He sat down and stuffed the first pancake into his mouth without a second thought. Then he picked up the tea cup and drained it in one go.

When the colonel came in from the garden a few minutes later, Josh got the impression that he had been away for significantly longer than it would take to pick the vegetables he was carrying. He looked different: his hair was slightly longer, but nothing like as straggly and overgrown as before, and his beard had begun to grow back.

He was carrying a basket full of carrots, leeks, and potatoes, which from the state of his hands, had just been picked. A small black cat followed him into the house, winding itself around his legs as he set about cleaning the vegetables.

'I see you found the oatcakes. You'll need to replenish your energy levels. I find strawberry jam helps the blood sugar along quite nicely.'

Josh took a heavy handled knife and smothered the next oatcake with jam and then proceeded to devour it. The colonel dried his hands and removed his coat. He was wearing a mustard-coloured chequered waistcoat and moleskin breeches, like a head gamekeeper from some country estate. He sat down opposite Josh and poured out another round of tea.

After a few minutes, Josh began to feel more like himself.

'So,' said the colonel, pouring a little of his tea delicately into a saucer. The cat jumped up onto the table and began to lap at it. 'I assume you have a few questions?'

Josh's head was full of them, so many that it was hard to choose where to start. He finally opted for an obvious one.

'Did we really just go back in time?'

The colonel nodded. 'Technically not so much *go* as *displace*, but, yes, you could say we did that.'

'How?'

'Ah now, quantised spacetime, that could take quite a while to explain, and I'm not sure I'm the right man to do it — you need a rather large blackboard for a start. To put it in simple terms, we followed the timeline of the medal. It's a rare skill — there are very few with the ability.'

The colonel took the medal from his pocket and placed it on the table. Josh could see there were still lines of energy emanating from it. The cat hissed at it and jumped down.

When Josh reached to take another oatcake, the colonel noticed the burn patterns on his hand.

'I see that you're no stranger to the weaving,' he remarked as he grabbed Josh's hand and pulled up his shirt sleeve. 'Very recent activity too. Don't worry — it fades in a few days.'

'Weaving?'

'That's what we call it. When we're trying to locate the appropriate nodal event in the timeline — like rewinding a map.' The colonel moved his hand over the medal and the lines shifted subtly.

Josh pulled back his arm and put his hand under the table. 'I don't remember how I got it,' he admitted with a hint of embarrassment. He didn't want to mention that he was drunk when it had happened. 'What are you?' he asked, trying to change the subject.

'An Anachronist, a man of the Watch,' the colonel said proudly, 'part of the Oblivion Order — an ancient society of chronologically ambiguous individuals from a rather elite evolutionary branch known as Homo Temporalis.'

Josh wasn't quite sure about the 'Homo', but he liked the

thought of being part of an elite group, as long as they weren't all as deranged as the colonel.

'And this time thing.' Josh pointed at the medal. 'You can all do that?'

'There are a wide variety of abilities within the Order, but, yes, basically everyone can do that.'

'That's messed up. How come no one knows about this?'

The cat came back and began sniffing around the remnants of Josh's breakfast.

'Do you honestly think that anyone would believe you? You hardly believe it yourself. Our work is based on the premise that the human race is blissfully ignorant of what we can do. Time is not something to be trifled with — there are rules.'

Every answer seemed to create more questions, and Josh's brain was having difficulty prioritising them.

'Why me?' was all he could think to say.

The colonel began to clear away the cups and plates. 'Who knows? It's random, doesn't follow any kind of perceivable pattern — that's the universe all over.'

Josh grabbed the last oatcake before the cat could get too close.

'Any of your relations show a penchant for history?' asked the colonel.

'No, not that I know of.'

'And your mother and father didn't have unexplained collections of things?'

Josh shook his head. He didn't want to go into the whole family history. There were too many gaps in it, ones his mother was unwilling to fill in.

'How old are you exactly?'

'Seventeen,' he said in between mouthfuls.

'I would have put you in your twenties. You're mature for your age — had a hard life, have you?'

'No, not really.'

'One thing you will learn about us is that it is pointless to lie about your past. Our own timelines are complex things, but they are there to be read just like the medal — if one has the talent to do it.'

Josh was not about to discuss his life story with a complete stranger, even if the crazy old man had just taken him on a round trip to Hitler's bunker.

'Back then, in the Wolf's Lair, what did you say to make Stauffenberg come out of the toilets?'

The colonel shrugged. 'Simple. I told him he was required by the Führer. Most officers know better than to keep their C.O. waiting.'

'So you were the one on the other side of the door? Before, when I was . . .' Josh felt the colour rise in his cheeks.

'Stark naked? Yes, that was me. It was a minor repair. In other versions of that scenario your appearance caused a lot more problems than a failed assassination attempt on Hitler — what we have now is one of the best statistical outcomes.'

'A repair?' Josh was confused.

'A temporal adjustment to ensure that the version of events stay within a pre-determined set of positive outcomes.'

'Determined by who?'

'By a whole department of brilliant boffins who spend a very long time assessing the alternatives before they decide on the best course of action.'

'I don't get it. How can we have gone back and —'

'Changed the past? That's the paradox of it all: it's already happened, and the world still seems to be turning.

Now, where did I put the biscuits?' The colonel began hunting through the kitchen cupboards.

Josh shook his head as if attempting to realign his misfiring brain cells.

'What you need in situations like this is a custard cream, or maybe even a Garibaldi. At the very least a chocolate digestive . . . Ah, here we are.'

The biscuit tin was Victorian — the hand-painted enamelling of a family Christmas scene around the dining room table looked like something off of the Antiques Roadshow — but when the colonel opened it the smell of freshly baked biscuits was overwhelming.

'Another perk of the job,' the colonel said, grinning like a six-year-old. 'Shopping is a rather more eclectic experience. By God, those Victorians really know how to bake!' He picked out a fig roll and popped the whole thing straight into his mouth.

Josh took one of the plainer ones and bit into it. The taste was so different from the usual budget stuff he was used to; it was as though the thing was melting on his tongue, butter, cinnamon and sugar crumbled apart in his mouth. He helped himself to two more.

'So what happened? Did Hitler survive?' he mumbled through half a biscuit.

'Yes. It took the Allies another year to end the war. Terrible bloody business.'

'Why not just go back and kill Hitler before? Or his dad? Or his grandad?'

The colonel paused for a moment as if weighing up how much to tell him.

'That's not how it works. Some things were always meant to happen; for good or evil, you cannot change the past too dramatically without disastrous consequences. You have to be more subtle.'

'Like telling someone they are needed urgently by their Führer?' Josh said flippantly.

'At the right moment, yes. One word can change the course of history. Never forget that.' He held up his finger to emphasise the point.

'But that wasn't how it should have been! Who are you to decide on who lives and who dies?' said Josh raising his voice. The image of all the names on the Churchill Park memorial ran through his mind.

The colonel's face grew serious. 'There are bigger things at stake here. We're trying to stop the human race from destroying itself. Sometimes that requires sacrifice — these decisions are not taken lightly.'

'So you're telling me that the hundreds of thousands who died because a bomb didn't go off were sacrificed for a good cause? You really are mental!' Josh stood up.

'Don't blame yourself. Greater minds than ours have been debating this event for hundreds of years. The Copernicans predicted a seventy-four-point-four per cent chance that a united Germany would have initiated another world war within seventy years, probably during the economic decline in 12.008-15, after the UK left the European Union.'

Josh took a moment to process the dates. 'No! I was there — it didn't happen! Your geniuses got it wrong!'

The colonel shrugged. 'That's statistics for you. No one said it was an exact science,' and began washing up the cups and plates in the sink.

'So is that it? Am I supposed to carry on as though nothing has changed?' Josh was shouting now. 'This makes no frigging sense!' and, with that, he turned and stormed out of the house.

The colonel sighed to himself. 'I think he'll find that everything about his life is about to change a great deal. Won't he, puss?'

The cat ignored him, realising that the opportunity for food had ended, and wandered out through the back door.

16

ABOUT MY DAD

It took three long, frustrating days to complete his community-service order. They didn't go back to Churchill Park, which was a relief as Josh didn't want to bump into the colonel. He needed time to think it all through.

Nothing seemed to make sense any more. He tried to ignore the changes, but something had been awakened in him — adding an extra dimension to the world around him. Everything had become more real, more vivid. Every object he touched seemed to pulse with history; every smell, sound or colour registered as if for the first time. He felt like he had superpowers, which perhaps he did. Josh ached to tell someone — to show them what he could do — but he knew he shouldn't. He didn't want to screw this up. This was the chance he had been waiting for, to be something really special, and he kept it close, kept it secret.

They had told him his mother was likely to be in the hospital for weeks and so, with his flat being a total train wreck, he had gone to stay with Mrs B. She was taking great delight in spoiling him. It was like being a ten-year-old again: tonight was chilli and chips, with Angel Delight for dessert.

Today was his final day of community service and as he packed up the tools into the minibus, he watched the other members of the crew goofing around: they had someone's phone and were throwing it to each other and pretending to drop it, while the kid who owned it flailed around, trying to intercept it. Everyone was laughing apart from the boy. It was juvenile and harmless. No one was going to get hurt — not yet, anyway. Josh knew that in a few years half this group would be doing time or dead. It was just a fact of life around here. Crime was a whole lot easier than working on a zero-hour contract and the pay was better, especially when drugs were involved.

Josh had never really been that into drugs — his mum took enough for both of them — but, when he did, it usually ended badly. Junkies were uncontrollable and random, ready to do just about anything for a hit; dealers on the other hand didn't give a shit. They got rich quick and, like lottery ticket winners, usually blew it all on pimped-up cars and tasteless bling.

'So, Mr Jones, this is it — our very last day,' Mr Bell said as he closed the doors of the van. 'Next time you'll probably be going straight to jail. Do not pass go.'

'No, sir.' Josh smiled. 'I'm not going down. Not like those retards.' He nodded at the rest of the gang.

'It's odd. Seems like I've known you for years. When was it now?'

'2013. Three years ago.'

'Yes. The fire, wasn't it? I seem to remember the school didn't reopen for weeks.'

'Wasn't my fault, sir. Wrong place, wrong time.'

Mr Bell laughed. 'It never is, Joshua.' He extended his hand. 'Your future is in your hands.'

Josh realised this was the first time Bell had ever treated him with any respect, and he could tell that the guy actually meant what he was saying. He shook his hand quickly before anyone could see and walked over to the group of boys.

'See you later, suckers,' he said, catching the phone as it spun past. He tossed it back to its owner nonchalantly and pulled up his hoodie.

'Got a message for you, Crash,' said Delland, who had a bandage over one hand. 'Lenin wants to see you tomorrow.'

'Yeah right,' Josh growled as he walked off.

The hospital ward was like a waiting room for the nearly departed. Visitors sat beside their sick relatives reading old magazines, sipping tea from cardboard cups or just staring blankly into space while they tried to think of something to say that didn't involve illness or death.

His mother was sitting up in bed with tubes running into each arm. She looked fragile and small, like a little doll. Her face had aged — as if the episode had drained her, but when she saw him the dark lines melted away under the warmth of her smile.

It was in these moments that he remembered how hard it was for her, never knowing when this disease would come back. She was damned to live a life of two halves: one spent suffering and the other waiting for it to return. There were only brief moments of happiness in between: when she would lose herself in a TV programme or score a small win on the lottery.

'Hi, Mum,' he said, leaning over to give her a kiss on the cheek.

'Hello, dear,' she whispered hoarsely.

'How are you feeling?' he asked.

'Oh, you know. Same old rubbish. Doctor said it would be a few weeks at least.'

Josh sat down and put the bag with her things into the bedside cabinet.

'Yeah, I know. I've brought you a few bits and pieces from home.'

'My tickets?' Her eyes widened.

'Yes. And some underwear and a toothbrush. The usual stuff.'

'And?' She was like a child at Christmas.

'And a lucky dip for the Euromillions. It's the largest rollover in two years apparently.' He handed her the ticket.

She held the paper as though it were made of gold. 'This is the one, Joshy. I can feel it in my bones. It will be ... what's the word? Kar- something.'

'Karma?'

'Yeah, like that. I always get a win when I'm ill. Check your diary thingy. You'll see.'

She was probably right. Her numbers did always seem to come up during her relapses — it came as a small comfort during the long nights to know that at least they would be able to keep the lights on for another week.

'Mum. About the flat ...' Josh faltered. There was a lump in his throat. He had rehearsed this conversation in his head all the way here on the bus.

Her face fell, the happiness vanishing as she shrank back into her pillow. 'I don't want to go back there,' she said, shaking her head.

That wasn't the answer he was expecting.

'The council have sent us a letter.' He produced the envelope, knowing full well that she wouldn't want to read it. 'They say we have to be out in a month. We're behind on the rent.'

'Good riddance. They can keep it.'

'But where are we going to go, Mum? You can't stay in here forever, and I'm sleeping on Mrs B's sofa.'

His mother looked away sheepishly, unable to look him in the eye as she spoke. 'I can stay with Aunty Julie for a while. Just till I get back on my feet. She came in yesterday and made me promise.'

Aunt Julie despised Josh. She had always blamed him for his mother's illness and hadn't ever been afraid to hide her feelings about him.

'Think of it as a holiday, love.' His mother tried to make light of it. 'Just while the council finds us another flat.'

She had no idea that they were about to get evicted. Josh had hidden the letters and the final demands. He knew that the stress would have kicked off another episode.

'What about our stuff? What am I supposed to do with it?'

'Burn it for all I care. There's nothing worth keeping.'

'But it was our home!' he said a little too loudly in the quiet ward. People began to stare.

She put her hand on his as if to calm him.

'They are only things, love. Bits of rubbish that we've collected over the years. As long as we have each other, we don't need anything else.'

'But Dad's stuff. It's all I have of him.'

She scoffed. 'Oh, Joshua. Your father never gave us a thing. I just made it up to keep you from asking too many questions.'

'The photo? The one at the beach?'

'That was taken by some stranger who was passing.' Her eyes closed and she sighed deeply. 'I have been thinking about it while I've been stuck in here — it's time you knew the truth. There never was anybody that you could call a dad. Just one stupid night at a party. I don't remember much about it, to be honest, but what he gave me was the best present I could ever wish for.'

She stroked his cheek, her eyes glistening with tears. 'I'm sorry, son, but I don't want you to waste time looking for something that never existed.'

As she spoke, the facade that he'd built of his father crumbled away. For years he had pasted layer upon layer of false memories over the gap where his dad should have been — using half-remembered stories or photographs he'd found in boxes of old polaroids. Like old wallpaper, the layers peeled off in one go to expose the isolation he'd been hiding from for so long, and he realised it didn't matter.

He'd never had a father — no amount of wishing for one would change that. His mother was all he'd ever known and that was enough. So he didn't have much to show for the last seventeen years. A few fading photographs and two swimming medals didn't really sum up his life — his criminal record was far more extensive and they were about to be sealed by the courts.

This was his chance to start again.

He was a survivor. No matter what life had thrown at him so far he had adapted and overcome it. All for her, she was the only thing he cared about, the reason he took the risks. The doctors were hinting that soon she would need full-time professional care. He couldn't bear the thought of her stuck in some residential home with a bunch of strangers, but he was running out of options.

He needed a plan. First, he had to get Lenin off his back and move his mum away from the estate — into a better neighbourhood. Perhaps he could even use her condition to get placed higher up the waiting list.

Her breathing had softened, and he knew she had fallen asleep. He'd wanted to tell her about the colonel — not the whole time-travel thing, but something to whet her appetite. He wasn't sure how it was going to help them, but he had a feeling that it was an opportunity to get them out of their situation. He just needed to find the right angle.

17

TRAINING

J osh went back home to pick up the last of his things: some clothes, his diary and a shoebox of old photos, which he had hidden under a floorboard in his bedroom.

He didn't realise there was someone else in the flat until he was leaving. The electricity was off, and it was getting late — making it virtually impossible to see who was rummaging around in the front room. He put down the last of his belongings carefully and picked up the baseball bat they kept behind the door. He gripped it tightly, as if he were going in to bat for the Redsocks.

There might not be much of his home left, but it was still all he had. It was probably a squatter or a junkie looking for somewhere to bed down for the night. He didn't care. This would be retribution for all the shit he'd been put through in the last week.

Josh crept quietly towards the front room, catching the woody aroma of pipe smoke as he got closer. Squinting into the gloom, he could just make out a large figure sitting in the armchair; the unmistakeable frizzy outline of the colonel's hair was silhouetted against the glow of the street lights that shone through the window behind him.

'What the hell are you doing here?'

'Joshua. I've been waiting for you,' the colonel's gruff voice announced. His face was suddenly lit up by flame as he re-ignited the pipe and puffed furiously on it. Josh couldn't help but notice that his beard had grown back to its usual bushy size again. He looked like a dark Santa Claus.

'They appear to have done quite a number on your home,' the colonel observed, once his pipe was alight.

Josh looked around the room. Someone had used the walls for graffiti practice while he was out. If it had been a car, they would have set it on fire by now. He dropped the baseball bat onto the sofa and sat down.

'Not my home, not any more,' Josh conceded, as if finally admitting defeat.

'Nonsense! This is merely temporary. We could go back a few days and fit better locks on that front door of yours — or even a better door if you wish?'

'No — it's OK. I'm done with this place,' Josh replied. He got the impression that the colonel had been drinking.

'Good,' the colonel said, getting unsteadily to his feet. 'Then I have a job you can help me with.'

'Why?'

The colonel took out a candle and lit it, placing it on the mantelpiece where the fake fireplace used to be.

'Because you have a talent, and it would be a great shame to waste it.'

Josh had never been told he had a talent for anything, apart from stealing cars.

'Will I get paid?' asked Josh.

'What?' barked the colonel, seeming rather taken aback by the question.

'Well, I kind of need cash — and you said "job" so I'm thinking I should get paid?'

The colonel burst into raucous laughter, the kind that came up from the belly and took a while to die out.

'What's so funny?' Josh asked.

The colonel wiped a tear from his eye and blew his nose on a large handkerchief.

'Sorry. It's been a while since I've had a good laugh.'

'So?'

'So you're the first apprentice that has ever asked to be paid.' He chuckled again.

'Well, the others must all be mugs, then. Or loaded.'

'Sorry. Yes, of course. It's just I haven't thought about money in such a long time. You forget what it means to not have it.'

Josh had never thought of the colonel as a rich man. In fact, he had always assumed the opposite. By the look of his clothes and the state of his house, it was reasonable to think that he didn't have a penny.

'Are you rich?' asked Josh curiously, 'like some eccentric millionaire?'

'Not as such no . . . But let's just say my "employers" make sure that I have everything I need.' The colonel walked around the room picking random objects up off the floor and placing them back into their original positions. Josh was astonished to see that the old man knew exactly where they should go.

'So they have a lot of money?'

'Amongst other things.'

'So I get paid then, yeah? Say, like, three hundred quid a day?'

'Whoa! You don't even know what the job is yet! Three

hundred pounds may seem awfully low when you find out what it is we have to do.'

Josh shrugged. 'Well, I need three Gs by tomorrow. So is it worth as much as that?'

'Where we're going, tomorrow will feel like a lifetime away.' The colonel took out his watch and tapped one of the many dials, as if it were stuck. 'This is not the place to have this conversation. Let's take a walk back to my house and I'll tell you all about it.'

Josh was about to leave when he remembered the diary and ran back into his bedroom to retrieve it. He took one last look around his room and waved it a mental goodbye — he had a feeling he was never going to see it again.

'Got your own almanac, I see,' the colonel said, pointing to the diary. 'Useful things, books.'

'There is just one other thing,' Josh said as they walked out into the hall.

'Ask away.'

'What is it with your hair? Three days ago you looked totally different. Does travelling through time make your hair go weird?'

The colonel looked at himself in what was left of the hall mirror and patted his hair down.

'Three days may have elapsed for you, but it's been more like three months since I saw you last — I realise it may take some time to get used to all this.'

Outside the rain lashed the pavement. It had cleared the streets of all but a few of the hardiest of pedestrians. A gang of boys sat silently on their BMXs under the cover of a dripping walkway watching the colonel and Josh as they made their way out of the estate.

'What's Crash up to now?' asked one of them.

'No idea,' said another, taking out his phone and typing:

CRASH HANGING OUT WITH CRAZY COLONEL. WAT 2 DO?

Lenin's response was almost immediate.

FOLLOW.

18

THE FIRST LESSON

'Before we embark on anything too adventurous, there are a few ground rules I need to go through with you,' the colonel said as he pushed the overloaded shopping trolley of bric-a-brac along the pavement. There wasn't a lot of room under his pink umbrella and Josh was beginning to question whether he should even be seen in public with the man; he smelt of booze and was acting strangely. Yet, certain things he'd said were starting to make sense — which wasn't a great indication of Josh's own mental state, but he ignored the alarm bells in his head — he needed the money.

The rain was beginning to tail off as they walked through the shopping arcade. They passed the last of the late-night shoppers who were slowly dragging themselves homeward — arms loaded with plastic bags. Josh watched the way they actively avoided the colonel and his trolley. It was a clever defence mechanism; no one made eye contact with a crazy man, especially one who was pushing a load of rubbish. A perfect way to make yourself unapproachable, if not invisible. Josh would've had exactly the same reaction as everyone else a couple of days ago.

'First, and most importantly, you never go back into your own timeline,' instructed the colonel, holding up his index finger as if to indicate there would be at least four more rules.

One of the wheels stuck on the trolley, and he spent a minute kicking it back into alignment.

'Changing your own line causes all sorts of complications and paradoxes, and it's not something you'll even remember afterwards. Like drinking a bottle of tequila, you almost always end up dead or worse.'

'What could be worse?'

'Excised. Expunged. Redacted. Removed from history, disappeared, never having existed.'

Josh wasn't sure that was really worse, since the dead didn't tend to care if anyone remembered who they were, but he decided now was probably not the right time to push the issue.

'The second point is about the future —' the colonel began as they came to the corner of the high street and he proceeded to walk straight out in front of an oncoming bus. Josh instinctively reached out to grab him, but the old man was too quick. The bus driver had to slam on the brakes to avoid hitting him. Passengers on board went flying forward, and the driver blared his horn and swore at him through the glass.

Josh went after the trolley as it began to rattle down the road under its own steam. The colonel, meanwhile, was gesticulating at the driver.

He managed to control the trolley and drag the colonel to the other side of the road before the bus driver got out of his cab.

'What is *wrong* with you?'

The colonel grabbed Josh's hand and tapped a button on

the side of his watch — time reversed around them —
seconds later they were back on the other side of the road
waiting for the bus to pass. This time, the colonel waved at
the driver as he went by.

'Nobody can travel into the future. As Shakespeare said:
it's *the undiscovered country*, too many unknowns, too many
variables. There are no paths to follow.'

'You're fricking crazy,' Josh said under his breath,
watching the bus disappear round the corner.

'An unfortunate side-effect of the job. Years of a non-
linear existence can slightly disconnect you from reality, like
jet lag. By the way, I don't care for the attitude. It really
doesn't suit you.'

'All right, Grandad. What century are you from anyway?'

'Well, since you ask. I was born in 940 — in your terms,
that's the tenth. We tend to use a different system, though,
one that has a longer perspective.'

They turned onto Churchill Avenue.

'So you *have* travelled into the future,' Josh stated
smugly.

'Yes. In the same way that most people do. One day at a
time.'

Josh calculated the man's age in his head, maths had
been one of his only strong points at school. 'That makes
you over a thousand years old.'

'If you take into account that I've spent more than
three hundred and fifty years in the past, I'm actually
nearer to fourteen hundred. Ageing doesn't stand still
when you go back, you know. You're still subject to the
same temporal laws of the universe, but they seem to affect
us less.'

'So how long do you live?'

'Barring accidents and other terminal situations, fifteen-hundred years, but some of the High Council are allegedly nearer two millennia.'

'So you're, like, nearly immortal?'

'Now you're beginning to understand my predicament. A lot of memories to try to keep track of,' the colonel said, tapping the side of his head, 'and birthdays are not quite what they used to be.'

He left the trolley in the front garden and marched up the front steps of No. 42 two at a time.

19

CABINETS OF CURIOSITIES

The first floor of the colonel's house was like a museum, in stark contrast to the chaos of the hallway and stairs. The large Victorian rooms on this level were full of glass display cabinets, each containing meticulously labelled artefacts.

'These are cabinets of curiosities — mementoes from previous missions,' the colonel said proudly. 'Each one represents a point in history that I've had to repair.' He tapped on the glass of a case. 'So which one shall we try for your first real test?'

Josh walked along the line of cabinets until he reached one with a vicious-looking cutlass lying on a bed of purple silk; it looked like something out of a pirate movie. The label read 'Ocracoke Island, 22-11-11.718-Nexus 20'.

'What was this for?' Josh asked as he tapped on the glass.

'That would be the cutlass of Edward Teach. Interesting chap.'

'Who?'

'Edward Teach, more commonly known as the pirate

Blackbeard.' The colonel opened the cabinet and carefully took out the sword. He examined the edge with his finger and then began to swing it around his body in a series of deadly scything arcs.

'Nice weapon for close combat,' he observed, stopping it millimetres from Josh's chest. 'Well balanced.'

Josh stared at the sword. 'So you're telling me you've met Blackbeard?' He couldn't quite hide the disbelief in his voice.

'Yes, I'd been second mate on his flagship, *Adventure*, for nearly a year when Lieutenant Maynard finally caught up with him. Nearly didn't happen. I had quite a job making sure she ran aground when she did — he almost made good on his escape.'

'So why exactly did you have to stop him?'

'See for yourself.'

The colonel offered him the sword, and as soon as Josh grasped the hilt he felt that tingling sensation. The same feeling he got from breaking into cars, but a hundred times more powerful. As the lines of history began to unravel from it, he caught fleeting glimpses of ships, and smelt the gunpowder of a battle. As he concentrated harder, the past expanded around him — suddenly he was looking at a young man standing on the deck of a ship in the middle of a wide blue ocean. He could smell the salt air and feel the wind rushing through his hair. It was a strange, dislocated feeling, like standing between two worlds — one foot in each.

'Our predictions indicated that Blackbeard's fleet would have intercepted this particular gentleman before he reached his destination.'

Josh didn't recognise the tubby, bespectacled passenger

dressed in knee breeches, waistcoat and white frilly shirt, but he didn't look to be much older than himself.

'Who is it?'

'Have you heard of Benjamin Franklin?'

The name was familiar. He had a vague memory of his mother shouting it out in answer to a question on the TV. 'Wasn't he one of the American presidents?'

The colonel took the sword back and placed it carefully onto the silk. Josh felt slightly dizzy, as if he'd just been on a waltzer. It took a while for the room to come back into focus.

'Not exactly. More like the founding father of the United States. He liked to dabble in meteorology and electricity, and was one mean chess player. When he was about your age, he ran away to London. In one version of events the ship he was travelling on was boarded and sunk by Blackbeard's fleet. Franklin would have died without ever realising his potential, and the USA would have been a very different place entirely.'

'So you took out Blackbeard?' Josh said, trying not to sound too astonished.

The colonel shook his head. 'No. We just selected one ending from a number of many possible outcomes. It is all planned very carefully to ensure we create the smallest number of side-effects. The sand bar at Ocracoke Island was calculated to be the least impactful event, even though it turned out to be one hell of a battle. I think it may be a little too hairy for your first planned excursion.'

Josh walked around the room. The cabinets were filled with the most random collection of historical objects: scissors, eyeglasses, a letter, some old brass keys, a ship's compass, four coins fused together by fire, a shoe, an old flintlock pistol. Each item had a date and a location, although some of the ink on the labels had begun to fade.

'So do you get to keep these after each mission?' Josh asked, thinking about how valuable some of them might be.

The colonel chuckled. 'It's actually the other way round. We need the artefact to find the path.'

'The path?'

'To travel safely back through time you need a path, a map, if you like. We use the timelines of man-made objects like these.' He waved his hand across the room. 'They each have an inherent history, one that you can use to navigate back to certain events, like a kind of bookmark or waypoint. If the object was particularly personal, you could even use it to reach certain people.'

Josh's eye was drawn to an old sepia-toned photograph of a beautiful young Victorian woman posing in a tight-waisted corset.

'So what was her story?' he asked, pointing at the picture.

The colonel walked over and produced a large ring of keys, which he fumbled through until he found the matching number and proceeded to unlock the cabinet door. He signalled to Josh to take the photo out, which Josh did tentatively, trying not to dislodge the other things that had been carefully arranged around it.

When Josh turned the photograph over, he saw the colonel's now familiar copperplate handwriting.

'Mary Somerville, 11.833,' he read slowly, trying not to reveal his dyslexia.

'Now Mary was a most interesting lady. She introduced Ada Lovelace to Charles Babbage.'

Josh stared at him blankly.

'The father of the computer? She also inspired John Couch Adams to discover the planet Neptune. Something I have to take a little credit for.' He performed a mock bow.

Josh turned the picture back over to study her image close up.

'Now I think that she would make the perfect test,' the colonel continued. 'Would you like to meet her?' He plucked the photograph out of Josh's hand and began to talk to it as if she were at the other end of a Skype call.

'What kind of test?' asked Josh, who was more than happy to meet such a good-looking woman; he just didn't like the sound of having to do any kind of exam.

The colonel stopped muttering and turned back to face Josh.

'A test of your range, of course! Each of us has an inherent limit. We need to know how far you can go back. A hundred years makes you a Centurion, a thousand and you're a Millennian. So far, we know you can travel back as far as 1944, which that means you're at least a first-level Centurial, but I want to see if you can make it back to 11.833!'

The ribbons of light were arcing about the photo now. Josh could see symbols dancing around it as the colonel moved his fingers over them.

'Can't do this kind of thing with digital photography, electrons too bloody erratic. Ah, there we are — nice safe point to drop into.' He reached out and brought Josh's hand towards the photo. 'Can you feel it, boy? The pulse of history running through your fingers?'

Josh put his fingers tentatively into the web of light and felt the tingling sensation like a cool burning over his skin. There were knots in the lines of light where the symbols were clustering. He moved one of his fingers and felt the knot slide underneath it. There was a feeling like remembering as he heard a voice, smelt the fragrance of a woman's perfume, then it was gone again.

'Did you feel it?' the colonel asked again.

Josh nodded. 'I think I heard her speak.'

The room twisted away, and the world dimmed for a second.

20

FENIANS

[London, England. Date: 11.833-02-21]

As Josh's eyes adjusted to his new surroundings, he realised that he was staring at the vaulted brick ceiling of a basement. The cold marble slab that pressed into his back made him shiver, and the sickly smell of chemicals did nothing to help the wave of nausea that swept over him. It was weaker than the last time and he managed not to throw up. He propped himself up on one elbow and saw that the colonel was busy rummaging through a wardrobe that was built into one wall.

It was then that Josh noticed the pale, lifeless bodies that were laid out on the three remaining marble-topped tables. From the look of the surgical instruments and glass jars that were arranged along the other walls, he guessed that they had landed in some kind of Victorian morgue.

'Glad to see you're feeling better,' the colonel said as he came back with a set of clothes.

The jump had reduced both of them to their underwear; the ones the old man had insisted on wearing, describing it as a 'Union suit': basically a white cotton onesie, which would be good all the way back to the fourteenth century.

The colonel laid out the clothes on the slab. 'Sorry about that. Perfectly natural reaction. I still find the sight of corpses hard to stomach. I probably should have mentioned this was a house of the dead.' He had picked out a white shirt and a green three-piece suit for Josh.

'This is one of our temporal safehouses — an outpost. They usually operate as a business to explain the comings and goings of strangers, one that doesn't raise too much interest from the general public. Funeral director is particularly popular — no one tends to pry into the preparation of the deceased. You can always rely on these places for sanctuary, food and an abundance of clothing relevant to the era.'

The suit smelled of cologne and cigars, the shirt of carbolic. It obviously belonged to a dead man, but Josh was too cold to care and, besides, he figured the other guy didn't need it any more.

As he got dressed, he could feel the quality of his clothing in the beautiful silk lining, the tailoring that was so fine that he couldn't see the stitching. Regardless of the jacket being slightly too big for him, he felt like a gentleman.

'Now we're both respectable, let's see what's left up in the pantry, shall we?' the colonel said, rubbing his hands together.

Josh could see from the weak light of the gas lamps that the colonel had selected a brown houndstooth suit with a red waistcoat. His hair was slicked back, and his beard combed. He reminded Josh of a portrait of Charles Darwin that he'd seen once on a school trip to the Natural History Museum. He remembered it well, especially the feel of

Monica Fellowes breasts as they were snogging during the film about dinosaurs.

'Why do I keep losing my clothes?' Josh asked as he followed the colonel out of the morgue and up the dark cast-iron staircase.

'It depends on their chronological inception. Man-made fibres especially don't make it back past 1937.'

'Why 1937?'

'That was the year Carothers invented nylon. Whilst he was working at the Dupont Experimental Station.'

It had never occurred to Josh that stuff like nylon had been invented by a bloke in a laboratory. It was something that he had read on every label he had ever washed of his mum's things. To him it was nothing more than just another setting on a dial at the launderette.

'The Order prefers older materials, like cotton and wool, materials that have been sourced from the seventh millennium — around 3000 BC. It's called 'jura' and they use it in our standard-issue travelling robes. Can't abide them myself — they just make you look like a damned monk.'

As they climbed to the ground floor, Josh began to realise how different the house was to the one they'd just left. The hall was decorated in heavy velvet wallpapers and thickly woven tapestries. There was no electric light, and the whole effect was made more gloomy by the weak glow of the flickering gas lamps. The colonel walked along the hall and adjusted the valves of each one with an audible hiss. Josh smelt the peppery scent of unburnt gas.

There was a bell near the front door and the colonel rang it once and then listened for some kind of response.

'Seems we have the place to ourselves.' The colonel shrugged. 'Let's find something to eat.'

. . .

The dining room was panelled in a heavy dark oak with ornately carved sideboards and cupboards stretching the length of the room. It had a vast, highly polished dining table with places laid out for at least twenty guests. The cutlery looked as if it were made of solid silver. Josh had to restrain himself from slipping a few of the smaller spoons into his jacket.

In the middle of the table and along the top of both sideboards was the strangest collection of stuffed animals in glass bell jars: Kittens playing with moths — frozen in a moment of intense play, bats in mid-flight, and many glass-eyed birds.

'Taxidermy was also rather popular in this period,' the colonel explained as Josh studied them closely. 'You'll find that the Victorians are more than a little obsessed with death,' he added as he disappeared through a door.

There were two oil paintings hanging at opposite ends of the long room: portraits of aristocratic figures. Josh thought he recognised one of them and went closer to read the bronze plaque that had been screwed into the gilded frame.

In a fine italic script it read: *Vc. Dalton Eckhart. 11.821.*

Josh stepped back to study the image. The subject was a good likeness of Caitlin's arrogant friend. Dalton was portrayed in a hunting scene with all the accessories: deerstalker hat, shooting stick, cartridge belt and shotgun, there was even a dog by his side proudly guarding a dead pheasant. They both stared out from the image straight at Josh. It was unnerving and not a little spooky.

A few minutes later, the colonel came crashing through the kitchen doors like a drunken butler, balancing a silver tray in one hand and his almanac in the other.

'Change of plan,' he blustered. 'I have to get to 11.866!'

The tray was piled high with cold meats: chicken, ham

and some thick sausages. There were two large glasses of a dark beer strategically balanced at each end.

'Causality crisis,' he said, opening his notebook and pointing at a page of symbols and formulas that were constantly changing around a branching set of lines. He went to one of the drawers in the long sideboard, and took out a velvet-lined box full of watches.

'Need to return you to the present. Give me your arm.' He muttered as he began strapping it to Josh's wrist. 'This is a Tachyon Mark IV, a timekeeper. One of its more basic uses is functioning as a homing device. I have set it to return you to the most chronologically recent point in your timeline — the moment you left the present.'

Josh examined the watch. It had a dial comprising clockwork gears and brass symbols, all encased in a series of concentric brass circles, each marked with fine lines and numbers. There was something underneath the dials that was emitting a faint blue glow, but he couldn't make out what it was.

'Why can't I come with you?' Josh asked, grabbing a sausage and following the colonel into the next room, which turned out to be another 'Curiosity' collection. The colonel was running his greasy fingers along a shelf of leather-bound books and counting off the years under his breath until he reached II.866. He took the volume down from the shelf.

'Encyclopaedia Britannica goes back to II.768. Can't beat it for chronology. Every safe house has one specially printed on twelfth century vellum.'

'I said, why can't I come with you?'

The colonel shook his head. 'Oh no. Far too dangerous. This causation involves Irishmen and explosives, never a good mix in my experience. I suppose you could wait here for Mary if you would prefer?'

Explosives sounded far more interesting than meeting some Victorian woman, no matter how hot she was. 'But I'm never going to learn anything if I don't see it for myself. I've been to the heart of a Nazi bunker and survived — how bad can this be?'

The colonel paused for a moment as if considering the consequences of taking Josh.

'Nice try, young man. But I don't think you're ready for this.'

'But if things get too hot I just use this,' Josh said, pointing to the tachyon on his wrist and smiling, 'and — *boom* — I'm back home safe and sound!'

The colonel scratched his beard. Josh noticed he did that a lot when he was pondering over a problem.

'You have a point. I'm probably going to end up regretting this, but I don't have the time to argue.' He placed the large leather book on the table. 'Remember you die just as easily in the past as the present. The first sign of trouble and you push this. Understood?' He pointed at the larger button on the side of the watch.

While Josh was studying the watch, the colonel went over to a tall cupboard and unlocked it. The cabinet was a lot larger on the inside. It contained a room full of weapons, each one carefully displayed as if at a museum. There were swords, daggers, blunderbusses and all manner of pistols and rifles from the last century. The colonel took a moment before selecting one particular pistol.

'Colt single-action army revolver. Model P — also known as the Peacemaker. It has a revolving cylinder, takes six bullets,' he said, snapping the chamber open and showing Josh the bullets inside. He handed one to Josh. 'Do you know how to use one of these?'

Josh had only held a gun once before: the one that Lenin had thrown into his lap. These were heavier than he expected. As he held it, he began to feel its history — the men that it had killed — as though it were warning him of what it was capable of. Josh had never liked guns. He had known too many people end up dead because of them. He shook his head and gave it back.

The colonel placed both of them into holsters inside his coat. 'Ah. Yes, with training you can learn how to control that. There are some simple exercises that can help you.'

Josh had never been that good at anything other than driving cars, something he had taught himself. This was different, like a superpower or an evil curse. He was beginning to wonder if this was something he could walk away from.

'Do I have a choice?' he asked. 'Do I have to join your Order?'

'I suppose you do have a choice, but I don't believe anyone has ever turned us down. Most accept it as their destiny — they're usually much younger than you. They tend to enjoy the thrill of their new abilities.'

'So there's more like me? Us?' Josh looked back to the picture of Dalton at the other end of the room.

'Yes, many more. Not all in this milieu of course, but spread out through time. We're stationed at various points throughout the last twelve thousand years. I have particular fascination for the petroleum age; the twentieth and twenty-first century obsession with fossil fuel has created some amazing technological advances, especially in space travel. So I was more than happy to be posted to the twenty-first, although there weren't many other takers, to be fair.'

'Why not?'

'There are many factors. Your time is seen as a hostile territory: electricity, nuclear weapons, intrusive technologies, social injustice, terrorism and of course you're very close to the Frontier.'

'Frontier?'

'The point at which the future and the present meet — where the known meets the unknown. We call it the Frontier. The younger members of the Order seem to be drawn to it, but many of my generation are scared of getting too close. They prefer staying further back in a nice safe posting in the past — they're a bit chicken shy.'

'Chicken shit,' Josh corrected.

'Exactly.'

Josh imagined what it must be like to be posted to the other end of history, just hanging out in caves and hunting with spears. He couldn't remember if the dinosaurs had died out before there were humans — he wished he'd paid more attention in his history lessons.

'So we need to get to the twelfth of December 11.866,' the colonel said, leafing through the encyclopaedia.

'You mean 1866?' Josh corrected him.

'Yes, but the Order work to a longer timeframe, one that starts at the end of the last Ice Age, over twelve millennia ago — so our years have an extra digit. It is more commonly known as the holocene calendar.'

The London Underground in 1866 was very different to the dirty, overcrowded, outdated version that Josh was used to. The train carriage was more like a decadent dining room than a commuter train: the seats were covered in a sumptuous velvet pinned in place with brass buttons, the electric lights were ornate brass lamps with glass shades — there were even curtains at the windows.

The colonel had made himself comfortable in one of the seats. He was pretending to read today's edition of *The Times* while puffing happily on a pipe. The very thought of smoking on the tube was so alien to Josh that he found it hard to believe it was allowed — yet nobody seemed to care. In truth, the colonel's smoke was nothing in comparison to the grey, soot-stained clouds pumping out of the steam engine and filtering through the vents in the windows.

Josh blinked back the sweat from his eyes. It was sweltering inside the tunnels. He couldn't understand how the other passengers, who were mostly men in black coats and bowler hats, were able to stand it. There were a few women in heavy-looking dresses delicately wafting themselves with Japanese paper fans.

It was a surreal feeling to be standing in a carriage with a crowd of people that you knew would most probably be dead in the next few minutes. Someone within this group was a terrorist, their suitcase full of explosives, waiting for the right moment to detonate.

Josh studied their faces, looking for a sign of guilt or a facial tic that would give them away, but found that most people looked pretty pensive on this train. He had to remind himself that in this time people bought tickets just for the novelty of taking a ride — rather than actually going to a destination. It was a carnival attraction for many, or so the colonel had told him when they'd appeared at Farringdon.

While they had been waiting for the train, the colonel had briefed him on the 'Fenians' — Irish freedom fighters who were planning to attack the railways as a protest over the occupation of Northern Ireland. The fact that Josh was standing less than ten metres away from a real terrorist was making him nervous. He'd contemplated testing the button on his new watch, but the colonel had caught his eye and given him a reassuring wink. Josh could see the pistol handle nestling inside his jacket, as if to say he had it all under control. He assumed that bombs needed fuses and timers in this era; there was no such thing as remote detonators, so the Fenian had to be on this carriage.

His first suspects had been a couple of navvies standing at the far end of the compartment. According to their coats they worked for the Thames Ironwork Company. Rough-looking men, their hands were like sledgehammers, scarred and solid from years of manual labour. Each of them carried a canvas bag, the cords of which were wound round their wrists so tightly he could see the red welts where they'd cut into their skin. He ruled them out when they got off at Smithfields, taking all their possessions with them. This left him with what appeared to be a respectable bunch of potentials with very little to separate them. Josh knew they would have to have a case, virtually every one of them did, and he assumed that they would leave it behind and get off at the next stop. The netted luggage racks were full of various valises and leather Gladstone bags, so knowing whose was whose would be impossible.

The colonel looked at his watch again. He had been doing it every couple of minutes, like the white rabbit out of Alice in Wonderland. Suddenly there was a loud crash from the next carriage and the screeching of metal against metal as the engineer applied the brakes. Everyone was thrown forward, and Josh found himself in the lap of a young gentleman with a very odd-looking moustache. When Josh put his hand out to steady himself, he touched the man's case.

His mind caught the image of something odd, a memory of a mineshaft and gunpowder. Josh apologised and pushed himself back up, trying not to be too obvious as he studied him more closely. The man was no more than twenty years old, with a chequered brown suit and derby hat, and he was looking around nervously now, trying to avoid eye contact. He put his hand into the bag.

Josh nodded to the colonel to indicate that he was sure this person was the one they were looking for, and the colonel smiled as if he already knew.

The train wasn't moving, and the other passengers were getting frustrated. There was a general murmur growing among the more disgruntled ones about 'inconveniences' and 'infernal machines'. The colonel stood up and came over to Josh.

'Ready?' he asked, folding up the newspaper.

Josh nodded even though he'd no idea what he was going to do next. His heart began to race inside his chest.

Something happened to the young man's case as the colonel grabbed Josh by the arm and clicked a button on the side of his watch. Time slowed down. He watched an orange ball of fire blossom from the bag when the bomb detonated inside it. Josh gaped as he watched the destructive force tear apart the body of the man, his body slowly scattering across the confined carriage. The pressure wave blasted the other passengers like dolls caught in a hurricane, and then, just when he felt the heat hit his chest, the world started to vibrate and flicker as time went into reverse.

[<<]

In a blink of an eye, they were back in the carriage of two minutes before. The navvies were still on board and the train was gently rocking along the rails. It took Josh a minute to register that they had just jumped back from the explosion, but he didn't have time to take that in before the colonel nudged him and walked over to the young man in the brown suit.

The punch completely threw the Fenian off his guard. Josh hadn't expected something so brutal either. The colonel hit the man square on the jaw, which caused the other passengers to stand back in amazement. It gave the colonel enough time to grab the case and throw it to Josh, who caught it instinctively without even thinking about what it contained. The colonel produced his revolver and waved it at the others, shouting something about being from Scotland Yard. He took the man by the arm and bent it behind his back as the train pulled into Smithfields Station.

The two navvies, who'd taken a great deal of interest in the commotion, picked up their bags and got off as they had before. The colonel pushed his prisoner out of the carriage and Josh followed with the case. As the train pulled away, the colonel released the man, who immediately ran off down the platform. Josh dropped the bag and began after him, but the colonel caught his arm and pulled him back. Josh turned, half expecting the colonel to be taking aim with his pistol, but the gun was back in its holster. The colonel simply nodded toward the escapee and whispered 'watch' under his breath.

As the man reached the gate near the end of the plat-form, his body shimmered as if going out of focus and then faded away. Josh scanned the crowd for the man, but he was gone. He looked back at where he had dropped the bag, but that too had vanished.

'What the —'

'The paradox of time,' said the colonel rather smugly.

'The real mission objective was to find out exactly who carried the bomb onto the train; there were no real leads from the historical data. Once we had identified the culprit, someone — probably me, would go back and stop him from ever being on the train or even involved with the Fenians. Quite neat really.'

'But didn't this happen, like, a hundred and fifty years ago? How come it is suddenly a crisis?'

'Takes a while to process. Copernicans are thorough if not a little slow.'

There was a scream of metal on metal again from inside the tunnel.

'Unfortunately we couldn't stop the other disaster,' he sighed as he began to walk away from the dust and smoke that came swirling out of the mouth of the tunnel. 'The first accident recorded on the London Metropolitan Railway. Workmen dropped a load of steel girders onto the tracks. The driver wasn't able to stop. The train derailed and crushed three people on the train coming in the opposite direction.'

'Can't we go back and save them too?' asked Josh as a panic-stricken stationmaster ran past them towards the disaster.

'Not authorised, I'm afraid.' The colonel tapped where his notebook sat in his jacket. 'I think we have overstayed our welcome as it is. Time to try out your tachyon.' He pointed towards Josh's watch.

Josh pulled back the sleeve of his jacket to see the dials whirring under the glass. He had no idea what they represented, although one pointer had now moved to a different number. He pressed the button on the side, and the Victorian station twisted away.

21

THE RIVER

The study was a strange and wonderful collection of seventies memorabilia. Interspersed between the impressive array of books were photos of space launches and collections of Apollo mission badges in neat frames. Hanging from the ceiling on short lengths of fishing line were meticulously painted model aircraft. A half-finished Concorde was resting on the upturned box at the edge of his desk and in an alcove was an ancient-looking turntable with a huge collection of old vinyl records stacked carefully underneath.

The colonel was sitting behind a large desk, struggling with an antiquated typewriter. He'd brought Josh into the study for a debrief on the mission. Apparently, this was all part of 'normal procedures'.

It was only now they were safe that Josh realised how late the colonel had left it to pull them back from the detonation. He'd actually witnessed the bomb ignite, saw its devastation in slow motion — the colonel had cut it fine, a little too fine, now he thought about it. It was a different experience to a jump. Time had slowed down and then rewound like a movie. He had felt something like it before, in the graveyard with Caitlin and the posh twat.

'The rollback — a very useful defence mechanism,' the colonel explained when Josh asked him how they had survived the blast. He was struggling to feed three sheets of paper into the typewriter.

'It gives one a few minutes' grace to avert, avoid or rectify a bad situation.' The paper jammed as he cranked a wheel on the side of the machine. 'It's a simple panic button. The Mark IV gives you about two minutes. The official term is "induced temporal retrogradation" — most of us refer to it as a rollback, rewind or even déja vu.'

'So I hit this and go back two minutes?' Josh asked, pointing at the topmost of the two brass buttons on the side of the watch.

'Yes. As I explained before, the other one is set to bring you back to the present, thirty seconds after you left — to ensure you don't bump into yourself.' He thumped the typewriter until it released the pages. 'Damn triplicate forms! What do they take me for? A bloody filing clerk?' He pulled a paperclip out from between two of the sheets and threw the ruined document in the bin.

Josh pressed the rewind button and the room flickered as he watched the last two minutes roll back.

[<<]

'So, how come I remember our conversation?'

'Which conversation?' The colonel went to put the form

in the typewriter once more. Josh stayed his hand and pulled out the hidden paperclip from between the sheets.

'The one about déja vu,' he said, handing back the paper and throwing the clip in the bin.

'Ah. We've had that chat, have we? You just tried the Mark IV out I suppose. Fair enough, I would've done the same. You're still travelling forward in your own timeline. It's a little hard to grasp — Eddington would be able to explain it better.' He took a fountain pen from his pocket and began to draw a series of lines on the back of one of the forms. 'I always think it's best to imagine time as a river, flowing ever forward.'

Josh could just about make out that the sketch was of a winding river with dots drifting down it.

'Now linears — normal people — are in their own personal boats, floating along with the current. Some sink, others misplace their oars, all eventually fall away.' He scratched little Xs over some of the dots. 'But members of the Order experience time in an entirely non-linear way. They have their own streams, which can be diverted away from the main flow: the continuum.' He wrote the word along the middle of the river, and then drew lines that looped away to join early bends in the stream. 'Yet we are still travelling along our own timeline, even when we go back, so we remember everything we experience, at least in most cases.'

'And you can control the direction of this continuum?'

'Not exactly.' He scowled. 'I may have over simplified the analogy. It's more like we're trying to keep it flowing in the right direction.'

'And that is?'

'Towards the best possible future of course! Which is a

conversation for another day. Now back to the report.' He turned back to the typewriter.

'So how would you describe the young Fenian's moustache?' the colonel asked.

'Fake?'

At the end of the day, as he lay back on Mrs B's sofa, Josh was still coming to terms with this new reality. The fact that he'd spent twenty-four hours in 1866 and come back to the same day he'd finished his community service made him appreciate what the colonel meant by tomorrow being a lifetime away. Josh knew that the future was waiting for him somewhere ahead — down the river — but he could deal with it when he was ready, and that gave him a great feeling of relief.

22

A BETTER LIFE

His mum was looking more like her old self when Josh went to visit her the next day. He still hadn't come to terms with the fact that the present was only one day older — even though he'd spent more than forty-eight hours in the past. The colonel had paid him in used banknotes, some of which Josh had to give back as they weren't legal tender, or at least not since decimalisation. There was also a 'bonus' — a guest room where he could stay whilst they continued his training. The cash came to just over £600, and it was burning a hole in his pocket when he turned up for visiting hours.

'Hi, Josh,' his mother said weakly.

He could see how drained she was and it made his heart ache to see how fragile she'd become. He'd bought her a box of her favourite chocolates — Malik had a deal going on them; they were fire-damaged stock from one of the shops on the high street which had suspiciously gone up in smoke the week before.

Her face beamed as she dug through the contents looking for the most precious of them all — the hazelnut cluster. If Josh was lucky, he might be able to get a couple of toffee fudges, but it was always a bit of a gamble.

'So how have you been keeping? Is Mrs B looking after you?' she asked before popping a whole cluster into her mouth.

'Great. She's a legend,' Josh replied. 'I have some good news.'

'Really, love? Have we won the lottery?' she asked with a broad smile.

'No, Mum, better than the lottery. I got a job — pays three hundred quid a day.'

She stopped chewing and looked at him with wide eyes. There were tears forming in the corners.

'You're not working for that bad boy are you?'

'No, Mum. It's legit.' *Well kind of*, he thought. He wasn't quite sure what to tell his mother that would sound convincing. 'I'm helping out this antiques dealer. House clearances and stuff.'

She smiled and went back to her quest for another sweet. He wasn't sure if she believed him.

'The lady over in bed four told me that her son has a job in the city. Something to do with computers. She says they can earn up to five hundred a day.'

'You know I'm not good with technology, Mum. This is proper work. Look.' He took out an envelope full of notes.

'Put it away. You never know who is watching.' She waved her hand at the money. 'I just want the best for you. I know it's not been easy.'

Here we go, he thought to himself. This was always the prelude to the monologue about how they 'never had any luck' and wasn't it about time they 'got a break' or the classic: 'if only their numbers would come in' they would be able to 'buy that house on the corner of Chamberlain Street'.

As she talked, he collected the growing pile of discarded wrappers off the bed, his mind wandering as he helped himself to another of the chocolates. The fire had melted them into strange shapes, and there was a white bloom on them from the heat. Still, they tasted the same, and his mother wasn't stopping to inspect them before they went into her mouth.

She always finished with some variation of 'if only I had never got ill', and how 'she should have married Mr Timmins when he'd asked'. Mr Timmins was a parasite who lived a few doors away. He was very welcoming when they moved in, making all the right moves and saying all the right things. Flattering a single mother with a young child wasn't hard, and he did a good job of pretending to care about them until his mother got ill and then he disappeared without trace.

The memory of 'Timid Timmins' did remind him of something else that the colonel had asked about.

'I'm fine, Mum, honestly, but there is something I have been meaning to ask you . . . Was there anyone in our family that was kind of special?'

'What do you mean?'

'You know, like, *gifted*. Did any of our ancestors have special abilities, weird psychic stuff, like seeing ghosts or having visions?'

She thought for a moment, chewing on a rather sticky toffee penny. Josh could see the wheels going around inside her head, one of her fingers twitched as if she were counting something.

'Well, your Great-aunt Agatha was supposed to be able to talk to animals, and my mum's uncle George claimed he'd met Napoleon. But he was definitely mad, and Agatha just spent too much time on her own with her cats. Why?'

'What about on my dad's side?'

Her expression soured as though the toffee had pulled out a filling.

'I've told you before — there's nothing to say about your dad. Don't ask me any more about it. I'm tired.' With that she closed her eyes and shuffled down on the pillow.

Josh took the hint, adjusted her blankets and put what was left of the chocolates in the bedside cabinet.

'Try and stay out of trouble,' she whispered as he left.

23

SECOND LESSON

[Paris, France. Date: 11.971-02-21]

J osh spent the next two days researching a test mission that the colonel had prepared for him. He knew it was going to be set somewhere during the French Revolution; the clues he'd been given were: a painting of a woman with a swan, an address in Paris and the words *liberté, égalité, fraternité* — which had meant nothing to him.

To complicate matters further, the colonel had taken him back to a safe house in Paris in 1971. There was no internet, and no computers to work with, just the books in the house's extensive library.

'Can't I at least work in a time with a search engine?' Josh complained as he leafed through the second volume of Encyclopaedia Britannica.

'You won't always have the luxury of Google at your disposal,' the colonel muttered as he read a French newspaper. 'A good watchman has to be able to work with what he's got.'

'But I'm rubbish with books,' said Josh, not wanting to admit to his dyslexia.

'Then think a little harder about how you would approach the issue,' the colonel answered without looking up. 'Humanity seems to have done quite well without search engines for the last twelve thousand years.'

Josh looked over his notes. He'd learned some interesting facts about the revolution: how the republic took shape around certain key figures like Robespierre and Danton, and how the masses had gone on a rampage that had destroyed palaces and churches all over France. Many of the most precious artworks had been 'liberated' from the aristocracy and taken to the Louvre for the benefit of the masses. This had been his first breakthrough: the address turned out to be the 'Tuileries Palace', which was once the home of the French King, Louis XVI, until he was deposed and replaced by the National Convention, who turned it into a court of justice for the rich during the 'Reign of Terror'. It finally burned down on the twenty-third of May, 1871, exactly a hundred years earlier, which Josh knew couldn't be a coincidence.

'So how about we go to the Louvre?' Josh suggested. He wanted to get out into the fresh air. Two days locked up in the house was beginning to make him a little crazy.

The colonel nodded and smiled. 'A fine idea,' he agreed, grabbing a hat and coat from the stand. 'You'll learn that institutions such as galleries and museums become very useful in our work.'

That made a lot of sense, Josh thought. *They would be full of old artefacts*. He kicked himself for not having thought of it before.

· · ·

The sun was shining on the gardens where the Tuileries Palace had once stood. The Louvre was sitting to the East and behind him was the River Seine. It was a serene place, a cultivated garden that gave no hint of the turmoil and horror it had seen during its history. There was nothing left here for them to work with. He turned to the colonel, who was sunning himself on a nearby bench.

'Dead end!' said Josh in frustration.

'Not quite.' The colonel pointed to the Louvre building. 'Let's go and visit one of my favourite places.'

Josh had read that the Louvre was once a grand palace, the exclusive playground of the rich and powerful. Back in 1971, the iconic glass-pyramid entrance had not yet been built, and the large square was flanked on three sides by the colonnaded facades of the three wings. Above each portico stood a sculpted figure staring blankly down over them. Josh wondered whether the architecture alone would have enough history for them to work with, but as he moved his hand out to touch one of the columns the colonel caught his sleeve.

'We try not to use stone,' he whispered as he shook his head. 'Natural materials tend to be too messy, something to do with their geological origins. Too bloody old.'

Josh shrugged and followed the colonel as he made his way to the ticket queue. The seventies were a bit of a culture shock; the line was full of long-haired hippy types with bad body odour and ridiculous flared trousers, taking photos of everything with clunky wind-on cameras. From their accent he could tell they were Americans. One of them wore an anti-Vietnam T-shirt with the words 'Make Love, Not War' on the front and — 'Weather Underground' on the back.

'What's the weather underground?' Josh whispered as they shuffled slowly inside the building.

'Bunch of militant anti-war protestors, formed at Michigan University — started a bombing campaign of government buildings in the US as a way to force them to stop the war. They usually gave enough warning to get the buildings cleared, but they did manage to blow themselves up once in Greenwich Village.'

'I thought it was all about making love, not war?'

'Not all of them,' said the colonel as he showed a piece of paper to the one of the attendants, and she waved them through. 'The weathermen declared war on the US government over Vietnam and the whole civil rights issue. They were put on the FBI's ten-most-wanted list in 1970,' he chuckled.

'What's so funny about that?'

'Weatherman means something else in the Order — one who cannot predict the future accurately — a fool, basically.'

The interior of the Denon wing was even more stunning than its grand facade promised. The vaulted ceilings were painted with images of angels and gods, framed in gold that seemed to float in the air above their heads. Along each side of the long corridor stood Greek and Roman statues on marble plinths.

'Ah, the blind heroes of antiquity,' the colonel said in admiration. 'Look on my works, ye mighty, and despair.'

He turned to Josh for some kind of reaction, but Josh had none, he didn't really get art — especially sculpture. He never really had the time or the opportunity to appreciate it, and didn't really see the point of it.

'This way,' ordered the colonel, opening a service door.

Behind it stood a stony-faced guard, who simply nodded and moved aside to let them through.

'Aren't we going to the exhibits?' Josh asked under his breath, looking back towards the guard, who was paying no attention to them whatsoever.

'Those are for the tourists. Never did see what all the fuss was about — *Mona Lisa* is nothing more than Da Vinci in a dress. No, the best part of the collection lives below stairs.'

Josh knew about the *Mona Lisa*. It was probably one of the only paintings he could name if asked.

He followed the colonel down a series of poorly lit stairs until they came to a large metal door that would have looked at home in a bank vault. In front of it stood another, even more surly looking guard with his arms crossed.

'Tempus fugit, Marfanor,' recited the colonel, pulling back his sleeve to reveal a tattoo on his forearm. It was a snake eating its own tail. 'Young man here would like to take a look at your Reign of Terror archives,' he added in perfect French.

Josh had seen the symbol before, but couldn't remember exactly where.

The stoic Frenchman's face cracked into a smile and he replied in English. 'Rufius. So good to see you.' He waved the tattoo away. 'You think I have such a bad memory that I can't remember that face? Who could forget it? Eh?' Marfanor winked at Josh as if asking for agreement. 'Even if it is covered in all that fur.' He produced an enormous set of keys and turned towards the massive metal door. 'So La Terreur is it? Not a very safe place to take the boy. I assume he's on probation?' he asked, looking Josh up and down. 'Bit old for that, though, no? Which test?'

'Ferrara. Leda and the Swan.'

'Ah.' There was a nod of approval as the locks on the door clicked. 'Say hello to Madame Déficit.'

The Louvre was built on the site of a much older castle, and as they entered it became apparent that the vault was the only remaining evidence of its existence. The walls were made of large grey stone blocks from the medieval fortress. It was damp and very cold. Josh could see his breath the moment they walked through the door.

Marfanor led them through a maze of long corridors, each lined with carefully wrapped paintings, vases and other precious objects until he stopped at another metal door with II.790-793 engraved in roman numerals. The key he used to open it was even more intricate than the previous one.

He waved them in. 'Good luck, my friend! *Bon chance!*'

'Another time,' said the colonel, shaking the man's hand.

The door closed behind them with a thunderous clang, one that reverberated along the metal walls of the tunnel in a neverending echo. It was as if they had walked inside the barrel of an enormous gun.

'So,' the colonel said, blowing on his hands, 'can we get a move on? I'm freezing.' He pointed to a row of mannequins dressed in revolutionary costumes as if to say: 'Help yourself.'

Josh chose a slightly torn blue velvet jacket and white, bloodstained breeches, along with a pair of muddy black boots. Near the lapel, the coat had a rosette of red, white and blue pinned over the seared edges of a bullet hole.

From his research, Josh recognised that the colonel had opted for something more militant; taking his inspiration from the 'Sans-Culottes' — the revolutionary army. He wore a red waistcoat, leather overcoat, red-and-white striped trousers, and a tricolour sash. Neither costume smelled as if it had been washed in decades, which he guessed was the kind of detail that kept you alive — turning up in a freshly pressed uniform in the middle of a revolution was as likely to get you killed as a powdered wig.

He looked around for some kind of weapon, but there were none, which was kind of a relief — they weren't expecting to get into a fight on this mission.

The metal vault was long and quite dark. The lights were kept low for reasons of preservation, the colonel told him. There was a timer switch by the door, as well as a set of clockwork flashlights.

The colonel took a torch and began winding the handle until the bulb began to glow. Josh did the same, and soon they had enough light to make their way down the central aisle. The space was divided by old wooden shelving that ran along the length of the space for at least twenty metres. As far as Josh could make out, it was a vast storehouse of objects from the French Revolution. He began browsing the shelves with no real idea of what he was looking for, but knew that just one of these valuables would be able to set him and his mother up for life.

There were all manner of treasures. It was like shopping at a B&Q that had been restocked by the Antiques Road-show. Each item was neatly wrapped in hessian or brown paper and labelled with a brass tag that had a long-date stamped into its tarnished metal. He assumed from the amount of dust surrounding them that they had been there for a very long time. Josh brushed at a few of the objects with his fingers and caught flashes of memories of dark rooms in forgotten palaces.

'You will have to be quite selective in your choice. There are many objects here that are not relevant to our task. Try to find something with resonance that would have intersected with your target destination.' The disembodied voice of the colonel spoke from somewhere beyond the light. It seemed distant and weak in the oppressive silence of the vault.

'Why exactly are we doing this?' whispered Josh. 'I know it's a test. But why this one? Art doesn't really make a difference to history, does it?'

The colonel coughed. His voice sounded even further away.

'Without art, what do you have? A bunch of books about logic and algebra? Art is the very expression of life! Of our hopes and dreams. Imagine how dull the world would be without artists like Da Vinci, Michelangelo or Picasso. Who would help us to celebrate the beautiful complexity of life?'

There wasn't time to celebrate as far as Josh was concerned. Art was for people who could pay their gas bills.

'Don't forget this was before photography. It was also one of the only ways to capture the zeitgeist,' added the colonel, suddenly standing right next to him.

Josh had no idea what a zeitgeist was and was far too proud to ask.

He walked on a little further until he spotted a stack of letters that had been tied carefully with a red ribbon. There was something odd about them, they seemed to shimmer slightly, and he realised that unlike the rest of the shelf there was no dust on them — they'd been recently moved.

'Ah, the diamond necklace affair,' sighed the colonel, picking up the parcel of notes. 'Eighty-seven point five per cent chance that this scandal was responsible for the downfall of the French monarchy and the instigation of the Revolution — I think this will do nicely.'

He handed the bundle to Josh, who immediately felt the strange prickling sensation as the timelines unwound from the surface of the paper. The black ink seemed to lift from the page as faint and sinuous moments rose like smoke, curling around his fingers. Josh began to explore the expanding matrices of the past, tentatively teasing out the knots of events. He caught glimpses of the people and places that had been involved in the affair: the woman who pretended to be the queen, the cardinal who was tricked into believing that she wanted such an extravagant necklace, and the secret room in the palace where the incriminating letters had been locked away for so many years afterwards.

He tried to pinch at a point with his thumb and forefinger, but it slipped away.

'Take your time. You need to find a point before the room's discovery. It was very close to the queen's trial,' the colonel advised gently. 'Let the time flow — don't snatch at it.'

Josh steadied his breathing and relaxed his mind; the line of events stretched out once more, and he followed it again until he came to the night the room was discovered. He watched the fine silver lockpicks in the rough hands of the locksmith as he worked on the secret door in the king's apartments. Then he moved slowly backwards to a few hours before.

'Now concentrate on that moment. Imagine yourself standing there in that room. Find something to focus on,' the colonel whispered.

Far off, Josh could hear the cries of the crowds as they bayed for the death of another aristocrat. As he focused on the noise, he felt the floor shudder and vault fall away.

24

THE PALACE

[Paris, France. Date: 11.793-09-21]

T he sounds of the crowd grew louder as he felt the space around him stabilise, and he found himself standing in the apartments of the King of France. Ignoring the small, lingering wave of nausea, he went to the secret door and when he touched the smooth wood, looking for a seam or hinge, he sensed the power of the history that pivoted on the objects stored within it.

There was no sign of the colonel. The baying of a rabble cursing at the top of their voices came from outside the apartments and Josh tentatively opened the door and went outside.

He followed the sound until he came to a balcony. Peering down into the ornate theatre below, he could feel the violence and hate emanating from the crowds. A woman in a torn gown was standing within a circle of very angry-looking peasants. Her wig had been thrown onto the floor and what was left of her own hair was stuck to her head in limp strands. There was blood on one side of her mouth, and one eye was nearly closed with the swelling. She sobbed silently as a grim-faced judge sat on a theatrical throne, reading out something in French from a long sheet of paper.

Josh searched the faces for any sign of the colonel. He didn't like the thought of being alone in one of the most violent periods of French history — especially when he couldn't speak a word of their language.

The cries of '*Guillotine!*' needed no translation as the woman was dragged away in hysterics. The crowd parted to allow her to be escorted out by two burly guards in the red-and-blue uniforms of the Sans-Culottes. As they passed underneath his balcony, Josh saw the familiar face of the old man — the colonel was helping the woman out of the room.

Josh had read that the Tuileries Palace had been used by the Revolutionary Council as a kangaroo court for the sentencing of the aristocracy — including royalty. Their leader, Robespierre, had been a lawyer and insisted that they should follow the rule of law when they prosecuted the gentry. His Jacobin deputies were not so bothered about justice. They were the ones that eventually brought Robespierre down and had him executed as well.

Josh visualised the floor plan of the building in his mind. Maps were something of a speciality, as if he had an internal GPS that instinctively told him the right way to go — useful when evading cops at 90mph through the back streets of London.

He moved quietly down the marble staircase, passing through the mass of onlookers who were using the stairs to get a better view of the spectacle. They were hysterical, like wild animals — spitting and screaming for blood as the prisoners were brought before the court. The crowd had become judge and jury, and the chief prosecutor was playing up to them as if it were some deadly game show. Josh had read that life had been hard for them under the king, but the hatred that was being unleashed in this room was the worst side of humanity he had ever witnessed.

Reaching the ground floor, he forced his way through the crowds towards the gilded doors that the colonel had used. He kept his head down, trying not to make eye contact with anyone. He had hated languages at school, and couldn't remember anything more than '*pardon*' and '*merci*'. His route was diverted by the surging crush of the crowd; many were drunk and only standing because of the press of bodies around them. Others were moving closer to get a better view as the names were read out. By the smell of it, no one had had a bath in months, the room was a seething mass of body odour, garlic and sour wine-breath.

The door was shut and as he went to open it a man's arm barred his way.

'*Non!*' a voice commanded. '*On ne passe pas!*'

Josh turned to the man and made out like he needed to piss urgently. The man grunted and pointed at a door a few metres away. He was a huge, thickset brute with a low brow that made him look like a caveman. His hands were the kind that could snap your neck in an instant, certainly not the type with whom you picked a fight in the middle of a lynch mob. Josh nodded to him, and made for the other door.

The room was a jumble of requisitioned artefacts looted from the mansions of the wealthy. They had been casually dumped wherever there was space. Priceless treasures were piled on top of one another, crammed into every available nook and cranny — like the back room of a charity shop. Standing amongst the clutter, Josh became aware of the buzzing drone of flies and the distinct tang of urine in the air. As he followed the sound, he began to realise that every

Ming vase, Grecian urn and silver punch bowl was brimful with a dark, pungent, straw-coloured liquid.

Josh scrambled over the clutter to the nearest window, pulled back the curtains and opened the latch just before the breath he was holding ran out. Sucking in lungfuls of fresh air, he looked out over the gardens towards the River Seine. The view reminded him of the one he'd seen in 1971. When he looked closer, he could see that it essentially was the same — except for the lack of cars, modern art and ornamental sculptures.

Smoke was rising over the rooftops of the houses on the far banks of the river. He watched as mobs of peasants ran rampage along the streets, destroying everything in their path: it was a war zone, though there were no police, no army, nothing but pure anarchy, pure rage and it was horrifying.

All the other doors in the room were blocked by stacks of furniture. Josh's eyes swept the room for anything useful. It was just his luck to have picked a room with no other exits and a hoard of piss-filled treasure he couldn't take back with him — even if he'd wanted to.

He thought about hitting the reset button on his tachyon and going back to the present, but that felt like admitting defeat and he wasn't about to quit. Instead, he began rummaging through the drawers and boxes in search of anything that he could sell: a coin, a ring or even a silver spoon from this age would be worth a fortune back in the present, or could at least be used as a marker for a return visit.

Then he saw the swan.

The picture looked as if it had been hidden by someone who wanted to keep it safe. It was placed carefully behind a tapestry and a stack of ornate golden dishes, but there was no mistaking it — there was his mission objective, his prize. *Leda and the Swan*, the missing masterpiece created by Michelangelo for the Duke of Ferrara. The colonel had been correct about one thing: art did have a value — he knew this one was worth millions.

The subject was of a naked woman entwined with a swan. The sexual undertones were not lost on Josh, but he wasn't interested in subliminal sixteenth-century porn. He just wanted to get it and get out of this madhouse.

He moved the other items aside so he could see it properly. This painting had been missing for more than three hundred years and in his time there were many collectors who would pay a fortune for it. All he had to do was follow its timeline back into the present and then take it to the right dealer, and he would be rich.

Josh slowly reached out with his hand until his fingertips brushed the paint. He could feel the lines of energy resonating just beneath the surface of the canvas; the sinuous flowering of its history rose at his touch.

Then suddenly he snatched his hand away.

The temptation to leave the colonel and claim his prize was a powerful one, but it was too easy. He had no idea what the old fool was doing next door. For all Josh knew this could be part of the test. There was a moment when he had nearly convinced himself that it would be better to just look after himself and take the path within the picture, when another cry of '*Guillotine!*' went up from outside the door and he dismissed the idea.

The thought of spending the rest of his days looking over his shoulder for the colonel or one of his Order was not something he relished — especially if they had the power to go back into his past and wipe him out.

Josh picked up one of the golden chairs, rammed it under the door handle and sat down on it, resting his head in his hands. He needed a plan. He needed to know what was going on in the next room, but couldn't see how he'd do that without going out of the window and facing the marauding gangs. The smell from the pots was getting worse, and the flies were starting to pay more attention to him than the festering piss buckets.

Then he had an idea — he was thinking too linearly.

25

LOST TREASURE OF THE BOURBONS

The colonel was standing amongst a desperate-looking bunch of guards as they played dice for what was left of Marie Antoinette's jewellery. The former queen sat weeping quietly on one of the stolen sofas, her dress torn and dirty, with a ridiculous mess of a wig balanced on her head, trying to retain some dignity.

Josh was slouched in a chair at the back of the room pretending to be a drunk sleeping off the booze. A half-finished bottle of wine sat in his lap, a propaganda leaflet was screwed up in one hand and a stolen hat pulled down over his face. From beneath the tattered brim he'd seen the colonel enter with the queen, and watched how the old man had protected her from the worst of the beatings from her guards.

As far as Josh could make out, they were waiting for her transport, which had been delayed by the chaos outside. The colonel was arguing with one of the other guards over her shoes when he first noticed the drunk in the corner — there had been the slightest hint of recognition, a creasing around the eyes, and then he had gone back to his disagreement.

It had taken Josh a while to get himself into the locked room. He'd gone through the timelines of the pisspots to find the moment when the guard had left his post to take a leak. It was possibly the most disgusting thing he'd ever had to do.

There was no one to be seen, and the room into which the colonel would escort the queen was empty. With nothing else to do but wait, Josh spotted a comfortable place to rest, found something that resembled food to eat, then went to sleep for a couple of hours.

The first time he awoke, the room was full of revolution-aries, all armed to the teeth. He panicked, attracting too much attention and ending with him having to use the 'rewind' button on his watch before getting stabbed with various sharp objects.

The second time he woke slowly, keeping still to appear as though he were asleep.

For the next two hours, he watched in silence as desperate men and women of the aristocracy were dragged through the antechamber. It was a waiting room for the damned. Their desperate pleas for mercy as they went into the court would haunt him. Robespierre himself came in at one point to check a list of names with one of the men.

When the colonel finally arrived, Josh realised that he hadn't thought his plan through. He'd been so wrapped up with how to get into the room that he hadn't considered what the colonel was doing in there in the first place. What was keeping them here? Was he seriously trying to save the queen?

While the men were busy with the dice, the colonel went over to the lady and whispered something in her ear. She nodded and turned towards Josh. A weak smile moved across her lips as she dabbed her eyes with the corner of a lace handkerchief. It was like some kind of signal. She looked calmly at something above Josh's head and then back at him her eyes widening a little as if to say, 'Look up.'

Josh pretended to yawn and sat straighter in his seat. No one paid him any attention as he scratched at his neck and took a swig from the bottle. He turned his head up to look at what the queen had glanced at and saw a lamp flickering in front of the now defaced portrait of her husband Louis XVI. It was delicately balanced on the mantelpiece and teetering above a large bundle of papers and pamphlets that had been dumped in front of the fireplace.

Josh turned back to look at the colonel who was holding the hilt of his sword as if ready to draw — his thumb was marking time on the pommel and one of his feet was tapping along to an unheard tune. It was clear that he was waiting for Josh to do something.

Josh stood up and stumbled as if still drunk. He reached out with his hand to steady himself and inadvertently knocked over the lamp, which fell and smashed over the papers setting them alight — seconds later, the fire was raging fiercely. Josh stepped out of the way as he watched everything the flames touch immediately ignite.

Guards jumped up and took off their jackets to beat back the flames. Others ran to the doors and windows to make their escape, but the additional draughts of air just fed the fire. Josh could see that the colonel was using the diversion to make a hasty exit with the queen, now wrapped in an old cloak, and he quickly followed them through the outer door into the gardens beyond.

'Majesty,' the colonel whispered hoarsely in between fits of coughing. 'We need the key. It is the only way to save your children.'

The queen nodded and produced a small iron key from inside her mouth. Josh watched in total confusion. He had no idea what the hell was going on.

A minute later the guards realised their most precious prisoner was missing and came running out onto the lawns in search of her. When they saw the colonel had the queen, they praised him like a homecoming hero, shaking his hand and patting him on the back as if he had single-handedly saved the revolution. Josh could see the colonel was struggling to play the part of the captor.

The queen was forcibly marched to a waiting carriage. As she stepped into the coach, she looked back and Josh thought for a second he saw her smile before they slammed the door.

When they re-entered the palace, the fire was being doused by a chain of bucket-wielding, smoke-stained soldiers. The court had been adjourned. With the spectacle abandoned, the crowds had dissolved and gone in search of other terrors. From the tired looks on the faces of the firemen, it was clear this was not their first call and probably not their last. Fires were an inevitable consequence of the revolution, Josh guessed. *Nobody ever thinks about who has to clear up the mess.*

The colonel took him back up to the king's apartments.

'So,' he said, closing the door gently, 'you seem to be able to think on your feet at least.'

'It was the only way to get into the room,' Josh said quietly.

'One of the ways. It was an interesting point in time that you chose. No one has ever been brave or stupid enough to choose the moment Marie Antoinette was in the room. Generally they take a more stealthy approach, like when everyone was asleep.'

'So the queen was not part of the test?'

The colonel shrugged. 'One never knows. It changes every time we play it. It all depends on where the student decides to drop into the timeline.'

'What did you say to her? What is the key for?'

The colonel took it out of his pocket and handed it to Josh.

'See for yourself.'

Josh held the small iron key in the palm of his hand and felt the familiar sensation as its path unwound from it. He saw images of a secret room full of plans and letters, then he moved back along its history until he saw a wooden chest full of gold.

'That, literally, is the key to the lost treasure of the Bourbons,' the colonel said, tapping on the wooden panel that hid the room.

Josh smiled. Finally, he thought, this was the kind of history he could relate to.

'The room is the Armoire de Fer, the secret antechamber of the king. A locksmith by the name of François Gamain discovered the room in 11.792. The diamond necklace and other financial correspondence would eventually discredit the royal family and end the right of kings forever in France.'

'And the treasure? The diamond necklace?'

'That had always been a mystery, until now. We've never been able to trace it: in every scenario we tried, we could never convince Marie to let us have the key.'

Josh held the image of the gold-filled box in his mind, trying to memorise the symbols that had swum around it.

They were obviously some kind of location marker, and it wouldn't take him long to work out how to find it, once he had learned what the symbols meant.

'Shall we go?' asked the colonel, taking the key back. 'I think that's quite enough excitement for one session.'

'And the missing Michelangelo?'

'A simple test, to see whether you follow orders or think for yourself . . . the Antiquarians will be interested to know of its whereabouts. It will be catalogued and stored for future rediscovery in some old monastery.'

'So. Did I pass?' Josh asked as the colonel studied something in his notebook. He looked distracted and Josh wasn't sure he'd even heard the question.

'What? Yes, of course,' he murmured, looking at his watch.

Then he was gone.

Josh took one more look at the hidden panel and visualised the symbols — he would be coming back very soon.

26

LENIN'S PLAN

'Where did you get this from, bro?' asked Lenin, waving the banknotes in front of his face like a Victorian lady.

They were sitting in Lenin's kitchen, one of the only parts of Lenin's flat that wasn't full of cartons of PlayStations and flat-screen TVs. The rest of his crew had unboxed one of each and set it up in what was left of the front room. They were playing Grand Theft Auto V.

'I won it — on the dogs. Had a good tip from Eddie.'

'No shit! Bastard never gives me anything.'

'You have to catch him in a good mood,' said Josh, relaxing a little. He knew Lenin wouldn't believe any story about him actually working for it, and he didn't want Lenin to know about the colonel, or what he was really up to.

The old man had paid Josh £2,000 this time. He'd given half to Lenin and kept the rest back for himself as a deposit on a flat.

The colonel had told Josh that he had done well and hinted that there was more work to come. Josh knew he mustn't screw this chance up. Nothing in the Job Centre was going to come within a million miles of this opportunity. He smiled as he thought of how the job description would look on the board: 'Time-traveller's apprentice required — must be able to . . .'

'So why you all happy now?' enquired Lenin, catching Josh's smirk. 'We ain't square. You ain't out the woods yet, dude.'

There was a shout from the crew on the PlayStation. They were shooting up another gang in the game — joking about how they were going to do it for real. Josh noticed there were Uzis lying on the table in front of them.

'So, if I get you the rest of the cash tomorrow we're even?'

Lenin shook his head. 'We ain't never going to be even, are we, Crash? But this job I got for you might come close.'

Lenin had always been there, like an older brother. He'd protected Josh long before he'd pulled him out of the car that day. He basically owned him and he never let Josh forget it.

'What's the job?'

Lenin's eyes gleamed as he leaned in to whisper, 'Come and see my war room.'

The so-called war room was basically a bedroom. A half-naked girl was asleep in the bed, her upper body was covered in tattoos. The walls were covered in maps of South Kensington and pictures of Imperial College. Lenin had drawn all over them with a black marker.

'This is Elena. She's Ukrainian or Lithuanian or some shit, but she can cook. You know what I mean?'

Josh did. Lenin was talking about making meth, which he'd thought was way out of Lenin's league.

'Yeah, Crystal,' said Josh.

'Exactly! Iceeee,' sang Lenin grinning.

He walked over to the map and pointed at an area on the university campus.

'See this? It's the chemistry department. Do you know what they got? Ephedrine. Which she tells me is all we need to make our own crystal.'

'So we're going to walk in there and just take it?'

'Damn straight. I need at least thirty litres to get started.' He picked up the discarded crack pipe. 'This shit is worth at least 20K.'

'What about the Feds?'

Lenin shrugged. 'Who gives a shit. It's about time we looked after our own.'

Lenin used to be smarter than this, Josh thought. The drugs were definitely making him a little crazy. The Turkish 'Fedaykin' or 'Feds,' had been running the Class A's for as long as he could remember and they were going to be pretty pissed off about Lenin moving in on their action. He was going to start a turf war with guys who would sell their own mother for a couple of grams of cocaine.

'So how big is thirty kilos?' asked Josh, thinking about the Renault Clio he had stolen.

'Like an oil drum,' Elena answered in a husky, East European accent as she pushed herself up into a sitting position and lit a cigarette.

Josh was not accustomed to seeing naked women. He tried very hard to stare at her face.

'I will send you a picture of the label so you know what to look for.' Her accent was strong and kind of sexy. 'Lenin, get phone!'

Josh had never heard anyone give Lenin an order, or see

him take it without question. He guessed they were probably shagging because Lenin did exactly as he was instructed.

Elena swiped through her photos until she found what she was looking for and then looked up at Josh with big, dark-rimmed eyes.

'Number?'

Josh was a little stunned. 'Don't have one. Sorry.'

Elena swore in her own language and turned to Lenin. 'Where did you find this guy?'

Lenin shook his head and shrugged. 'Tell me about it. He's a nightmare. They just seemed to die on him.' He picked out an iPhone 5s from a drawer and threw it to Josh. 'It's a burner. You can chuck it after the job.'

Josh looked at the cracked screen and read out the number to Elena whose fingers blurred as she tapped it into her phone.

A second later a notification popped up on his screen. There were two new messages: the first was a picture of a chemical label, the kind you saw on the side of lorries. The second was a nude picture of Elena with the words 'YOU WISH!' burnt into the image, obscuring her nipples.

Josh swallowed hard and looked back at her, she raised one eyebrow at him as if daring him to show Lenin.

Lenin took out a marker and began to hi-light different points on the floor plans as he explained the location of the security systems in the chemistry building.

'I thought I was just driving?' said Josh.

'Everybody's going in. Don't want any second thoughts, and that thirty-kilo drum is going to need at least four of us to get it out, or a forklift if we're lucky.'

They went through the details of the job. Lenin was meticulous, going over each of the various different entrances to the university using Google Streetview images. Josh studied the maps closely, pointing out routes that would be potential hazards, and shortcuts that would help them lose the police. It was a simple job but he found his mind kept wandering: he went from wondering how easily he could do this if he still had the Tachyon Mark IV, to the naked image of Elena, to what the colonel had said as he took the watch back that morning.

'Don't do anything out of the ordinary. Don't draw attention to yourself.'

He wasn't sure this qualified as normal to the colonel — what was ordinary to a time traveller anyway? This was the only life Josh had ever known, one where you took what you needed rather than waited for it to be given. He had little choice but to see this through. Lenin would be seriously pissed if Josh tried to duck out of it, and then there would be consequences that you didn't need the colonel's notebook to predict.

'Enough with the talking,' Elena snapped.

'Let's give the lady some privacy,' Lenin said as he guided Josh out of the room. Elena threw off the sheets as they left and Josh had to use every ounce of willpower not to look back.

Lenin's crew had finished their game and were busy bagging up dope into plastic wraps. The sound system was banging out something ridiculously loud, and Lenin had to shout over the noise.

'Saturday morning. Two a.m. You finally get to go to uni!' He held up two fingers in a gangster salute and waved Josh out.

Elena walked out of the bedroom towards the bathroom wearing a thong and a cropped black T-shirt. The guys started whooping and banging on the table as she walked down the hall towards the toilet.

As Josh went through the front door, he heard Lenin shouting.

'Elena. For God's sake. Put some damn clothes on, you prick-teasing bitch!'

27

ANOTHER COLONEL

Collecting his things from Mrs B had taken longer than Josh had anticipated. Her ability to fuss over the smallest things drove him to distraction, but he patiently waited for her to finish the usual speech about trying to 'stay out of trouble for your mother's sake' and then took the two carrier bags and left.

There was a letter from the council taped to the metal grille where his old front door used to be. As he passed, he read the words 'EVICTION NOTICE' in bold red type on the envelope. Josh was less bothered by it than he'd thought he would be; it had never really felt like home — more like a prison where he'd just served five years.

He felt an unusual sense of relief as he walked off the estate with everything he owned. The carrier bags were mostly full of clothes: boxers, socks, T-shirts and another pair of jeans, enough for a week — not much to show for his life. He'd put his photos and diary inside his coat, but the pockets were ripped, and the thing had fallen inside the lining, which was probably the safest place for it anyway.

He was a mess, but for the first time in his life, he felt like something was actually going to change for the better.

The colonel showed him to the guest room. It was a large bedroom with the slope of the roof encroaching on one side. There was a round window high at the end, which let in just the right amount of light. A large double bed took up most of the floor space and an old wooden wardrobe sat against the opposite wall — it was enormous, the kind that could take you into Narnia.

'You can put your clothes in there,' said the colonel, nodding at the cabinet, 'but I should warn you that it's pretty full already — space is a premium here, I'm afraid.'

Josh opened the door to find it full of uniforms and outfits from at least two centuries.

'I took the trouble of requisitioning you some gear — standard-issue stuff, really — should see you right back to the sixteenth.'

Josh threw his bags into the bottom with the boots and shoes then sat down on the bed and felt the mattress. It was like sitting on air.

'Right, get settled in. Dinner's at eight. Then we have a few things to discuss,' the colonel said, closing the door.

Josh lay back, shut his eyes and let the bed carry him away.

They ate in the kitchen on a table that folded out. The colonel made some excuse about the dining room being out of order, but Josh didn't care — the old man had a real talent with food: it was some kind of red meat, not exactly steak.

Josh devoured it all. He was starving, and it tasted even better than Mrs B's.

'So, Joshua,' the colonel said, pushing his plate to one side, 'you have a few questions I would hazard.'

Josh nodded. 'More than a few.'

'I may not be allowed, or able to answer all of them, but fire away.' The colonel poured a large glass of red wine from a dusty old bottle dated 1723.

'What is it about that book?' Josh asked, pointing to the battered old leather journal on the table. The colonel consulted it more than most people used their mobile phones.

He picked it up and handed it to Josh.

'Take a look for yourself. It's quite a thing to behold the first time.'

Josh opened the book at one of the many dog-eared pages and stared in wonder as the writing on it changed before his eyes. He flicked through the whole book, and every page was the same: covered in notes, diagrams and cyphers that seemed to be in constant flux as though someone was continuously re-writing it.

'What the —' exclaimed Josh.

'I know, it's quite hypnotic, isn't it? I can still remember the first time I saw it,' said the colonel, taking the book out of Josh's hand before he dropped it in the remains of the béarnaise sauce. 'This, my dear chap, is an almanac, a sympathetic book dating back to the sixteenth century where it is currently being revised and rewritten by the Guild of Copernicus: a group of mathematicians and statisticians who calculate the possibilities and consequences of our actions. You are quite literally watching history being written.'

Josh remembered the symbols from the secret room in Paris; they were obviously co-ordinates.

'So that's like a map?' he said, pointing at the page of moving lines.

'A map of the possible. Yes, I suppose it is.'

'So what do all these symbols mean? Are they like algebra?' Josh had always hated maths — especially abstract stuff like formulae.

'Those are temporal glyphs: probability coefficients, abstractions and equations that have been developed to help us calculate future outcomes.'

'But you said we can't go into the future.'

'No, but we can make a bloody good guess as to what is going to happen. Well, at least some of the time. It's complicated.'

'So these Copernicus dudes spend all their time trying to work out what's going to happen next?'

'They pride themselves on their predictions — nothing lower than a seventy per cent certainty is ever accepted.'

'Will I have to learn how this works?' Josh asked, staring at a page that had stopped moving for a moment.

'Eventually — we all have to. For now, you will have a mentor, such as myself. You never go back on your own, especially not without this.'

He took the tachyon out and gave it back to Josh.

'So is there some kind of college? Do I have to go school?'

'No.' The colonel laughed. 'You are apprenticed. Everything you do, you learn on the job, and we have all the time in the world to teach you, don't we?'

Good, thought Josh, this was his kind of education.

. . .

The colonel had told Josh to take some time to relax and recuperate after the first set of training missions. He'd mentioned something about quantum dilation; that his body's cells would take a while to get used to it — like an extreme form of jet lag. He woke late the next morning. His sleep had been disturbed by a crazy dream: headless noblemen swimming after him down the Seine, while weird ghosts stood on the bridges as he swam underneath them.

When he came downstairs, he found the house unusually peaceful, which could only mean that the colonel was out. He was one of those people who was incapable of doing anything quietly; just breathing seemed to require a cacophony of coughs and verses of song.

Josh was still getting used to the idea that the colonel could be in another century or just down the shops buying some biscuits.

After searching the kitchen cupboards for something that resembled a 'normal' breakfast, and there were many things that didn't, he took some brioche and jam out into the conservatory and began to flick through one of the books the old man had given him the night before.

The colonel's cat magically appeared on the chair next to him and began eyeing the food. Josh stroked it absent-mindedly as he read. The textbook described the properties of temporal glyphs, each symbol laid out on its own page. The text was small and he had to concentrate hard to stop the letters jumping around. He tried to find one of the those that had been tagged to the gold, but they were hard to visualise the morning after. The memory of them was fading.

Josh had finished his breakfast, or at least the part he'd managed to rescue from the cat, when he heard the first crash. It wasn't the usual clatter of things being knocked sideways by the coat-tails of the colonel, but the sound of something being dropped from a great height and breaking into a thousand pieces, and it had come from the study and not the front door.

This was followed by a second noise, quieter than the first and more in the form of a low groan, as if someone had hurt themselves badly and hadn't the strength to call out for help.

Josh moved stealthily towards the study door, looking for something to use as a weapon. He wanted to believe that the colonel had been working in the study the whole time and had hurt himself getting something from one of the higher shelves, but he knew that someone had probably broken in through the window and had injured themselves in the process.

He pushed the door open enough to look through the crack and saw a large man sprawled on the sofa. The coffee table looked as if he'd landed on it first: parts of model aeroplane and wood were scattered over the floor.

He was talking to himself and Josh recognised the colonel's voice, although the robes and the shaved head made him think twice. He put down the brass poker he had been holding for purely defensive purposes and went over to the old man.

'You're not looking your best,' Josh said as he spotted the blood seeping through the old man's clothes. He was dressed in a white toga, like someone from an old Charlton Heston movie.

'Seventeen to the fourth, Tiberian. Twenty-five. Nine. Fourth branch, ninth parallel,' panted the colonel.

'Where have you been? Looks like Rome or Greece maybe? You want me to call an ambulance?'

The old man coughed and lifted himself up on one elbow. He looked very odd with no beard or hair, like a well-scrubbed potato. He shook his head and repeated: 'Seventeen to the fourth, Tiberian. Twenty-five. Nine. Fourth branch . . .'

'Yeah, I got it.' Josh repeated it back to him.

'Good,' sighed the colonel. He closed his eyes and disappeared.

'Well, that was weird,' muttered Josh, looking at the bloodstain on the sofa.

'So you're sure it was me?' the colonel asked with a grave look on his face.

'Yeah, you turned up with all this blood and . . .'

'Stop. I told you not to tell me any of the details.'

'Why not?'

'Because it hasn't happened to me yet. Something very bad must have occurred if I have come back into my own timeline — it's called an intercession.' He was stroking his beard with one hand and still holding the bag of shopping in his other.

'But don't you want to know what he — you said?' Josh found it weird even saying that out loud.

'Absolutely not! Under no circumstances can you tell me. It breaches about a hundred or so clauses of the Temporal Act.'

'What act?'

The colonel paced around the study trying not to look at his own bloodstain on the sofa.

'The Temporal Act is the basic tenet of all our laws. The Protectorate will come down on us like a ton of bricks. We'll both end up in Bedlam!'

'The Protectorate, are they like time police?'

The colonel shook his head. 'Police no — more like secret service, the Stasi maybe. They really do make people disappear.'

'To Bedlam?'

'If you're lucky. You must never mention this, ever. They aren't particular about who they lock up in these situations.'

Josh shrugged. He had no idea what was going on and the only person who did wouldn't tell him.

The colonel paced around for a few more minutes, and then seemed to make a decision.

'All right, I have a plan. It was about time I introduced you to them anyway. Grab a coat. I'm going to take you to meet a few friends of mine.'

28

OTHERS

J osh had never seen the colonel inside a car. It reminded him of one of those Russian bears imprisoned in a zoo where the cage was far too small for him.

'The Order has a series of staging posts at key points in time,' the colonel began as he tried and failed to get his window to go down further than an inch. 'They are commonly known as Chapter Houses and can always be relied upon for sanctuary. Usually they're run by a family, or at least a husband and wife, who act as hosts and can comfortably accommodate over a hundred people at any one time.'

'And why exactly are we going there?' asked Josh, still at a loss as to what was stressing the colonel.

'I need to go and find out what happened, and you can't come with me.' He held up a hand as Josh began to protest. 'This is for your own protection. Where I may have to go is strictly off-limits and very dangerous. This Chapter House is a safe place, and it's run by people I trust. You can continue your training with them until I return.'

Josh didn't like the idea of being dumped with a bunch of strangers.

'So do I have a choice? Can't I stay at your house?'

'Not really. Anyway, I'm sure you'll find some of their guests are far better company than an old codger like me.'

The cab stopped outside a decrepit second-hand bookshop. The colonel unrolled the strangest collection of banknotes, peeled away a suitable number and handed them to the driver.

'Trouble is that the house tends to move about so the best way to get to it is through a waybook.' He nodded toward the bookshop.

The inside of the shop was cramped and musty. Dust, disturbed by their entrance, swirled in strange and unusual eddies around the naked light bulbs that barely lit the cluttered shelves. There was no sign of a shopkeeper, even after the bell that hung over the door had rung itself out. The colonel didn't seem to care; he knew what he was looking for. Josh followed him through the book-lined maze to a section labelled 'special interests' where he began to pull various books out and inspect them.

'Books are one of the best ways to navigate back through the last couple of thousand years. Although the earlier ones are rather hard to get close to. You'll find that most second-hand dealers and even some charity shops can get you back a good two hundred.'

He stopped when he found a small tattered copy of *The London Guide*.

'You can tell a waybook by the author — J. K. Bartholomew — it's like a codename. Now where is it?' He flicked through the pages. 'Here we are: "The Charitable House of the Hundred", fifty-six Mendover Place, Camden.

Interesting — hasn't been situated there for over eighty years. Alixia must be working at the British Museum again.'

The Charitable House was nothing much to look at from the outside. A slightly run down, terraced Edwardian town house in a quiet side street of Camden; it didn't really match up to the gothic mansion that the colonel had described, and its three, slightly wonky storeys certainly didn't appear to be able to accommodate thirty — let alone a hundred people.

They climbed the worn stone steps up to the black lacquered front door. Josh noticed the circular brass knocker was shaped like a snake eating its own tail — a match for the colonel's tattoo.

The door was opened on the third knock by a bone-white old man dressed entirely in black. He stared directly at them with dark, haunted eyes.

'State your business!' he snapped sharply as his nose sniffed the air. 'We don't take kindly to costermongers and hawkers!'

'Arcadin, you're in the wrong century again, you blind fool. It's me, Rufius!'

Arcadin's face turned sideways as if looking past Josh. 'And the boy?'

'Apprentice. Under my charge.'

Arcadin stood aside and waved them in. 'You'll have to change. We are in the middle of luncheon,' he wheezed.

They walked into a reception area. Before them stood a large arched wooden door with the snake symbol carved into it. On the wall to his left was a smaller door marked 'Ladies' and to his right 'Gentlemen'. The colonel was already making a beeline for the Gents.

Arcadin motioned to Josh to follow the old man. 'It would be advisable to change for lunch, sir,' he said with a sneer as his blank eyes inspected Josh's clothes. Josh had to hold back the urge to punch the guy in the face, and he dutifully followed the colonel through the door.

The changing rooms were like something from an exclusive golf club, lined with wooden lockers and pegs. There was a row of coats hanging along the wall. Josh estimated that there were at least twenty or so, all from very different periods in time. The colonel took off his greatcoat and hung it on the next available peg and took a long cloak from the locker marked 'Westinghouse'. Each locker had a brass plaque with names like 'De Freis', 'Makepiece' and 'Newton'. He was about to ask about the last one when he saw one with his own name. Opening the door, he found a dark set of robes, nowhere near as grand as the ones the colonel was wearing, but, still, they seemed to fit well.

He checked himself out in the mirror — he looked like an entirely different version of himself, one that had just graduated from university.

'I see they got my message,' the colonel said, checking Josh's robes to see if they fitted.

'Why do we have to wear these?' Josh asked, holding out his arms like wings.

'Partly for practical reasons. The house has had a few modifications over the years, doesn't exactly exist in any one time period, so it is advisable to wear something made from an early millennium — to cover one's modesty, as it were.'

'And the other part?' Josh thought this was the most ridiculous thing he had ever seen.

'Tradition. It is part of who we are. Our robes are a symbol of the Order's origins, just as this' — the colonel pointed to the symbol of the snake devouring its own tail on his breast — 'Ouroboros. Symbolises the eternal circle of life and death.'

Arcadin was standing by the large door with an approving look on his face. The dress code now satisfied, he could let them into the house. He took out an ornate key and placed it in the lock. The metal snake released its own tail and rotated 180 degrees as the sound of heavy gears grinding echoed from behind the wood. Suddenly the door broke into two and swung away to reveal the entrance hall of a seventeenth-century mansion.

Josh had to take a moment to come to terms with the scale of the place. The hall was vast, with a grand sweeping staircase flowing down from the floors above. There were chandeliers with real candles flickering above his head and large portraits of various nobility hanging on the walls.

There was an odd sensation as they stepped through the arch, as though the floor was an inch or so lower than he expected, Josh stumbled and the colonel had to steady him.

'As I said, the house is not actually all in one time. You get used to it after a while.'

Josh turned back to the door and went back through, much to Arcadin's disapproval.

'Don't dawdle, boy!' ordered the colonel as he walked off down the hall. 'I don't have time to explain. Methuselah will be able to answer all your questions later.'

'What is that smell?' Josh asked as the doors closed behind him with a deep resonating boom.

'Lunch!' the colonel said rubbing his hands together. 'And if my nose isn't deceiving me — the main course. I would say it's Carpathian boar, one of Methuselah's specialities.'

They walked quickly, passing many closed doors, each inlaid with a golden symbol. As they got nearer to the delicious aroma, Josh could feel his mouth watering. It was a mixture of herbs, spices and rich dark meats, like a thousand Christmas dinners all rolled into one.

The colonel stopped in front of the last door and motioned to Josh to go in. 'Guests first. It's another tradition. You'll find we have quite a few.'

Josh could hear a murmur of voices behind the door but couldn't make out how many there were. He was trying not to let the butterflies rise in his stomach; it was okay to be scared, he told himself, just don't let anyone else see that you are.

The door opened on to the strangest feast Josh had ever seen. The room was like some kind of Viking banqueting hall. Stone walls were decked out with animal skins, and the wooden beams of the roof were hung with shields and axes. Running down the centre was a long table at which a dozen or more people were eating and talking at the top of their voices. At the far end of the table was an enormous hunk of roasted meat. Judging by the tusks sticking out of its snout, it was some kind of prehistoric pig.

A tall Arabian man stood carving the haunches of the boar with vicious-looking sword. He reminded Josh of a villain from a Disney movie. His beard was black and sharply pointed, and his dark hair was swept back to expose his widow peaks. He was olive-skinned: 'Swarthy' was how his gran would have put it. There was definitely more than a touch of the gypsy about him. To his right sat a petite woman with immaculate poise, and skin like porcelain. She held up a plate for the man to lay generous slices of meat onto and then handed it down the row of guests. Josh watched as the plate was passed along. He studied the faces of each of the eccentric-looking diners as it progressed until it came to the group of young people who had collected at the end of the table nearest to him.

They were dressed differently, but he recognised most of them from the night in the pub. Sim nodded at him as soon as their eyes met. He was sitting between a boy and a girl who, judging by their features, were obviously siblings. There was another girl with her back to Josh. As she turned to see the new arrivals, he saw that it was Caitlin. His smile dissolved at the look she gave him — she wasn't pleased to see him. The posh boy, Dalton, was sitting next to her saying something in her ear and chuckling to himself.

'Rufius, you old dog. Welcome!' bellowed the Arabian man. 'Pull up a chair and have some of this delicious boar.' He knocked over his wine as, with a wide gold-toothed grin, he waved the sword around. The lady next to him began to fuss over the spillage and deftly took the sword off him before he did any more damage.

'Methuselah,' replied the colonel. 'Alixia.' He bowed slightly to the lady who performed the smallest of curtsies in return.

Methuselah reminded Josh of the Grand Viseer from Aladdin, replete with jewelled rings, long silk-woven robes and a hint of something magical in his dark eyes. He swept over to greet the colonel with a hearty handshake that turned into a bear hug.

'So who is this young whelp you've brought me?' Methuselah asked, examining Josh with a cool, calculating glance. 'There's hardly anything of him.'

'This is my latest foundling. Joshua Jones. Joshua, I have the great pleasure of introducing you to one of my oldest friends, Methuselah DeFreis, and his beautiful wife, Alixia, and their family.'

Josh shook Methuselah's hand and bowed awkwardly to

his wife. Everyone had stopped talking and turned to stare at him as if expecting him to say something.

'Hi.' Josh was at a loss as to what to say next.

'Man of few words. Like myself!' Methuselah grinned as he slapped Josh on the shoulder. 'We're going to get on famously. Have a seat, my boy, and let's see if we can get some meat on those bones.' Methuselah placed Josh next to Sim and passed him a plate of food that his wife had been busily preparing.

The colonel went and sat with their host at the other end of the table, leaving Josh alone with Caitlin and her friends.

'Good to see you again,' Sim said, handing Josh a drink.

Josh had initially thought that they were similar ages, but now they were close he could see that Sim may be a little younger.

'Is it true you solved the *Leda and the Swan*?' Sim asked with a little too much enthusiasm.

'Er, yeah. What the hell are you lot doing here? Are you all——'

'Anachronists?' Sim chuckled. 'Yes, I guess you could say we're all fate-shifters of one sort or another.'

Josh looked around the group as they talked and ate. Caitlin was having some kind of quiet argument with Dalton.

'I take it Caitlin never told you before the gig?' Sim asked as he handed Josh some cutlery.

'Nope,' Josh said, carving off a piece of the boar. It was delicious. He seemed to be constantly hungry these days. The incident with the other colonel had spoiled breakfast, and that had seemed like hours ago.

He watched as Dalton made some snide remark to

Caitlin whose face flushed red as if she were going to explode.

Sim was oblivious and continued. 'You know that has never been solved? No one has ever made it out of the room. Let alone got the key to the Bourbon treasure from the Queen. Everyone has been talking about it — even Dalton.'

Josh looked back over at Dalton, who raised his wine glass as if to congratulate him. Caitlin, on the other hand, was ignoring Josh. He wracked his memory, trying to remember what had happened that night. He'd obviously screwed up and it was probably to do with getting drunk, which usually meant waking up in a stranger's bed with only a vague idea of how he got there. In most cases, he'd never seen the girl again so it hadn't mattered. Caitlin was different though. He'd wanted her to like him; he'd wanted to impress her.

'Sim,' Josh lowered his voice so none of the others could hear, 'are Dalton and Caitlin an item?'

Sim laughed and then realised that Josh was being serious. 'Er. No. He just acts as if they are.'

Josh watched the two of them for a few more minutes as he finished his meal and answered Sim's never-ending list of questions about the Paris mission.

'Strange to have found him so late,' Methuselah said as he watched Josh chatting to Sim at the other end of the table.

'It happens. I was nearly fourteen when Dolovir found me,' the colonel replied, helping himself to another slice of boar.

'Yes. But the gift is usually apparent by ten — Copernicans boast they can track them from as early as eight!'

'And we know how accurate their predictions can be!'

Methuselah scratched at a scar that ran down one side of his face. 'Only too well, my friend. Only too well.'

The colonel turned to Methuselah. 'He's not a bad lad. I would appreciate it if you would look after him for me — I have some urgent business to attend to.'

Methuselah took a bottle of fourteenth-century red wine from the table and poured the colonel a large glass.

'My friend, we have known each other longer than I care to remember. If you need my assistance, you have it without question.' He held up his own glass so that they could toast each other.

'But of course you will ask the question all the same,' the colonel quipped as he raised his glass.

Methuselah grinned. 'Would I be me if I did not?'

The colonel let the fine wine roll around his mouth for a moment as he considered how much to reveal.

'I have to go back to the founder.'

'Serious business, then?'

The colonel nodded.

'Not that old story about the Fatalists again? He won't entertain any more of your conspiracy theories, old boy. He'll just send you straight to Bedlam and into the ministrations of the Grand Seer!'

The colonel let out a long sigh. 'Not the Fatalists. This time it's about something far more personal.' He leaned in close to Methuselah's ear and whispered, 'An intercession.'

His friend's eyes went wide, 'Oh, how . . . ? No, don't tell me — the last thing I need right now is the Protectorate on my back! It's bad enough as it is bringing up four teenagers!'

'I wouldn't,' the colonel said sullenly, 'not after the last time. How is Caitlin?'

Methuselah shrugged. 'She has good days. Your boy seems to have sparked her interest.' He motioned towards

Josh with his glass. 'From what I hear, she has been arguing with Dalton about him all day.'

Caitlin had turned away from Dalton as if they'd fallen out. She was listening intently to the conversation between Sim and Josh without actually appearing to be. It was a trick she learned as a child, and only he could spot it.

'Dalton says he's a thug. Apparently, the boy put him on his backside with one punch.'

The colonel snorted. 'Yes, Josh does have a bit of a short fuse, but Dalton probably deserved it.'

'And if he insists that we revoke him?' Methuselah asked in a serious tone.

'If the Protectorate had their way, we'd never have any new recruits. Did Dalton read him?'

Methuselah nodded.

'And?'

'He can't tell. Seers are not known for their modesty, but Dalton admits that he couldn't get much in the way of a history.'

'So he retrograded him?'

'Of course. Dalton is one of the best, no matter what you think of his allegiances. He is a master of amnesia — he made sure the boy has no memory of the event.'

The colonel scratched his beard. 'He's got a lot of potential. He'll be a millennial, I'd bet my beard on it. He just needs some polishing.'

'Another rough diamond?'

The colonel stood up and drained his glass. 'Aren't we all? I'll bid you adieu, my friend. Give my best to Alixia and tell her I'll be back soon to admire her latest botanical restoration.'

Caitlin wrapped her arms around the colonel when he came over to say goodbye. Josh could tell that he meant a lot to her. They hugged for a long time as the colonel whispered gently into her hair. 'I'll be back soon,'

He turned to Josh when she finally let go of him. 'Walk with me.'

Josh followed the colonel out into the hall.

'There's a good chance I may not be back for a while. These are good people; they're family. Try to stay out of trouble and listen to Methuselah.'

'Can I still visit my mother?' Josh asked.

'Of course,' he said, patting Josh on the shoulder. 'It's not a prison. You can come and go as you please. Arcadin knows you now.'

CHAPTER HOUSE

S im had volunteered to show Josh to his room. Navigating the Chapter House was like walking through a maze without a map: corridors and doors led off in all directions, making the interior of the house far greater than it appeared from the outside.

Their quarters, as Sim called them, were situated at the top of the house and involved climbing endless flights of stairs. Sim told him there was a quicker way, and that he would show him once he was 'orientated'.

Josh was breathing hard by the time they reached their floor. Each storey of the building looked like it was from an entirely different period: the decor moved from Baroque to Victorian to modern. It was like climbing through an architectural journal.

The rooms were larger than he expected. They each had a bedroom with an en-suite bathroom and there was a communal space that Sim had filled with all sorts of cool gadgets: an Xbox One, a PlayStation 4, a huge flat-screen TV and a very powerful-looking PC with a strange pair of goggles — Sim called it a 'VR headset'. It felt weird to be back in a room that resembled present day — albeit far from the world that he knew. He had to keep reminding himself that he hadn't broken into the house of some rich kid, that he was actually a part of this.

Sim had booted the PC and was babbling on about some game or other that he had just completed. He was proudly showing how he'd found all the collectables and gained a very rare sword, but all Josh could do was wonder how the hell he'd got to this house and how long it would last. He couldn't believe that these guys were seriously suggesting he could join them — that they wanted him to be part of their Order.

As Sim launched a driving game, Josh tried to explain to him that he had never really got on with computers. Sim dismissed his objections with a comment about 'holocronic flux interference', sat him down and placed the VR headset over his head.

Josh found himself in a Ford Mustang on the start line of an indie car race. The revving of the engines of the other cars buzzed in his headphones, and he found himself looking round a completely 360° environment. He felt Sim slide some pedals under his feet and a steering wheel in his hands just as the lights turned green.

Ten minutes later Josh was an indie champion. He took off the headset, and grinned at Sim. 'That's insane!' he exclaimed.

'Yeah, and you're really good at it!' agreed Sim. 'No one else wants to play video games here. They are all far too serious.'

'No shit. What's this thing called?'

'Oculus Rift,' Sim replied, taking the headset back. 'Want to try something else? Portal is mental on this!'

Josh shook his head. 'No. It makes me feel a bit sick.'

'That's motion sickness — your brain can't work out why your eyes are telling it you're moving when your inner ear says you're not.'

Josh spun round in the chair. 'So which is my room?'

Sim took him down a short corridor to a bedroom stylishly furnished with a bed, TV, walk-in wardrobe and bathroom. Josh had never seen a rainfall shower, let alone a bidet. But for him the most impressive feature by far was the glass wall that framed the most incredible view of London. He could see the River Thames, but it took him a while to work out where they were.

'This is a penthouse suite in Chelsea. You like it?' Sim asked. 'Dad added it when the chance of you showing up spiked.'

'You knew I was coming?'

Sim glowed. 'I was the closest by two hours. Don't be offended — it's what we do.'

Josh found it a bit creepy that they were planning out his life.

'We can change it if you don't approve?'

'No, it's great,' said Josh. 'I like his style. But doesn't someone own it? Won't they, like, come back and wonder why I'm here?'

Sim suppressed a chuckle. 'There are a few things you need to understand about chronostasis before my explanation would make any sense.' He held his hand up as Josh began to protest. 'I'm not saying you're stupid — it's just temporal mechanics is not one of the colonel's specialities, so I'm guessing he hasn't really taught you much about the science behind our abilities?'

'No. He's more of a doer than a thinker,' Josh agreed.

'OK. Think of it like this is all frozen in time like a photograph, on a kind of loop. No one but us can interact with it, although obviously in other parts of its timeline it continues to function as normal. I can draw you a diagram if it helps.'

'I'll take your word for it.'

'OK. So do you want to change out of those robes?' Sim asked, pointing to a mirrored wall. 'There are some new clothes in your cupboard. If you don't like them, we can ask the Antiquarians to send something else. They can do it retrospectively so it takes no time at all.'

Sim closed the door behind him as he left. Josh went to the wardrobe door and slid it aside. He smiled to himself as he looked at the rails of classic brands: Burberry, Abercrombie & Fitch, Ralph Lauren and many, many more — compared to the colonel their fashion sense was at least in the same decade.

He spent the next hour or so trying on various outfits until he found the right combination of understated cool, and then lay back on the bed and laughed. He tried not to do it too loudly, but it was unstoppable. Something inside him couldn't stop thinking how insanely ridiculous the whole situation was, that nothing in his wildest dreams had ever come close to this: hanging out in a Chelsea flat wearing Issey Miyake with a bunch of geeks that could travel through time.

Josh seriously considered whether he might be in some kind of coma and this was just all some drug-induced hallucination. It was unlikely; he couldn't have made this kind of stuff up — not in a million years. He wondered what his mum would say if she could see him now. If he told her about it, she'd never believe him, and if *she* didn't there wasn't a chance in hell anyone else would.

Just have to go with the flow, he thought. The colonel's away for a few days, Mum's in care for at least another week and Lenin is off his back till Saturday, so just sit back, relax and enjoy the ride.

There was a knock at the door.

Josh sat up, conscious that his laughter may have been a bit too loud.

'Hello?' Caitlin's voice came through the door. 'Josh. It's Caitlin. Can I come in?'

His heart skipped a beat.

'Yeah, one second,' he said, getting up and checking himself in the mirror before opening the door.

'I've been instructed to look after you,' she said with a look of grim defiance.

'It's OK. Sim can do it if you don't want to,' Josh replied, trying to sound disaffected.

She chewed her lip as though she was holding something back — he didn't like the way she kept avoiding looking him in the eyes.

'I have to give you the tour,' she insisted after an awkward silence. 'Sim has work to do. Come on.'

He went to follow her, but she raised a hand to stop him. 'I suggest you put your robes back on.'

As they made their way up another set of stairs, the silence between them was deafening. For the first time in his life, Josh was at a loss as to how to start a conversation. He watched Caitlin's long hair sway as she walked up the steps ahead of him and tried to find the right word for the colour: auburn, brunette — it was a kind of gingery-brown, not a term you could use about a girl's hair without getting a slap.

Caitlin stopped on the next landing. There were numerous corridors leading off from it, each one reminiscent of a museum with glass cases running down each wall.

'There are currently fifteen storeys attached to this house; each floor is based in a different era, except this one. These are our collections,' she started to say. 'We use them for —'

'Your mementoes — the colonel has one just like it,' he interrupted, a little too eagerly — he was still trying to impress her.

She crossed her arms and glared at him. 'Do you want the tour or not?'

'Yeah.'

'Stop interrupting, then,' she snapped as she turned away. 'Bloody think you know everything.'

Halfway along a corridor of some of the strangest arte-facts he'd ever seen, they came to a brass spiral staircase.

'Roof garden,' she said coldly, ringing a small bell that hung on the railings.

Nothing seemed to happen, but after a minute of waiting another bell sounded from somewhere above them. Caitlin strode up the stairs two steps at a time and Josh followed until they came up into what appeared to be a jungle.

The garden was warm and tropical, and full of large, Jurassic Park-looking plants. It was enclosed under an elegant glass and metal dome on the roof that reminded Josh of Kew Gardens; colourful birds flew in slow circles above the large ferns and butterflies flocked around the exotic hothouse flowers.

'This is my stepmother's herbarium, or aviary — basi-cally, it's a botanical garden. She studies extinct species of flora.'

'Extinct?'

'Yes, like, dead forever. She's cultivating plants and birds that were wiped out years ago.'

Josh walked a little way into the garden, and felt a warm

mist wet his face. The humidity was extremely high, making his clothes stick to his skin.

'How long ago?'

'Oh, a hundred thousand years or more, back into the last Ice Age.'

At least she was talking now, he thought, not shouting or telling him off — this was progress.

'How far can you go back?'

Caitlin expression changed at the question — she was obviously proud of her abilities.

'To the end of the Quartarian period, about ten thousand years. That makes me a Tenth Millennial.'

Josh tried to look impressed, although he had no idea whether that was good or not. 'I've only been back a couple of hundred so far.'

'Then you're just a Second-level Centurial,' she said in a tone that emphasised that he was weaker than her.

'So what's the furthest anyone has gone back?'

A flicker of anguish crossed her face, but she quickly masked it. It was enough to make him wish he'd never asked; everything had been going quite well up until that point.

'No one can go back beyond the last Ice Age, twelve thousand years ago,' she said through tight lips, and turned away.

As they wandered through the garden, Caitlin pointed out various species of birds, ferns and trees that had been saved by her stepmother. Beneath the centre of the dome they found Alixia de Freis repotting a row of small cuttings into large ceramic jars; she looked like a Victorian beekeeper with her long leather gloves and large netted hat. There was another small bell next to her on the table.

'Don't come any closer,' Alixia ordered sharply without

looking up from her work. 'This is *Verbasium noctorfloris*, probably the deadliest flower that ever existed.'

Josh took a little more interest in the delicate purple lily that Alixia was carefully extracting from its old container. He watched the vine-like tendrils unfurl and wrap themselves round her arm as she transplanted it into its new home. The vines reluctantly released their hold as she carefully poured what looked like blood into the soil around its roots. She placed a large glass jar over the plant and stuck a label with a large skull and crossbones on it.

'There now. Much better,' she said, rolling back the netting of her hat. Alixia patted the glass as if the plant were a pet. 'The extraneous feeler roots contain a deadly neurotoxin that can bring down a wild ox, let alone a human. They were the carrion eaters of the Pliocene,' she added as she removed her long leather gloves and held out one delicate little hand. 'How do you do, by the way? I don't think we were ever formally introduced. I am Alixia De Freis.'

Josh took her hand carefully. It was thin and cold, as if she were made from very fine china.

'Josh. Joshua Jones, I'm —'

'He's Uncle Rufius's new protégé,' Caitlin interrupted in a sardonic tone, making 'protégé' sound like a curse.

'I know, dear,' her stepmother said calmly. 'I wasn't totally distracted at lunch. You are the one that completed the challenge in Paris.' The way she pronounced Paris hinted at her European upbringing, as a Frenchwoman would, not pronouncing the final 's'.

'Yes, I was. But I don't know what all the fuss is about. It was easy.'

'Ha,' Alixia scoffed, 'you are too modest. Two candidates died trying to solve that particular conundrum and many others have failed entirely.'

'Including Dalton,' Caitlin added dryly.

There was a moment when he saw a glimmer of satisfaction in Caitlin's eyes.

'And you will be staying with us for a while I think?' said Alixia, changing the subject. 'It will be good for you to be around people of your own age. Rufius Westinghouse is a crazy old man who has spent far too long by himself!'

There was a rustling in the bushes behind them. A large bird with short wings and a huge beak burst through the foliage and careered down the walkway, almost knocking Josh over.

'Lentement! Maximillian! Slowly!' Alixia chastised, as it disappeared into another bush.

'Dodo,' observed Caitlin, 'stupidest bird that ever lived.'

Josh laughed and so did she. It made her eyes shine.

Alixia produced a thin sliver of fish from a small metal bucket and held it between finger and thumb. 'Would you feed Max for me, Josh? He's hiding in that thicket of *Rhacophyton.*'

Josh nodded, took the fish by the tail and wandered over towards the giant ferns that the dodo had disappeared into.

'Caitlin, a word,' Alixia said softly when they were alone.

'Yes, ma'am?'

'Aren't you being a little harsh on the boy?' Her voice was hard but maternal.

'But he attacked Dalton.'

'He failed — this is true. But it was not a fair test. Master Eckhart made it impossible for him to pass, did he not?'

Caitlin shrugged.

'You will learn that men are simple creatures, my dear. It is unfortunate that we must endure their faults, but he is not such a bad boy and he could be a great man — with the right guidance.'

Alixia kissed Caitlin on the cheek and gave her a hug. 'Now stop this petulant act and be yourself.'

Josh returned looking pleased with himself and with an obedient dodo chirping merrily behind him.

'So have you shown Joshua the baths?' Alixia asked as she began to cut up raw steak and feed it to the largest moth Josh had ever seen.

'Not yet no,' Caitlin groaned as if it were the last place she would have thought of taking him.

'Take him to the baths,' Alixia said, waving her hand. 'They are by far my favourite place in this crazy puzzle-house, and where I keep my most interesting specimens,' she added with a wink.

The baths were down in the basement, a subterranean spa filled with warm blue pools that steamed slightly in the flickering light of the oil lamps.

'Don't tell me,' Josh said as he admired the mosaics of sea horses and nymphs that lined the floor of the nearest pool. 'Roman?'

'Close enough — Byzantine,' Caitlin said with a smile. She apparently enjoyed being the know-it-all.

The cavern was a series of vast brick-lined vaults that seemed to tunnel out in different directions. Every ten metres there was an arch with a sculpture of an aquatic god or leaping dolphin. Along the central chasm, Josh could see a large fountain enshrined in sunlight and spouting giant flumes of water.

'They certainly knew how to build a swimming pool,' he observed, thinking how good it would be to swim over to the fountain — if he'd had a swimsuit.

There was a splash behind him, and he turned to see Caitlin in the water — naked.

'So. You coming in?' she asked, and there was that smile again.

'I don't have a costume!' he protested.

'Really? Didn't have you pegged as such a wuss! Don't worry no one's watching.' She dived under the water.

He turned his back to her and threw off the robes. The air was cool on his skin and he jumped in before he could check whether she had kept her end of the agreement.

'Nice abs,' she said, swimming away from him giggling.

Josh dived down into the deep blue water. The floor fell away sharply, and Josh could make out vague structures deep below him that looked like old buildings. A large shadow moved between them, and he came back up to the surface with a gasp.

'What's down there?' he asked, trying not to sound too concerned.

'Oh, fish mostly — Alixia has been known to keep aquatic mammals in here sometimes. They're usually harmless.'

'Like *whales*?'

She had swum off, and he couldn't hear her reply. He ducked his head back in to check there wasn't a prehistoric shark or something equally nasty coming to get him and then swam off towards the fountain.

The water was clearer and cleaner than any swimming pool he'd ever been to. There were no chemicals to sting his eyes and the temperature was warm and soothing, like a bath. Josh stopped after twenty metres so he could take in the view. The walls were decorated with the mythology of an ancient culture: warriors with tridents were defending yellow-haired maidens from sea dragons.

'Classic story: girl meets dragon, boy kills dragon — not

much has changed in a thousand years.' Caitlin's laughter echoed off the walls like silver bells.

As they swam towards the fountain, Sim's brother and his sister surfaced. Josh couldn't help but feel a little disappointed at finding they had company.

'Hi, Cat,' Lyra purred.

'Lyra, Phileas, meet Josh.' Caitlin moved aside to give them a better view of Josh who was still a good ten metres behind her.

'He's cute. Which guild does he belong to?' Lyra giggled.

'Shhh,' Phileas chastised his younger sister, 'he's still a novice.'

Lyra dived under the surface.

'No!' shouted Caitlin and Phileas in unison, but it was too late. Lyra was on an intercept course and was by far the fastest swimmer.

The first Josh knew of Lyra was when he felt something tugging at his ankle. At first, he thought it was one of Alixia's pets, then he caught sight of her yellow hair as she pulled him down into the deeper, colder waters. She was strong and fast. He'd never been that interested in swimming, other than to stop himself from drowning, and as he watched the surface disappear above him, he began to wish he'd paid more attention.

Lyra's face appeared in front of him like a beautiful water nymph, her hair framed by blonde tentacle-like tresses that drew him in. She placed her hands on either side of his face and kissed him hard on the mouth.

He felt the world turn as they moved through time. He felt her body close to his, warm in the deep, colder waters. There were memories moving between them, parts of his past were being unearthed and discarded as she dug through his timeline.

And then suddenly it stopped, and he was being pulled to the surface.

He broke through the water and sucked in air. It was as though he had forgotten he'd needed to breathe.

Caitlin was next to him trying to say something, but his ears were full of water so it was too muffled to make any sense. He held his nose and tried to equalise the pressure.

'. . . she's a bloody nightmare. Sorry,' was all he caught of Caitlin's apology. Phileas was reprimanding his sister on the far side of the fountain.

It took a few minutes for him to get his breath back enough to speak. 'Was she trying to kill me?'

'Hardly,' Caitlin said calmly. 'Lyra's a seer.'

'Which involves drowning people?'

'No, let's get out and I'll explain.' Caitlin started swimming towards the entrance.

'Seers are usually a bit eccentric,' Caitlin began. 'They're special, they can read people — their timelines I mean.' She was sitting by the fire drying her hair in one of the 'caldariums', a kind of sauna that the waters of the baths passed through on the way to the main pool. Both of them were wearing towelling robes and drinking something intoxicating that Caitlin had poured from a stone jar.

'So she was reading my life story?'

'Basically. She was a little over-enthusiastic in her methods, though. Lyra is very impulsive — she's mostly just hormones.'

'So how do you know if you're a seer?'

'You would know. It's something that happens very rarely and very early. Dalton is one too. The Order treat them as if they were blessed. Virtually every one I have ever met has been an arrogant asshole or a bit bonkers. We are trying to stop Lyra from being either.'

Josh laughed. 'Dalton is a dick.'

She smiled. 'But a powerful one all the same. He's ambitious, and his mother is the Chief Inquisitor for the Protectorate.'

'The secret police?'

'The most powerful group in our Order. They enforce the laws and govern us by them. They only report to the founder — Lord Dee.'

'And they can send you to Bedlam?'

Caitlin looked at him quizzically, 'what do you know about Bedlam?'

'Not much. The colonel mentioned it the other day.'

'The colonel?'

Josh smiled. 'A nickname the kids use for Rufius.'

Caitlin thought for a moment. 'Yeah, that kind of fits.'

'Have you known him long?'

'Uncle Rufius has looked after me since I was ten.' Her expression hardened a little. 'As for Bedlam, it's been a prison and a hospital — for the insane mostly. Depending on what you have done you can get sent to a different period of its history. There are quite a few seers in residence as well as a number of radical Chaosticians.'

Josh had never heard the colonel talk of anyone other than the group that sent him messages through his almanac. 'Are they like the Copernicans?' he asked, trying to sound like he knew something.

'Copernicans! No,' she exclaimed. 'Radical Chaosticians are those that take direct action on the past, without permission or consequence protocols. Copernicans are the opposite, most are interfering old coin flippers. Did Rufius tell you about them?'

'A bit. He said they try to predict the future?'

She shook her hair and then wrapped it in a towel. 'That's the general idea. There is a joke that goes something like "How many Copernicans does it take to change a lightbulb?" '

'How the hell should I know?'

'Exactly!' she laughed.

Josh couldn't see what was so funny, but Caitlin was too busy giggling to notice.

'I should warn you that Sim is an Actuary. That's what they call you when you first join the Copernicans,' she added once she realised that he hadn't got the joke. 'They spend most of their time staring at statistical analyses and risk factors. It takes them forever to make a decision about anything and even when they do they talk about probability rather than actual actions.'

'Why did he join them? He's more of a geek.'

'Oh, Sim loves tech — the Copernicans have some of the most amazing computers.'

'I thought you couldn't take technology back into the past.'

She was impressed. 'You can't, but I didn't say these were like present day PCs — these things are massive, like cathedral-size mechanical analytical engines. You have to see one to believe it.'

'So did they predict that I was coming to the Library?'

Her cheeks flushed a little. 'There was a sixty-three-point-two per cent chance that someone like you would be there, yes.'

'How did they know?'

'Because of the Watzenrode hypothesis. The change you made to history was predicted hundreds of years ago. It was one of two theoretical directions for the end of the Second

World War and was debated for many years. There was a Copernican Master by the name of Lucas Watzenrode who was convinced that it was the correct course, but many others disagreed, and so it was never acted upon.'

Josh couldn't conceive how anyone would have thought of something that far ahead — he had trouble deciding what to have for dinner tomorrow.

'So this Whatshisface predicted that I would be in the library last Saturday?' It was then that he realised it had only been a week since he'd stolen the medal. Elapsed time was hard to keep track of when you weren't always in the same century for more than a day.

'No, a difference engine and a whole floor full of actuaries probably did that, but they predicted it with a high probability.'

'Sixty-three per cent isn't that high,' he objected.

'It is for a Copernican. Most of their calculations never give you better than a fifty-fifty probability.'

'So why didn't the colonel just put it back the way it was?'

'Because he was told not to.'

'By the Copernicans?

'Probably the founder. Uncle Rufius is a Watchman — his orders can be overridden by the Council.'

Josh's head was full of questions, and every answer seemed to lead to new ones.

'Why did Lyra kiss me?'

'Seers need physical contact to make the connection. She is a little wild, likes to shock — it's nothing personal. Unless of course you want it to be?'

Josh blushed a little and shook his head. 'She's a bit young for me!'

Caitlin smiled. 'Don't be distracted by her appearance. She's over a hundred, which is young for us, but not for you.'

'What were those marks on her arm?'

Caitlin sucked breath through her teeth. 'Ah. Yes, those.'

Josh realised then that Lyra's scars and wounds were obviously from self-harming and that he'd touched on a sensitive subject.

'Seers tend to become obsessed with trying to understand the ways of the universe. They are a bit like poets, pondering the imponderable — the total opposite of the Copernicans with their logical minds.' She stared into the fire as she continued. 'Anyway, some of them become very interested in what happens at the point of death, how our timelines end and what occurs after...'

Josh could see the pain on her face even though she'd turned away. She was playing with something on her necklace.

'Lyra used to try to take herself to the edge to see for herself. It's called Reaving, and there are quite a few seers who have died or gone completely mad chasing the reaver.'

The moment was interrupted by Phileas walking in. He sat down next to Josh with a wet thud.

'Sorry about that, Josh. My sister is a complete tart.'

They laughed, and Caitlin poured out some more Byzantine brandy.

'The first order of business,' Methuselah announced over a lavish breakfast the next day, 'is to complete the assessment of Josh's range.'

They would begin each morning with a mission briefing in the Library, which had been annexed to the house and was only accessible via a portal at the back of the garden shed.

'Why the shed?' Josh asked Phileas as they walked down the garden path.

Phileas had been late down to breakfast and was holding half a bacon sandwich in one hand and a mug of tea in the other, alternating between the two as he tottered along the brick pathway. He was a couple of years older than Josh, who was sure he caught the distinctive whiff of booze on his breath.

'It's not really a shed,' Phileas said before cramming in the last of the sandwich. 'He calls it that to make it sound normal for the neighbours.'

From the outside, it looked every bit the kind of wooden shed that could be found at the bottom of any garden in England. Someone had chalked up some cricket stumps on one side of it, and there was the rusted iron ring of a netball hoop hanging redundantly above the door.

Methuselah, Caitlin and Lyra had already disappeared inside when Phileas and Josh reached it. The musty smell of oil and old grass cuttings engulfed Josh as he entered the dimly lit clutter.

'Smells like a shed to me,' Josh said to himself. He'd seen quite a few in his time.

'Keep going,' urged Phileas as he repositioned a hoe that had fallen from its peg.

Josh soon discovered that it was more like the entrance to a warehouse, albeit a long, thin corridor with what seemed an infinite number of shelves and cupboards. Along each side were hung every kind of garden tool imaginable, carefully placed on wooden pegs. They dated back hundreds of years. Josh picked up a scythe and examined the well-oiled blade.

'Dad can't help himself,' Phileas said, taking the scythe back and hanging it on the wall. 'Everyone in the Order is a bit of a collector — they tend to have their own personal storehouses.'

'Why not just add the library to the house as another floor?'

'It used to be. Mum had him move it out here a few years ago. She doesn't like guests turning up unannounced and the library is a nexus for the Order; so any entrance to it is also an exit. She likes to know who's coming.' He pointed ahead of them. 'Now here's the portal.'

The door looked as if it has once been part of a castle. It was constructed from a grid of small wooden panels, metal studs had been driven through it at the cross sections to add strength. The lock was heavy, black iron with a brass key protruding from it.

'Why does everything have to be so Gothic with you guys? And where exactly is this library?' Josh asked when he realised the door was only leaning up against the wall rather than being part of it.

Phileas put his tea down on a bench cluttered with mugs, placed his hand on the key and grabbed Josh's robe. 'I think you meant *when* is it?' he smirked as he turned the key and the world twisted away.

The library was an immense cathedral of knowledge.

Towering columns of ancient books disappeared into an unseen ceiling far above him. It was as if someone had taken every book that had ever existed and built a Babylonian ziggurat around them.

As Josh's eyes adjusted to the gloom he could make out a network of metal gantries and walkways stretching across the faces of the shelves; tiny figures moved across them on wired harnesses like trapeze artists. He looked back the way they had come and saw the small shed door propped against the wall — for some reason it reassured him.

'Please take your seats!' Methuselah's voice rang out from somewhere up ahead. Josh and Phileas quickened their step towards it.

A group of kids were sitting in a small auditorium, a series of benched seats that went down into the wooden floor. Each of them had been keenly preparing to write every word that Methuselah was about to say until Phileas and Josh arrived, at which point everyone turned to stare at the late arrivals. It reminded Josh of his first day at his last school, after yet another exclusion; kids always had a partic-ular way of staring at newcomers that was meant to destroy

any form of self-confidence, but Josh had grown immune —
he had been through it too many times.

'Right. I only do this particular lecture once,'
Methuselah began, his booming voice disturbing the other
scholars, creating a background of tutting and grumbling at
the end of each of his sentences from the floors above them.
He was standing in the centre of the auditorium with a book
in one hand and a piece of chalk in the other. There was a
blackboard with some of the temporal symbols that Josh
had seen in the colonel's book.

'Today you will each receive an almanac. This is for
training purposes only and is not to be used for keeping
notes or writing love letters to each other.' There was a definite undertone of a drill sergeant about his delivery. 'For the
next twelve weeks this document is your bible; I will use it
to set you tasks, missions and to find you when you stray off
the path. Guard it with your life — you will keep it
throughout your entire second year of training. Those of
you who have not passed year one, please be so kind as to
take yourselves to Novicius in 11.728, where Miss Cavendish
is expecting you.'

Three students disappeared in quick succession.

'Does that include me?' Josh whispered.

Phileas shook his head.

'The almanac is a precious artefact,' Methuselah
continued as Lyra and Caitlin appeared from behind a
nearby stack and began to hand around worn-looking jour-
nals as if they were songbooks at choir practice.

'You must treasure these with your life, they are one of
your only lifelines, without this or your tachyon you're lost
to us, not even the Draconians will be able to find you.'

As Lyra walked past Josh, she handed him a book and

winked, he took it and opened it to find a hastily scribbled note.

'Fancy another swim later? L. X.' He looked up and caught Caitlin scowling at her stepsister. Methuselah was busy drawing something on the blackboard.

'So this term we begin with the basics of ...' his voice sounded like every other teacher Josh had ever endured, and he began to zone out. He started to flick through the rest of his book. At first glance, it was completely blank, and then suddenly it wasn't; words and symbols began to appear across the surface of the yellowing paper — he thought it was never going to settle, but then slowly it coalesced into a flow chart of hieroglyphic pictures and numbers.

'Your first assignment?' Caitlin asked, peering over his shoulder.

'I guess so. I've no idea what it means!' he replied, showing her the book.

'I think Methuselah has assumed you have completed the basics. I can help you with that.'

She walked off into the maze of books and he duly followed. He could still hear Methuselah's voice in the background, but it was growing weaker.

'So how long does the training take?' Josh asked as they walked between the stacks. Each one was filled with old leather-bound volumes with golden hieroglyphs stamped onto their spines.

'Depends on which guild you join.' Caitlin's voice was barely more than a whisper. 'Basic training is four years, after that you specialise — unless you're a seer of course then you're in it for life.'

Above them, the moveable metal walkways clanked and whirred as the ladder systems reconfigured. Josh watched the small figures fly from one stack to another, collecting books in baskets on their backs like bees gathering pollen.

'So who has the shortest training?'

Caitlin turned to look at him, 'are you serious?'

'What? I'm just asking!'

She sighed and began to enumerate on her fingers, 'Fifteen years for Copernican, Scriptorian is eighteen, Draconian is only eight but you need to be invited. You can't join the seers unless you're born into it, so that leaves the Antiquarians which is an easy ten.'

'Ten years! To do what? Catalog art?'

'Time is a serious business — it's not something you can just jump into and blag it.'

'So how long does it take to become a Watchman?'

Her eyes narrowed. 'That's not a route many would choose to take it's not really a guild as such. They're kind of outcasts — most don't tend to live very long. Uncle Rufius is a bit of an exception.'

'Great. Sounds like my kind of job.'

She ignored him. 'So this first symbol 百 is "Bai". It's Chinese for "century". The second is "Afoset", which I think it originated from Akkadian. Anyway, that means fifteen or twenty-five, depending on how it's used.'

'So it's basically a date?' Josh said, staring at the characters as they moved around the page.

'Yes, kind of. You have to learn to read the context. More like a riddle. The codification of time is not a concept of absolutes.'

'Can't you just tell me what it says?' he pleaded, holding out the almanac.

She shook her head. 'That would be cheating. You'll never learn anything that way.'

She was right, of course, but cheating had got him

through school and would have done the same for college if certain people had kept their mouths shut.

Caitlin took a book down from the shelf and handed it to him. The title was in English, but it looked as if it had been printed a thousand years ago: *Codex: The Principal Symbols of Time*.

'I'm not good with books.'

'Yes, I remember. *Codex* is mostly pictures and numbers. The best way is to take a couple of them at a time. Methuselah told me you need to test your range anyway, so we can kill two birds with one stone.'

'Okay, where are we going in the fifteenth century?' asked Josh, staring blankly at the other symbols on the page.

She took a pencil out and wrote down a series of numbers on the page. As she drew a line between each symbol and number, it seemed to pin it in place — like kites tethered in the wind.

'The first one is a kind of longitude, not the one that you will have used on Google maps, but an older system — one the ancient Sea Kings were using thousands of years before Harrison rediscovered it in 11.770. It was one of the things that drew me to the Great Library of Alexandria — there is so much you can tell about a civilisation by their maps.'

'So what do we use?'

'I find Mercator's projections are quite a good start,' she said, pointing towards a large brown globe sitting in the middle of the table. 'He was one of our best Nautonniers.'

Josh shrugged. 'I have no idea what that means.'

'Means navigator or pathfinder. They're a specialist part of the Draconians. They chart the blank spaces in time, the forgotten eras. Temporal cartographers, if you like.' She became introspective and started to fiddle with her necklace.

'And how long does it take to become one of them?' he asked, trying to lighten the mood.

She punched him hard on the arm and smiled.

Thirty minutes later, Josh had scribbled a dozen or so notes next to the symbols and had an answer; he had enjoyed decrypting it, like a puzzle. It was more than just learning a new language.

'So we're going to Portugal, to find a lost map?'

'Not just any map. This one shows the Antarctic coastline,' she said excitedly.

'So?'

'So, it's been covered by layers of ice for ten thousand years. This is proof that someone surveyed it a long time ago. We can use it to find out more about them.'

'But why 1572?'

She sighed. 'Try to use the Holocene time format, otherwise you sound like a linear.'

'A linear?'

'Someone who experiences time in one direction. Not one of us.'

'1572 would be —'

'11.572. It's easy — you just have to add 10,000 and then divide by a 1,000.'

Easy for you maybe, thought Josh.

'If you had bothered to read the mission brief, you would know there was an admiral known as Piri Reis. He was supposed to have discovered it and brought it back home in 1572. Shit, now you have me doing it!'

They both laughed.

She was looking around for the nearest staircase. 'Our best bet would be in cartography. The Portuguese had a school dedicated to navigation; we're bound to have some of their work. I think it's four floors up and over there somewhere,' she pointed above his head, 'but they may have moved it. The Scriptorians are always reindexing stuff. They can never agree on the best system.'

'Scriptorians?'

'The guys on the flying trapezes,' she said, pointing straight up. 'The guild responsible for cataloguing everything — you would call them "Librarians", I guess. It's actually my guild,' she said proudly.

31
FIRST MILLENIAL

O ver the next few days, Josh learned the basics of using the almanac. Each morning they would go to the library, and a new challenge would appear on another page of his book. To his disappointment, other members of the De Freis family took it in turns to mentor him after Caitlin, each one helping him a little less as he became more confident with the basic symbology of time.

He travelled back further with every mission. Phileas took him to the fourteenth century to observe the Black Death, then he went to the Crusades with Lyra in the twelfth and Madame De Freis took him back to 10.920 to the last Mayan capital. These were not sightseeing trips; there was a purpose to each mission. Most involved saving some artefact from being destroyed, or reacquiring a lost skill or piece of knowledge — every one had to be written up in triplicate when they returned.

By Friday Josh had covered over 1,200 years of jumps and was beginning to wonder where the colonel had got to. He brought up the subject at breakfast.

'Ah. Yes,' Methuselah coughed from behind a newspaper, dated 1878. 'He's been put on a special assignment. Something very hush-hush apparently.'

Sim, Caitlin and Dalton were sitting close by and overheard the conversation.

'Protectorate business,' said Dalton in an officious tone, 'not something that goes through the book.'

'How does that work?' asked Josh without thinking.

Dalton sneered. 'Don't you know anything?'

Caitlin went to speak, but Josh caught her eye and shook his head.

'Why don't you explain to our guest?' Sim hissed at Dalton. There was a heavy emphasis on the word 'guest'.

'Only those within the council can order a direct action; rare events where even having the Copernicans involved could change the outcome, causations that threaten the very fabric of the continuum.'

'Basically he's gone dark — like special ops,' translated Sim for Josh's benefit.

'We're not even supposed to discuss it,' said Caitlin, glaring at Dalton.

'No. Quite so,' said the chastised Dalton.

Josh liked the sound of dark missions, he missed the thrill of riding shotgun with the colonel. While he was still enjoying their company and learning a lot, it was all a bit safe, and rather dull — like going on holiday with your parents.

'So, anyway, I have some other news,' Methuselah announced.

They all looked up from their breakfasts as he tapped the side of his teacup with a butter knife.

'It has been a while since I have had the pleasure of doing this.' He paused and nodded to his wife who was preparing something in the Viking equivalent of a kitchen.

'Joshua has passed a key milestone yesterday: he is now a first level millennial. Congratulations, my boy! Here's to your next thousand!'

Caitlin and Sim clapped, Dalton sneered and Mrs De Freis came over with an impressive-looking cake with a single candle and the numerals for a millennium iced onto it.

Josh couldn't remember the last time anyone had made him a cake. When he was younger, birthdays were generally something he had organised for himself, usually involving a packet of Jaffa cakes and a DVD — after a while, even he had forgotten to celebrate them.

'Well done,' Alixia said, smiling warmly, and then turning to Methuselah. 'I think today we should have a break from all this tedious studying. We should treat Josh to a little game.'

'Treasure Island?' said Sim, jumping up and clapping his hands like a five-year-old.

'No,' Caitlin shouted. 'Huntsman!'

Others were shouting at the same time. Josh could tell it wasn't often that they got to play, and assumed that none of the games were as normal as they sounded.

Methuselah waved his hands to calm them all down and then paused as he thought about it.

'Captain's Table?'

'Yes!' came a resounding shout from the others. Even Dalton seemed excited about that one.

32

CAPTAIN'S TABLE

The rules of the game appeared to be quite simple: by dinnertime, they had to have found the most interesting artefact to present to the 'captain', who was, of course, being played by Methuselah. They would recount its history and why it was so unique. The most fascinating find would be deemed the winner and placed in the 'collection' — which was apparently a high honour.

There were some forfeits and side rules around how you couldn't steal another team's prize nor use an existing or 'known' object from the collection, and that there was a limit on how long you could spend in the past: no more than forty-eight hours. Once the objects had been placed on the table, there was no going back and changing your mind after you saw what the others had brought.

Sim was excited. This was a rare treat — played only once a year at best. He told Josh that Dalton and Caitlin had both won five times each, so this was to be a tough game, and neither would be taking any prisoners, which was also one of the side rules — Josh knew what he meant.

Josh could see from Caitlin's look of concentration that

she was determined to beat Dalton. He began to wonder whether it would be safer to team up with Sim, but Methuselah had effectively ordered, and Caitlin had grudgingly agreed, to allow Josh to ride shotgun with her. Which Josh felt was a little unfair — he was convinced he was ready to go solo, but Methuselah wouldn't allow it, no matter how hard both Josh and Caitlin protested.

They were all gathered around a beautiful oval table in the middle of the curiosity collection on the second floor. A few other guests had heard about the game and joined the group. Dalton was standing at the opposite end of the table to Caitlin, flanked by a couple of his cronies — who Sim had informed Josh were going to work as 'tails' to report back to him with updates regarding the era in which the other teams were searching.

Josh knew Caitlin was unhappy that she'd been saddled with him. His level-one status was like a handicap that meant she would only be able to work within the last thousand years.

Methuselah appeared. 'So, gentleman, ladies . . .' He was dressed like a pirate, wearing a long velvet housecoat and a three-cornered hat.. 'Usual rules apply. No weapons, no stealing, no rewinds. My word is final and may the best prize win. As usual, the mission time is a maximum of forty-eight hours, and back by eight this evening?'

They set the dials on their own tachyons and then one by one disappeared, leaving Josh on his own with Methuselah.

He stood in the room feeling like an idiot. Had he missed something? Did Sim not tell him what to do next?

There was an awkward silence as he wondered if Caitlin had decided to dump him after all when she suddenly reappeared.

'Sorry. It was quicker if I did the first bit on my own.' She handed him a small coin. 'Here, take this and open it.'

He felt the timeline unfurl in his palm, and she pointed a path that led to the British Museum in 11.920.

'There, meet me in anthropology after closing. I have to shake off one of Dalton's minions.' With that, she disappeared again.

Josh focused on the time point until he could expand it enough to see the room where the coin had been stored, and then moved forward a few hours until the museum was closed.

He slowed his breathing and let his mind drift inside the timeline.

The room was dark and still, and there was a strong aroma of sandalwood and dead things. Josh realised he was in the wrong place when he saw the cabinets were full of stuffed animals and jars of pickled fish, their dead eyes staring blankly out at him through a viscous green liquid. The stillness was a strange, menacing silence that played tricks on your mind, triggering the imagination — conjuring life in the long-dead exhibits, so that they were only waiting for the right moment to jump out on him.

There was a noise from further down the hall. Instinctively he hid behind a cabinet, and his fingers found his tachyon in case he needed to make a quick exit.

The shadow of another visitor flickered on the far wall as their lamp swept the next room: it was the night guard. Josh could hear the man's keys jangling on his belt as he shuffled around muttering to himself and rattling cabinet doors — as if he too was checking they were all safely locked away.

A few long minutes passed by. Josh tried hard not to make a sound, then he heard the footsteps recede and the lamplight fade away.

He stepped out of the shadows to see Caitlin standing next to a cabinet full of small monkeys. The whole place was beginning to remind Josh of some kind of dead zoo.

'What are you doing in Zoology?' she asked, looking at a large, stuffed dodo that was the spitting image of Maximillian.

'I didn't want to get caught,' Josh explained. 'I thought the idea was not to attract attention to yourself.'

'Not in museums, dummy,' she tutted, 'and certainly not from Albert. Anyway, I told you to go to Anthropology — stuffed animals are no use to us.' She opened a nearby cupboard and took out a small lantern.

'Albert's one of us?'

'They all are. The Antiquarians run every museum as far back as the Great Library of Alexandria.'

'So what would you have done?'

'Just show him the mark.' She pulled back her sleeve to reveal the snake tattoo. 'Or in your case, the almanac. Since you don't have the mark yet.'

She turned a knob on the lamp and clicked a button until it lit. 'He's used to bumping into novices out of hours. The Order use this place as a testing ground all the time. Now we need to find a stepping stone.'

'A what?'

'Something that can get us back further, one that doesn't exist in the future. How do you feel about becoming a third-level millenial tonight?'

'Fine by me. Where are we going?'

She moved off between the exhibits, the beam of her

lamp flicking from one side to the other until she found the sign.

In golden capital letters were the directions to the various departments.

'Anthropology is on level four,' she sighed. 'We're on the wrong bloody floor.'

33

DALTON'S SPY

J arius had worked for Dalton for three years, although 'work' was probably the wrong term; there hadn't been any payment for what he did, only the very vague promise of a position of power once Dalton became a member of the council.

He'd followed Caitlin unnoticed through the various diversions she'd taken in time — it was his speciality. If there had been a need for such skills within the Order he would have risen through the ranks, but there was not. Nobody needed anyone followed. The Copernicans knew where everyone was at any given time and therefore made his innate skills rather redundant. The Draconians were the only other natural choice for his abilities and even he wasn't suicidal enough to want to join them.

He watched the two figures, haloed in the sphere of lamplight, as they climbed the stairs to the floor above and knew that Dalton had been correct in his assumptions:

'She'll take him to the Great Library, probably via the Egyptian exhibition of 11.920,' Dalton had told Darius during his briefing. 'Follow her until you know for sure and then come back to me.'

'So who won last time?' Josh asked as they climbed the stairs.

'Dalton,' she answered through gritted teeth. 'He brought back the chronometer from HMS *Beagle*. The ship that Darwin was on when he came up with his theory of evolution.'

'Doesn't sound that great. What's so special about a clock?' Josh said before realising that was probably the wrong response.

'It was one of the six owned by the captain, Robert Fitzroy — without them he would never have found the Galapagos Islands.'

Josh wasn't entirely sure what difference that made to anything. 'Sounds boring.'

'Darwin thought it was very entertaining — Yes, he's one of us,' she growled. 'I'm going to beat him this time.'

'You still haven't told me how.'

They stepped out onto the landing and Caitlin made straight for the entrance to the 'Exhibition of the Pharaohs', as the banner declared — stretched between two golden sarcophagi.

'He thinks I'm going to the Great Library. It's where I usually start, but this time I'm changing it — this time we're going to think a little bigger.'

'Great! So we're going back to the Pharaohs?' Josh asked with wide eyes as he admired the golden objects arrayed inside the display cases.

Caitlin didn't look up as she kept walking 'No, we not

going there, especially not the second dynasty — it's forbidden.'

Before Josh could ask why, they left the opulence of Tutankhamen and walked through into the next section. This hall was dull by comparison, flanked by two massive sculptures of winged men with the bodies of lions and immense beards.

'Assyrian,' Josh read from one of the displays.

'Too far back for you.'

'How far?'

'At least five thousand years. I promised Methuselah that I wouldn't take you beyond the tenth epoch.'

'I could do that easily. I'm not a kid.'

'Do you know what happens to those who go outside their range?'

'No, but I guess you're going to tell me.'

'That's the thing, nobody knows. They never return, and not even the best Draconian has ever been able to reach them.'

Josh wondered what it was like to get lost in history. To end up somewhere with a bunch of cavemen sounded as if it would be quite a laugh.

'So who are these Draconians anyway?' he asked, changing the subject.

They were nearly through the Assyrian collection and Josh could tell from the way she was walking that Caitlin's patience was wearing thin.

'Do you mind if we put the lessons on hold until I've won this stupid game?'

The next room was full of old books, ancient manuscripts were laid open to display a beautiful illustrated panel or letterform. Josh tried to read some of the texts, but most were in German or Latin. The heavy characters of the words were so perfect he thought they could had been printed, but in places, he could still make out the pencil lines of the scribe who had prepared them.

'Here it is,' she whispered, as she opened the glass case of an ornate leather book, which was held shut with a series of iron bands.

'What is that?'

She unlocked the book, and the leather cracked as she lifted the cover to reveal the frontispiece.

'It's a Wallachian Bible. It was from the time of Vlad the Impaler.'

'Who?'

'Dracula?'

'No shit.' Josh was suddenly very interested. 'When was he?'

'11.431.'

'I've gone further back than that! I thought you were going to take me back another thousand!'

'I said that in case one of Dalton's minions was listening. Do you want to come or not?'

Josh held up his hands in surrender, he wasn't going to turn down a chance to meet the original Lord of the Vampires. There was a small thrill as he placed his hand on the page, he was beginning to think he might enjoy this time travel thing after all.

Darius walked up to the Wallachian Bible, closed the cover and shut the glass case. He was glad he hadn't left when he'd seen them enter the Egyptian section. Dalton had been wrong, and he was going to enjoy telling him so.

34

DRACUL

[Transylvania, Romania. Date: 11.431]

The castle was cold, really cold. It was as if the stone were actually made from blocks of solid ice. Josh felt a shiver run down his spine as they crept down the spiral stairs of one of its towers. A storm lashed at the walls outside; the stairs were slick with the driving rain that sluiced through the arrow slits on every full turn of the staircase. Torches guttered in the icy wind that drained the heat from the flames, leaving only the faintest glimmer by which to see the ever descending steps.

'Where are we going?' asked Josh as quietly as he could through chattering teeth.

Caitlin was either ignoring him or couldn't hear above the howl of the storm and continued down into the dark. Josh tried not to hear the distant screams of pain that were carried in on the wind or think too deeply about what the awful smell was that was rising up from somewhere below them.

He was so caught up in his thoughts that he didn't

realise she'd actually stopped, and he found himself flailing around for a handhold to prevent himself from knocking her down.

They came to a landing. The walls were adorned with tapestries and a portrait of a medieval knight was hanging on the end wall.

'Not much of a looker, is he?' said Josh, unnerved by the way the eyes seemed to follow him around the hall.

'That's Vlad Dracul II,' she whispered, 'father of the impaler.'

'Dracula had a dad? I thought he was immortal?'

'Even if he was immortal, which he wasn't, he would still have to be born, and that happened in the winter of 11.431. The father has just been invested in the Order of the Dragon, hence the epithet Dracul.'

'So when did he start biting people?'

'He didn't. You do know that was just a story Bram Stoker made up in 11.897?'

He smirked. 'So no need for the garlic or the crucifix, then?'

Caitlin wasn't listening. She was distracted by something she was holding. It was a small ball made of glass.

'What's that?'

'A lensing prism. Lets you split out the various possibilities.'

'You mean you don't know where you're going?'

'Shut up. I'm trying to concentrate,' she snapped, closing one eye and holding the prism up.

Josh wandered over to inspect a collection of old shields and swords hanging on one of the walls. Their edges were pitted and nicked as if they had seen a great deal of action. He ran his finger along a blade, sensing the echoes of the terrible battles. Below them were a set of daggers with strangely carved bone handles. Josh took one and felt the weight of it in his hand. These were real historical items, ones that didn't need a timeline to see what they had experienced.

'Shit!' Caitlin cursed under her breath.

Josh turned to see her putting the lens away and taking out a blade and looking around nervously.

'What's up?'

'Monads — real vampires. We have to hurry!'

She grabbed him by the arm and walked quickly down the hall towards the portrait.

There was a door to the right, a small insignificant door with the symbol of a dragon on it.

'I thought you said there was no such thing?'

'Not now!'

'Shouldn't we just leave?' Josh asked, but Caitlin was obviously not about to give up her plan. She opened the door slowly, trying not to make the hinges complain too loudly. The room was lit with an amber glow. The heat from a large open fire warmed their faces. It was a finely furnished bedroom with a sumptuous four-poster bed and furs covering every inch of the floor. In one corner was a cot in which a child slept soundly. The nanny sat snoring in the chair next to it. Caitlin nodded to Josh to watch the sleeping nurse, which he duly did — although he had no idea what to do if she woke.

Caitlin went over to the cot and carefully took a look inside.

The fire crackled, and the nanny stirred but did not wake. Josh looked over to the hearth.

Caitlin whispered his name, and he turned back to see her waving at him. He walked over to her, the fur-lined floor muffling any sound of his step.

The boy was no more than four or five years old. He was fast asleep and looked completely innocent of the life to come. Spinning slowly above the child's head was the talisman of a dragon eating its own tail. Josh assumed that this was why Caitlin had called him over, but when he reached out to touch it she held his hand back and shook her head. She held out a small white tooth in the palm of her hand.

'What's that?'

'His first tooth.'

Josh scoffed. 'Really? Of all the things you could take? You want to play tooth fairy?'

'Sometimes it's not about the value of a thing, but what it represents. Haven't you learned anything about what we do yet?'

'Obviously not,' Josh said with a mystified look.

Suddenly there was an inhuman scream from the other side of the door.

Josh saw Caitlin go white, her eyes wide, and he turned to see a ghostly figure walk through the very solid-looking oak door. The thing had no eyes, and a dark hole where its mouth should have been. Its body was distorted, like a bad copy of a corpse.

Josh instinctively opened the timeline of the dagger he was holding and pulled Caitlin into the first time point he found.

[Northwest Europe. Date: Unknown]

J osh woke slowly, surfacing from a dream in which he
had travelled back to Dracula's castle and been killed
by a werewolf — who'd been the boy's nanny. He'd
been cold, frozen to the core — which must be what death
felt like.

He tried to move but found that his arms were held
down by something warm and thick. He attempted to open
his eyes, but it was too dark to see.

'Lie still,' a woman's voice whispered in his ear. 'They'll
find us soon.'

He could feel her body warm against him, her breath on
his neck, and he closed his eyes once more and fell into a
dreamless sleep.

The next time Josh woke he felt more alert and this time
when he opened his eyes he saw daylight. His arm brushed
the furs that covered his naked body and without needing to

turn he knew that Caitlin was curled up behind him. He listened to her breathing and felt her body rise and fall against his back. It was triggering all sorts of sensations. His heart started to beat faster as the blood began moving exactly where he didn't want it to.

Josh tried to think of something else. Looking up, he saw that they were in a cave, although what they were doing here was a mystery. He could remember nothing after he had used the dagger to escape the monster.

'You're awake. I can tell from your breathing,' Caitlin whispered in his ear. 'Don't move.'

There was a shock of cold air as she wriggled away from him, dragging some of the furs with her.

'And don't get any ideas. We had to conserve body heat, and this was the best I could do.'

He could hear her feet slapping against the rock floor as she walked away.

'OK. You can look now.'

He raised himself up on his elbow to find that he had been lying on a bed of tatty old furs in a cave full of skulls of creatures he'd never seen. Caitlin was wearing a mixture of skins and fur that covered most of her body. She threw something at him that looked like a long vest made from animal hide.

'Put that on,' she ordered, and disappeared further into the cave.

He could hear gurgling from somewhere, and a few minutes later Caitlin returned with a crude wooden bowl full of clear spring water.

'Drink this,' she ordered in a tone that inferred she was pissed off with him.

He did as he was told. The water was freezing and tasted

of rock, but it was refreshing, and he drank the whole bowl in one go.

She sat down by the remnants of a fire and poked at it with a bone, then slowly added dry tinder and sticks until it was burning well.

Josh was disorientated, his head was still fuzzy and his stomach was empty, which made him feel weak. He sat down opposite her and let the fire warm his body.

'You should put something else on,' she muttered. 'We have to stay here for a while. Until they come.'

'Who?'

'The Draconians, of course. They're the only ones who can find us. Probably once we've died of hunger,' she said through gritted teeth.

'What happened?'

She looked at him through eyes filled with fire. He could see the storm building in her. '*You* happened, that's what happened. What were you thinking? What was your brilliant plan? I'm dying to hear it.'

'I don't know. I panicked.'

She picked up the handle of the dagger, there was nothing left of the blade. 'You used a natural. Do you know how dangerous it is to use natural materials?'

He shook his head.

She waved her hand around the cave and then at their furs. '*This* dangerous. You made a jump into the periphery — the unknown past. We're off the grid. I have no idea how far back. The tachyons don't even work back here.'

He looked at his own watch. She was right, the dials had all frozen — it also explained why their clothes had disappeared.

'But these Draconians will find us?' he said, trying to sound hopeful.

'They should be able to. The tachyons will be found in the future and then traced back.'

'How far into the future?'

'Oh, I'd say in about fourteen thousand years. By the look of the ice, I would estimate we are somewhere in the Mesolithic.'

They sat in silence for a few minutes. Caitlin poked the fire absentmindedly while he tried not to think about how hungry he was, but he didn't dare ask if there was any food.

'Why didn't you just use the tachyon to take us back,' she asked, breaking their reverie.

'Then you would have lost the game.'

'It was only a game — no one was supposed to die,' she sighed.

'We're not going to die,' he said, pulling another fur around himself.

The wind roared, driving the snow into the cave and over his feet. Josh stood at the cave entrance; he could feel his hands going numb and went to put them in his pockets — which was when he realised he didn't have any. The furs were warm, but they weren't stitched together, and the cold air had an exceptional ability to find the gaps.

Caitlin was inspecting the bone handle, holding it up to the firelight to get a better view of the carvings. 'This is a ceremonial handle, probably for a stone blade. They used them for skinning animals.'

Josh was only half listening; the noise of the wind was overwhelming. He watched as it scattered drifts of snow across the tundra. A herd of mammoth was making slow progress across the short stubby grassland, their coats matted with ice as they battled into the winds. He took a long, deep breath of the sharp, cold air — it was pure, as if the world were just waking from a long winter's sleep.

Caitlin had said something about a land bridge and that the plateau before them would be the English Channel one day. They could walk to France, or Eurasia as she called it, if they could survive the cold.

Josh went back into the cave. 'So what was that thing that came through the door?'

'A monad — time wraith,' Caitlin replied.

Josh dropped the gorse bushes that he'd collected on to the meagre pile of other burnable stuff they'd found. He rubbed his hands over the fire to warm them. They were raw from the cuts of the prickly thorns.

'Wraith? You mean like a ghost?'

'More like a vampire — one that likes to feed on your memories.'

'How?' was all that Josh could manage. He was weak from the lack of food.

'They are from beyond the continuum, outside of time — a place we call the Maelstrom. There are many dark and terrible things out there, and they all like to feed on the energies of our timeline.'

Josh wondered why the colonel hadn't mentioned this. It was the kind of health and safety video he would have expected on day one.

'How did it find us?'

She shrugged her shoulders. 'Wild ones need a breach, a hole in time, but I'm guessing that this one was a captive, although we won't know now after your brilliant escape plan.'

'So what exactly would you have done?'

'I'm quite capable of dealing with a monad. They're not

the worst thing I've had to take on.' She flipped the dagger handle over and threw it at him.

Josh caught it with one hand. 'If this monad was captive, then it was a trap?'

'No shit, Sherlock. It's not the first time Dalton has played dirty.'

'He doesn't like losing, does he?' He came and sat next to her.

'No, he doesn't. It's a shame. I thought Dracula's first tooth was a definite winner — it had a certain irony,' she said to herself.

'Yeah. It did,' he laughed. 'I would love to have seen Dalton's face when you dropped that one on the table.'

She smiled, and then they both laughed for no other reason than it was better than crying.

'How long did this ice age last?' he asked as he poked the fire. It was getting low, and the sun was setting outside; the temperature would drop drastically soon, and they would have to work hard not to freeze to death.

'The last one? About 300 million years,' she said without taking her eyes off the fire.

'And the chances of anyone finding us in the next couple of days?'

'Not great.' She shrugged. 'This far back, there are hardly any man-made artefacts. It's mostly tribes of nomadic hunters and cave art.'

'So what's further back than this?'

Caitlin shivered and moved closer to him, pulling the furs around them both. 'It's not been mapped. The Draconians are the only ones allowed to travel into the ice ages, and they have forbidden anyone from going back. It's too dangerous.'

He could hear her stomach groaning through the furs.

She was being brave, and he knew that he would have to do something soon. They couldn't survive on water and grass.

'So tell me about these Draconians. They sound like a crazy bunch of mothers.'

She chuckled. 'Funny you should say that. My mother was one, and my father.'

He had wanted to ask what the deal was with Methuselah, Alixia and the Colonel — it was obvious they had been looking after Caitlin for a while.

'They were both Draconian Nautonniers, specialist navigators who travel into the forgotten parts of history, literally the spaces on the map. You ever heard the saying "Hic sunt dracones"?'

'Nope.'

'It means "Here be dragons". It was what the old cartographers used to put on the blank parts of their maps — when they didn't know what to draw.'

'I like their style.'

'So, anyway, when I was ten they were sent on a mission, some kind of anomaly in the Egyptian second dynasty. I can still see them getting ready — they always went on missions together,' she paused as if cherishing the memory. 'But they never came back, none of them did. I've been staying at the Chapter House ever since. They're like my second family.'

'I never knew my dad,' Josh volunteered without thinking. He'd never said that to another soul. It felt kind of good.

'I don't remember much about mine. Only what Uncle Rufius would tell me when he used to take me on our adventures, as he would call them, usually around the fifteenth century.'

'Looking for lost Italian art?' Josh joked.

'No, our fifteenth century, about 9000 BC. We used to explore, hunt and fish, the usually outdoorsy kind of things.

We'd camp out for weeks and he'd tell me stories about what my mum and dad had done.'

Josh thought back to the childish fantasies he used to have about having a father: going to football matches, camping, learning to drive — they'd all died a long time ago.

'So you actually know how to survive back here?' Josh looked mildly annoyed.

'I guess so, but it doesn't matter — the Draconians will come soon.'

'So why haven't they found us yet!' Josh snapped as he got up and went searching around the cave.

'I don't know,' Caitlin replied, moving his discarded furs over her legs. 'What are you looking for?'

'Something sharp. Didn't you say there were hunting tools here?'

'Yes, over in the corner by the tusks. What are you going to do?' She sounded concerned.

'I think I know why they haven't come. We die here in this bloody cave, and no one ever found us.' He kicked over a pile of bones and pulled out the broken end of a spear. 'I have never sat around and waited for someone else to rescue me — that only happens in the movies. We have to survive, Caitlin. We have to go out there —' he waved the spear towards the blizzard that was battering the world outside — 'and we have to make a difference — start a village or a religion or something. We have to make our mark on history. Think of it like a signal flare. They will find it and come for us.'

'I don't know if I can. I'm tired and it's too cold,' she muttered, moving deeper inside her furs.

'Not now, but tomorrow when the sun comes up, we need to make a go of it. If I'm right, they will come. If not, well, it's still better than dying in this cave.'

She was drowsy, and he had to shake her awake.

'Caitlin. The colonel didn't teach you all that stuff so you could die in the middle of the Mesolithic, did he? You make the best of what you got. That's what my Nan used to say.'

She roused at the mention of her uncle, her beautiful green eyes looking deeply into his, and he saw the flash of anger once more.

'And now he's disappeared too, just like they did! They've been doing it for years and still couldn't save themselves. What chance have we got?' She stood up and shouted at him, the cave amplifying her voice. Her eyes were blazing now, all traces of sleep gone. He knew he had to push her further.

'Well, maybe he wasn't as good as you thought he was. Maybe he just ran off with another woman?'

She punched him in the face with such force that he fell back into a pile of old bones.

'You never, ever talk about my parents again! You hear me?' The heat had risen in her cheeks and her eyes were brimming with tears.

'Fine. No problem,' Josh replied rubbing his chin.

'Fine. If we're going to survive we need food and soon.' She walked over to the old tools, 'And we should move south, it's warmer there. Now help me make some kind of weapon out of this shit.'

Later that night there was a noise from the mouth of the cave. Josh woke first, his arms wrapped tightly round Caitlin. In the dim glow of the dying fire he could just make out a figure at the cave entrance. It was covered almost entirely in snow, a few moments later another arrived. Josh urged his frozen fingers to reach for one of the spears they had made that afternoon and hid Caitlin under the furs.

The first figure signalled to the second, and both marched into the cave. They wore large bulky furs with hoods that covered their heads. It wasn't until they came nearer that Josh saw the insignia on their bags.

'Well, you took your time,' he said as he bent down to wake Caitlin. 'Wake up, Cat. The cavalry has arrived!'

36

CONSEQUENCES

Josh couldn't believe Dalton's mother was a high-ranking official in the Protectorate. Ravana Eckhart sat behind the captain's table; her face gave no hint of emotion as she studied the report. On either side of her stood two menacing-looking men in full face masks, dressed in black leather armour with tubes running into the backs of their heads. This was the first time Josh had seen officers of the Order's police force — the black glass of their eye lenses reflected nothing.

Before the chief inquisitor sat the various prizes from the game, including the tooth that Caitlin had taken from Dracula and the crudely carved bone handle of the knife that had taken them back into the Mesolithic.

Methuselah stood beside Josh. Caitlin had been confined to her bed for two days by Alixia, and no amount of pleading would change her mind.

He was still trying to come to terms with the fact that his plan had worked; somewhere in another branch of time they had survived long enough for the Draconian team to find them. There was a life back in the Mesolithic that he and Caitlin had made together, enough time to make themselves stand out.

'Methuselah, you were warned that he was impulsive,' Ravana said. 'You should have known better than to allow such childish games to go unsupervised!'

Methuselah knew better than to respond.

She picked up the bone handle. 'Jones. What an earth made you choose this?'

There had been numerous conversations in headmasters' offices where an object, either broken or stolen, would be placed in front of him, and an explanation demanded.

'Instinct?' he replied, not quite knowing what to say.

Dalton's mother grimaced and put the handle back with the other trophies.

'You do realise that you went back more than fourteen thousand years? The Draconians inform me there was less than a one per cent chance of ever finding you had you stayed in the cave. Ms Makepiece tells me that it was you who persuaded her to move out into the wilderness.'

Josh nodded. There was a chance he might get away with this.

'She has pleaded for leniency on the grounds that you weren't aware of our rules.' She glanced at one of the officers. 'Rules that have stood for a thousand years, ones that have never been broken in the history of the Order.'

Ravana stood and placed her hands on the table. Her knuckles went white as she leaned forward and her eyes narrowed. 'I blame Westinghouse for all of this. Do either of you have any idea of his current location?'

Josh shrugged. Methusaleh shook his head.

'You leave me no choice. You cannot go crashing around in history as you wish. The consequences of your actions could affect hundreds of millions of lives. You must learn to consider the implications of your actions, Joshua Jones. Until then you are hereby barred from the Order.'

The two guards came and stood either side of Josh. He could see strange dials wired into their gauntlets.

'Escort him from the premises, confiscate his almanac and tachyon, and inform Arcadin that, until further notice, he is no longer welcome.'

37

EXILE

Beyond the doors of the Chapter House, the world was grey and dull. Storm clouds gathered in the sky above him as if conjured up by his mood. The colonel would never have let it come to this, Josh told himself — where was the old man anyway?

As he trudged along the street towards the tube station, he thought back to the night before and the way Caitlin's body had felt beneath the furs. He longed to be back there again, relive that moment of quiet intimacy, just the two of them alone in the middle of nowhere. He'd never really got that close to another human being, let alone a girl. A smile crossed his face at the thought of what they must have got up to after that night. The Draconian patrol that had found them refused to give him any details, but it must have been something quite epic to have attracted their attention.

Then the reality of his situation kicked in: there was never likely to be another night like that, no more adventures in history, no more Caitlin, no more money — he had screwed it up like he always did, trying to impress her with some ridiculous stunt, putting her life in danger.

Suddenly the mobile Lenin had given him started vibrating in his jacket. Josh took it out and saw a list of unopened messages; the forgotten phone must have been off the network the whole time he was in the Chapter House.

Three were naked selfies of Elena, which he deleted with a swipe. The others were from Lenin, the later ones all threats, escalated over time by his lack of response.

There were also missed calls from various numbers. He scrolled up and down through them and picked one at random and dialled it.

'Yo,' a voice answered after a couple of rings — it was Billy.

'Sup?' replied Josh.

'It's Friday, dude. Where the hell have you been? It's like you dropped off the planet.'

'Yeah.' Josh had no idea what day it was, let alone which century.

'The man wants to know if you have everything, you know, like, sorted?'

'Totally. What time we up?'

'One thirty tomorrow morning.'

Josh dropped the call, deleted all the messages, pulled the sim card out and dumped the phone in the nearest bin. He had little choice but to go through with Lenin's plan now — it was the only way out.

All he had to do was this one last job and he was home free. He had a few hours before he had to meet them, time enough to go to see his mum and sort out a plan B.

They'd moved his mother to a different ward after she'd had some kind of relapse. The doctor said they'd tried to contact him, but there was no answer at the last known address. They all tried to play it down, telling him everything would be all right, but Josh was not in the mood for being treated like a kid. He knew how bad it could get, and no one knew her condition better than he did.

She was in a side ward in her own room. The TV was on with the sound turned down. Her eyes stared blankly over the oxygen mask that hid most of her face. He took her hand and sat on the bed.

'Hi, Mum,' he whispered.

Her eyes blinked but didn't move from the screen. They must have given her some serious sedatives, he thought. Her hands felt tight, the tendons in her forearms still corded and rigid from the spasms.

'Listen. I've got a plan — it's going to sort us out for good this time. I promise,' he whispered as he stroked her hair. 'You have to believe me, Mum. You were always the one that believed me.' There were tears running down his cheeks. 'I can fix this once and for all. For good.'

He sat there holding her hand until a nurse came in with a trolley and he knew it was time to go. He kissed his mother on the forehead and left.

38

AT THE COLONEL'S HOUSE

The colonel's house was dark and unusually quiet as
Josh climbed up to one of the back windows. He had
persuaded the old man to change the locks on both front
and back doors, which was fine if you had a key, but that
had been confiscated along with his tachyon and almanac at
the Chapter House.

Glass crunched under his trainers as he stepped over the
window ledge and into the study. He could just make out
the bloodstain of the other colonel on the sofa, and heard
the words:

'Seventeen to the fourth, Tiberian. Twenty-five. Nine.
Fourth branch . . .'

He wondered where the old man was right now and
whether he knew or even cared about Josh being kicked out.
The cat wandered in, licking its lips. It wound itself round
his leg, and he could feel the purring through his trousers.

'Yeah, I miss him too,' he admitted as he gave it a scratch
behind the ear.

He imagined the old man would have quite a lot to say
about his expulsion. Josh wanted for nothing more than to

have the colonel give him a bollocking, but that wasn't going to happen — he still had another reason to be here, and it wasn't to check on the cat, who seemed to be looking after itself perfectly well.

Even though he could tell the house was empty, Josh still crept as quietly as he could up the stairs and into the collection room. He used a torch to find the cabinet where the photo of Mary Somerville was displayed. It had been propped up against one of the stuffed animals the colonel had taken from the Victorian safe-house.

A few minutes later Josh was standing in the dining room in 1833, staring at the painting of Dalton as he strapped a brand-new Tachyon IV to his wrist.

There was something quite comforting about having one back on his arm again. He wondered how long it would be before the Order would notice it was missing and send someone after him. Then he realised that they would have been waiting for him if they had — the whole time-paradox thing was hard to get your head around, but he was slowly getting the hang of it.

39

THE HEIST

Lenin got into the front seat of the Renault dressed entirely in black army surplus gear, including a balaclava which made him look like some kind of chubby Ninja. Two of his boys jumped in the back in similar outfits. As Josh got back in, he wondered whether he should have changed into something more appropriate.

All of them were carrying guns.

'You sure this car can take it?' Lenin asked as he rolled up the balaclava and put his shades back on.

Josh nodded. 'I took everything out of the boot. I guessed we wouldn't be needing the spare tyre.'

Lenin took his gun out and snapped back the barrel to load it.

'What's with the guns? You expecting trouble?'

'Drive,' was all he got in the way of a reply.

He started the car and pulled out onto the main street. It was 1.32am and the roads were empty except for the occasional taxi driven by pale-faced ghosts.

Josh had gone over the journey to and from the University until he had memorised all the best routes, ones that didn't involve too many traffic lights, CCTV cameras and dead ends. He had stolen the licence plates from another car and swapped over at the last minute so they wouldn't flag up on the automatic recognition systems for a while — everything was a go, as NASA would say.

They drove past the main gates of the university to check that the guards were still at their posts. Lenin had chosen to use the smaller back entrance, opposite the Royal Albert Hall, which had a pair of locked iron gates. Josh parked up in Kensington Gore at 2.15am, fifteen minutes ahead of schedule.

'We've got to get to the Separation Science Lab in the Blackett Laboratory,' Lenin instructed them as he scrolled through the map on his phone. 'The ephedrine is stored in the basement, two floors down. Billy, you keep a lookout at the back door. Crash, Tek, you're with me.'

'Shouldn't I stay with the car?' complained Josh.

'We've been over this,' Lenin growled as he took out a university security card, one of Tek's creations no doubt. 'You're coming. Now, Tek and me are going to sort the power to the gates — you back the car up and leave the engine running. Got it?'

Josh nodded.

Lenin and Tek got out and ran towards a wooden door with the words 'Roderic Hill Substation' spelt out on terra-cotta tiles above it. Josh waited for them to disappear inside and then allowed the car to creep forward until it was in line with the entrance. When he saw the magnetic locks on the gates disengage, he reversed quickly into the alleyway as Lenin pushed the gates aside.

'Smooth,' commented Billy from the back seat.

Tek was climbing down a pole as they pulled into the delivery yard. He had put some kind of device on the CCTV that was covering the back entrance. Billy pushed the front passenger seat forwards and jumped out. 'So you coming or what?' he whispered as he got out.

'Don't suppose I have a lot of choice,' Josh replied, pulling the handbrake up and leaving the car idling in neutral.

Lenin was already at the back entrance of the building, which was clearly marked: 'Faculty of Chemistry and Molecular Sciences'. Billy ran off into the shadows to find a suitable lookout point as Josh and the others went in.

The lights in the corridor flared into life, startling them until Tek pointed out that they were controlled by motion sensors. Josh realised too late that a mask would have probably been a smart move; there were CCTV cameras, following every step of his progress. The run to the stairs was ten metres of pantomime as he tried to hide his face.

As they descended, Josh noticed that each of the doors they passed had increasingly more serious warning signs; with the additional droning hum of machinery it was beginning to feel like something out of a Bond movie — like they were entering the underground headquarters of Dr Evil.

Tek was stripping wires out of the keypad on the door when Josh caught up. Lenin had pulled up his ski mask and had his gun in one hand. He had an insane smile across his face, the kind that told Josh he was seriously overmedicated.

Tek was a technical genius, hence the name. He could get you free calls on your mobile, or hack into your email, but his real talent was credit cards. His skill with cash machines was legendary. It was said that he had once organised an attack on HSBC that had resulted in £75,000 being withdrawn from cashpoints in London in one day. It had taken two days for the bank to get their systems back up and running after that.

The doors beeped meekly and slid open. Tek gave them the thumbs up, and Lenin pulled the mask down once more and raised the gun as he went in — like he was playing a video game.

The laboratory was empty, no self-respecting student was going to be working at this time, they would all be in the bar trying to get laid or drunk, or both.

Josh watched as Lenin crept slowly among the metal benches, each one stacked high with fragile experiments made up of plexiglass tubes, beakers and bunsen burners. He was heading towards the storeroom at the far end of the lab. It was a large metal door with more signs warning about hazardous materials, which Lenin ignored as he slid it aside and went in. Tek followed close behind with a trolley.

That was when Josh first noticed something odd.

He had the strangest feeling he was being watched, but when he looked around there were no active cameras, thanks to Tek, and nowhere for anyone to hide. He could hear the two of them shifting containers around in the store room, they were both too busy to keep an eye on Josh, but he still couldn't shake the sensation, all the hairs on the back of his neck were standing on end.

Then Josh noticed the numbers on the lift panel next to the stairs. The number was descending — someone was on their way down.

He began to wish he hadn't thrown the phone away, he couldn't even text Billy to see if everything was OK upstairs.

As the number continued past 0, he heard the wheels on the trolley squeak and saw Lenin come charging out like a shopper on black friday. Tek was running too, carrying a couple of metal cylinders tucked under his arm.

'What are you waiting for? Get the freaking lift!' Lenin shouted as he waved his gun towards the doors.

There was no time to explain to them that someone was already on their way down, Josh just watched events unfurl in slow motion. As Lenin reached the lab doors, they opened automatically, at the same time the lift doors slid apart and a night guard stepped unwittingly into Lenin's line of fire.

In slow motion Josh watched Lenin shoot the man in the chest. His body flew backwards into the back wall and slid down into a bloody pool. Lenin was shouting something at them, but Josh didn't wait to listen, he pressed the rewind button on the tachyon.

[<<]

The lift number was still above ground on the indicator, Josh knew he had less than two minutes to try to stop the guard getting killed. He looked around for a weapon or something to distract Lenin when he came through the door. There was nothing but glass and chemicals in the lab, he had no idea what any of them were for. He guessed acid would do the trick, but everything was labelled with scientific symbols, and he had failed Chemistry in Year Nine.

They were seconds away from coming out of the store room when Josh noticed the fire alarm. He grabbed some paper towels and lit them from a Bunsen burner, then held the makeshift torch up to the sensor. The water cascaded from the sprinkler system and soaked everything in seconds. Alarms went off all over the building. The lift stopped on the floor above and did not come down any further. Josh breathed a sigh of relief and turned to find Lenin staring at him in disbelief.

Tek was furiously trying to disable the alarms behind him but was shaking his head as if it were a waste of time.

Josh couldn't hear what Lenin screamed at him as he raised the gun towards him, his hand reached for the tachyon but it was too late, the butt of the gun struck him across the temple, and he went down.

40

THE PROFESSOR

There was a blinding pain behind his eyes when Josh came around. His hands were bound, his clothes were soaking wet and the seat he was sitting on was hard and uncomfortable in the way that only school chairs could be.

His head was resting on a table. Someone had made a pillow out of his hoodie to try to make it more comfortable, which it was not.

He wasn't sure what had happened after Lenin had hit him. The alarms had stopped, which helped with the headache, but everything else after that was a blank. His fingers blindly searched for the tachyon — it was missing. An icy feeling gripped his stomach at the thought of Lenin with a time device. He groaned inwardly at the idea of having to explain that to Methuselah or the colonel.

He could hear muffled voices talking on the other side of the door. The room was nothing more than a storage area with a few lockers and a table — he was being held prisoner by someone, but not Lenin — this wasn't his style. He looked around and spotted a health-and-safety poster, which told him he was still in the university.

'I'll deal with this!' a man's voice commanded. 'You go and wait for the police outside.'

Josh swore at the word 'police'. This was the kind of situation that was always made dramatically worse with the involvement of the cops — especially when weapons were involved. Hopefully they didn't know about the guns.

The door opened, and a tired-looking, middle-aged man walked in. The security guard hovered outside like an over-eager puppy, his nightstick ready in one hand. The academic waved him away and then closed the door and locked it.

Josh was not contemplating escape, not yet anyway. His head was still throbbing, and his usual quick wits had been dulled considerably by the blow from Lenin's gun.

'So,' began the man as he sat down opposite Josh. 'My name is Professor Fermi.'

He had a European accent, which Josh couldn't place exactly. His glasses were heavy and thick-rimmed, and he wore a tweed jacket over a black turtleneck.

'The guard believes you were one of a gang that tried to break into Blackett's this morning.'

Josh made no comment — he knew better than to talk. It would be bad enough for him when the cops arrived. The last thing he should do was answer a bunch of incriminating questions.

'I realise that you probably don't want to talk to me and that we are somehow breaching your human rights by holding you in this way.'

He had a point, Josh thought. This probably was against the law too. The guy was either dumb or after something else.

'So before the police turn up and make things complicated, I will try to simplify the outcome.' He took something from his pocket. It was a clear plastic bag, the kind they used on CSI for evidence. Inside, much to Josh's relief, was the tachyon.

'I know you were after our ephedrine. Predictable if not a little dramatic.' He made a gun shape out of his fingers.

Shit, thought Josh, he knew about the weapons.

'I don't care about that,' he said with a wave of his hand. 'The chemicals can be replaced.' He took the tachyon out of the bag and held it up. 'This, on the other hand, interests me very much.'

Josh watched the dials on the face of the device move round. He tested the bindings on his wrists, but they held tight.

'Do you know what a Quantum Singularity is?' Fermi asked.

Josh shrugged. This guy was a talker. He knew it was best to let him rattle on until he saw a chance to make a move.

'No, I didn't think you would. Which is what has been bothering me since my sensors picked up the signal from the other side of the quadrant — not something one expects to encounter outside a black hole. Your timepiece is giving off a very strange signature.'

Josh tried to look blank. He guessed the Order would be very unhappy about a scientist getting their hands on a tachyon.

'I should explain,' Fermi continued. 'I have been researching quantum field theory for many years, mostly ways of measuring the slightest gravitational disturbances in our universe. This device just registered off the scale on every one of my monitoring systems. May I ask where you acquired it?'

Josh was sure the professor really wanted to say: 'steal', but was giving him the benefit of the doubt. The tachyon was his only means of escape, but this guy was looking at it like it was the Holy Grail.

'I stole it.' Josh had always thought that a half-truth made for the most authentic-sounding lie, 'from some old guy.'

The professor looked disappointed, as if he were hoping that somehow Josh was a secret quantum physicist who just hung out with drug dealers for kicks.

'This old man, would you remember him if you saw him again? Do you know where he lives?'

'Yeah. I could show you, but,' and this was the chance he was looking for, 'not if I'm in a police cell.'

The professor nodded and stepped out of the room with his mobile phone pressed to his ear. Josh's freedom was obviously a small price to pay for the secrets of the tachyon.

The watch sat on the table, gleaming in the neon light like a new Rolex. It was the first time he had a chance to study it properly — the craftsmanship and intricate detail were astounding. Josh was tempted to try to trigger it with his nose, but the ties bit into his hands when he moved the chair.

A minute later the professor returned.

'So the police are dealt with. We can finish our discussion about the old man.'

'My hands are hurting,' Josh pleaded with a look of pain.

'Ah yes, my over-zealous colleague.' He got up and cut the zip ties with a lock knife he produced from his pocket.

'Thank you,' Josh said, as the blood rushed back into his

fingers — he massaged his wrists to soothe the tingling sensation.

'Now. The owner of this timepiece, where can I find him?'

Josh was tempted to just rush the professor and grab the watch, but the guy was still holding the knife in one hand, and Josh didn't care to find out how good his reactions were.

'Have you managed to get it open?' Josh asked knowingly. The man had probably blunted every drill and screwdriver he owned trying to get into it. The Order built them to survive just about anything, the colonel had told him.

'No. Have you?'

Josh nodded and saw a glimmer of excitement in the professor's eye. This was what the man secretly wanted. He held out his hand. 'Let me show you.'

The professor reluctantly gave up his prize, laying it gently in Josh's palm. The watch warmed in his hand as he stroked the dial with his thumb. He felt the power of the device vibrating within it, the power of a black hole, apparently.

'So, it's simple. You just need to turn the dial like so . . .' Josh spun the outer dial to the symbol 'phi' just for dramatic effect. It made no difference to what he was planning to do next. 'Now watch very carefully. I just push this button and —'

'Wait!' shouted the professor, reaching out and grabbing the watchstrap.

As he pulled it away, Josh touched the homing button and disappeared.

41

FIND THE COLONEL

Josh reappeared back in the middle of the colonel's collection room. That had been way too close for comfort — without the tachyon he knew he would have been in serious trouble.

Realising he was no longer holding the watch, Josh looked around the floor, assuming that he had dropped it. Then he checked his pockets and under the surrounding furniture. Each new search getting a little more frantic, until he had to finally admit that he must have left it behind with the professor.

'Shit. Shit. Shit,' he shouted, kicking over a small stack of books. Today was turning out to be one hell of a bad day: he'd managed to get thrown out of the Order, lose the best chance of a girlfriend, get involved in a stupid robbery — get caught, and then leave an invaluable piece of time-travel technology with a guy who was totally obsessed with trying to understand how it worked. Definitely not one of his best days.

He was just considering helping himself to something from the colonel's whisky collection when he heard a noise from downstairs. It sounded remarkably like the front door closing, and Josh felt a small spark of hope ignite in his chest — the colonel had returned; the one man who could fix all of this had finally come back. Josh ran out into the landing and down the first flight of stairs, expecting to see the crazy mad brush of hair and the big old greatcoat.

Instead he saw the face of Caitlin staring up at him.

'Er. Hi. What are you doing here?'

She looked at him with dark, stormy eyes.

'What am *I* doing here? What are *YOU* doing here?' she said in a voice that was trying hard not to scream.

Josh wasn't quite sure where to start. He thought about telling her the truth, but that would involve a lot of back-story and he wasn't ready to explain about Lenin or the shit he'd got himself into. Nor did he think it was a good idea to mention stealing a tachyon and then losing it — which left very little of today that could be deemed to be appropriate.

'Don't tell me!' she added as she took off her coat and shook out her wet hair. It must have been raining outside. 'I probably wouldn't want to know.'

'I thought you were supposed to be in bed?' Josh said, trying to change the subject.

'They tried. But when I found out that Dalton had you excluded, I told them where they could stick their recuperation.'

'Dalton?' Josh exclaimed.

'Yes. Bloody Dalton. Interfering little bastard told his mother. Our little adventure was all he needed to have you kicked out, and he's claiming that Dracula's tooth should be disqualified!'

She walked into the kitchen and grabbed a towel to dry her hair.

Josh wanted to run his fingers through it, pull her close

and kiss her, but Caitlin was cold and distant. The closeness they had shared in the cave was gone. Her emotional defences were locked down, as if she were ready for a fight.

'So why did you come here?' he asked.

'I wasn't looking for you, if that's what you're thinking.'

'No, of course not.'

A tiny smile flashed across her mouth and vanished.

'The Council has declared Uncle Rufius officially missing in action. Methuselah sent me here to see if there were any clues as to where he might have gone. I have a sneaking suspicion that Methuselah might have known you were here too — since he told me to bring a spare tachyon.'

She reached into her coat pocket and produced an older-looking model. 'It's only a Mark Two, but its functions are basically the same, just a bit heavier.'

Josh let her strap it to his wrist. Her fingers were delicate and precise as they threaded the leather band and closed it. He tried not to think about the new Mk IV that was probably being disassembled in the basement of the university at this very moment.

'So Methuselah doesn't agree with my exclusion?'

She shook her head. 'No! Neither do I, not after what you did for me. It's a formality imposed on him by the Protectorate. There is some kind of emergency meeting going on. All the elders have been ordered to attend — including Methuselah.'

'To do with the colonel? I mean Rufius?'

'I think there has been some kind of leadership challenge by Dalton's mother. She has many friends in the council — including a faction that disagrees with the way the continuum is being managed. They call themselves "The Determinists". They have a major issue with the way we allow for so much random variation within our calculations.'

'What kind of challenge?' Josh asked, imagining some kind of old-fashioned duel.

Caitlin shrugged her shoulders. 'Dalton was boasting the other day that his mother has some new revelation, but he wouldn't tell me what it was.'

Josh imagined the ways in which he could inflict pain on Dalton. There were many and most involved sharp, pointed things.

'You do know you have the right of appeal? About the exclusion I mean,' Caitlin added.

'No. Why didn't anyone tell me?'

She frowned. 'You would need Rufius to speak on your behalf. It's not usual for a prospect to lose his mentor just as he's getting excluded. In fact, I think you're the first.'

Josh looked around the kitchen. 'Then I'll have to find the old man, won't I? Don't the Copernicans know where he went? Shouldn't they have a trace on his notebook?'

She shrugged. 'Apparently he didn't take his almanac or it's been destroyed. There is a "statistically low possibility of recovery",' she said, putting air quotes round the last phrase.

Over the next three hours Josh and Caitlin searched the entire house. On the top floor, Josh found rooms that he'd never known existed. One was full of random notes and clippings pinned to the walls, each connected to another by lines of red twine — it looked like the work of a madman. He called to Caitlin, and she came running up the stairs. Her eyes went wide at the sight of it.

'I knew that Uncle Rufius was a bit obsessive about the

fatalists. We don't really talk about it — the Protectorate aren't too happy about some of his theories.'

They took different sides of the room, following the string as it crisscrossed the space, connecting one random event to another in no apparent logical way.

'Did he ever speak to you about this?' she asked.

'No. Who are the Fatalists?'

'A group of fanatics that believes the Order shouldn't be meddling in the timelines. Rufius believes they are sabotaging the past,' Caitlin said as she stopped at one particular area of the wall.

There were a large number of red lines converging on a single sheet of torn newspaper. It was a report on the discovery of a new tomb in the Valley of the Kings from the *Times* dated 1933.

'My parents investigated this one. They never came back from it.'

Josh couldn't think of anything to say. He put his hand on her shoulder, but she shrugged it off and wiped her eyes.

'We haven't got time for that now,' she growled.

Josh spotted a number written by the side of the pin that was holding the twine in place.

'What does this mean?'

'It's a time co-ordinate. Written the old way, there are still some that say it's more accurate.'

He remembered the night the injured colonel had appeared in the study. The old man had been babbling on about a random set of numbers.

'I think I know where he might be.'

42

THE COPERNICANS

[Richmond, England. Date: 11.580]

When Josh told Caitlin about the co-ordinates that the colonel had made him memorise, she'd nearly hugged him. She made him repeat them to her over and over again, but she couldn't quite figure it out, so she decided that they would have to go back to someone who would be able to help them.

Caitlin left Josh in the Grand Nexus, the atrium of the enormous Copernican building — the largest structure Josh had ever seen. Like a plaza, it was a long, thin, cathedral-like nave with a high, vaulted, stained-glass ceiling through which sunlight filtered down in rays of ruby, topaz and emerald. Hundreds of floors were stacked on each side with metal stairways providing access to the inner workings of the building. Its components occupied every available space and filled the hall with the sound of a thousand gear wheels — giving the overall feeling of being inside a massive old clock.

A crescendo of bells rang out from the far end of the

hall. Josh turned to see an enormous rotating dial made up of concentric rings turning through 180° as it marked the hour. Each ring was inscribed with numerals and symbols that, by Josh's limited understanding, told the time in at least ten different millennia. In unison, everyone on the floor around him took out their own timepieces and checked them, then went back to their work.

The floor was tiled in a marble chequerboard of black and white, with symbols etched into the obsidian squares. Josh assumed that it was some kind of signposting since there were no other obvious ones. Hundreds of men and women in various coloured robes walked to and fro across the concourse. They were all absorbed in their work, adjusting strange-looking abacuses or flicking through thick books. An old man with a long white beard passed him, tossing a coin repeatedly and calling out 'naive' or 'caput' to a young boy who followed behind, keeping tally on a beaded rope.

'The Venerable Von Neumann — he's testing the random coefficient,' said a familiar voice behind him. Sim was wearing an elegant-looking blue robe with the seal of Copernicus stitched into the front. The clothes made him look older somehow. He offered his hand as he approached.

Josh was happy to see him and shook his hand warmly.

'Every century they have to check how far off S.R. — Standard Random — the continuum has moved,' Sim added.

'Random has a standard?'

Sim looked at him in disbelief. 'Of course. How do you think we compensate for it?'

'By tossing a coin?'

'Classic Bernoulli process. Sometimes the simplest solution is the best.'

'So how long does he have to do that for?' Josh asked, beginning to wish Caitlin would hurry up with whatever she had gone off to do.

'Oh, not long, maybe a year or two. It depends on the asymptotic equipartition property.'

Josh watched the man wander off, his coin rising and falling through the iridescent rays above them. He had no idea what Sim was talking about, but he had a lot of respect for the old man's dedication.

'Amazing place you have here,' Josh said, changing the subject.

'Yes, she's a beauty isn't she?' Sim agreed, looking into the upper levels. 'It houses the most advanced difference engine the sixteenth century could engineer.'

'Can I see it?'

Sim laughed. 'It's all around you, Josh. This whole building is one giant computational machine. She can process over a hundred thousand pph — probabilities per hour,' he explained proudly.

Josh looked at the building and began to notice some of the details, the cogs and gears turning in the walls, the cables and pipes carrying punched cards across the space above them.

'Caitlin tells me you've run into a bit of trouble,' Sim whispered, reaching inside his robe.

Josh caught a glimpse of many pockets in the inner lining as Sim pulled a small almanac out from one of them.

'Here, take this. It will allow me to contact you wherever you are.'

Josh took the book and hid it inside his own robe 'Thanks.'

Caitlin came out of a set of doors followed by a tall, thin

man in a dark, sombre gown. He walked beside her with all the distinguished bearing of a priest.

Sim turned to see what Josh was looking at and whispered, 'Stochastic Professor Eddington. He's always had a soft spot for Cat.'

Caitlin's face cracked into a broad smile when she saw Sim, and she rushed over to wrap her arms round him, hugging him tightly. Eddington was obviously uncomfortable with such a public show of affection.

'Professor Eddington, may I introduce Joshua Jones, Acolyte of the Fourteenth?'

Eddington raised his eyebrow slightly and bowed. 'Fourteenth . . . That is impressive for an Acolyte — I would say in the ninety-fifth percentile.'

Caitlin shook her head as Josh went to offer his hand and he quickly withdrew it.

'Yes, it was kind of an emergency —'

'I have told the professor about Rufius,' Caitlin interrupted, 'and he thinks he may be able to help us.'

'Yes.' Eddington nodded. 'What is your milieu of origin?'

Josh looked blankly at Sim.

'He's from the present, sir,' Sim intervened.

'Terrible place!' The professor grimaced. 'Now, if you would care to follow me. Master Simeon, do you not have work to which you must attend?'

Sim looked sheepish and made his excuses before bowing to the professor and leaving quickly.

They walked behind the austere figure down the length of the hall towards the giant clock. Josh tried not to be distracted by the amazing mechanical systems around him, but it was virtually impossible.

'What does all this actually do? Other than tell the time.'

'*Omnia fieri possunt* — all things can happen,' said

Eddington without turning around. 'To calculate the near-infinite possibilities and probabilities of the future and select the best course for the continuum.'

'But why not use computers?'

Caitlin grimaced, and Josh immediately realised he'd said the wrong thing.

Eddington spun on his heels to face him, his placid expression replaced with a red flush of anger. When he spoke it was through gritted teeth.

'Ms Makepiece, please be so kind as to explain to our young friend here why we cannot use ELECTRON-ICS!' He turned back and strode off at an even faster pace.

Caitlin sighed and pulled Josh along after the disappearing form of the professor.

'You can't bring that kind of technology back here.'

'I know that,' he said. 'You can't go back to before it was invented. But you could set all this up in the twenty-first century.'

She shook her head. 'Too close to the present. The frontier has a distorting effect on the convergence of random variables the closer you get to it.'

'The frontier?'

'Where the present and the future converge.'

'So why can't you just bring back the plans for computers and build them here?'

She coughed. 'That's possibly the stupidest thing you've ever said. Can you imagine what would happen to the future if we built advanced technology and it got out into civilisation?'

Josh shrugged.

'Second rule of the Order: "No advancement of earlier milieu by imparting of future knowledge or events." It screws up all their calculations for a start.' She waved around at the Copernicans.

'And what was the first rule again?'

She made an exasperated groan, then saw that he was joking and punched him in the arm.

Professor Eddington had calmed a little and was waiting impatiently in front of a large door with a globe embedded at its centre.

'The map room. You should be honoured. Not many get to see beyond these doors,' she whispered.

'If you are quite finished with your horseplay, perhaps we could proceed?' Eddington said, taking out a strange-looking key that hung from a chain round his neck. He placed it into the centre of the globe.

The doors ground open slowly. They were over a metre thick and made from some kind of metal. Josh assumed this was a kind of vault, the room beyond the doors was dimly lit, and he couldn't make out the details of what lay beyond.

'Follow me,' Eddington said, putting the key back round his neck, 'and don't touch anything.'

Josh's eyes slowly grew accustomed to the low light until he could recognise some of the shapes around him. At first, he thought it was a planetarium: there were large spheres on metal rods that idled around each other on rotating discs, and pinpricks of tiny white light shone down from the high ceiling, creating a star field of constellations he couldn't name.

'This is the Orrery, or Universal Engine as some refer to it,' echoed the voice of Eddington from somewhere out of the darkness. 'With this model we are able to show the arrangement of the universe at any given time in the last twelve millennia.'

As impressive as the machine was, Josh had no idea how

this was going to help them find the colonel and was about to say something to that effect when Caitlin's hand slipped into his and squeezed it gently as if to say, 'Wait and see.'

He heard the professor move a series of unseen levers, and the silent spheres began to whir around above their heads. Like a carnival ride, they watched the universe turn round a central orb, which began to glow, obviously signifying the sun. As the illumination intensified, Josh tried to work out exactly where the earth was. A minute later he spotted a small insignificant blue sphere the size of a golf ball in comparison to the gas giants of Jupiter and Venus.

'This model is of course not to scale,' the professor said from the pulpit of controls on the far side of the model. 'It has been a somewhat contentious issue over the last few hundred years. The fourteenth century was still debating whether or not the earth was flat, let alone the centre of the universe.'

Josh couldn't imagine what it must be like to live in a time that didn't understand basic stuff like how the solar system worked — things that any six-year-old took for granted. To not know that the earth was round or that the reason the sun came up every day was because the planet was spinning round it at 1,000mph. The knowledge was so fundamental that it seemed as if it had always been there. This was the first time Josh actually appreciated the little education he had received; he realised he knew more about the universe than most of the scientists of the fourteenth century.

'Now, those co-ordinates if you please,' the professor requested.

'Seventeen to the fourth, Tiberian. Twenty-five. Nine.

Fourth branch, ninth parallel,' Josh repeated, and Eddington manipulated the controls of the machine to send the universe spinning backwards in time.

The shape of the model changed before their eyes; the Earth grew larger as the other planets shrank and disappeared beneath the floor. As the blue sphere expanded, the metal plates of its shell slid over each other like layers of an onion, each adding more detail until he could make out the continents, oceans and topographical details of the various land masses. Place names appeared over the surface in old-fashioned copperplate — Josh saw the coast of England flash by with 'German Sea' written in place of the channel. France was called 'Gaul' and there were other older terms for other places, but their outlines were unmistakeable.

'This is Earth circa 9.914.'

Josh tried to do the maths in his head.

'Eighty-six BC,' Caitlin whispered in his ear, her breath sending a tingle down his spine.

'The co-ordinates that Rufius gave you refer to Ogylos in Greece, now known as Antikythera.'

A brass-ringed magnifying glass larger than their heads swept round and centered on the small island just above Crete. Josh could see model buildings, trees and even ships in the harbour.

'At this time it was being used as a base by a band of Sicilian pirates, but Rome was very dominant and still had a permanent fleet stationed off the coast.'

'And this is where the colonel is?'

'Perhaps,' answered the professor, appearing out of the dark. 'It is most certainly where he wanted you to go.'

'Why Greece?'

'That, Mr Jones, is what you are about to find out.'

43

THE ANTIQUARIANS

C aitlin thanked the professor and took Josh down a
series of winding stairs to an underground train
station where the platform was nothing more than a waiting
room with a few benches.

'The Copernicans aren't collectors,' she said once she'd
checked to see if they were alone. 'We'll have to go to the
Antiquarian department before we can make the jump back
to ancient Greece.'

'Aren't the Antiquarians the ones who run the
museums?'

'That is one of their roles.' She tried not to sound too
condescending. 'They are essentially the custodians of all
historical artefacts, and their collection goes well beyond
what you see in a museum.'

The windows of the waiting room began to rattle. Josh
felt the ground beneath his feet shudder as if some massive
juggernaut were passing through. A moment later, a
gleaming black steam locomotive slowed into the station. It
was pulling a single metal carriage. Josh could see a rather
eccentric-looking man standing at the controls, wearing an

old leather flying hat and goggles. He spoke into a tube, and a tinny voice came through a metal grille in the ceiling. 'Next stop: Antiquarian Archives. Please have your designations ready.'

'That's us,' Caitlin said, standing up.

Josh followed her into the carriage, which was empty except for a strange collection of railway memorabilia. They sat down on one of the less uncomfortable-looking benches as a bespectacled old guard appeared through the back door.

'Tickets, please.'

'So the Antiquarians are based in the same century as the Copernicans?' he said, trying to sound as if he wasn't a complete newbie.

Caitlin handed the guard a ticket, and he inspected it through thick-lensed glasses. 'Not exactly,' she said. 'They use redundant timelines to deal with the storage issue. It's the only way to keep everything organised.'

'I don't get it.'

'You'll see.'

The guard clipped their ticket and announced, 'Grecian,' in a monotonous tone into a speaking tube, moving a series of dials on the device that hung round his waist. Seconds later the train set off at speed.

The Grecian archives of the Antiquarians was equally as impressive as the Hall of the Copernicans. It was like a museum but hundreds of times bigger. Caitlin explained there were thousands of artefacts carefully catalogued and stored in rooms spanning centuries from 5000 BC.

They were deep underground. There was a sense of the subterranean about the place: no natural light, the air smelt old and there was an oppressive feeling of thousands of tonnes of rock suspended above your head. The walls were made from white stone blocks that were more than a metre square and formed hexagonal rooms over twenty metres in diameter. Each wall had a large arch leading to another similar space.

There were no maps or signs, only a Roman numeral above each arch. Josh assumed they were supposed to indicate the century the artefacts belonged to.

They wandered from one room to the next. Every so often Caitlin would stop and admire a piece of art or pick up a manuscript. Nothing here looked that ancient. Many items looked as if they were new — which made them look like replicas. Josh found it hard to believe that these three-thousand-year-old antiques could actually be in such pristine condition, but that was a linear way of looking at the world, and he knew he would have to learn to think differently about history.

They saw no one. Caitlin told him that unlike the Copernicans, who seemed to be everywhere, the Antiquarian was a solitary calling, and those who chose this vocation tended not to play well with others. There was probably only one supervisor assigned to this part of the collection. Josh thought back to the guard in the Louvre, who had seemed genial enough, but when he mentioned it to Caitlin she laughed.

'Marfanor isn't an Antiquarian. He's probably been assigned guard duty as a punishment.'

'Like a detention?' Josh asked, his voice sounding lost in the volume of silence around them.

'Kind of. He tends to get himself in trouble on a regular basis. Think of it more like a community-service order. There aren't that many Antiquarians, for obvious reasons, and so the council use guard duty of the more accessible archives as punishment.'

'What did he do?'

She screwed up her eyes as if thinking really hard. 'I think the last time was stealing from the US government. He caused some kind of financial crisis back in 12.008.'

'They put a thief in charge of valuable treasures?'

'Yeah, it's kind of ironic when you put it like that.'

They reached an arch with the numerals IXMVIICL carved into the stone.

'This is our century. Now we need to find something from Antikythera.'

It took a few hours of searching before they found some coins from the island. There were scarcely any other options, and Josh realised how difficult it must be for Draconians to find their way back into the forgotten periods in time. Once you went back further than the printing press it was like being a detective on a case without any clues, all you had to go on was money, art and the odd clay tablet. The trouble with knowledge was that unless you wrote it down on something that could last, there was a damn good chance it would get lost.

Clothes from that time were hanging on the usual set of rails next to a set of screened changing booths. These Antiquarians were methodical if nothing else, he thought, as he changed into a rough woollen toga.

When he reappeared, Caitlin was already waiting for him with an impatient look on her face.

'What took you so long?' she asked.

'The bloody shoes,' he said, pointing at the leather thonged sandals. 'They're like some evil puzzle dreamed up by a knot fetishist!'

Caitlin looked stunning. Her hair was coiled into ringlets and tied back behind her head. A necklace of small golden coins hung around her neck, and she wore a thin blue cotton dress that was slightly transparent. The memory of the way her body had felt against his came flooding back.

'What? Is this too much?' she asked, fiddling with the necklace.

'No,' he replied with a smile, 'you look like a perfect little Greek princess.'

'Γιατί σας ευχαριστώ είδος κύριε,' she said with a mock curtsey. 'How is your Hellenistic Greek?'

He pulled a face. 'I've never been any good with languages.'

'I take it the colonel never showed you how to intuit?'

Josh shook his head.

'No,' she frowned, 'it would have been too early in your training.'

'What does it do?'

She tapped the side of her head. 'Allows us to share memories.'

'How?'

'They're another form of energy, just like your personal timeline. Seers do it all the time. It takes a lot of practice to isolate the branch you want. Otherwise, it can get a little too personal.'

'So you can teach me to speak Greek just by giving me the memories.'

'No. Language is hard. It uses so many different parts of the brain.'

Josh looked disappointed.

'But,' she added, 'we do have specialists that can help us with that.'

She turned and walked over to a shelf of glass jars with what looked like large pickled walnuts inside. She went along the row, reading the labels out loud.

'Dianthus, Peteor, Jullian de Meer. Ah, here we go —

Janto Sargorian.' She lifted the jar down from its resting place and set it on the table, then began attaching electrodes to metal contacts on each side of the glass.

'That's not —'

'A brain? Of course it is. What else would you store memories in?'

'But . . .' He couldn't think what to say next.

'They donated their minds to the Order. It's seen as a very noble gesture.'

'But they're dead!'

She opened a drawer in the table and pulled out a metal crown to which she attached the other ends of the wires.

'Stop being a pussy. Sit down and put this on. It's not like I'm going to make you eat it!'

Josh sat on the edge of the table and let Caitlin place the crown on his head.

'Now, according to the label, this mind has been dormant for the best part of four hundred years, so he's not going to take too kindly to someone banging around in his personal space. Try to tread lightly, and whatever you do don't let it get too deep into your mind — just keep thinking about the coin. Okay?'

Josh nodded nervously, playing with one of the metal discs. 'I thought you weren't supposed to mess in other people's timelines?'

'Not living ones. These are more like filing cabinets of accumulated knowledge. Not as systematic as a library, but a hell of a lot faster for acquiring knowledge than a book.'

Josh felt the contacts on the crown warming against his temples.

'Now lie back. I find it helps to close your eyes and focus on your breathing,' she said as bubbles started to form in the liquid around the brain. 'He's waking.'

Josh felt the presence of the mind gently reach out to probe his own; it emoted warmth and friendship — like a child waking. Colours and shapes began to form on the edge of his consciousness, not like the timelines of an object: these were more abstract, more organic. It was impossible to make out any distinct branches.

WHAT/WHO/WHEN?

The questions formed inside his head. There wasn't a voice; the words were not exactly like speech, but more like the meanings of a thought.

HELP? Josh replied without speaking.

The shapes changed, reformed and flowed into one another as if searching for the right response.

WHO.WERE/ARE. YOU?

JOSHUA JONES.

There was a stillness and the colours faded into purples and blues as the mind contemplated his answer.

I. JANTO. LAST. SARGARIAN. YOU. REQUIRE/NEED. HELP/ASSISTANCE/GUIDANCE?

The mind was probing him now. Josh could feel it spreading across the surface of his mind. He concentrated on the image of the coin as Caitlin had instructed — imagining the small round disc spinning over and over like the Copernican flipping it in the hall.

HELLENIC COIN > CIRCA 9th MILLENNIA?

'Tell him you need a lexicon memory for Hellenic Greek,' she whispered in his ear.

Josh did exactly as he was told.

WHY? Came the response.

'He wants to know why,' Josh repeated to Caitlin through gritted teeth.

'He's playing games. Tell him it's a temporal imperative. Level Nine-Beta-Five.'

ACCEPTED>PREPARE> LEXICON FOLLOWS:

Josh saw a complex geometric form appear from the abstract swarm of information. It was full of sounds and symbols, and flashes of imagery. As it solidified, he felt the usual sensation that he experienced with a timeline, and allowed his mind to enter it.

It was like watching a thousand movies at once. His head ached as the information flowed into his memory. He felt like his mind was going to burst, and he reached up to pull off the crown, but Caitlin stopped him.

'It will pass,' she said. 'Just relax.'

A few minutes later it stopped, just as if someone had pulled out the power. Josh felt able to breathe again and opened his eyes.

THANK YOU. He imparted to the other mind as he felt it separating from his own.

WHO WAS FATHER?

Before Josh could respond Caitlin removed the crown and the connection was broken. He sat up and rubbed his temples.

'That was some pretty crazy shit.'

Caitlin laughed as she took the jar back and placed it on the shelf.

'What's so funny?'

She turned and smiled. 'You're speaking in fluent Greek.'

44

LENIN AND THE PROFESSOR

'Go back and loop over those last fifty frames,' Professor Fermi instructed the security guard who was operating the CCTV playback. He was staring at a bank of monitor screens all showing various angles of the same scene in the lab just before Josh triggered the fire alarm. There was a point in the footage where the face of Josh, grainy from the multiple magnifications, had gone from looking confused and scared to calm and determined — in a split second.

'Tell me, Boyce, would you say that looked like the same man?'

The guard shook his head. He wasn't sure what the professor was trying to prove from the change in the kid's expression, but the overtime paid double.

'OK. Go back to the other guy. The one with the gun.'

The footage wound back until Lenin appeared from the store room with the trolley laden down with canisters.

'STOP!' the professor commanded 'Enhance that guy and print me out a couple of copies.'

The guard did as he was told.

'Now, what I still don't understand is why our friend here.' He pointed at the blurry figure of Josh. 'Sets off the sprinklers and jeopardises their mission. Run it forward again.'

The video continued, and they watched as Lenin struck Josh with the butt of the gun, then took one look at the lift and ran up the stairs.

'Go back to the point where they are watching the lift. There!'

Boyce stopped the recording.

'Now wind it back a frame at a time. You were coming down in the lift until the fire alarm went off. I'm guessing they are programmed to stop automatically when the alarm is triggered. Yes?'

Boyce nodded.

'So, he stopped you coming down to the lab. I think, my friend, that boy might have been trying to save your life. Put a copy onto this.' Fermi handed him a USB stick. 'And leave the printouts on my desk.'

It had taken less than twenty-four hours to find out who the kid with the gun was. Boyce, who had taken early retirement from the police, still had a few friends on the force and had little trouble finding out that the perpetrator was a local gangster and drug dealer known as Lenin.

Fermi had lived in Italy long enough to know how to deal with racketeers. They were simple animals, driven by a pathological need to dominate and an almost suicidal lack of respect for authority. The only thing they cherished more than power was money, and Fermi had a lot of that.

His father had left him a vineyard in Piedmont that had an annual revenue in the millions. He had no interest in viticulture and had recruited a South African estate manager by the name of 'Dieker' to run operations so that he could pursue his research into quantum fields. Research that had been entirely self-funded up until now, but that was all about to change since his systems had picked up the gravitational wave given off by the watch.

He moved the microscopic camera further into the body of the device. The inner workings of the watch were more intricate than any circuit board; fine gears and wheels moved in perfect regularity above an iridescent crystalline structure. Fermi guessed that the quantum heart at the centre of the crystal was being held there in some kind of stasis, but knew better than to start breaking it apart. Black holes were highly unstable and incredibly powerful, and the scientific method required him to observe and analyse, not smash it open with a hammer.

He looked down at his notes. The sheets of paper were covered with sketched diagrams of the mechanism, copies of the symbols from the fascia and comments on what they might represent. His current hypothesis was that the dials were some kind of measurement of time, but not marked in hours. He calculated that the total possible number of configurations could span twelve thousand years at least.

What he couldn't reconcile was how and why the boy had such a device. It was evident from the way he had used it to escape that he knew exactly how it worked — which would save Fermi a great deal of time and frustration if he could find him again.

This was where the notorious Lenin came into the equation. Boyce's associates had no problem tracking him down and even providing the names of his known associates, including a certain Joshua Jones aka 'Crash', who had just finished his latest round of community service for some petty burglary.

Fermi read the charge sheet again. The boy had been in trouble since he was ten years old. The crimes were mostly all misdemeanours, apart from one serious incident when he was twelve — a boy had died in a car accident in which Jones was driving, and many others had been injured.

There had been nothing but an empty, boarded-up flat at the last known address the police had on file for Jones. Someone had sprayed a ghost tag over the metal gratings that covered the windows. It was a menacing symbol of which Fermi had seen similar versions in the streets of Naples. It was a 'Segno Nero' — the black mark — Jones was literally a dead man walking.

Fermi wondered if he might make an alliance with Lenin. They both wanted the same man and Fermi had something that Lenin needed, Ephedrine — vast quantities of it. The professor was willing to do anything to get his hands on Joshua Jones.

The guy was not as stupid as he looked, thought Lenin as he watched the stranger park up on the opposite side of the multi-storey car park. There weren't many who knew about the CCTV in this place; the security had been knocked out months ago and no one had the time or the money to repair it. He watched in the rearview mirror as a well-dressed, middle-aged man stepped out of the black Landrover and held up his hands as if to say 'I'm not armed' — his driver, however, who remained at the wheel, looked like he was ex-military.

Lenin patted the gun that was tucked inside his jacket and got out of the car.

'Stay here. Keep an eye on the jar-head in the other car,'

he ordered the two boys who had slid down on the back seat.

The stranger walked confidently towards Lenin and stopped halfway; Lenin did the same, and each studied the other for any signs of betrayal.

'You are Lenin?' the stranger asked with a slight Italian accent.

'You got the meth?' Lenin asked, not bothering to acknowledge the question.

The stranger smiled. 'Straight to business. Very good.' He motioned to the car, and the driver came out with a briefcase, he was massive and walked with an air of confidence that made Lenin wonder if a bullet would actually stop the guy.

The stranger took the case and held it out to Lenin. 'A sample of our new partnership.'

'Open it — slowly,' Lenin instructed.

The stranger shrugged in that Mediterranean way and flicked the locks to reveal two metal cylinders with 'ETHANOL HYDRATE' printed in large type down the sides.

'That's not what we agreed!' Lenin complained, his hand drifting towards his gun. 'You said you could get me thirty litres.'

'This is better. It is hydrate, smaller and easier to transport — it just needs water. With these two you can make sixty litres. Ask your chemist.'

Lenin thought about calling Elena, but somewhere at the back of his drug-addled mind, he knew that what the guy was saying made sense.

'OK, hydrate — cool,' he said, taking the case.

'So, what about my part of the bargain?'

Lenin nearly pulled the gun on the guy, just to see what

would happen. The contact who had set up the meeting had said something about this dude wanting to know where Josh was, but Lenin hadn't seen him since he screwed up the job at the university.

'So you looking for Crash?' Lenin sucked air in through his teeth.

'That was the deal.'

'He's a dead man.'

'Perhaps, but first I need to talk to him. Twenty-four hours should be all I need, and then he's yours.'

'No one's seen him — he's gone dark.'

'He is in hiding. I was told you would know how to find him.' The professor's voice was strained.

'Not him,' Lenin took out a joint and lit it. 'His mother. She's sick. He's a devoted son. It's a simple case of waiting.'

Lenin turned back towards his car and started walking.

'And where do I find his mother?'

'Barts. Neuro ward. Josh'll be there, he's always been a mummy's boy.'

Fermi went back to his car and got into the front passenger seat.

'Everything OK?' the driver asked in a thick South African accent.

'Yes,' replied Fermi thoughtfully. 'Get in touch with Professor Turner at St Bartholomew's. Tell him we need to organise a patient transfer to Harley Street.'

'Sure thing.'

45

ANTIKYTHERA

[Antikythera, Crete. Date: 9.914]

The market was an incandescent bazaar, packed with traders and their customers haggling over figs, oil, carpets and a thousand other trinkets. The warm evening air was full of the scent of oil lamps, citrus and a myriad other exotic fragrances that Josh couldn't name. Everywhere he looked he saw something unusual or bizarre: small monkeys in cages peeling figs for the passers-by, a tattooed scribe selling spells drawn on scraps of paper, even a stall that sold live snakes.

He was trying hard not to be a wide-eyed tourist, but the experience of an ancient culture close up was overwhelming — especially when you were quite literally standing in the middle of it. There were too many new things to take in: the clothes, the jewels, the beautiful women, nothing looked familiar — his brain was constantly searching for a frame of reference, some glimmer of normality.

His newly acquired language skills weren't helping either; being able to understand the babble of the crowd was only useful if you had some kind of context of what they were talking about — understanding and knowing were two entirely different things. He had that weird feeling that you get when you jump into the sea and realise you have no idea where the ocean floor is.

There were Roman soldiers everywhere. Their presence overshadowed the otherwise easy-going feel of the place. He watched the traders as they shrank back when the guards marched by — everyone was cautious, on their guard. Compared to the poor merchants they were an intimidating sight with their polished armour, spears and heavy shields. The Romans seemed not to care, they had the look of battled hardened men who would rather be anywhere but policing a street market.

Caitlin had told him not to look anyone in the eye, especially not the Centurion. Josh kept his head down as they passed, hiding himself amongst the crowd. She was standing a few metres away, her head covered with a cowl to hide her hair. There weren't many redheads in this part of the world; virtually everyone he had seen had dark black hair and olive skin. She'd made some remark about not wearing any deodorant earlier, and it was only now he appreciated what she meant: in the close proximity of the crowd, the smell of their collective body odour over-whelmed him.

After the patrol had passed, they made their way to a fountain in the centre of the market square. He took the wooden cup she offered him and drank; the water was cool and sweet.

'You okay?' she said in Greek.

'What's with all the Romans?' he replied, taking another cup of water.

'I forgot to mention the island is under Roman protection. They've invoked martial law. The locals aren't too happy about it. I think it's getting close to the curfew so they'll be closing down soon.'

As she spoke, he could see the market was dispersing. People moved out into the side streets with baskets balanced on shoulders, the wealthier ones followed by heavily loaded servants.

Josh looked up into the tree that hung over them. It was old, with a thick trunk and a wide sprawling canopy. The leaves were dark green, and ripe succulent oranges hung from its lower branches. Josh reached up and picked one. He peeled it and gave half to Caitlin. The fruit was deliciously ripe and refreshing — the two of them sat in silence and savoured the taste.

'So, where do you think he will be?' Josh asked when he'd finished.

'Not too far from the harbour, I would guess,' she said, wiping the juice from her chin and pointing down the hill to a spur of land that reached out into the moonlit waters of the bay. Josh could make out the dark shapes of fishing boats moored close to the jetty and the lights of a larger fleet of warships anchored in the deep water. Two beautiful silver sandy beaches stretched out either side of the bay. Both were deserted — it was the picture of an unspoilt little fishing port.

How different it will be in the future, Josh thought, *when the tourists turn up with their jet skis and party boats.*

'They're quinqueremes,' she said nodding to the large dark ships, 'they're part of the Roman navy. The Macedonians may still be at war with Pompey. I can never quite remember when it ended.'

'Great. I should have guessed he would be somewhere near a war.'

Another Roman patrol marched past. Some of them were carrying torches and others were thumping their swords against their shields. The traders scrabbled around, packing up their stalls as they approached.

'They're going to move us on. You up for finding him now?' she asked, keeping one eye on the troops.

'What if he's in some kind of trouble?' Josh said, looking at the swords. 'Shouldn't we have weapons?'

Caitlin turned and patted her thigh. 'I've already thought of that.'

Josh could see there was a dagger-like lump under the layers of her dress.

An old lady was hurrying away from the guards carrying a small basket of bread and figs. She tripped and the shopping spilled out onto the cobblestones. Caitlin stood up and went to help her.

'Venerable grandmother, would you know where I might find a soothsayer or an oracle?' Caitlin asked, once they had everything safely back in the basket.

The old woman gave Caitlin a toothless smile — her face broke into a thousand brown creases.

'Of course, my child. The seer you seek resides in the temple over yonder.' She pointed up with one bony finger at a single white building on a distant hill that overlooked the bay.

It had taken them most of the night to get out of the town. They had spent hours carefully avoiding the Roman army, hiding in alleys and side streets until they'd got clear of the patrols. By then it was late and the moon was obscured by cloud, making it too dark and dangerous to navigate along the cliff path. They had slept huddled under Josh's cloak listening to the sound of the waves below.

The next morning they ate one of the loaves the old lady

had given them and watched the fishermen preparing their boats.

'The Order has a variety of roles we can assume for times when we need to stay in one period — soothsayer is one of the more standard ones,' Caitlin told him as she pulled apart the bread and handed him a piece. 'The Draconians are well known for integrating themselves with the local cultures — going native. They once created an entire religion around the Oroborus symbol in ancient cultures just to ensure our safety.'

'So we can always get a job as the local fortune teller?' Josh joked.

'Hardly. Oracles were more than just sideshow acts back here. Look at that place,' she said pointing up at the impressive temple towering above them. 'I guarantee you that he's probably one of the most revered men on the island, and probably has ten or so acolytes at his beck and call.'

The view from the top of the cliffs was breathtaking. Sunlight danced off the cerulean blue of the Aegean Sea as it stretched out along the curve of the horizon. White sails of the warships looked like tiny postage stamps on the flat, glass-like surface of the water.

The temple was silent as they entered. The cool marble floor was a relief after the rough stone paths they'd just walked up. On either side of the entrance hall were benches beside long rectangular ponds full of golden fish. Caitlin sat on one and beckoned to Josh to join her.

'Don't we have to bang a gong or something?' he whispered.

She smiled and removed her cowl, shaking her hair loose. 'They know we're here.'

There was a tinkling noise, like tiny silver bells, from the far end of the chamber. A beautiful pale woman in a thin white dress appeared from an unseen door and stood waiting for them.

Josh and Caitlin followed her inside the main chamber. She motioned them to stand in the middle of the circular room, and, as they did, a procession of a dozen or so equally beautiful women surrounded them — each one smiling beatifically. Josh found it very difficult to stop staring at their dark nipples, clearly visible through the gossamer of their dresses.

Once the circle was complete, one of their number stepped forward. She was slightly older than the others and wore a golden snake amulet wrapped round one upper arm.

'I am Sybil. Priestess of Apollo.'

'We are travellers,' said Caitlin as she pulled her sleeve back to reveal the mark of the Order.

'The traveller is most welcome in the temple of Apollo,' said the lady, who turned towards Josh as if expecting him to follow Caitlin's example.

'He is my servant,' Caitlin added quickly.

Sybil smiled, placated by the explanation and her attention moved back to Caitlin.

'What do you desire, mistress? We are at your service.'

'I am looking for the sayer. I was told he was here within your temple.'

Something unspoken passed between the others as Caitlin spoke. Josh was studying the group while she was talking and noticed them shiver in unison. It was obvious that something had happened to the old man.

'The sayer does not commune with mortals. We are his eyes, his ears, his mouth. You may ask what you wish, we will convey it to the blessed one.'

Caitlin looked a little put out by this. Josh could see the

flush of colour on her cheeks — that was always an early indication of her temper building.

She bit her lip, the second sign of approaching anger. 'Would you be so kind as to relay to the sayer, that Lady Caitlin of the Scriptoria requests a private audience.'

Sybil seemed to take a moment to process the request before something changed in her expression.

'My apologies, my lady, but you seem to misunderstand — only we may commune with the Sayer.'

Josh wanted to interrupt, but knew that he was supposed to remain mute — Caitlin had made that very clear when she'd introduced him as a servant, but there was something wrong with the situation that he couldn't quite put his finger on.

'This is ridiculous, are we not blessed?'

'You are, my lady. But we have to preserve the grace of his holiness. His state must not be corrupted with the affairs of the corporeal plane. I must ask you for the last time to speak your business or begone.' There was a subtle underlying threat in Sybil's tone.

Caitlin turned towards Josh her eyes glowering. She drew a long thin blade from her skirts and disappeared.

A second later she reappeared behind Sybil with the dagger against the pale white skin of her neck.

'Where is he?' she demanded.

The circle of women surrounding them hissed and their skin began to crack and peel away as the hideous creatures beneath discarded their vestal virgin disguises and revealed the twisted bodies of haggard old crones. Their naked skin was scarred and covered in ancient tattoos. They leered at Josh, licking sharpened teeth with black tongues and cutting themselves with black edged knives.

'*Strzyga!*' Caitlin cursed, and pushed the blade a little deeper into Sybil's neck.

'Hold!' ordered Sybil, who still retained her human appearance.

Josh was surrounded by the ugliest collection of hags he'd ever seen. He choked at what he'd been fantasising about doing with some of them. Caitlin was shouting something at him — he was too busy trying to work out what the hell they were. The threat on their leader seemed to be holding them at bay, but Josh was too far from Caitlin and too close to the others. One of the nearest creatures reached out towards him and then reeled back screaming as its severed arm fell bleeding onto the white marble floor. Caitlin's blade was stained black, but it was as if she hadn't moved.

'Nobody touches him,' she threatened.

'What are they?' Josh shouted in English, hoping they wouldn't understand.

'Strzyga. Witches. Time whores. We're in some kind of trap — I should have spotted it.'

'What do we do?'

'Don't let them touch you. They won't risk anything while I have this one — but they will try to get to you.'

The Strzyga were growing impatient, their heads twisting from side to side as they tried to understand the strange language their prey were speaking.

'Stand very still — I am going to try something,' she said through gritted teeth.

Caitlin disappeared, and Sybil immediately opened her mouth to command her followers to attack. As she did so, a vision of Caitlin appeared behind every one of the surrounding women and sliced off their heads. There may have been a heartbeat between each one as the thud of their skulls hit the floor, but by the time Sybil had uttered the first syllable her entire entourage had fallen.

Sybil let her own disguise drop away, and the stench of putrefaction had Josh fighting the urge to throw up — it smelt like a corpse. The woman, if woman she had ever been, was a bloated mass of writhing body parts, as if many different bodies were being held within the skin of one being. Eyes and mouths appeared at random on various points on her body, while her head boiled with snake-like tentacles, each ending in a vicious-looking array of teeth.

The many Caitlins had become one and she was busy laying a circle of black dust round the monster.

'What are you doing?' shouted Josh.

'I'm binding her to this moment with coal dust, it will absorb her powers for a while. When they turn to diamond we're out of time.'

'Why not just burn her?' said Josh before his brain had time to process the word 'diamond' properly.

'Because I think somewhere in there —' she pointed at the bulging mass — 'is Uncle Rufius.'

'Shit.'

The thing-that-used-to-be-Sybil writhed and cursed inside the black circle, she cursed them in many different voices, all speaking at once in a hundred different languages, the sound was like a demonic choir and made the hairs on the back of Josh's neck stand on end.

'So, I am going to need your help,' Caitlin said, pushing the hair back out of her eyes. 'We need to access the most recent part of the Rufius timeline, which I'm assuming is the night he appeared and gave you the co-ordinates.'

Josh thought back to that event, running over the scene until he had it clear in his mind.

'OK. Not sure how that's going to help.'

She gave him the look that meant 'just do as you're told' — and held out her hands as if trying to do some kind of Jedi mind trick. The monster turned towards her, one of its hands blindly reaching out over the carbon barrier, and the dust began to turn grey.

Beads of sweat started to break out on Caitlin's forehead.

'OK — now reach into the circle and grab her arm.'

'Are you mental? That's like saying stick your hand in the nice crocodile's mouth! I thought you said I shouldn't let them touch me.'

Caitlin scowled again.

'Do it. It's not going to bite you. It doesn't know you exist.'

Josh slowly reached in and found the least disgusting part of her arm to grasp — the skin felt rough and leathery. It leeched the heat from his hand as he made contact.

Lines of energy began to pour out of the point at which they touched. A collection of thousands of unconnected timelines unwound around him, each one an entire lifetime subsumed into the Strzyga's body.

'Now use the memory of Rufius as a beacon, a lifeline. Look for a pattern that matches.'

There were too many lines to recognise any one individual timeline, but he knew better than to mention that to Caitlin. Instead, he went inside his own timeline and looked for connections. As he examined the moments around that night, he saw tendrils reaching out from the Strzyga. Like feelers they curved sinuously out from the central mass — as if attracted to a fresh victim.

'There's not much time,' said Caitlin as the grey circle began to turn white.

Suddenly one line struck out like an arrow from the

turmoil, it connected with the moment and Josh recognised the signature of the colonel and pushed into it.

He was still in the temple but it was the middle of the night. It was dark except for one oil lamp that flickered in the corner of the room. There was a body lying on the floor.

'Do you see him?' came Caitlin's voice from somewhere far away.

'Yes. I think so.'

'Wake him up. He needs to realise he's about to be attacked — he should be able to do the rest.'

The colonel was bald. Every hair on his head, including his beard, was gone. His skin was brown — he looked a bit like a reclining Buddha.

'Colonel?'

The old man stirred, but it was like trying to wake a drunk. Josh rolled him over onto his back and saw that he was totally out of it. He assumed that Sybil must have drugged him. The wound in his chest was only just beginning to soak through his toga — as if it had just happened. There was a dagger lying next to him — Josh recognised the handle immediately. It was the same one he had stolen from Dracula's castle.

On the floor around the colonel, someone had drawn a set of glyphs in blood. They were arranged on a five-pointed star, which was beginning to glow.

'There's a star on the floor. Made from his blood, and it's glowing.'

'That's a summoning portal. You must wake him now!'

Josh shook the colonel harshly, but got nothing more than a groan. He tried harder, this time accidentally touching the blood on the old man's tunic and felt the immediate connection with his timeline. Knowing he had little left in the way of options, he focused on the twisting ribbons and entered the bloodlines.

It was a chaotic mess, a jumble of intersecting events, experiences and emotions that seemed to have no beginning, middle or end. Josh could understand why seers went crazy trying to unravel the complex web of the human psyche.

As Josh tried to make sense of the chaos, he noticed that certain events seemed to have more paths than others. Their collected memories stood out like large knots of light — marking them as times to which the colonel returned regularly.

Josh opened one and realised why: it was the birth of a child — there was a woman cradling a newborn baby in her arms. Josh left the event and moved to another more powerful one. This time, it was a funeral, a grave surrounded by the De Freis family and many others — again he extracted himself from the memory and moved on.

As the lines of the colonel's lifetime wove around each other, they were drawn towards one point, a terminus. It was a dark, black hole into which every winding path was drawn. There was a powerful force at work within it — Josh could feel the pull of unknown events emanating from inside the infinite darkness. He knew it represented death, the country of no return, and fought back the urge to explore its depths. He realised this was what drew the reavers, this was what Lyra had become obsessed with.

As he tried to resist, Josh noticed that nearly all the paths were moving in a slowly decaying spiral into the darkness, all but one. He moved his mind across the dark space towards it and as he reached it he knew what to do.

. . .

He'd taken the colonel back into his own timeline — Josh was the one who'd brought the old man back to his house that day, breaking God knows how many rules. He looked around the study — his earlier self had yet to enter the room; the colonel was as he remembered, laid out, bleeding, on the sofa, his hand covering the wound.

'Rufius. Can you hear me?'

The colonel grunted.

'You're about to be absorbed by a Strzyga — someone set you up — I think it was Dalton. Caitlin says you would know what to do.'

The colonel opened his eyes and nodded. Josh heard himself talking to the cat in the other room and guessed that bad stuff would happen if they met.

'I've got to go. Caitlin is holding back one ugly queen bitch while I'm connected to one of your lifelines inside it. Tell the other me these coordinates — I'll work it out eventually.'

He repeated the co-ordinates to the old man and jumped back into the darkened temple.

The colonel's body had disappeared, which Josh assumed was a good sign. He was searching the room for clues of when he heard the howling. Strzyga began to materialise inside the circle, each one more hideous than the last. Josh found himself facing the horde instead of the old man and was on the verge of pulling out of the event when he heard the colonel's voice.

'Stay very, very still.'

Josh turned to see the colonel holding a strange-looking vase. It was clearly ancient; there were lead seals around the lid and arcane symbols across its surface, ones that he could tell were warnings without being able to read them.

The colonel waited until the last of the Strzyga had appeared, then lifted the vessel above his head and smashed it down onto the floor at Josh's feet. A faint wisp of smoke rose from the ashes inside the broken pot. The hags hardly paid it any attention as they fought each other to reach Josh. The swirls of dust began to gain mass — collecting other motes together as it moved through the air until it had taken a shape. Slowly, a grotesque spectre formed above the Strzyga and Josh saw them shrink away from it. The ghostly apparition waited a long, painful second before descending on them like a bird of prey.

Josh turned towards the colonel who simply winked and said: 'Probably best if we go now.'

'Thank you,' the colonel said to Caitlin and Josh as they tucked into the trays of food laid out on the floor in front of him. 'You took a great risk coming after me.'

'What an earth were those things?' Josh asked with a mouth full of pitta and hummus.

'The Strzyga? They're one of the elder races. They prey on the lost and the fallen. They've a sweet spot for members of the Order, feeding on their extended timelines. A sort of quantum vampire, I suppose.'

'So you sent a monad after them?'

Caitlin looked up from her food. 'Monad?'

The colonel looked uncomfortable, as if Caitlin wasn't going to like the answer.

'It was awesome — they were shit-scared of it.' Josh waved his hand around where the bodies of the Strzyga would have been a few minutes before.

'You released a monad!' exclaimed Caitlin.

The colonel shrugged and nodded. 'It seemed like the only thing to do at the time,' he said sheepishly.

'What's so bad about that?' Josh asked, dipping his bread for the second time into the hummus.

'No double-dipping!' Caitlin said, slapping his hand away. 'A monad is a seriously dangerous entity, and stealing a captive one is highly illegal.'

'Well, the Strzyga weren't too pleased to see it, that's for sure.'

'I'm not surprised. The temptation of a three-thousand-year-old soul would be more than it could resist. Monads are particularly fond of Strzyga — but it won't be long before it follows your trail to us.'

The colonel shuffled uncomfortably and cleared his throat.

'I left a note. The Xenos will have contained it by now. So, anyway, you took it upon yourself to come find me — why? I assume there isn't a Draconian brigade waiting outside.'

'Not as such no,' Caitlin said demurely. 'We're kind of it — and the Xenobiology Department has better things to do than clear up after you.'

Josh was intrigued. 'Are they like Ghostbusters? How many other monsters have you guys forgotten to tell me about?'

'More than I care to remember,' sighed the old man, staring into the distance.

'Methuselah sent us. He was concerned after the Council listed you as MIA,' Caitlin added. 'Something is going on in the Council. There is some kind of challenge by Dalton's mother and the Determinists.'

'That could explain why the Protectorate wanted you out of the picture,' Josh mused.

'How an earth is this related to the Protectorate?' exclaimed Caitlin.

Josh handed her the dagger. 'I found this by his body and the last person I saw with it was Dalton's mother — she asked me if I knew where you were.'

'Ravana wouldn't stoop that low,' the colonel mused.

'No, but Dalton would,' Caitlin added. 'Or one of his minions.'

'Joshua may be on to something,' said the colonel thoughtfully. 'I think someone may have been trying to eradicate me. My research is seen by many as heretical,' his voice dropped to a whisper. 'I believe someone may be intentionally manipulating the continuum, bypassing the Copernicans.'

'We know about your research — we found the room, the one in the attic,' Caitlin admitted.

'What are they trying to do?' Josh asked, helping himself to the meat. It tasted a little like chicken, but he was afraid to ask in case it wasn't.

'Your Greek is very good by the way — I'm impressed,' said the colonel, trying to avoid the question. 'How long have you been here?'

'We used a mind,' Caitlin interrupted. 'We got here yesterday. Please answer the question, Rufius. What are "they" trying to do, and why here?'

'Ah, a mind. I bet that was an interesting experience for you, Joshua.'

Caitlin squealed in frustration.

'All right, I'll tell you,' he said, picking up a fig and tearing it open, 'although you may wish I hadn't.'

46

FATES

The colonel shifted on his seat as if to make himself comfortable.

'Around 11.900, a group of sponge divers discovered a shipwreck off the coast of Antikythera.' He pointed out of the west window. 'At first, they thought it was a Roman ship that had sunk whilst taking the spoils of the second Punic War back to the republic; the scientists carbon-dated the ship back to 9.795 — around 205 BC,' he added for Josh's benefit. 'The treasure consisted mostly of statues and amphorae, as well as a whole cache of coins from around this period, but by far the most valuable find was nothing like anyone was expecting. Have either of you heard of anyone discovering an "out-of-place" object in the continuum?'

They both shook their heads.

'No, even the Draconians won't admit they exist, but it has been a pet project of mine for many years. I've discovered there have been a number of incidents involving archaeologists who've uncovered modern items fossilised in much older rock — mostly things like steel bolts in the strata of four-million-year-old riverbeds. These sponge divers found a small wooden box on that shipwreck and inside was what could only be described as an analogue computer.'

Josh coughed on the grape he was chewing and spat it out. Caitlin was not impressed.

'I thought you couldn't take technology back in time?'

The colonel nodded. 'You can't, not physically. But you can take the knowledge back and teach someone how to do it.'

'But that breaks the prime directive,' Caitlin said with a look of astonishment.

'Indeed it does, and no one in our Order would ever contemplate such a thing. Not even the Determinists.'

'Are there others like us who haven't joined the Order?' asked Josh.

Caitlin rolled her eyes as if he'd just opened a can of worms.

'Yes, I believe there are. Although I seemed to be the only one,' the colonel replied, looking at Caitlin cryptically. 'I call them the Fatalists, or Fates for short, and I believe these renegades are working against the Order.'

'To do what exactly?'

'From the little I can ascertain, I believe the Fates want the Order to stop interfering in the timeline altogether, to leave the future to pure chance — they are throwing curve-balls at the continuum.' The colonel tossed an olive stone out of the window. 'I have no idea what their real agenda is — there have been more than a couple of incidents, ones that cannot be explained away as coincidence — a word that one should never use in front of a Copernican by the way.'

'So you needed to find this computer?' Caitlin interrupted.

'Actually, I think I am the one who has to sink it. There will be nothing like this technology for another fourteen hundred years, not until the Renaissance. I want to make sure it doesn't reach Rome, and more importantly find out who made it.'

'Why?' Josh asked naively.

Caitlin coughed into her drink. 'Er. Because the advancement of technology breaks our prime directive, and would probably result in the extinction of the human race!' She turned back to the colonel and added, 'surely the Council know about this?'

'Well if they do — they're not doing anything about it. Not that they would admit to the existence of a secret organisation of anarchists — it would undermine their stochastic ideals and play directly into the hands of the Determinist Party. They've been pushing for tighter controls for years — we would end up in a police state.'

Josh grimaced at the word 'Police.'

'Do you think my parents might have known?' Caitlin asked quietly.

'I don't know my dear,' the colonel said, taking her hand, 'they were the bravest and brightest Draconians I've ever met, and they ranged far off of the map, who can say what they would have seen.'

Josh could see how much the colonel meant to her. He'd missed the old man too, and he had no idea how he was going to explain about getting kicked out of the Order yet, so he asked the next most obvious question.

'So, how exactly are we going to sink it?'

'For that,' the colonel said with a smile, 'we're going to need a Pirate.'

47

SELEPHIN

Silent waves lapped at the sides of the boat as they rowed their way out into the bay. Josh fought back the impulse to throw up every time the water hit the prow. It wasn't going to be long before he lost control, but he was going to hang on to it as long as he could.

The dark shapes of the colonel and the two oarsmen sat in front of him, their sinewed arms carving the oars through the water at a rapid pace. Caitlin sat behind Josh looking up at the canopy of stars, which were magnificent, but not something he could really appreciate properly while trying to focus on keeping down his last meal.

'Do you ever wonder if there's another boat out there somewhere on a sea just like this?' Caitlin asked as she trailed her hand through the water.

'No,' replied Josh, feeling his stomach lurch again.

'The chances are slim I know. According to the Drake equation, maybe less than one in a hundred million, but I like to think there is someone looking up at our sun and wondering the same.' She moved and the boat rocked. 'Just look at Cassiopeia. When did you ever get to see the Milky Way so clearly in your time?'

Josh was having trouble concentrating on what she was saying through the rising nausea. His skin had gone clammy, and his tongue felt too big for his mouth.

'Caitlin, stop teasing the boy. Josh, for God's sake, get it over with,' the colonel interrupted.

Josh let physiology take over. It was beyond his control and he surrendered to it, venting the contents of his stomach into the sea.

'It's all right,' he heard the colonel say. 'I'm sure some-where in the infinite vastness of space someone else is suffering from *mal de mer* at this very moment.' He passed Josh a small flask. 'Here, I find this helps on such occasions.'

It was a sweet, citrus spirit that instantly made Josh feel a hell of a lot better.

An hour later they reached the ship. It was anchored far out in the bay, a large wooden vessel with three rows of long oars on each side and two huge masts with their sails furled. The hull was a vast hulking wall of barnacle-encrusted wood and tar that dwarfed their boat as it rose and fell in front of them like a floating castle. Suddenly a rope ladder was cast down from the deck, and voices called out in various languages for them to climb aboard.

In the dark, cold night it seemed suicidal for Josh to leave the relative safety of the small boat and climb up the side of the heaving wall, but the colonel jumped up and pulled them towards the ladder with a boat hook. Then, with Caitlin following close behind, the colonel climbed up the swaying ropes. Josh came last. The two oarsmen were keen to leave and virtually threw him out on to the ladder as their boat pitched and dipped in the ship's wake.

He climbed the wet rungs slowly, trying not to look down between his feet, but stinging salt water ran off the bulkhead and into his eyes when he looked up. There was nothing below him but the dark, brooding sea and he closed his eyes and forced himself to keep moving upwards — with only the sound of Caitlin shouting at him to 'move your arse' barely audible over the boom of the waves.

There was nothing more satisfying than the feeling of the deck beneath his feet when he was finally dragged over the gunwale by one of the crew. Josh felt like a complete idiot for being so pathetic. He wanted to explain to Caitlin that he'd never been this close to the sea — other than the time at the beach when he was six, the largest body of water he'd ever seen was the local swimming pool. But then she would realise that he'd never been anywhere and he didn't want to admit to that.

'You okay?' Caitlin asked, as the ship lurched and he fell against her.

'Yeah. Just need to get my sea legs.'

'It will be easier when we get under way,' she said, trying to reassure him.

'Do the waves get smaller then?'

'No, but we get faster.'

'Great.'

A few minutes later the colonel returned with an unusual-looking man dressed in a baroque chest plate and what Josh could only describe as a skirt.

'Caitlin, Josh, I would like to introduce you to a very old friend of mine — this is Selephin Maltraders, former

Draconian Commander of the Ninth and the especially excellent captain of this marvellous vessel.

Selephin had a broad smile that exposed many of his pearly white teeth and what appeared to be jewels embedded within them. The scars across his face were deep and old and only mildly less distracting than the tattoos that covered the rest of his entirely hairless head.

'Welcome to my humble vessel!' Selephin said in a clipped English accent, holding out a hand that was covered in rings and bracelets. 'A fine evening for a fight, don't you think?'

Josh shook his hand, and then watched as the captain took Caitlin's hand and kissed it very gently.

'We are blessed to have such beauty aboard. Your fairness doth outshine the moon.'

Josh tried not to laugh, but when he saw how flattered she was, he changed his mind.

'Now the tide is about to turn,' Selephin observed, and barked out a series of orders to the crew in something that sounded like Arabic. It was pretty obvious from the way the crew responded that he'd just told them to make sail: a troupe of men appeared from various hatches on the deck and clambered up and down the rigging, hauling thick ropes, and unfurling the sails. Within a matter of minutes, the ship was ploughing through the water at speed, the night winds pushing them forward into the darkness.

Selephin took them to his cabin: a small, cosy space at the stern of the ship. It was full of charts and chests, but in the centre a space had been cleared for a table, where a map of the surrounding seas had been laid out.

The colonel consulted his almanac and then picked up

some small coins that lay discarded on top of the map. 'So this is us,' he said, placing the first coin down near the island marked Ogylos. Then he took another coin and put it near the island labelled Kretes. 'The ship in question left Crete approximately two hours ago.'

'She will be fighting the wind,' commented Selephin. 'We have the advantage.'

'Good,' said the colonel, 'she is also heavily laden, full of prizes for the patricians.'

'Ha,' spat Selephin. 'Damn the senate and their accursed patricians! My men will be only too happy to relieve them of one of their prizes. Their ships have been very bad for business lately — this war never seems to end!'

Selephin took an unusual-looking bottle and a handful of glasses out of a cupboard. 'We have a three hours before the dawn and much to discuss.'

Caitlin and Josh made themselves comfortable on the captain's couch and whiled away the next few hours listening to Selephin's and the colonel's stories. Caitlin grew tired and slowly nestled down against Josh's shoulder and dozed off. Josh was too intrigued by their anecdotes to notice. The two veterans recounted one adventure after another as the rum flowed, each one became more daring and outrageous than the last.

'Do you remember Thebes?' the colonel asked with a drunken chuckle.

'The time you broke Nefertiti's heart? How could I forget? We were only supposed to locate her tomb, and you took it upon yourself to bed the wench before we'd even found the architect, let alone the temple he was building for her!'

'Nothing compared to that time you wagered Hannibal that he couldn't ride a troop of elephants over the Alps.'

'Well, someone had to,' Selephin said with a knowing smile.

The colonel conceded and raised his bottle to the old pirate. 'We've had some interesting times you and I, but I've never quite understood why you took early retirement.'

Selephin reflected over the answer for a few moments. Josh thought he saw a flicker of sadness in the man's face as he replied.

'There have been many times when I have asked myself the same question. I am Draconian, always have been, always will be. It is my calling, my reason to live, but when you watch too many of your friends disappear —' he looked over at the sleeping Caitlin — 'you begin to question why we do this, and then, when you can't find a good enough answer any more, you know it is time to stop.'

The colonel nodded. 'This life does takes its toll, of that there is no doubt. But why here, why this era?'

'Ah, my friend, we each have our own special milieu, do we not? A favourite century to while away a few hours when time — and the damn clackers — allow. This is mine, aboard my own ship in the middle of a great war. I have no desire to die in my sleep.'

They both drank then to 'an interesting death' and sank into quiet contemplation of their own mortality and those they had lost. Josh found himself thinking about Gossy and wondering what it would have been like if he hadn't died. With his new abilities, it should be a simple exercise to go back and change it, but it was forbidden — the colonel was very clear on that point, and Josh was in enough trouble already.

Selephin's snigger broke his reverie.

'Do you remember that time we had to inspire Newton?' he asked, wrapping air quotes around 'inspire'.

'How many apples did you have to drop on him in the end?'

'Fourteen. He was never the sharpest knife in the drawer.'

48

DAWN

D awn broke as they stood at the prow, lighting a dark thunderhead of clouds that stretched across the horizon — bruising the sky with the purple shades of storms. Josh could smell the rain on the wind that raced toward them. The sails flapped idly above him, their lines swinging loose, untied from the wooden belaying pins. The ship was deathly silent, ghost-faced men with vicious knives and axes crouched on the deck, their faces painted white to resemble skulls.

This is the real ghost squad, Josh thought.

The colonel surveyed the widening dawn through an archaic leather telescope. Like the others, he too was wearing armour: a sturdy-looking chest plate and bracers as well as a heavy bronze sword that hung from his waist. The colonel had been adamant that Josh and Caitlin were not going to be joining the boarding party, and inwardly Josh was relieved — Caitlin was still fast asleep in the captain's cabin and he didn't fancy his chances in a sword fight with the Roman navy.

'So this device would change the future — I mean the present?' Josh asked.

'It would accelerate the advancement of the human race,' the colonel replied without taking his eyes off the sea.

'And that's a bad thing? What if it could help find new treatments — you know, like for MS?'

The colonel sighed and lowered the eyeglass. 'Invention is a powerful agent of change. Your own millennia is proof that the human race is only just capable of controlling its self-destructive tendencies. Civilisation needs time to mature before it is ready for such technological advances — this is like handing a loaded gun to a six-year-old.'

'So if we don't stop this ship?'

'Rome would conquer the known world in under a century, creating an empire unlike anything we have ever known. Science would develop exponentially based on their new calculus engines and within another three hundred years weapons of extinction-level destruction would have decimated the planet — give or take fifty years or so. Humanity would never make it out of the Middle Ages.'

'Shit.'

'Exactly. A time for everything and everything in good time.'

Suddenly a sail broke over the line of the horizon, distorting the edge of the world for a moment. The colonel snapped the telescope up to his eye once more as the first rumble of thunder rolled across the dark seas.

'Go back to the cabin and don't come out again until I say. She will fight you every minute she's locked up in there — so you'll have your work cut out for you.'

Josh watched the ship try to outrun them for a while. It was obvious from the way she sat so low in the water that she was far too heavy to get away.

He went down the hatch as the grappling hooks and lines sprang across the gap between the two boats. They were so close now that he could make out the faces of the Roman crewmen as they frantically tried to chop through the ropes.

Caitlin was still fast asleep, curled up under the furs that Selephin had given them. Josh watched her for a while. There was a contentment in her sleeping face that he never saw when she was awake. A stillness in the way she breathed that warmed his heart. Her skin was perfect, the faintest sprinkling of freckles brought about by the Greek sun across her cheekbones.

The sound of the two hulls scraping together resonated throughout the ship, and she sat bolt upright.

'What are you doing?' she snapped.

'Nothing,' he said shyly.

'Were you watching me while I was asleep?'

'No. That would be weird.'

She threw off the furs and stood up and stretched. 'You totally were. Weirdo.'

The conversation was suddenly drowned out by the howls of Selephin's crew as they began to board the Roman Galley.

'Shit. Has it started?' she asked, hurrying to one of the windows. 'Come on, Josh! We're missing it!'

'It's not safe. The colonel told me to keep you down here,' he said, moving in front of the door.

'Did he now? Why do you care?' she scoffed. 'Not because I'm a girl? Get real. I can kick your ass any day.'

There were screams from above and sounds of clashing metal as the hand-to-hand combat got underway.

'There are people getting killed up there! It's not like you have some kind of magic force field — this IS real, you could die.'

'And you think I don't know that?' She had a steely look in her eyes, and there was a flush of red in her cheeks. 'I don't need a protector — you're not some kind of knight in shining armour. You're just . . .'

'Just what exactly?' He too could feel the anger building as he asked her. It was a question he'd been mulling over for weeks.

'A complete pain in the backside!' she declared. 'You never think things through properly! You just jump in with both feet, and you have that *stupid* idiotic smile that you *think* makes everything all right!'

He tried not to smile as she said it.

'Don't!' she said, raising one finger. 'Do not say a word. Just get the hell out of my way.'

'I will if you just answer one question,' he said, wearing his best poker face.

Her eyes glared into his like lasers. 'What?'

'Do you ever wonder what happened to us back in the cave?'

'No,' she said, averting her eyes.

'Well, I do. The Draconians wouldn't tell me anything, but we must have *survived*! We must have had some kind of life! It took them *forty years* before they could locate us.'

She turned away from him, and he could feel the tension draining away.

'Well, I probably saved your butt back then too,' she said, looking around the room.

'Yeah. I don't know what I would've done without you. Probably had to marry the daughter of some Neanderthal chieftain.'

She smirked as she turned back towards him. 'Unlikely. They died out a long time before the Mesolithic.'

'Okay, so maybe I shacked up with a polar bear, or something equally large and hairy.'

She smiled knowingly.

'What?' he asked. 'Did the Draconians tell you what happened?'

She tried not to look too smug.

'They did, didn't they?'

Her smile grew wider, and her eyes flashed.

'Tell me!' He wanted to shake her, hold her, kiss her. His mind was going over all the things they must have got up to in that cave.

'Maybe. When this is over.' She backed away from him as he advanced. 'And only if you behave yourself.' She knelt on the couch and peered up out of the window again. The sounds of the battle were louder now. 'It's a Praetorian ship — Pompey's elite fighting force — and Rufius and his merry band of pirates are trying to take them out. Don't you think he needs all the help he can get?'

'But he gave me an order not to let you out! I need to keep on his good side, remember?'

'And what if the old fool doesn't make it? Who's going to speak up for you then?' she said stubbornly. 'I'm sure if Sim were here he'd put the odds at five-to-one against.'

Josh thought back to the events he had seen in the colonel's lifeline, how close the strzyga attack had been to the point of death. He knew then that this battle might be his last.

Caitlin was rummaging around in one of the wooden chests. 'You never struck me as the type who would leave a man behind,' she said taking out a breastplate and a long sword.

'I'm not. Where did you find —'

'The colonel isn't the only resourceful one on this mission. If I remember rightly, didn't I take down a horde of ugly demon bitches yesterday?'

'Yeah, okay,' Josh said, moving away from the door, 'but won't I need a weapon too?'

'Do you even know how to use one?' she joked, handing him a short sword from one of the chests.

49

THE FIGHT

Blood and rain dripped down through the cracks in the decking as they walked through the deserted lower decks.

Josh's heart was thumping like a drum inside his chest, his senses heightened, every sound and smell magnified a thousand times — he had never felt so alive.

Caitlin made her way to the ladder and looked up at the small square of thunderous sky that loomed over it. She carefully placed one foot after the other until her head was just below the level of the deck and then peered out. What she saw seemed to drain the colour from her face. When she looked back down at Josh, there was nothing but fear in her eyes. He shook his head as if to say, 'Don't go,' but she ignored him and leapt through the hatch.

He felt a cold shiver run down his spine, then followed her up and out into the fight.

Corpses littered the deck. An indistinguishable mass of limbs and assorted body parts lay scattered across the planks, which were slick with rain, blood and entrails. There was no way to tell how many had been lost from each side.

Through the sheeting rain, Josh caught a glimpse of Caitlin as she disappeared into the centre of the fight. Selephin, the colonel and a small band of what was left of the crew were surrounded by a circle of heavily armed Roman soldiers.

The colonel's bald head towered over the helmets of the guards. It was covered in blood — he was wielding a large sword like a dervish in wide, deadly arcs, but the Romans were well drilled and held their ground, waiting for him to tire.

Josh could see the old man's arm wavering a little more with every stroke and knew he was running out of steam.

One of the soldiers spotted Caitlin and turned to engage her. She leapt over a fallen body and struck high with her first blow, knocking him slightly off-balance. As she landed, she went low and sliced his leg with another cut above the knee. He went down quickly, and her sword buried itself into his neck.

Illuminated by a flash of lightning, Josh saw another soldier turn to attack Caitlin while she tried to free her blade. Josh picked up a discarded spear and threw it as hard as he could at the man.

The shaft buried itself in the chest of her attacker, and he crumpled. She turned and nodded her thanks before having to parry the blow from another legionnaire.

With the fight divided on two fronts, the Roman circle opened and gave Selephin and the colonel the break they needed. They carved their way through the ring of steel, and the fight fractured into a series of one-on-one melees across the deck.

The ship rocked violently as the storm-tossed waves did their best to throw them all into the sea. Josh was soaked to the skin and wiped his eyes free of the stinging salt water. He knew he would do more harm than good with the sword, so he found another spear and managed to take down a soldier who was about to gut one of the crew.

A few minutes later, the last of the Roman guard fell.

The storm calmed to a persistent drizzle, and an eerie silence fell over the survivors. Selephin gathered the remainder of his crew together, and they started dropping the dead unceremoniously overboard. A crewman lay struggling for breath close to where Josh was standing. He knelt down to help him, but Caitlin caught his hand before he made contact.

'Best not to touch the dying,' she said, panting with exhaustion. There was blood splattered across her cheek.

'Why?' he asked, pulling back his hand.

'Bad things happen at the end of timelines.'

There was a tremor in her voice that spoke of something terrible. The man's eyes rolled, he let out a last groan and was gone.

Josh looked out into the sea, realising that the men they'd killed were sinking slowly into the deep. It was an odd feeling to know that he could do it. Taking another life was very different when they were trying to end yours — it was a primitive survival instinct that required no emotion, no remorse — nothing like when Gossy had died. That was a cold, empty place in the pit of his soul, one that had taken years to stop staring into.

Caitlin knelt beside the dead man for a few seconds as if in prayer, then stood up and took off her chest plate.

'Nice throwing arm you've got there,' she said, tossing the dented armour over the side.

'Remind me not to pick a fight with you,' he replied, handing her a water skin that he'd found near one of the dead. It was hard to feel victorious standing amongst so many bodies, ones that had breathing a few minutes before. Selephin's men seemed to have no qualms about it. They were already helping themselves to the captured wine barrels.

The colonel came over to them. He looked drained. His sword had been left in the body of the last man.

'You disobeyed me.'

Josh nodded. 'Guess I did.'

'I think your training is over.' He was panting and there was blood running down his arm when he slapped Josh on the shoulder. 'Well done.'

Caitlin shot Josh a look of concern, but, before they could ask, Selephin swung back over on a rope carrying a polished wooden box. The colonel opened it and showed them all the small bronze astrological clock that lay inside.

'So that's what all the fuss was about?' asked Selephin. 'What is it?'

'Analog computer, fourteenth century.'

'OK, so now that you have your clock, I assume the rest is booty?' Selephin smiled. His crew had already begun to transfer the contents of the captured ship to their hold.

'The device must sink with the ship,' the colonel said, handing back the box, 'and we'll follow this back to its maker.' He held up a small gear wheel. 'And don't forget you need to leave enough treasure to look convincing when you scuttle it.'

Selephin was already standing on the gunwale, preparing to swing back over to the other ship.

'Of course, my friend! Just enough to keep them guessing.'

The colonel turned to Caitlin and Josh. 'So you two have earned a break. I'll follow this one up.' He pocketed the gear wheel. 'Go back home and get some rest.'

Caitlin shook her head. 'Not before we get you to a doctor.'

Josh caught the colonel as he stumbled. He was like a dead weight. Caitlin unbuckled his armour to reveal a large red slash below his ribs. Josh realised it was in the same place as the dagger wound used to summon the strzyga.

Caitlin grimaced. 'We need to get him to Dr Crooke right now!'

50

BEDLAM

[Bishopsgate, London. Date: 11.647]

Doctor Helkiah Crooke was an imposing figure in his long black cloak and humped back. To Josh he looked more like an evil wizard than a physician — especially when his surgery had all the trappings of a medieval torture chamber.

A stern-looking woman dressed in a nun's habit ushered Caitlin and Josh out of the room, telling them that the colonel's treatment would take many hours, and banished them to the outer rooms.

Josh was tired and sore. He'd wasted enough time in waiting rooms and had grown to despise them. It seemed that no matter which era you were in, they always had a lingering odour of disease weakly masked by chemicals.

'Is there a garden or something?' Josh asked as he paced around, trying not to look at the pale organs that sat in fluid-filled specimen jars on the shelves.

'There's a herbarium,' Caitlin replied. 'It's a garden, or we could go back to the chapter house?'

'No. I just want to get some fresh air.'

The herbarium was set within the main quadrangle of Bethlem hospital, or Bedlam as it was more commonly known. On every side, the old redbrick walls were covered in ivy and climbing roses. It was midday and the sunlight bathed the small garden, which had been divided into four sections, each with a planter full of medicinal herbs. In the centre was a neatly clipped lawn with a small stone fountain surrounded by a circular bench.

Josh sat down heavily on the bench and dipped his hand into the cool waters of the fountain. As he rubbed the cold liquid into the back of his neck he watched the swallows diving in and out of the eaves — it was good to feel the sun on his face, to chill out after everything they had been through.

Caitlin wandered around the herb garden, bending over to smell a flower or pick the odd leaf and eat it. His stomach growled at the thought of food.

Drowsy from the warmth of the sun, he watched her through half-closed eyes as she inspected the plants. There was an intensity about the way she examined everything, as if each petal were the most precious thing in the world.

She walked back over to him with a handful of strawberries. 'Hello, sailor,' she joked, popping one into his mouth.

He couldn't reply. The taste of the fruit was overwhelming his senses.

'Good?'

He nodded and took another from her.

'Always got to keep an eye on your blood sugar after that kind of action. Don't want you having a hypo.' She dropped the rest into his lap and went off to search the other side of the garden.

·   ·   ·

'Before,' Josh began after they'd finished another batch of fruit, 'when I was rescuing the colonel from the strzyga, he had a wound in exactly the same place as he has now.'

Caitlin lay beside him on the bench, her head in his lap as she watched the birds. A nun was wandering around the garden with a basket over her arm picking off the dead heads of the roses.

'That was a fated wound,' she replied dreamily.

'A what?'

'Some things will always happen, no matter what.' She pulled back the sleeve to reveal a fine scar on her upper arm. 'I got this when I was seven playing with one of my father's swords. No matter what I did to try to avoid it, however many times I rewound and tried different ways — it still happened. My father told me later that there are certain events that cannot be changed. "The continuum will have its moment," he used to say. The Order refers to them as cornerstones.'

'Cornerstones?'

'Moments that define who we are. They shape our future. We all have them — mine was losing my parents.'

Josh had never given it a name, but in that moment he saw that losing Gossy had changed his life irreversibly. Since the accident, his fate seemed to be a never-ending catalogue of disasters.

'What if there was one thing that you could change? Would you do it?'

'An intercession?' she whispered as if it were a cursed word.

'Yeah.'

'No. There are too many consequences. Changing your own timeline is one of the cardinal sins. The Protectorate will lock you up in here and throw away the key.'

'But what if it meant you could see your parents again?'

'She opened her eyes and he could see tears welling in the corners.'

'Don't think I haven't wanted to, but no matter what I tried they would still have gone on that mission. I couldn't change who they were.'

They sat in the garden until the shadows reached their feet. It was a small moment of sanctuary, even if it was surrounded by the insane, which was something that Josh could relate too.

'Got yourself a new one, did you?' the colonel asked as he nodded admiringly at Josh's tachyon. He was sitting up in a huge four-poster bed, bolstered by a hundred pillows. There was a large poultice pasted over his ribs and a series of glyphs written in ink over his bare chest.

'Sim gave it to him for passing his second Millenial,' lied Caitlin before Josh could think of a better excuse. He didn't want to explain how he'd left his previous one with the professor at the university.

The nun was busy at the other end of the room, washing out a bowl and humming to herself annoyingly. The colonel waved them closer and struggled to sit up. He whispered so the woman couldn't hear.

'Listen, you two, I appreciate what you've done, but I have unfinished business back there — need to find out who's been passing technology to the Greeks. Get yourselves back to Methuselah before someone notices you're missing. I'll be fine. Old Crooke's medicine smells like bat shit, but it works wonders.'

He winked at them and peeled away the poultice to show a newly healed lesion underneath. Josh was impressed — a few hours ago the wound had looked pretty fatal.

'Thank you for coming,' the colonel said loudly for the benefit of the nun. 'I should like to rest now.' Again a wink.

'Take care, Uncle,' Caitlin said, and she bent to kiss the old man on the cheek.

He took Josh by the hand and looked earnestly into his eyes. 'Be careful, Joshua. Your training may be over, but you still have a hell of a lot to learn.'

'Shall we?' Caitlin asked, taking Josh's hand. As they walked out of the room, she whispered, 'Rufius suspects that the old battle-axe is a spy for the Determinists. Did you notice how she was always hovering around us?'

'Why would they be so interested in him?'

'Oh, it's not *him*,' she said, turning to face Josh. 'It's you.'

51

PRIVATE HOSPITAL

Professor Fermi left the nurse settling the patient into her private room. He'd already spoken to the clinical specialist and knew there was very little left they could do — other than continue her current treatment and make her comfortable. Multiple Sclerosis was a terrible illness, one that eroded the body and the mind. There were new therapies, ones that she would never be able to afford, trials that only those with the right connections could try.

'It's the fate of the poor to suffer,' his father had once told him as they watched the grapes being harvested by the local villagers.

Fermi was a pragmatist. He took no pleasure in her suffering. He simply needed her to get to her son. She'd no idea of his whereabouts, the sedatives had made her confused, so it was just a case of waiting for Josh to resurface and come looking for his mother — which Lenin had assured him he'd do very soon.

52

THE TEXT

Caitlin had left Josh at the colonel's house and gone back to the Chapter House. She'd promised to come back after dinner, or if she couldn't then they'd agreed to meet the next day in the local library. Josh had forgotten that she had a day job, and that in terms of the present they'd only been gone for a few minutes.

Josh sat alone in the study. The room was still a mess. He had set a fire in the grate, which was slowly warming the unheated room; the house had no central heating, and the nights were cooling quickly as the summer came to an end.

He sat in the colonel's worn leather armchair and flicked through his old diary, rereading the notes he'd made all those years ago. Amongst descriptions of his mother's symptoms and daily medication schedules were doodles of knights and spacemen, dragons and castles. As Josh ran his fingers over the badly drawn figures, he could feel the pen in his eleven-year-old hand, drawing them on his mother's bed as she lay sleeping. They were quiet moments of escape when he let his mind wander — daydreams of adventures he thought he would never have.

He came to a week of blank pages, June 12th, 2011, the day of the accident. He couldn't remember much about that day. The doctor told his mother it was some form of post-traumatic stress that would heal in time — it never did. The empty pages were like a mirror of his memories, a missing week in his life. All he knew was that when he came home his best friend was dead, and there were no more doodles in the diary after that.

The coals on the fire sputtered and hissed as rain fell down the chimney. The Grecian storm seemed to have followed him back to the present. It was sheeting rain outside, and there were flashes of lightning behind the curtains.

The house was too quiet, too empty. Josh went over to the stereo, which was some kind of retro-turntable model. He knew the colonel was a purist when it came to music. He was always complaining that digitising sound lost some-thing — preferring vinyl to MP3s or CDs.

Josh thumbed through the collection of albums and picked *Ella Fitzgerald Live at Mister Kelly's*. It reminded him of his gran. She was always singing — her favourite song was called *You Don't Know What Love Is*.

He pulled the shiny black disc out of its sleeve and placed the needle carefully on track six of the B side. The speakers crackled into life. The music was a pure, beau-tiful tone that surrounded him. He stood in the middle of the study and let the warm notes flow over him. It was as if the band were in the room — playing just for him. He'd never experienced anything quite as moving as when Ella's deep velvet voice sang the first words of the song.

In his mind Josh could see her standing in a dimly lit nightclub. Her blue dress shimmered in the single spotlight, and her eyes were closed as her red lips trembled over every word.

His consciousness reached into the event, using the timeline that expanded from the sounds of the music, and suddenly he was inside Mister Kelly's club, could smell the cigars and the whisky. He was so surprised to find that he could enter the moment without any physical object that he pulled back. This was something new, an ability that none of the others had ever told him about, and he wasn't sure whether he was even supposed to be able to do it.

An hour later there was a knock at the door. Josh woke with a start, not realising that he had fallen asleep on the sofa. Assuming that Caitlin had forgotten her key, he jumped up in total darkness and fumbled blindly for the light switch as he went in the hall.

There was a package on the doormat. The knock had been someone posting it through the letterbox. Josh picked it up and turned it over. It was badly wrapped in the torn pages of a Dark Knight graphic novel. Batman stood high above the cityscape of Gotham. Written over the sky were the words 'open me' in a thick black marker.

He tore off the packaging to find a cheap Nokia phone nestling in bubble wrap. It was already powered up, and there was a message waiting for him.

'WE HAVE UR MUM. U OWE ME 20K. L.'

Josh read the message twice before chucking the phone at the wall. It bounced off a stack of newspapers and landed in one piece on the floor.

He went over to stamp on it, but then thought better of it. The colonel had no landline — he was convinced that they were continuously monitored. Josh picked up the Nokia and went back into the study and dialled the hospital. It was a number he'd memorised a long time ago.

'Neuro,' the ward sister's voice crackled through the crappy speaker.

'Hi. My name is Joshua Jones. Can I talk to my mother, please?'

'One moment.' There was a click and the line hissed a little. Josh looked at the bars on the display; the signal was weak. He moved closer to the window.

'I'm sorry, Mr Jones, your mother has been transferred. Her notes say it was processed this morning.'

Josh was looking out into the garden as he listened to the woman's voice. A flash of lightning lit it up, and for a split second he saw the silhouette of someone standing with what looked like a gun pointed straight at him. Josh dropped the phone and ran for the back door, grabbing a carving knife from the drawer as he went.

By the time he got down into the garden, whoever it was had gone. The rain soaked him to the skin as he searched the bushes, shouting and slashing at anything that moved.

When he finally came back into the house, he was drenched. He grabbed a towel, threw more coal onto the fire and sat down in front of it, trying to rub some warmth back into his hands.

The discarded phone lay on the mat, and he picked it up carefully, his hands shivering. He swore under his breath as he read Lenin's message once more, then hit 'reply' and typed: 'Where? When?' and hit 'send'.

Josh found that there was less than a thousand pounds in legal currency in the colonel's petty cash. He'd always assumed the Order had some kind of bank account, although he'd never seen the old man with a credit card or go anywhere near a bank — let alone a cashpoint. There was probably some kind of treasury at the Chapter House, but he had no chance of getting near that.

It was the middle of the night, and Josh was so tired his eyes ached. Neither the colonel nor Caitlin had returned — which they guessed might happen. She'd been away without permission so he was sure they had grounded her again.

The Nokia sat inert on the desk. There had been no reply from Lenin and, no matter how many times he checked, it refused to give him the answer he needed.

Josh tried not to think about where his mother was or what they were doing to her. There were hundreds of places Lenin could have hidden her. He had a network of empty flats all over the estate, evictions or sublets — the kind the council had given up trying to work out who should be the legitimate occupier. Every one of them would be a damp, squalid hole with no running water, heating or electricity. Josh just had to hope that Lenin would keep her warm, that he still had some remnant of decency.

Josh went into the curiosity collection looking for something valuable — anything he could trade or sell. As he went from one cabinet to the next, he realised that most of the objects were just everyday things, old and well loved, but not especially valuable in their own right. It was as Mrs B had said: they were only priceless to those that had owned them.

There were, of course, items such as Blackbeard's sword, but that would need a specialist buyer, and he really didn't have time to find one of those.

Josh thought back to the treasure that Selephin had

taken off the Roman galley and cursed the fact that he hadn't thought of keeping any for himself. It wasn't like him at all; he'd spent too much time with these people, and it was making him soft. He needed to look after his own now — no matter what the cost.

Then he remembered the key that Marie Antoinette had given the colonel. Hadn't he said something about the treasure of her children? He tried hard to recall the old man's exact words. Something to do with Bourbons, which he thought was odd at the time — he had always thought of that as a biscuit.

He began looking through each cabinet carefully, trying to remember what it had looked like; it had not been a big key, but it had been ornately carved with a motif in the fob. The letter 'M' and an 'A' were intertwined, the insignia of the Queen of France.

It took a long time to find it. The colonel hadn't actually labelled it as yet. In his usual disorganised way, it had been thrown into a tin box with a dozen other random mementoes from 11.792.

Josh took the key out and felt the history radiating from it. Patterns of energy arced around his hand. He knew Caitlin would say this was wrong, but he had no choice. His mother needed him, and the only thing Lenin understood was money. He would have to get enough to pay him off and set them up somewhere far away from London. There were a lot of new advances in MS treatment in America, he thought. Anywhere that was far enough away from his old life.

As he turned the key over in his fingers, he watched its history unfurling: Marie Antoinette locking the chest in front of her children, a nobleman taking it away towards some kind of church in the middle of nowhere. Then years of darkness, watching the stones around it age and crumble to ruin. No one had ever found it. The crypt in which it had been hidden had collapsed over the centuries. He wound back to a point a few days after the courier had left it in the crypt and let himself step into that part of history.

53

ORVAL

[Orval, France. Date: 11.795]

The crypt smelt of rotting wood, or so he told himself. The chamber was damp, moss coated the crumbling stone walls and water dripped down on hair-like roots that had penetrated the roof where it had begun to sag and crack. There were tombs on either side with the illegible names of dead French nobles slowly fading from the crumbling surface of the stone. In another hundred years there would be nothing left to identify them — time and nature were erasing them from history.

The crypt was pitch black, and he had to step carefully between the rubble that was strewn across the flagstones using the glow from his tachyon to light the way. He swept it slowly across the room, looking for any sign of the chest.

The beam found the base of an iron-bound wooden box, but as he moved the light up to the lid he found that there was a foot placed squarely on top of it.

Josh jumped back, nearly dropping the tachyon.

Someone switched on a torch and he found Phileas staring back at him.

'What the hell are you doing here?' Josh said in a whisper, as if trying not to wake the dead.

'I was about to ask you the same question,' Phileas replied.

Josh's mind ran through a whole list of lies and excuses and then settled on a simple one.

'The colonel, Rufius I mean, he sent me to collect the treasure.'

'Caitlin said you might say that.'

'And how would she know?'

'I'm afraid that was down to me,' said another voice from the shadows.

Josh jumped again and turned towards the second voice — it was Sim.

'Jesus! You're going to give me a heart attack! Is there anyone else in here that I should know about?'

'Only little old me.' Lyra appeared next to Sim and winked.

There was only one person missing.

'The Protectorate has put her under house arrest,' Lyra answered his unspoken question, 'while they investigate what happened in Greece.'

Lyra always made Josh a little uncomfortable. Her eyes always had that look, like she knew all his secrets.

'It took me a while to calculate your next move,' Sim added apologetically. 'We couldn't be sure whether it would be the warehouse or one of your previous missions.'

'So you KNEW I was going to do this? I thought you guys couldn't see into the future.'

'But we do know about your past,' Lyra said with that look again.

'And we did some digging,' Phileas added more seriously. 'My department has to do background checks on every candidate. It's nothing personal.'

Josh couldn't think of anything more personal. The thought of them knowing about his past, all those stupid mistakes he had made — the way he used to be. He was ashamed of that life, and he realised that wasn't who he was, nor ever really had been — he had just been trying to survive any way he could.

'So I'm guessing you're not going to let me borrow a little of the treasure?' Josh half-joked as he kicked the chest. It was made of a thick, dark wood and didn't move an inch.

'I'm afraid not,' Phileas replied. 'Its fate is best served here. The Antiquarians will archive it in another hundred years or so.'

'Why? If no one is going to ever use it?'

'Because,' Sim answered, 'there is a ninety-seven-point-three per cent probability that it would end up getting you killed.'

Josh knew better than to argue with Sim's statistics.

'Fine. So I am guessing Caitlin has another plan?'

'Funny you should say that,' Lyra replied.

54

CONTACT

The professor was sitting at a desk in a half-built laboratory — one that the university knew nothing about. Fermi had bought a secure industrial warehouse specifically to work on the device that Joshua had left behind. He sat amongst a chaotic collection of cardboard boxes as white-suited technicians were busy constructing complex machines and computer systems, all following his carefully planned instructions.

'So he's made contact?' the professor said into his phone. He was using an encrypted VOIP app which he'd bought a significant stake in a few years before the NSA had starting monitoring everyone's communications.

'Yeah. Just as I said,' the voice of Lenin replied through the speaker. 'He wants to know when and where.'

'Let's say midnight tomorrow. Where do you suggest?'

'I know a place. What about the money?'

He liked the directness of the boy. He was ambitious and smart. In other circumstances he would have made a great politician or general, but the fates hadn't been kind. Drugs were a one-way street to disaster. Lenin would probably be dead within five years.

'You will be compensated once I have him.'

Fermi ended the call. A few seconds later, a map location appeared in the message tab.

One of the technicians came over with an iPad held out in front of him. There was a technical schematic displayed on its screen.

'The magnetron needs a 400amp supply. We're pretty sure this place doesn't have the capacity for that kind of load.'

Fermi put his phone away and ran his fingers through his hair.

'*Che cavolo!* Do I have to do everything around here?' he said, taking the tablet from the man.

55

CLOCKMAKER

[Naxos, Greece. Date: 9.913]

T he clockmaker's old hand trembled as he placed the last bronze gear into the mechanism — this was to be his masterpiece, his finest work. Vikardis had imagined creating such a device since he was a young apprentice, a machine that could plot the transit of the sun and other heavenly objects across the sky.

There was a precise logic to its design, one that could only be realised in the angles of Euclidian geometry. It was a manifestation of mathematics that had no equal and it would ensure that his name would be revered alongside those of Pythagoras and Plato.

The fact that it wasn't his idea was something that history would forget. The traveller who'd visited him so many years ago, who'd sat for days with the young apprentice as he memorised the workings and gearings required, was now nothing more than a ghost. He was a stranger who'd asked for nothing in return for the knowledge, stating that his motives were 'for the good of mankind and science'.

Putting the last piece in place, Vikardis sat back and admired his invention. As he kneaded his aching shoulders, unravelling the knots that the hours of painstaking work had created, he knew there was nothing left now but to send the work to Rome and wait for the summons to the senate.

His reverie was disturbed by a noise in the outer court-yard — a cat most likely chasing a meal. Before he could rise to investigate, he realised there was a man standing in the doorway.

Vikardis quickly covered the device with a cloth and stood up. 'You are welcome stranger,' he said, bowing his head and assuming a benevolent tone to mask his irritation at the unannounced interruption.

'Ave, Master Vikardis,' the stranger said, bowing low. 'I have come to talk to you about your latest commission.'

Suspicious of the stranger, who wore the robes of a senate official, the old clockmaker moved in front of the device.

'My humble apologies, master, but how do you know of my work?'

The stranger smiled and produced the seal of the Consul Lucius Cornelius Sulla.

'Sulla was most interested in your last report and are very eager to see a working model. "Go to Vikardis", he commanded. "See how he advances!"'

The old clockmaker bowed his head deferentially. 'Sire, this is most timely — I have just recently completed the only working prototype.' He proudly removed the cloth from his invention.

The stranger came closer to the object, his eyes wide with amazement. 'It's a wondrous thing. A veritable master-piece — you truly are a master craftsman.'

The old clockmaker glowed with pride — this was all

he'd dreamed of, to be brought to Rome, to live the good life. He offered the stranger a seat and poured them each a cup of dark, rich wine.

The stranger sat down opposite the watchmaker, took a sip from the cup and scratched his beard.

'Now tell me about the man that showed you how to make this.'

56

THE PLAN

'You've got to be kidding,' exclaimed Josh, 'I thought that was forbidden. Don't you have rules about messing with your own timelines?'

They were sitting in the colonel's kitchen, Sim was busy cooking something Lyra had caught in the grounds of the Abbey at Orval and Phileas and Lyra were pouring over a collection of time maps and notebooks spread out on the table.

'Literally hundreds of them,' agreed Sim, 'but Caitlin is convinced an intercession is the only chance of resolving the crisis.' He crushed some herbs into the steaming pot of stew. 'She made me run the numbers — they do look rather good.'

Josh wasn't sure he could believe what they were asking him to do — something he'd spent most of his life wishing he could.

They wanted him to go back and save Gossy.

'It's not as if you would be directly interacting with your own timeline anyway,' said Lyra, pointing to something on one of the lines on the map.

Josh didn't need to be convinced, but he remembered how the colonel had reacted when his other self had shown up. 'Isn't there some kind of temporal law that could wind up with me just disappearing?'

The others smiled as if sharing some kind of in-joke.

'What?' asked Josh.

'That's what they tell all the new recruits. It's supposed to stop them playing the Grandfather Paradox,' said Lyra.

'Going back and killing your grandfather, so your dad never existed,' Sim added. 'It's classic Novikov self-consistency conjecture.'

Josh looked at him blankly.

'The universe seems to have a few built-in safeguards to stop that kind of thing from happening,' Phileas interrupted, trying to sound reassuring. 'All we're going to do is make a small adjustment to the outcome of one particular car crash. The effects of which will be so localised as not to have any impact on the broader timeline.'

'It may not seem like a big thing to you —'

'But we know that it will change your life and those around you,' Lyra interrupted.

'Will I remember how it was before?'

Sim put the lid back on the pot of stew and sat down next to Josh.

'The truth is, we don't know, and neither will you until we do it. These kind of changes are strictly off the books, and therefore don't tend to be well documented.'

'So tell me again how this is going to help resolve the problem with Lenin?'

Sim went to grab one of the drawings.

'The non-technical version,' Josh added, pushing the papers away.

Sim seemed to be a little put out. Phileas stepped in to explain.

'We think that cornerstone — the death of your friend — caused a significant shift in your timeline. Lenin became a far more dominant influence in your life as a result — your guilt stopped you from challenging him. The belief that you were solely responsible for Gossy's death, and that he saved your life, has allowed Lenin to exploit you for years.'

Phileas reminded Josh of the psychotherapist they'd sent him to after the physical injuries had healed. There was a lot of talk about a missing father figure and authority issues.

Sim leaned forward and pointed to something in one of the notebooks. 'Caitlin thinks if we alter the outcome of the accident here, it will release you from the subservient role that you have assumed ever since.'

'And he won't abduct my mother?'

'Basically yes.'

'Or we could just pay him the money — I know the Order can afford it.'

Lyra smiled. 'Yes, we could. A thousand times over, but it would never end. He would always find another way to bind you to him. He thinks you're his property — like a slave, I suppose. You will never be able to free yourself until one of you is dead. It's quite the most destructive kind of relationship.'

Josh had never really thought about it that way. He'd always hated the way Lenin bossed him around, and had lost count of the ways he should take him down. But there was always that small voice in the back of his head that reminded him of how he'd saved Josh's life — he could never shake the feeling that he owed him.

'Okay. I suppose it can't hurt to try. Can it?'

'Good, now we need something from that time. Do you have any personal effects here?' Phileas asked as he looked around the kitchen.

'I have a diary that goes back that far.'

'Perfect. Let's have something to eat and go over the plan.'

Sim grabbed some bowls and began to ladle out the food. It smelt amazingly good for four-hundred-year-old rabbit.

57

SPLITTING UP

During the meal a text came through from Lenin. It read, 'PIRATES MIDNIGHT 2MORROW.' Josh replied and switched off the phone. He didn't want to think about the future when he was about to relive the worst moment of his past.

There was a slight issue with his diary, as they discovered when he showed them the blank pages from the time of the accident.

Lyra tried to read his memories, this time without sticking her tongue down his throat. She gently took his face in her hands and slid her mind into his. He caught glimpses of old events as she sifted back through his long-term memory, but when she reached the right time frame she shrank back in horror. Her face went ashen, and Sim had to catch her before she fell over.

'What happened?' Josh asked as they all went to help her.

Lyra pushed them away and got back to her feet. Phileas gave her a glass of water.

'You've got some pretty serious defences blocking those

memories. It's kind of like scar tissue, but with added demons, all wrapped around a six-metre-thick wall of pain.'

'So you can't get in?' asked Sim.

'I didn't say that,' she snapped. 'I just think, well, it's like an old carbuncle — you wouldn't want to be around when it burst.'

Phileas was sitting on the sofa deep in thought. 'How are you with music?' he asked casually.

Josh thought back to Ella's song the night before. 'I can use music to go places. It's weird — I don't even need to touch the record.'

'You may have latent audiophilic abilities. Sound can be a very powerful vestige, but only some of us can use it to actually move through time.'

Josh shrugged. 'If you say so.'

'Okay. So think back. What were you listening to around the time you had the accident?'

It was a track that Josh had spent years trying to forget about. It wasn't something he ever wanted to hear again.

'It's not something you guys would have heard of,' Josh said, trying to avoid the subject.

Phileas laughed. 'We're not all into Mozart and Sibelius, you know.'

Lyra could see Josh was uncomfortable and took his hand. 'It's alright, Josh. I know this isn't easy.'

Josh sighed. 'It was called "Speed of Light", by —'

'DJ Laser. I know that one,' Sim said. He pulled out an old iPod and started flicking through the songs. He went over to the stereo and dropped the iPod into a dock. 'Rufius tends to be an old fart when it comes to music. It took me ages to persuade him to get one of these.'

'Does he ever use it?' Josh asked. He couldn't imagine the colonel using anything so modern.

Sim shook his head, cued the song and turned up the speakers. The others stood in a circle around Josh as the bass kicked in.

Josh felt nothing. The song was right, but it didn't initiate any timelines or events for him.

'Something's wrong. It's not like the last time with Ella.'

Sim scratched his head and shrugged.

Lyra stepped in. 'It's digital, you idiot. We need an analogue recording.'

Sim's eyes lit up. 'Back in a min.'

He disappeared for less than a heartbeat and returned with a twelve-inch record under his arm.

'Bloody hard thing to find — this is a bootleg from one of their concerts. Took me nearly a day to track it down.'

He placed the shiny black vinyl onto the turntable and dropped the needle gently onto it.

> *You won't see it coming*
> *The power builds inside*
> *Motion taking over*
>
> *Moving out into the night*
> *Taking on the world*
> *At the speed of light*
>
> *We're gonna go farther*
> *We've gotta go faster*

Josh let the music flow through him, feeling his heartbeat match that of the song. He was instantly transported back to all those times in the car, so many good memories of driving fast down empty lanes in the middle of the night, the music so loud he could feel the bass in his chest.

'Good,' shouted Lyra over the noise. 'Now focus on that time. Find the point nearest to the accident.'

He fast forwarded through the days until he got close to the time, then slowed towards the fateful day and stopped. He was close enough. He held out one hand, and Lyra took it. The others joined her and the room began to vibrate.

You won't see it coming
We gotta go faster
We gonna go farther

Taking on the world
At the speed of light

58

NCP

[London, UK. Date: 12.011]

A moment later they were all standing in the lower basement level of a NCP car park with the music playing somewhere close by. A Subaru Impreza squealed out of one of the far bays and sped past, skidded round the corner and onto the up ramp. Two boys were sitting in the front. The driver looked no older than twelve.

'Was that me?' Josh asked, trying to remember if he had ever stolen a Subaru.

'Uh-huh,' muttered Sim, checking his almanac. 'We need to make sure you don't actually meet yourself. Things can get a little complicated — unpredictable if you know what I mean.'

'I thought you said there were safeguards.'

'There are, but it's better if we don't have to find out what they are.'

Phileas checked his watch. 'We have an hour or so before the Copernicans send the Protectorate to investigate this — so we need to hurry up.'

'Where would your friend be now?'

Josh took a moment to think. 'I unlocked a Porsche for him on the second floor, but I left first. He must've had problems getting out. He was a couple of minutes behind me at the start.'

'Second floor, ten minutes,' said Sim, doing some quick calculations in his head. 'Okay, got it. Everyone hold on.'

They grabbed each other instinctively and shifted up to the second floor.

Josh spotted Gossy's mop of sandy hair through the window of the Porsche. He held his breath and watched the head of his friend bob around as he adjusted the seat — a car alarm was going off somewhere nearby.

'Is that him?' asked Sim.

'Yeah,' confirmed Josh. 'He always used to have trouble with the seat controls — legs were too short.'

'How are you planning to stop him?' asked Lyra.

Josh hadn't really considered what he was going to say to Gossy to stop him. It wasn't as if the kid would recognise an older version of his best friend, and telling him that he was from the future and that he was trying to save his life wasn't going to fly either.

'We could just lock him in the boot,' suggested Sim.

'No,' whispered Phileas, 'he needs to —'

Lyra made a strange kind of whimpering noise, and everyone looked around.

'Dalton is searching for you. He's close,' she said, holding up a lensing prism and rubbing her temple.

'We need to split up,' declared Phileas. 'Sim you stay with Josh. Lyra and I will create a diversion.'

'How?' asked Josh.

'Give me your tachyon. Dalton is probably using it to track you.'

Josh didn't like the idea of handing it over. He hesitated before giving it to Phileas.

'It's okay. You still have Sim. He can pull you both out of a crisis. Just make sure your friend survives.'

Lyra and Phileas disappeared into thin air.

'What are we going to do now?' Sim asked.

'I have an idea, but it means I have to do something illegal.'

'Great!' said Sim with a wide beaming grin. 'I've always wanted to do something bad.'

59

GOSSY

They were driving fast, trying to stay in sight of the tail lights of Gossy's Porsche.

Sim's knuckles were white where he gripped the seatbelt, and he kept making small frightened noises whenever Josh got too close to the car in front.

'Better than Xbox?' shouted Josh with a hint of sarcasm.

'Yeah,' Sim groaned through gritted teeth.

Gossy was pulling away from them. Josh had forgotten how good a driver he was. In his rearview mirror he could see his younger-self coming up on the inside lane. Weaving between the slower moving cars like a pro.

Josh had to stop himself from getting carried away. The car he and Sim had broken into was a late model Mazda MX5, and it had some serious power. His plan was to stop the accident by getting between the two cars at the right moment, but both of them were driving so recklessly that it was proving difficult not to cause an accident of his own.

Sim checked his watch. 'Two minutes, fifteen seconds,' he said nervously.

Reading the road ahead, Josh could sense an opportunity, and he pushed the accelerator to the floor. A car moved across to the middle lane as they came up the outside, allowing them to draw level with Gossy. Josh looked over to him. The twelve-year-old was staring straight ahead, his face set in deep concentration as he focused on his next move. Josh could remember the way the two of them had argued about who took which car — Gossy almost always went for the silver ones. He thought he was James Bond.

'One-minute-forty.' Sim's time check brought Josh back to reality.

His other self was only two cars back and gaining on them. Josh let Gossy move ahead and then slipped into his wake.

'I'm going to try and sit between them,' he shouted to Sim over the roar of the engine.

'Okay. Forty-five seconds.'

'Count me down from ten.'

He thought back to the way that Gossy had tried to block his attempts to overtake, playing through the memory of those last few seconds. He saw the cars and the lorries beginning to move into their final positions.

'Ten ... nine ...

Josh felt the ABS kick in as he braked hard to avoid a mini that pulled out unexpectedly. That hadn't happened last time. He felt the sweat begin to bead on his forehead.

'Eight ... seven ... six ...'

There was less than a metre between him and the back of Gossy's Porsche. Josh could see the approaching traffic through the windscreen of his friend's car. He saw Gossy look back in the rearview mirror and his hand come away from the wheel to flip Josh the bird.

'Four ... three ... two ...'

Josh pulled back into the middle lane, leaving a gap for his younger self.

'Hold on,' he screamed, spinning the steering wheel and braking hard. The rear of the vehicle kicked round, but he controlled it, counter-steering until he had the car sideways across two of the lanes.

The Subaru ploughed straight into them. He watched his younger self disappear under the airbag as it deployed and felt the judder of their collision run up his spine. An adolescent version of Lenin bounced in the passenger seat next to him, held back by the seat belt. As he'd planned, the front of their car buried itself into the back door of the Mazda, which crumpled as it absorbed the impact.

Josh looked to his right to see Gossy's car slipping ahead through the traffic.

'Now,' said Josh as the smell of fuel leaked into the car. Sim gripped his hand and activated his tachyon.

They reappeared amongst a stand of trees on a hill overlooking the scene of the accident.

The Mazda was on fire, and there were people running around with phones trying to get everyone away from the danger. Josh couldn't see any movement in the car with Lenin and his younger self, and there were no signs of the emergency services. Two brave men were trying to open the doors but they were having trouble getting anywhere near it.

'Did your calculations predict this?' asked Josh. 'What happens if I die?'

'You won't,' Sim replied confidently. 'Don't you remember what happened?'

'No — wait, what's he doing here?'

A familiar figure in a military greatcoat appeared from behind a truck and starting yelling at them to back off. The colonel marched up to the car and wrenched open the door.

Josh watched in amazement as the old man pulled both himself and then Lenin out of the car, and dragged them over to the side of the road.

'So Lenin didn't pull me out of the car?' Josh said under his breath.

'No, and Gossy survived. See?'

Josh could just make out the silver Porsche heading south, oblivious to what had happened behind him.

'Do you feel any different?'

'Nope,' replied Josh. 'Why? Should I?'

'No reason. It was just a pet theory of mine. Do you still remember what it was like to lose your friend?'

'I didn't lose him, he drove off and left me to die — selfish bastard.'

'So no memories of him dying?'

'What are you talking about? You saw for yourself he just took off.'

Sim made some notes in his book.

'Okay. Well, we'd better get a move on before Rufius sees us.'

60

BAD ODDS

'So did it work?' Caitlin enquired the moment Sim appeared in her room.

'Yes, and no. He has no memory of his friend's death, but for some reason Lenin is still holding his mother to ransom. He's not happy.'

Caitlin closed her eyes and chewed on her lip, something she only did when she was deep in thought.

'I'd hoped it would have fixed the mother issue too.'

'Too many variables. You know it's always difficult to predict emotional outcomes.'

'So there is no escaping the showdown?'

'It's plus ninety-five now,' Sim said, consulting his notes.

'Bugger.'

'Have Lyra and Phil returned yet?'

She nodded. 'Dalton didn't take too kindly to their little diversion. His mother's actually had them arrested,' she muttered, her eyes still shut.

Sim laughed. 'I wish I could have seen his face. When did they take him?'

'Oh, they dragged him around the seventh for a day and

then back to the second. You know how much he hates that particular millennia.'

She opened her eyes.

'Where is Josh now?'

'Safehouse in 11.884. I can't believe Ravana has actually locked them up!'

'Currently under investigation,' she said with air quotes.

'Wait until Methuselah gets to hear of it. He's going to crucify them.'

'I doubt it. She's getting more powerful within the Council and Dalton says she's destined for greatness, or so he keeps telling himself.'

'What did they ask you?'

'You know, the usual stuff. When had I been and where, but they already knew everything. The Copernicans had given Dalton a log of my movements for the last three months. It makes for quite interesting reading when you see it written down.'

'Josh has had quite an effect on us,' Sim agreed. 'Do you really think he is the one? Lyra has convinced herself.'

Caitlin's voice changed, becoming more serious. 'You have to keep him safe, Sim. Just for a bit longer.'

'I know. I'm trying, but he's so —'

'Impulsive?' she interrupted.

'I was going to say unpredictable, but impulsive is better — he just doesn't play by any of the rules. It's really hard to calculate his next move.'

'I know,' she said thoughtfully. 'Did you check the safe house for weapons before you left him?'

'No. Why?'

'Because he's angry and wants to take it out on Lenin. In their culture, that always tends towards violence. What do your latest calculations predict? I assume you have a scenario running at the moment.'

'Of course,' Sim replied with a wink as he opened his almanac — 'Shit!'

'What?' she asked, taking the book out of his hands.

'He's got hold of two Colt 45s and jumped to the meeting place.'

'Where?'

'Somewhere local.' He took the book back. 'Their old primary school. It seems to hold some special significance to the relationship between him and Lenin.'

'I'm coming with you.' She walked over to her wardrobe and took out a black coat and Samurai sword.

Sim shook his head. 'You can't, Cat.'

'Why the hell not?'

He held up the page of his book. Lines and symbols danced around her name. 'Because there is a fifty-four-point-six per cent chance you're going to get shot.'

'I've had worse odds,' she said, putting on her coat. 'Now lend me your tachyon and go back to Copernican Hall and re-run the numbers.'

61

HIDING GUNS

[London, UK. Date: 12.007-08-22]

Josh appeared in the middle of the old playground between the twisted climbing frames and broken seesaws. It was a sad sight: chains rusted slowly on swings with no seats, brambles flourished in the sand pit and the roundabout had completely rotted away.

He'd gone back to the night before the meeting with Lenin so that he could get his bearings, remind himself of the layout of the place and stash something somewhere for insurance.

He was wearing a long leather overcoat that he'd found in the safe house. It reminded him of the guy out of the Matrix and was also especially useful for hiding weapons. The Victorians really knew how to make a coat: it was waterproof and warm, which was comforting at five o'clock in the morning when the sky was full of dirty grey clouds chucking rain down on your head.

Inside the coat he could feel the weight of the two pistols

pressing against his rib cage. They were hard, awkward shapes that felt cold against his body.

The school building was in a bad way. It'd been closed down a few years ago and the 60s pre-fab construction hadn't stood up to the rigours of bad weather and vandals. The smashed windows and barricaded doors looked more like a scene from some zombie-apocalypse movie — broken glass and old bits of classroom furniture were scattered in front of the entrance, and grass and weeds had burst through the pavement as nature reclaimed its own.

The text from Lenin contained one important word: 'Pirates,' and it was all that he needed. There was only one place that meant anything and that was here, at their old primary school, where he and Lenin, or Richard as he was known then, had spent a few blissfully innocent years before everything had got serious. The school was the first and last part of his childhood: before his mum got ill, before he started stealing cars — when he still believed in Santa Claus and the Tooth Fairy, and his friends didn't stab each other over a disagreement.

Pirates was a game they used to play in the gym. It was one of his only happy memories of school. His gym teacher, Mr Morgan, was a typical man's man — an ex-rugby player who took no shit but didn't dole it out either. He had retrained as a geography teacher and worked in a private school until he got ill and had to take a career break, returning as a primary teacher two years later. It was strange that the only contribution Mr Morgan had made to Josh's life was one afternoon a week in which he got to play the best game ever invented.

It was a simple game, the best ones always were. They would put out all the gym equipment including ropes, bars, mats, benches, a whole array of equipment to jump and climb upon, and then with everybody taking their places Mr Morgan would blow his whistle, and the mayhem would begin.

No one could touch the floor, for it was the sea, of course, and full of sharks. One kid would be the pirate — usually this fell to Lenin, who even then wanted to take control, and he would recruit his crew by chasing them across the equipment and tagging them. Once on his team, they would go off recruiting on their own, and so on until everyone had either fallen into the sea or joined up. It was Spiderman, X-men, Batman and a dozen other things rolled up into one perfect afternoon.

That was until Mr Morgan's cancer returned and he had to take sick leave. Josh had cried at the assembly when they said goodbye. He was probably the closest thing he would ever get to a father figure. There were no more Pirate games after that, and they left the school a year later.

As Josh entered the building he had a flashback of his first day — it all seemed so big and scary back then. His mum had walked him to the gate and waited there as he disappeared inside. He'd watched her from the classroom. She'd stayed at the gate for hours in case he came back out, but he never did — by lunchtime, she was gone and he was busy kicking a ball around the playground with Billy and Shags.

He felt like a giant as he walked down the corridor to the main hall. In his day it had doubled up as the gym and had been the arena for their game. Everything around him seemed to have been designed for midgets. The coat pegs, noticeboards and what was left of the cupboards were all built at a metre high. Even the chairs looked like something out of a doll's house.

The walls were covered in the tags of the various gangs. Every budding graffiti artist came here to practice. Josh was not sure the old headmistress, Mrs Bowler, would have approved, but it did bring a certain street-cred to the place that his art teacher, Mr O'Connell, might have liked.

Water was dripping into pools from the ceiling where the flat roof had perished. The front of the school was a single-storey building and he had found his way up on to its black-tarred surface many times, hunting for numerous balls that had been accidentally kicked up there.

It was a ruin now, and he resented Lenin for bringing him back here. Knowing him, it was probably some kind of intentional psycho-bullshit that was intended to put Josh off his guard, but Josh had the luxury of time. He could deal with his ghosts and reminisce all he wanted — tomorrow was as far away as he needed it to be.

The gym/hall was a larger, two-storey extension at the back of the school. It was in a better state than the front of the building, probably because not everyone could be bothered to walk all the way down. There were a few gang tags sprayed across the walls and the scattered remnants of enough booze and nitrous oxide canisters to suggest there had been some kind of party here recently.

Every one of the windows in the hall had been broken, but somehow the roof had remained intact. Birds had nested in parts of the ceiling and what was left of the climbing bars; the stench of their droppings was overpowering.

Josh sat down on one of the old benches, its varnish scored with hundreds of initials of forgotten pupils. He felt the history reaching out to him, surfacing moments of his younger self bundling over the vaulting horse — of his friends screaming with delight as they chased him across the equipment. He longed to go back there and relive those moments, but he knew he couldn't focus on the past now; nothing was going to change the fact that he had to deal with Lenin once and for all.

Caitlin had told him that there were certain events that just had to happen, that no amount of changing the past seem to make any difference — this was going to be one of those moments, this was a cornerstone.

He wished she could be there. She would have been a good wingman for what was to come. Josh had been impressed with her skills on the ship — Cat had obviously seen more than her fair share of action, but Josh knew he had to do this alone, he couldn't ask anyone else to fight his battles.

He took one of the guns out and aimed along its sight to where he knew Lenin would be standing the next day. On the raised stage at the other end of the hall, exactly where the old headmistress used to witter on about the three Rs: 'Respect, Responsibility and Reflection,' something that no eight-year-old with dyslexia and undiagnosed ADHD had any interest in whatsoever.

Josh had been an anathema to most of the teachers. They automatically assumed he was just another 'disruptive influence', but he wasn't stupid — he was just bored. His grades were hampered by his reading and he fell behind target, finding himself consigned to a class full of misfits and rejects — he had no choice but to adapt to his environment.

Looking back, it was easy to see how his life had got messed up: the bad breaks, false promises and injustices that he'd experienced as both the system and his own choices let him down. He refused to hold his mother responsible for any of it, even though she blamed herself for everything: if they had been born in a different part of town;

if she'd helped him with his reading; if he'd had a father; if she had never got ill... there were too many ifs when you looked at your life that way. That was how Sim saw everything — a series of events that led to where you were now. Josh didn't want his life to be about probabilities and causalities; he wanted to be in control. He wanted to choose his own destiny. If travelling through time could never fix his mother's MS, or his dyslexia, then all he could do was use it to ensure that he made the best future for the both of them.

He pulled the second pistol out. It made him feel like a cowboy — a six-shooter in each hand. The guns had histories of their own. He could sense their past moving under the surface of their carved wooden handles. They'd been halfway round the world: carried by an officer of the 7th Cavalry at the Battle of the Little Bighorn; by a British soldier fighting the Zulu in Africa, and had even murdered a Russian politician on the Trans-Siberian Express.

He got up and walked over to the half-destroyed school piano and slid one of the guns underneath it. This would be his primary back-up tomorrow if anything kicked off.

The piano had been a fixture of the hall for as long as Josh could remember. Every morning Mrs Larkley had banged out 'All things bright and beautiful' on it, trying desperately to hide the tremors from her alcoholism as she played. He closed his eyes and let the history of the instrument unwind around him. He watched the panorama of events expand until he found a point close to the last game of 'Pirates' they'd ever played and moved into it.

. . .

Standing on the stage surrounded by gym equipment, Josh lost himself in the scent of sweat-stained crashmats and rubber-scuffed, waxed floors, then pulled out the tachyon, rotated the dial to bookmark this timepoint and threw the remaining pistol up into the air.

The gun spun slowly, end-over-end, up into the air as he tapped the watch and jumped back to the present.

62

MEETING

I t was close to midnight when he reappeared, the rain had stopped, and the sky above the school was clear and full of stars.

He could tell by the cars parked outside that Lenin had already arrived, and that he'd brought reinforcements. Josh was going to be heavily outnumbered. He didn't care — he wasn't going to be hanging around to get shot — he had a plan.

Josh stayed out of sight and crept quietly around the grounds of the school. Lenin had posted armed guards at every entrance. It reminded Josh of the time he and the colonel were scoping out the Wolf's Lair back in 1944; standing in the cold watching the Nazis seemed like so long ago now. He missed the old man and his crazy ways.

There was a noise from the bushes behind him, and a slight rush of statically charged air that signalled someone actualising nearby. Josh moved back into the shadows and waited to see who appeared.

It was Caitlin.

'What the hell are you doing here?' he whispered hoarsely to her.

She looked a little surprised, but it was quickly replaced with anger.

'Trying to stop you doing something stupid,' she spat back at him.

'This is my fight. Not yours. I don't go messing around in your life trying to put it right, do I?'

She looked a little taken aback.

'I wouldn't have to,' she said defiantly, 'if you weren't about to screw it all up.'

'It's mine to screw up! Who gave you the right to say what I do with it?'

Caitlin was about to reply when Sim appeared. He was wearing some kind of dark armour under his cloak — he looked like something out of a video game.

'Dalton is tracking us. According to my calculations, you're going to need some back-up. You can't go up against all of them on your own.'

'They have weapons — Uzis,' Josh warned.

'We know,' Caitlin said, producing her sword.

'What did you bring with you?' Josh asked Sim.

Sim opened up his coat to reveal an impressive array of fighting stars and just about everything else you could buy from a martial arts catalogue.

'So you're going to go all ninja on their ass?' Josh said with a laugh. 'Against automatic weapons.'

'You got a better plan?' asked Caitlin sarcastically.

'As it happens, I do.'

'Good. Well, let's hear it, then!'

Lenin had assured the professor that he knew the perfect place for a meeting. Fermi had his doubts, until he checked the plans of the old school and found it did indeed have everything he required. There was a basement that ran the length of the hall, where he could install his monitoring equipment out of sight in a matter of hours.

Fermi sat in what had once been the boiler room and checked his laptop: all the readings were stable. He could take a baseline of the gravitational background and then sit back and wait for the show to begin.

He took out the old watch once more and stroked its finely engraved surface with his thumb. There was something deeply satisfying about such a well-made piece; its construction exuded craftsmanship, a level of mastery he'd hardly ever seen. Fermi felt like a Victorian explorer studying an artefact from a lost civilisation — the symbols and glyphs around its intricate dials made no sense to him. It was a mystery wrapped in an enigma.

There was a subtle but highly localised distortion field surrounding the metal casement. He could feel the shifting waves when he ran his finger over it, as though he wasn't actually touching the surface but a micrometre above it. This really was a quantum device, he thought to himself. It was in a state of permanent flux: both here and not here at the same time — it was Schrödinger's watch.

Fermi couldn't imagine how the secrets of this device were in the hands of some itinerant car-thief, an opportunist who had stolen something he couldn't comprehend. Nevertheless, the frustration would soon be over, he told himself. Josh's need to rescue his mother would soon resolve the situation. Fermi's men would take him and with the appropriate amount of persuasion he would have the details of the original owner. Then the thief could be on his way, or at least be released into Lenin's care, whatever that entailed.

The boy's mother was recovering well under the ministrations of the private hospital; if all went to plan tonight, there should be no reason why she wouldn't live a long and healthy life — whatever that was for a woman of her age and condition. He wasn't sure he could say the same for her son.

There was an odd burst of static on the walkie-talkie, which coincided with a strange spike on his monitoring screens.

'Three bodies just appeared on the thermal. EchoSix,' a military voice crackled over the radio, 'walking south. Appeared out of nowhere. Over.'

Fermi felt a tremor of excitement as he put on his glasses and sat down next to the laptop.

'Bring the cameras online. I want everything recorded.'

'Copy that.'

A series of grainy images flashed onto the grid of monitors behind the laptop. The night-vision cameras capturing a trace of the group moving through the grounds of the school. They were painted in eerie hues of green. Their faces were obscured. Only the glowing points of light in their eyes gave him any hint that they were even human.

The fact that there were three of them disturbed Fermi — Lenin had told him that Jones would come alone, that he had no friends who'd have the balls to stand beside him in a fight. Fermi didn't like surprises. Hypotheses needed to factor all the variables.

'Scan every sector. Secure the perimeter!' the professor barked into the radio.

63

SHOWDOWN

Josh walked into the crowded hall with his head held high, looking into the eyes of each member of the ghost squad as he passed them. Caitlin and Sim shadowed him, their weapons still hidden beneath their long coats. By Josh's estimation, Lenin had brought everybody to the party, and every single one of them was armed. He could tell from the way they wouldn't meet his gaze that they were nervous, waiting for him to make the first move. Most of them had never fired a gun, except in video games. That could work to his advantage if he played it right, or it could end up with them all getting shot.

Gossy was standing in the middle of the room. His hands were empty, but Josh could see from the bulge in his coat that he was packing. They nodded to each other and Josh thought for a second he saw a glimmer of concern in his friend's face — Lenin obviously didn't have everybody's total allegiance.

Lenin sat on a makeshift throne they had built out of a couple of old crates on the stage. He was smoking a joint and tapping his feet to the beat of something loud and bassy playing on the PA system sitting next to him. He put his hand into his jacket and pulled a microphone.

'Ladies and gentleman, give it up, give it up — Crashman is in da house,' he rapped in perfect time to the beat. There were various hoots and chants from the crowd closing in around them. Josh could feel Caitlin's eyes burning into the back of his head.

'So,' Lenin took another drag on his spliff, 'do you have what I asked for?'

'Do you?' Josh replied, his voice sounded meek in comparison to the PA.

Lenin smiled and waved the mic at someone in the corner, who in turn tapped on a door and opened it.

Josh felt his resolve drain away as he saw the feeble figure of his mother appear through the doorway in a wheelchair. Her head was lolling to one side as if she were heavily sedated. He heard Caitlin gasp and felt the anger rise like a red wave. It engulfed him. He felt every sinew tense as a lifetime of domination under Lenin burst like a putrid ulcer.

Caitlin put her hand in his and squeezed it.

'Well, looks like Josh brought his girlfriend,' teased Lenin. 'When this is over, darling, we're going to party, yeah?' he added with a lecherous wink.

Josh squeezed back as if to say it was going to be OK.

They wheeled his mother on to the stage next to Lenin. She was dressed in a surgical gown with a threadbare blanket thrown over her legs. Josh could see there was still a cannula in her arm where there should've been an IV drip attached.

'So, Josh man, where's the cash?'

Josh placed a small Gladstone bag on the floor in front of him. It was one of the colonel's, like the one from the

Fenian bombing. They'd stuffed the bag full of old notes — Caitlin had gone to a 'collector' who wouldn't mind loaning them a few thousand.

'The interesting thing about loose notes is that they always looks a lot more than there really is,' she'd said handing him the bag. She'd liked parts of his plan, but had had some suggestions of her own. Before he could argue, she was back with the cash. Josh had to laugh at the idea of someone who 'collected' cash — in any other situation they would have been called 'rich' or 'loaded', but in Caitlin's world they were simply a curator of currency. He made a mental note to ask her more about that particular division of the Order later.

'Bring him,' barked Lenin.

Gossy went down and picked up the bag, holding it up to feel the weight. Josh could tell from his expression that he was impressed. The Victorian case looked odd in Gossy's hands, out of place next to his ripped jeans. Josh felt hands grab his arms and push him towards the front.

Lenin threw away the joint and opened the bag. He smiled at what he saw inside and began to pull notes out and throw them at his crew, who immediately forgot themselves and began scrabbling around on the floor for the fluttering notes.

'The power of money,' said Lenin smugly. He pulled out another fistful and flung it into Josh's face. 'You sure it's all here, Joshy?'

Josh stood directly below him, trying to look unimpressed. He was slowly counting down the seconds in his head.

Lenin nodded to Gossy and dropped the bag.

'Sorry, Crash. You did fine, but there's a man who pays better.'

The members of the Ghost Squad were busy chasing notes and squabbling over who should have the bigger share when another crew arrived. These were mean-looking men, mercenaries, ex-military types with hard eyes and crew cuts.

Josh leapt on to the stage as Lenin pulled a gun.

'Don't —' was all Lenin managed to say before Josh grabbed him and hit the button on the tachyon. They both disappeared from the stage.

Lenin and Josh appeared in the empty hall seven years earlier. The equipment laid out ready for a new game. Josh looked up and caught the gun he had thrown earlier as it came down.

They stood, silently pointing guns at each other. Lenin was naked except for his tattoos, Josh was shocked at how emaciated he'd become. His ribs were showing and the track marks on his arms were raised and sore. Lenin's eyes flicked nervously around the room looking for any sign of his crew, trying to process where and when he was.

'Put it down, Len. It's just between us now.'

Lenin's hand was shaking a little, and his fingers flexed on the handle of the gun as if to get a better grip.

'How the —'

'Shoot me and you'll never get back.'

'How about I shoot you anyway and work that out later?'

'No. You're not giving the orders any more. You aren't the boss of me,' growled Josh pointing his gun at Lenin's chest.

'Whoa, suddenly someone grew a pair!'

'Just telling it like it is.'

'Go on, then,' Lenin said, lowering his weapon and opening his arms out. 'Let's see if you've really got the balls.'

Josh stood his ground. The barrel of the gun didn't waiver.

'You're a pussy, Josh, always have been. Just remember who pulled you out of the car.'

Josh thought of all the times he'd heard this from Lenin, the debt of which he'd been reminded of so many times. He knew now it had all been a lie — their entire relationship for the last five years had been based on that one day, the day he'd nearly died, when the colonel had pulled them both out of the car and Lenin had taken the credit.

'You didn't save me, though, did you, Len?'

Lenin's eyes narrowed, and Josh caught the slightest flicker of guilt.

'You saying I didn't? You were totally out of it — I should have left you there to burn.'

'No,' said Josh, 'you see I went back — that's what I do now. I saw what happened. I saw the guy who pulled us both out of the car when everyone else stood back and watched.'

'Bullshit. You're seconds away from being a dead man,' threatened Lenin, bringing the gun back up.

Josh couldn't hold back any more. 'You made me think you saved my life! What kind of friend does that? Acting like you owned me. Like I owed you — and I believed you, feeling like it was all my fault! I would have gone on believing you until I found out I could do this,' he said, waving the gun at the gym. 'I went back there, I saw what happened and now this is all I need to totally screw up your life. Whereas this,' he said, waving the gun, 'doesn't solve anything.' He put the gun away and stepped closer to Lenin once more.

He held the tachyon in Lenin's face. 'Watch.'

Josh pressed the rewind, and they both disappeared.

Caitlin and Sim were holding their own against the rest of the room. In the chaos, the Ghost Squad had turned on the mercenaries, and it was hard to see who was winning.

She had done her best not to maim or injure anyone too badly. The weapons that she and Sim were using were deadly: but could be used to incapacitate an opponent rather than kill them. The Ghost Squad were easier targets than the mercenaries who were all skilled in hand-to-hand combat.

Josh reappeared with Lenin a few seconds after he'd left. Gossy couldn't quite work out what was going on, but Lenin was naked and still holding a gun, which was weird and dangerous, to say the least.

Josh went to his mother while Lenin blinked and looked around as if he'd just woken up. His nakedness went unnoticed in the chaos.

Gossy took a long look at the carnage unfolding around them: bullets, swords and blood were flying in all directions. His gaze met Lenin's and seemed to come to the same conclusion. He picked up the bag of money. It was time to get the hell out of there.

Lenin looked over at Josh and raised his gun. Gossy shouted a warning as he fired. Josh turned at the sound, causing the bullet to miss him and it hit his mother instead.

A red stain flowered on her surgical gown just below the shoulder. Josh screamed at Lenin and turned on him his eyes burning with tears.

'You —'

Lenin's eyes were wild as he raised the gun again.

'Josh!' shouted Caitlin from the middle of the fracas. 'Rewind!'

Somehow he heard her voice through the noise of the battle and remembered the tachyon. He closed his hand over it and went back two minutes.

[<<]

The hall reset, and he was back in front of Lenin. As before, Lenin nodded to Gossy and dropped the bag.

'Sorry, Crash, you did fine, but the man pays better.'

This time, Josh dived to the piano and grabbed the gun from its hiding place. As he rolled and brought the weapon up to fire, he saw Caitlin running across the room towards him. Lenin was raising his gun and Josh knew he would only have one chance to stop him. He fired and felt the pistol's recoil kick back into his arm. The bullet hit Lenin in the leg, knocked him off balance and he fired wide.

Josh saw Caitlin fall. At first, he thought she'd tripped, but when he got closer he saw the blood on her neck and knew where Lenin's bullet had gone.

He hit the rewind again.

[<<]

'Sorry, Crash. You did fine, but the man pays better.'

He had less than ten seconds to make a choice. This

time, he jumped straight at Lenin before he could pull the gun, before the military burst in.

He was about the same size as Lenin and knew that he could take him in a fair fight, but Lenin never did anything fairly, and as Josh took him down he felt a cold, sharp pain in his side — Lenin had stabbed him.

Gossy was shouting at Lenin as Josh rolled over on his side and saw the wound, it was not deep, but the blood was pouring out of it. He pressed a hand to the cut and raised himself up on one arm.

Lenin was staring at him, the knife in one hand and the gun in the other.

'I told him you'd be easy,' Lenin shouted. 'You were supposed to be a pussy! Now I'm going to have to end you.' He raised the gun to take aim.

Gossy came up behind Lenin and began to wrestle with him for the gun. Lenin dropped the knife and used his free hand to punch Gossy, but he wouldn't let go, and they bundled across the stage.

Josh got to his feet and picked up the knife. It was a small hunting knife. He remembered Lenin bragging about how many people he'd cut with it. The blade was too short to be fatal. Lenin had never been a killer — a sadist and an egomaniac, yes, but never a killer.

The sound of the gun going off brought Josh's head up. He saw Gossy had the gun. At first he thought he'd shot Lenin, then Gossy's legs crumpled, and he collapsed on to his knees. Lenin was injured too, but Gossy had a dark red stain on his back that was spreading fast.

Josh crawled over to Gossy, the pain throbbing in his side. His friend was still holding the gun, but his eyes were glazing over.

'Hey, Joshman,' he said weakly. 'You OK?'

'Yeah. Just a scratch,' Josh whispered as he tried not to look at the hole in the front of Gossy's chest. He managed to push himself upright.

'Couldn't let him take out my wingman.' Gossy tried to laugh, but the pain made him cough. There were bubbles of blood in his mouth. He fell forward on to Josh.

Josh held him, trying to think of what he could say. Lenin lay on his side, not moving, and the others hadn't noticed he was down. He felt the weak panting of Gossy's breath against his chest as his life slipped away. His blood was all over Josh's hands. Somewhere in the background noise he heard Caitlin shouting a warning to him as he studied them — he ignored her as his friend's lifeline spread out before him.

Just like the colonel's, Gossy's timeline was an elaborate web of interconnecting events and emotions. He could see and feel every experience that his friend had ever had — his life laid bare — not just crystallised points in time, but snapshots of his consciousness. It was hard to resist. There were so many emotions bombarding him as he immersed himself in Gossy's history.

There were good times and bad: Josh experienced the elation of his friend's first skateboard, the pain of the break-up of his parents, the kiss of Marie Withershall — all the little formative moments that went into making him who he was.

Then he came to the crash. There was something strange about the way the lines of time coalesced around the accident. Josh could see other fainter lines ghosting around the node as though it had been repaired. He could see that there were other ways, other paths that Gossy's life could have taken, and he couldn't help but explore them.

It was an odd sensation, as if he were looking down from

the top of an enormous skyscraper. He could see the many different lines stretching out from the day of the crash — some much longer than others. He saw how Gossy's life could have simply ended that day, whilst in others he lived — there was even one with a wife and kids. None of them ended in old age. There was something wrong with his heart, a biological time bomb waiting in his future. Josh knew then that Gossy was never meant to make 'old bones'. Nothing was ever going to change that. Was it better to live a short and happy life or a long and painful one? Josh couldn't make that choice. Gossy had chosen for him.

In the distance, the darkness was approaching, a numbing void that consumed the timeline as everything was drawn to it. Josh was still deeply embedded, unable to extract himself. The lines around him were burning out to nothing like sparklers on bonfire night.

He stared into the abyss, captivated by the hypnotic patterns of dying futures that coalesced along its edge. As he studied the emptiness that raced towards him, he was sure he could feel something inside the blackness: a malevolent presence watching him silently from the other side. This was what reavers like Lyra found so addictive, he thought. Why they risked everything to get close to death — they wanted to know what was beyond the veil.

He remembered Lyra's beautiful skin and the scars that she had carved into it, her lingering kiss in the deep waters of the baths and then something she'd said — a word, or more like an idea.

A remembering — a way back.

Gossy had stopped breathing, and his eyes were closed. Josh looked up and found Caitlin and Sim standing over him with weapons drawn and a look of shock on their faces. Around them everything had stopped. It was as though time had been paused. No one was moving; they were like a photograph of a moment.

From between the frozen fighters walked a set of dark figures in long sweeping robes, their faces obscured by masks. As they approached, Josh could see their insignia, the clock with no hands — the symbol of the Protectorate. They were searching everyone in the hall, using something in their gloves to scan them. When they reached Josh, their leader made a silent sign to the others.

Josh was sure he saw Phileas and Lyra at the back of the squad, but he had no time to wonder why before the officer's gloved hand touched his temple and the world vanished.

64

LENIN RECOVERED

Professor Fermi found Lenin lying on his side. The other members of his gang had fled — their loyalty dissolved at the apparent demise of their leader.

There was another body nearby, still holding the gun. Fermi knelt down beside the boy and checked for a pulse, but found nothing. He could hear Lenin's laboured breathing and went over to him. He was badly injured, the gunshot wound in his lower abdomen slick with dark blood.

'Can you hear me?' Fermi whispered into Lenin's ear.

Lenin grunted in response.

'You are going to die unless I call for help, but before I do you are going to tell me what happened.'

Lenin's eyes opened slightly, and he swore through gritted teeth.

'We had a deal. You were supposed to deliver me the boy, remember? Now tell me!' the professor demanded.

Lenin groaned, and through gasps of pain he told the professor what he could remember.

The professor pulled out his phone.

'Get the medics in here stat,' he ordered. The words

appeared on the screen followed by 'encrypting' and then 'delivered' underneath it.

He swiped the app away and pulled up the data that his monitors had captured. A series of graphs appeared, overlaid on a video feed of the hall. He sped through the first twenty minutes of the steady sinusoidal shape of usual background gravitational waves until he found the three-minute burst of activity. There was a cluster of lines overlapping each other, like a series of echoes. Each line registered a set of changes except one that started erratically and then went flat for over a minute — either one of his sensors was faulty, or someone had literally stopped time.

The medics arrived and went to work on Lenin. They turned him over on to his back and began to work on his injuries. One gave him CPR while the other unpacked the mobile defibrillator and switched on the charger.

'Wait!' said Fermi, as they tore his T-shirt open to place the paddles on his chest.

Fermi stood over them and held out his hand. 'His watch, if you please.'

The medic stopped his compressions, unstrapped Lenin's watch from his wrist and handed it to the professor.

'Now let's see if my theory was correct.'

He'd given the digital watch to Lenin before the meeting. It had been synchronised to the nanosecond with his own. He compared the two and as the screens lit up in the harsh red glow of their LEDs he smiled — there was a difference of 0.0000000022 seconds.

Lenin had travelled in time.

65

AWAKENING

[Bethlem Hospital, London. Date: 11.666]

J osh woke gradually, the sounds of the room seeping into his dream until he surfaced into consciousness.

'Josh?' whispered Caitlin. 'Are you awake?'

'I am now,' he replied sleepily.

She was close by, but not in the bed. He felt her weight shift the mattress as she sat down beside him.

When he opened his eyes, Josh realised he had no idea where he was.

The room was panelled in dark wood and sparsely furnished with a few chairs and a wardrobe that could comfortably house a small family. There was a real fire burning in the massive fireplace, and a tapestry of some idyllic hunting scene covered one entire wall. Through the door he could hear the muffled screams of the insane.

'We're in Bedlam,' she said in response to his unasked question.

'We're in trouble,' added Sim, who was sitting in a wing-backed chair by the fire.

'Your messing around with time alerted the Coperni-cans. They sent out an entire Protectorate brigade to investigate.'

Josh sat up and absentmindedly scratched at his belly. There was a bandage wrapped round his stomach where Lenin had stabbed him.

'Try not to scratch it,' Caitlin said, inspecting the bind-ings. 'Doctor Crooke says the wound will take another couple of hours to heal properly.'

'What about my mum?' Josh asked as his memory of the events returned.

'She's fine. They've taken her back in time to the neuro ward at Barts. It's like she never left.'

Then Josh remembered that Gossy had died before he could rewind again.

'The Protectorate — did they actually stop time?'

'More like slowed it right down,' Sim muttered. 'The armour they wear has tachyon tech built into it — they call them "stillsuits".'

'I thought I saw Lyra and Phileas.'

'Methuselah insisted they went along as witnesses. They do that when there's going to be an inquest.'

'An inquest?' Josh groaned.

'Oh yes,' she sighed, 'the court of inquiry has already been invoked. Officially we're all under arrest.'

'Thanks to Dalton's mother,' added Sim, swearing and prodding the fire with a metal poker.

Caitlin shook her head. 'I think it's bigger than that. This is political — the Determinists will use this to directly chal-lenge the Founder's authority. They will use every trick in the book.'

'Looks like you're going to meet the man himself,' Sim said to Josh with a smile.

'The Founder?'

'Lord Dee. The founder of the Order.'

'And what's he going to do to me?'

'If you are found guilty, it could mean excision,' Caitlin said quietly.

Josh stared at her blankly.

'They go back and remove you from history. Everything you've ever done, who you were, just disappears as if you were never here.'

'Shit!'

He sat in silence for a while and tried to contemplate what that would be like.

'No matter what I did I couldn't save everyone,' Josh said to Caitlin. 'It was a choice between my mum, you or Gossy. I couldn't see a way to make it end well — and then they turned up.'

'Interdiction,' Sim interjected. 'There are only so many times you can rewind before the Copernicans will pick it up and send the Protectorate to investigate.'

'Something catastrophic must have been about to happen,' Caitlin added glumly.

'I was inside Gossy's timeline when he was dying. I saw something in the darkness.'

'You were reaving?' exclaimed Caitlin. 'I warned you about that!'

'There was a kind of presence, like something was watching me.'

'The dying are in a state of flux. Only very experienced seers are able to deal with the unravelling timeline of the dying. You were lucky you didn't end up scrambling your brain.' Caitlin tapped the side of his head.

'You could have ended up in here for good' said Sim solemnly, pointing at the walls.

'I saw other versions of his life, what it could have been. Is that what Lyra sees when she —'

'It's why most seers end up going crazy, those that didn't start off that way. It's an overload, too many choices, too many possible futures.'

'And they just lock them up in here?'

'It's for their own good,' she said, getting up and walking over to Sim. 'Many reavers get obsessed with the idea that there is something beyond the continuum. They have to be restrained to stop them from killing themselves.'

'Religious nutters,' added Sim. 'They believe they can commune with elder gods.'

Josh thought back to the dark things he had sensed waiting in the void and a shiver ran down his spine.

There was a knock at the door, and Phileas came in. He looked as if he hadn't slept for a week.

'Good, you're awake. The court is ready for you now.'

66

STAR CHAMBER

I t was unlike any courtroom that Josh had ever seen: a vast circular auditorium with tiers of benches, stepped in concentric rings that went up into the dark ceiling hundreds of metres above him. He stood in the centre of a golden, six-pointed star that had been laid in to the chequered marble floor. Round him, sitting behind a raised desk, were the members of the High Council — made up of a single representative from each one of the guilds. Josh studied every one of the six in turn: there were four men and two women, each dressed in the ceremonial robes of their particular guild.

The audience was made up of the most eccentric collection of people, dressed in clothes from their respective periods. It looked like the annual gathering of the costume department of the V&A. Josh had spotted Caitlin and Sim sitting in one of the front rows with Methuselah, the colonel and Eddy. They were all in deep conversation, he assumed about him. Caitlin caught his eye and tried to smile reassuringly, but failed to pull it off and went back to the discussion. The colonel kept pointing at someone as he spoke and when Josh followed the line of his finger he found Dalton and his mother, the chief inquisitor, sitting on the opposite side of the round. Dalton looked very smug. The smile thinned a little as he caught Josh's eye.

The spectacle of a 'Grand Trial' had drawn a large crowd, and the chamber was buzzing with the sound of a hundred different voices all talking at once. Caitlin had warned Josh that these were rare events and would probably pack the house. There were Scriptorians in their dark purple robes and ridiculously thick glasses; Copernicans with their complex abacuses, calculating the probabilities of the outcome while making side bets with the Draconians; Antiquarians sitting awkwardly as far away from others as they could; and a whole host of minor guilds that he had never met.

It was the first time Josh had seen so many of the Order in one place. It was much larger than he'd imagined; Sim had said there was no official census on how many there were, but Josh had always assumed there were more chapters, like the one that Methuselah managed, spread out through time. Seeing everyone brought together in one place somehow made it more real. There were literally thousands of them, a well-organised gang with their own traditions and laws — ones that he had just violated.

A sudden hush swept around the chamber as a hooded figure appeared from the shadows and walked slowly out on to the floor, leaning heavily on a cane, which marked each step with metallic tap.

The whole court stood up in unison.

'Apologies for my tardiness,' the Founder spoke from beneath his cowl. His voice was deep but old and tired. He bowed to the council of six and took his seat on the far side of the circle.

'Proceed.'

So this was the Founder, thought Josh, the man who has the final say over my existence.

Dalton's mother stood up and walked into the circle. Her features were thrown into sharp relief by the harsh light. Like a circling bird of prey, she paced around the marble floor. The gold thread of her lawyer's robes shimmered as she addressed the gathering.

'Founder, honourable members of the council, delegates of the guilds of Copernicus, Scriptoria, Antiquaria, Draconii, men of the watch . . .' Josh tried not to zone out, but the list of names was extensive and apparently a legal requirement.

'. . . we have been assembled on this occasion to hear the case of the Order versus Master Joshua Jones, initiate and lately apprenticed to Rufius Westinghouse. He stands accused of temporal malpractice on three counts: the first, that he did willingly and with malice aforethought, endanger life in going beyond the temporal limitation; that on a second separate occasion did change the continuum without proper authority causing the continuation of war or wars beyond their original course; and, lastly, that he was found to have maliciously altered the outcome of an event to his own personal benefit, requiring the need for an interdiction. He stands before the court for judgment.'

One of the council of six stood up.

'Call the first witness for the defence!'

The colonel stood up and made his way down the steps and on to the floor. Josh could see that he'd attempted to comb his hair and had dressed in his most formal robes, on to which he'd pinned a set of medals.

He came and stood next to Josh without acknowledging him.

'For the record, please state your name,' ordered another of the six.

'Rufius Vainglorious Westinghouse,' the colonel repeated in a flat tone.

'Rank?'

'Guardian of the Twelfth, Master of the Initiates, Seventh brother of the Watch — you know the rest, Paelor Batrass.'

The man who was scribbling furiously on to a large piece of parchment looked up from his notes and waved the quill as if to say: 'carry on' and the colonel sighed and relaxed his shoulders.

'Master Westinghouse,' asked the inquisitor, 'for the records of the court, can you formally identify the accused standing before us today as one Joshua Jones.'

'I can.'

'And can you tell us how you came to meet the accused?'

'He broke into my house.'

There was a collective gasp from the crowd.

'And yet you chose to take him on as your apprentice?' the inquisitor continued.

'I did. He isn't a bad lad, and he showed incredible potential.'

'Yes. I believe you are referring to the second charge, that of changing the outcome of the Second World War.'

'It was an accident. He was not aware of his abilities at that time.'

'So the deaths of a million souls was nothing more than a mere accident.'

'That isn't what I said. The outcome of that particular

war has been hotly debated by many of us.' He turned to the Founder. 'Even my lord has been known to favour this particular scenario over the alternatives.'

There was a muttering from the crowd, mostly over the presumptuousness of declaring the founder's views in open court.

'The opinions of the founder are not under scrutiny here,' the inquisitor reminded him. 'Let us turn to the first charge, that he did endanger life in direct breach of the limitations placed upon him — by removing himself and Miss Makepiece to a time beyond the datum.'

The colonel drew a large breath and let it out slowly. 'I cannot answer for that one. I wasn't in charge of him at that point.'

'No? Then can you call on another to support his defence?'

The colonel turned solemnly towards Caitlin and said: 'I secede the defence to Miss Caitlin Makepiece.'

There was a ripple of whispers as Caitlin stood up and walked out on to the floor. The colonel walked off with his head down and slumped into his seat like a defeated man.

'Ms Makepiece, for the record, please state your name and rank,' Batrass the Scribe said without looking up from his parchment.

'Caitlin Verity Indomitable Makepiece, Scriptorian of the fourteenth,' she spoke clearly and confidently, looking directly at the council.

Ravana Eckhart stepped in front of her. 'Caitlin — may I call you Caitlin? Yes? Good. I believe you were left to tutor the accused. Is that correct?'

'No. He was placed in the care of the House of the Hundred. Methuselah de Freis was charged with his mentorship,' she corrected Dalton's mother, whose arrogance dissolved as Caitlin spoke.

She coughed and rephrased the question. 'How would you describe your relationship with the accused?'

'He's a friend.'

'And yet he endangered both of your lives?'

'There was no real danger.'

'According to the Draconian team that found you —' she made a dramatic point of waving at a stack of papers — 'you had gone back into the Mesolithic, over two thousand years beyond the limitation. Can you explain how that happened?'

'We were testing his range.'

'I believe that the standard tests are usually no more than a millennium? Can you explain how you came to be so far beyond the normal procedure?'

It was evident Caitlin was becoming uncomfortable with the inquisitor's line of questioning. Josh could see her confidence was beginning to evaporate.

'I used an ancient artefact to rescue her from a bad situation,' Josh intervened.

'Silence!' shouted the council in unison.

'The accused will be advised to remain silent until his time,' said the Founder in a monotone.

'Ms Makepiece please continue.'

'We were playing a game, Captain's Table, and we'd gone back to collect something from Vlad Dracul II when we encountered a monad.' She stared directly at Dalton. 'Which I now believe had been released by another team. Josh grabbed the first thing that came to hand and used it to escape. I know it sounds unlikely, but —'

'Indeed it does, Ms Makepiece. I believe that it took forty years before they found you.'

'But, we survived, we raised a family, a tribe in fact — we survived long enough to be located. He was the one that did all of that,' Caitlin shouted as she pointed directly at Josh. 'If it had been down to me, we would be dead in some cave!'

Josh watched her in awe. The passion in her voice set his heart alight. The Draconians had refused to tell him what had happened after they'd rescued them; he knew they must have survived long enough to have been picked up. It was odd to think that in some other timeline they'd been together — part of him was beginning to wish he could have stayed there. It would have been a lot less complicated.

'Thank you, Ms Makepiece. You may step down,' said one of the council.

Caitlin turned and went back to her seat without looking at Josh. He could see there were tears running down her burning cheeks.

'Turning now to the matter of the interdiction,' continued the chief inquisitor, raising her voice above the chatter of the crowd.

'The prosecution calls upon Stochastic Professor Eddington to bear expert witness to this most serious of crimes.'

Professor Eddington rose from his seat and walked slowly out on to the floor.

'Professor, would you please be so kind as to enlighten us to the actions of the accused.'

Eddington looked round the circle at each of the council members and then folded his arms behind his back, cleared his throat and spoke: 'I have studied all aspects of the recent altercation and it is my considered opinion that the accused was in a Nyman Paradox, meaning that his options were so limited that any action would have caused the demise of one, if not more of his party.'

Josh could see that the inquisitor was less than happy with this answer.

'But is it not true to say that the accused abused his powers by taking direct restorative action? Are you condoning the personal motivation behind the outcomes? Were any of them for the greater good of the continuum?'

There were shouts from the gallery of 'No!' and 'Bad judgement!' as the inquisitor appealed to them directly.

Eddington remained calm and spoke quietly. 'Yes, the accused was acting in his own interest, I concur, but the possible outcomes were, as I say, limited.'

'And, further to that point, you confirm he actually chose to allow the death of a boy he'd saved from a terrible end only a few days before?'

Josh looked at Caitlin, who had her head buried in her hands. Alixia was stroking her shoulders. Sim looked grey and ashen.

'I'm sorry, I don't understand the question.'

'Were you not aware that the accused had been involved in changing his own timeline no more than thirty-six hours before the interdiction? A crime that is still being investigated and I believe involves other members of the defence?'

Eddington's eyes narrowed. He was being out-manoeuvred. Josh couldn't understand how the prosecution could know something that a senior member of the Copernicans didn't. That was until he looked back towards Dalton and then it became clear; there was a smug grin plastered across his face. He put his arm round the girl sitting next to him, Josh hardly recognised Elena without all the make-up and piercings. She smiled wickedly at Josh when their eyes met.

'No, I did not,' muttered Eddington, staring at his shoes. 'My department is overworked and understaffed as you well know!'

'Thank you, Professor, that will be all,' said the founder in a tone that was not one to be challenged.

The professor walked slowly back to his seat, his face set in stone.

'The prosecution calls their first and only witness, the accused himself.'

The eyes of the entire chamber fell on Josh. He felt the weight of a thousand accusing stares press down on him and knew that there was no talking his way out of this one. He thought about his mother, how she would be without him in her life. He wondered if she would be happier. Would she still get ill? What kind of life would she have without the pressure of raising a kid on her own? Josh had made her life so difficult, he knew that. He was the one who'd done everything his own way, no matter what the cost to her. She was the one who'd waited patiently every night worrying about whether he was safe — if nothing else, he would save her that pain.

'Joshua Jones, you stand accused on three counts, each of which comes with the severest of sentences. Do you have anything to say in your defence?' the shrill voice of the chief inquisitor echoed around the silent chamber.

As Josh heard the words 'in your defence', it triggered something deep in his memory. A fragment of a forgotten thought awoke in his mind — like a whale surfacing from the depths.

It was from the incident in the baths with Lyra when she'd kissed him, a forgotten moment triggered by those three words. Her voice was inside his head saying: 'When you hear the phrase "in your defence", you reply: "I claim the Rite of Scrying."'

Josh had no idea what the Rite of Scrying was, but he had little choice. He could see from the stern expressions on the faces of the Council that none of the defence witnesses had made an ounce of difference to his case.

'Do you have anything to add?' asked the inquisitor again as if Josh were a little slow.

Josh took a deep breath and said, 'I claim the Rite of Scrying,' as confidently as he could.

There was a collective intake of breath from the audience followed by an outburst of outrage on all sides. The inquisitor lost all the colour from her face and shrank back. The council turned to one another in confusion. Whatever the Rite of Scrying was, Josh liked it just for the uproar it caused.

'Silence!' came the booming voice of the founder. 'The boy has invoked the rite. Call for the Grand Seer.'

Lyra was sitting quietly in the corner of the bench, trying not to look at anyone, when Caitlin came and sat beside her. The court was adjourned while they waited for the seer to arrive, and everyone was busy discussing the accused's unusual request.

'You didn't have anything to do with that, did you, sister?'

'It was his only option, Cat. I looked at all the other ways,' Lyra replied, flicking through her notebook. 'I have them all here somewhere if you want to see?'

'No, Lyra, that's fine, but the rite is a very dangerous route to take. He will see everything.'

'He will see what you see.' Lyra looked directly into her eyes. 'He's a good man, yet there is more to him than you think.'

'More of what exactly?'

Lyra's eyes flashed. 'Wait and see . . .'

· · ·

The colonel walked out to see Josh on the pretence of giving him a glass of water. A couple of court attendants had dragged a dusty old wooden rack into the centre of the floor and were busy trying to remember how to assemble it.

'So this Rite of Scrying, it's not some kind of medieval torture, is it?'

The colonel smiled.

'I did wonder if you knew what it was when you asked for it. Not many have ever heard of it — let alone used it. I think you have confounded the prosecution.' He looked over to Dalton and his mother, who were in the middle of a heated argument. 'What an earth made you choose it?'

'Just something Lyra told me once.'

'Ah. Do you remember talking about it or did it just pop into your head at a certain moment?'

'Just popped in — like I'd forgotten it.'

'Implanted memory. Very smart young seer that Lyra. She apparently thought it was your best chance of escaping this farce.'

'What will they do to me?'

The colonel scratched his beard, mulling over the answer. 'Edward Kelly is the founder's chief scryer, basically a very powerful seer — Lyra is one of his pupils. He's more than a little mad, believes he can commune with angels. Too much reaving, if you ask me.' The colonel waggled his finger near his temple.

'And this rite is going to show him I'm innocent?'

'Oh no. He's going to read your entire timeline from beginning to end. It's a rare talent. Not something many of us have ever seen, to be honest. Although I have read reports that it can be quite uncomfortable for the patient.'

'Shit.'

'Still better than being non-existent.'

'You think? Will everyone else know?'

'No. It's just you and him. At the end, he'll declare you innocent or guilty. It's a pretty medieval approach, as you say.'

The attendants came over and escorted Josh towards the wooden frame.

'So why the need for this?'

'Stop you from hurting yourself — that and he likes his subjects to be inverted.'

'What?' said Josh as they began to strap him in.

'Upside down.'

Edward Kelly was definitely the craziest-looking man Josh had ever encountered.

He walked into the courtroom wearing a long cloak made of dark feathers and a mask that resembled a long crow's beak. He proceeded to strut round the circle drawing a thin line with salt or chalk dust around the outer rim of the star. As Kelly walked, he would randomly jump on to one foot, turn and mutter some strange incantation at an invisible entity and then return to his task. When the circle was complete, he removed the mask and shouted at the top of his voice: '*Transit umbra, lux permanent!*' and then began mumbling some incoherent gibberish as he removed his gloves and feather cloak to reveal a sombre suit of dark velvet.

The attendants cranked the wheel and rotated Josh a hundred and eighty degrees until his head was level with the table that Kelly had placed before him. A large glass sphere was put between them so that Josh could only see a distorted view of the scryer's face. His eyes were entirely black.

'Relax, my young one,' he whispered as his hands stroked the surface on the opaque globe. 'I am the winter to your summer, the night to your day. You are but the wind, and I am a nighthawk who rises upon it.'

The words were soothing. Josh felt the man's mind reaching into his own. It was a soft, gentle sensation, as if he were half awake, and yet he could still sense the world around him.

'The line must be true. There is no time for dissembling. I must pierce the skein of your many-coloured mind and follow the river of memory,' the scryer continued in a high sing-song voice.

Josh felt his memories surrender to the questing consciousness and surrendered as the man routed through his past.

Kelly worked quickly, like flicking through a book. He skipped over parts that Josh would have thought important and dwelt on the tiniest of incidents, like a naturalist studying a moth.

He stopped at one early memory, the beach holiday from which Josh had kept the photograph. There was something unusual about the memory, something in the background. He examined it from many angles, but Josh didn't have time to work out what it was before Kelly was off again, digging deeper into his early childhood.

They reached his earliest memory and left his timeline altogether. Josh watched as Kelly moved to his mother and followed her back, through her pregnancy and all the suffering she'd endured during it. He wept as he watched his mother pull herself out of bed every day to go to work, knowing that part of her pain was the undiagnosed MS that would worsen because of him.

'Now to the father,' murmured Kelly.

Back still further into the first days of his conception, when she was a happy young woman, a student at the university with a bright future.

Then darkness.

'No. That is not the way. Things do not wind thus amongst the clockwork trees,' said Kelly, looking up from the glass and staring directly into Josh's eyes.

'Are you a chameleon? Jackanape? Changer of lines? We shall see . . . What doth thy future hold?'

The scryer sat down again and pulled once more at the fabric of Josh's timeline. He separated out the strands of his life and looked into his futures. There were many loops and knots within it, and the scryer became quite frustrated at the number of dead ends and blind alleys with which he had to contend.

Finally, exhausted, he collapsed on to the table and released Josh from his mental control.

'No more! Bring me wine and peppermint!' he demanded, slamming his fist down on the table.

The attendants stepped forward and rotated Josh into an upright position, but didn't remove his bindings. They handed Kelly a large cup of wine and a bowl of sugary white sweets. He popped two straight into his mouth.

'So, seer, what is your verdict? Is he guilty?' asked the founder.

'As guilty as the North Wind,' Kelly said with a hysterical chuckle. The audience laughed, enjoying the sideshow.

'Then innocent?'

'No more so than a virgin's kiss,' the madman replied, amusing the crowd again.

'Then what say you, fool? No more of your riddles.'

'He is the one. The strange attractor, the paradox,' Kelly said, and slowly he put down his wine and got to his knees before Josh.

The audience went deathly silent.

The founder stood up from his chair.

'State your case clearly!'

Kelly got to his feet and adopted the same pose of the founder: his hands on his hips, and his head held high.

'He is of tomorrow, the forbidden country. He is from the future.'

As Kelly spoke, he began to dance a jig, singing a song to himself.

'Please escort our learned colleague to his seat,' the founder ordered the attendants, 'and have the court cleared.'

There were various catcalls and protests from the benches as the crowd was ushered out of the room.

Caitlin walked over to Joshua as the attendants cranked the wheel until he was upright once more. Her face streaked with tears. 'Are you okay?'

'Yeah,' he whispered, 'not so sure about Kelly. He's off his rocker.'

Caitlin laughed. 'He just saved your life, you idiot!'

The founder threw back his hood to reveal the head of an old man with a grey beard and short white hair. His eyes were a vibrant shade of blue and shone with intelligence — Josh found it hard to hold his gaze for more than a few seconds.

The chamber was cleared of onlookers. Only the colonel, Caitlin and her extended family were allowed to remain. Dalton and his mother had to be forcibly ejected after protesting that Josh has somehow fixed the outcome and that Kelly had finally lost his mind completely.

The council of six had split up and gone their separate ways, although Josh did spot one or two of them having a quiet word with each other before disappearing into the exodus.

'Have you any idea what has just transpired?' asked the founder. His voice seemed less threatening now Josh could see his face.

'Not exactly, no.'

The founder's smile broke so suddenly across his face that everyone was taken aback by its appearance.

'Ha. The irony of it all. The Paradox stands before us! This will keep Eddington's department busy for centuries!'

The colonel smiled and patted Josh on the shoulder. 'I knew you were special, boy, but this really is quite outstanding.'

Caitlin turned to Lyra. 'You knew, didn't you?'

'Of course, silly. I wouldn't have done it otherwise,' Lyra said smiling.

'The problem now, of course, is what is to be done with you?' the founder said to himself.

'Well, I believe investiture would be a good place to start — don't you, my lord?' suggested the colonel.

The founder seemed to be lost in thought. 'What? Yes. Of course, we must invest him at once. Notify the dissignator.'

The colonel went off to a speaking tube in the wall and began to shout into it while plugging one finger in his ear.

Caitlin was staring at Josh in a way that was starting to make him uncomfortable.

'Can you please explain what is going on?' Josh asked

her. 'Did he find out who my father is or not? Can someone please get me out of this thing?'

Caitlin looked across at the founder, and he waved his hand as if to invite her to answer the question. Sim stepped forward and unbuckled the straps that held Josh in the frame.

'Kelly tried to find your father — it's standard procedure to review your lineage — but when he followed your time-line he found an anomaly.'

'What kind of anomaly?'

'A paradox loop, a line that goes forward rather than backwards as you would usually expect.'

'So you're saying my father was, is, from the future?'

She nodded. 'Hence the title "Paradox". You shouldn't exist, but you do.'

'And this has never happened before?'

'No, Josh. We have been waiting a very long time for someone like you,' replied the founder.

'But what does that even mean? How does that make me any different to you guys?'

'Since the inception of our Order we have known that time travel beyond the present was a distinct possibility. Something that goes beyond the dynamics of the continuum. Some have tried to deny that a Paradox could exist, but we've always been more open-minded. You were predicted, Joshua — more than a thousand years ago.'

Josh was confused. His head was still pounding from being suspended upside down for so long, and now they were telling him that his father — the imaginary being that he'd spent so many years wondering about as a kid — was from the future. It was a concept that his befuddled mind refused to accept.

Caitlin took his hand and looked into his eyes.

'What the founder is trying to say is that there is a very strong chance you can travel beyond the frontier, into the future.'

'What the —'

'They're ready for you now,' interrupted the colonel. 'Follow me.'

67

INITIATION

A s they walked, Caitlin explained that the initiation was usually a grand affair, steeped in traditional and ceremony. When they entered the Grand Hall, it reminded Josh of a church they'd gone to when they buried his gran — except the mourners weren't dressed like a grand order of wizards.

There were pews on either side of the central aisle, which led up to a raised dais. Walking slowly down the scarlet carpet, Josh saw that the symbol of the snake eating its own tail was emblazoned on banners and columns on both sides of the hall.

The founder led the way, followed by the colonel. Methuselah, Sim and Caitlin stayed beside Josh as the rest of the extended family followed behind.

An old woman stood on the dais dressed in robes that shimmered like the sun on water. In one hand she held a staff, in the other a finely carved wooden case just bigger than a shoebox.

The woman's hair was woven into long dark braids streaked with grey; a golden symbol had been woven into the end of each braid — she reminded Josh of Medusa with her hair of snakes.

The old woman began to tap out time with the end of her staff, and he found his steps matching the beat. Like a metronome, the rhythm of the sound brought order to the proceedings. The audience grew silent and watched as the entourage marched in deference to the beat, making their way slowly towards her.

When he reached her, Josh could see that the top of her staff was crowned with a snake holding a sphere, and that the box cradled against her breasts had a similar mark. Her face was masked by a golden veil, but he could see a dark pair of eyes studying him as he approached.

'I am Moirai, Aisa, Diké — the Goddess of Fate,' she announced dramatically to them all. 'You shall know me as Destiny, as Chaos and Calamity. I am your beginning and your end.'

As one they all stepped away from Josh, leaving him standing alone before the masked goddess.

'Who brings this soul to the continuum?' she asked, waving the staff over his head and bringing it down on his shoulder, forcing him to kneel.

'I do,' answered the colonel, stepping forward to stand beside Josh.

She lifted the staff away from Josh and handed it to an attendant.

'Time is a river. It flows through me like water.'

They all repeated the incantation solemnly.

'I am the navigator, the weaver, the guardian. I shall not shy from the consequences of my actions.'

Again the assembled repeated her words. As they did so, she brought the box up towards Josh's face.

'Behold the engine of the infinite. Within lies your past,

your present and future. Do you pledge them all to the service of the continuum?'

She nodded to Josh as if to prompt him to repeat the words. As he did so, the circular symbol at one end of the box irised slowly open to reveal a dark hole.

The colonel took Josh's right arm and guided his hand into the hole. At first Josh tried to resist, afraid of what might be inside. He guessed it was going to be a snake, but he knew this was some kind of test and that the colonel would never do him harm.

The inside of the box felt unusually cold. As he tentatively spread his fingers in search of the contents, he found that it was much larger than it looked from the outside. A familiar prickling sensation began to spread over his hand and up his arm; his mind began to sense the lines of energy as the darkness reached out of the box and took him.

It was pitch-black; he searched blindly for any point of reference in the formless void that surrounded him. The feeling of solitude and emptiness was overwhelming — isolated from any stimuli, he could feel his senses desperately scavenging for some kind of input.

'Do not be afraid,' said the disembodied voice of the goddess.

Her tone was like a mother calming her child — a deep, soothing, reassuring sound laced with maternal benevolence.

A small glimmer caught his eye and he felt the warmth of something under his hand. He looked down and found that he was touching a small black cube that glowed slightly where his fingers touched its surface. The cube was floating in a dark viscous liquid, like black mercury, in a shallow bowl. The dim light cast out in a small umbra around the bowl, encasing him and the column on which it stood in a sphere of pale blue light.

'Behold the continuum,' explained the voice.

Sparks of light issued from his fingertips spreading out across the surface of the cube. Like embers they glowed and died as they travelled along its sides, their trails igniting symbols and glyphs of ancient equations. Lines of power began to trace between the glowing symbols and as the number of lines multiplied, the lattice seemed to grow and spread outwards until it enveloped him and the space around him.

Suddenly Josh was standing in the middle of an intricate web of lines and symbols that revolved around him like a thousand galaxies.

'The continuum: the culmination of twelve thousand years of work. A model of every branch of history, every correction, and all of the possible futures contained within one beautiful and ever-evolving algorithm.'

As Josh focused on the swirling matrix, he recognised various markers and symbols; he could make out the centuries and the notes, the annotations and formulae that had been tagged to the various branches. Every change, every choice was marked with a series of numeric symbols and references as to who had sanctioned the action — it was a beautiful, intricate structure of infinite scale, it made him wonder what it was all for.

'The continuum must be maintained if humanity is to survive,' the voice of the goddess responded — as if aware of his thoughts.

His eyes were drawn to the clusters of timelines, like knots in the fabric of the lattice. There were key dates: world wars, the fall of empires and major events that attracted the most attention and generated more possibilities. He could see a pattern to their frequency, they were becoming more regular as the timeline approached the present.

The present itself had so many strands converging on it that it looked like a frayed rope end. As he watched in awe, he could see some of the possible futures weaving together into the main trunk while others were discarded, separating and dying off like a dead tree branches.

'Tomorrow can never be known entirely. We who study the past must use it to forge the foundation of a better future.'

He turned slowly round, taking in the size and complexity of the model. There were so many layers; information hid microscopically so that detail was only revealed when you focused on a particular area of it.

He shifted his attention to the earliest part of the timeline, searching for the period in which he and Caitlin had been lost— the Mesolithic. There was no record. The first date, the datum point, was a simple symbol with one line branching out from it. Year zero was only twelve thousand years ago. Josh knew that there was something else before it. As he pushed his consciousness past the date, it expanded, and other symbols appeared.

'Enough!' commanded the voice, and the timelines emanating from the cube contracted and the lights went out.

'Open your eyes,' she whispered.

He could feel her breath on his skin. She was close, and the hand that had been inside the box was now being held by another.

He blinked back the intensity of the light as his eyes acclimatised to the vibrant colours of the real world once more. His arm was still tingling, and he looked down at it to find the snake tattoo now burned into his skin. The goddess released his hand, and he lifted his arm closer to his face, tracing the already healed scar tissue with his fingers. There was no pain, just a fading warmth as if something hot had been lifted from it a few minutes before.

The tattoo was different to Cat's.

In the centre of the circle made by the snake's tail was a small dot, like a tiny island. He turned to Caitlin and showed her the anomaly.

'It is the mark of the one,' she whispered quietly.

The goddess stood before him. The box had disappeared, and she was holding the staff once more. He saw her eyes widen at the symbol on his arm. She went down on one knee and touched her free hand to her forehead

'The continuum has selected a chosen one. May all the paths of time bend before him.'

Josh wanted to laugh, to tell them to stop messing around, but saw in Caitlin's expression that they were all taking this very seriously

'Quite,' said the founder, breaking the reverie. He was obviously finding the over-dramatic performance a little too much. 'Now that all the formalities have been dealt with, I believe there are quite a number of people who will be wanting to talk to you, my boy.'

68

GOLDEN HOUR

L enin was strapped to a hospital bed surrounded by machines. His head had been shaved, and an array of wires were taped to his skull.

Professor Fermi was making the final adjustments to one of the machines and checking the various monitoring devices. This was to be his epiphany, his moment of glory — after so many years of researching he had the proof he needed to demonstrate the potential of his research. A group of very influential people were watching from the observation booth, a mixture of high-ranking officers from the military and various other government departments.

He turned to the large glass window and signalled to one of his assistants to switch on the mic and start the video recording.

'Welcome, ladies and gentleman. Thank you all for coming today.'

He walked over to one of the larger machines, a white ring-like torus with an object suspended in the central field. As he neared, a blue glow began to radiate from the edges of the ring.

'This is a quantum field generator, a research project I have been working on for some time. You will have read in the briefing notes that this is a unique device, similar in power to the Large Hadron Collider, but with a considerably smaller footprint and energy consumption.'

He could see some of his guests were amused by that remark.

'So, the question on your minds is — what can this do for us? I hope you don't mind if I answer that particular concern with a practical demonstration.'

The professor motioned to another of his assistants, and a series of medical diagnostic interfaces appeared on the displays beside him. They were paired to screens in the observation room.

On one of the monitors, the observers watched as a guard walked up to Lenin's bed, took a gun from his jacket and shot Lenin directly in the chest.

The observers seemed unconcerned, and Fermi explained: 'As you can see from the diagnostics, our patient has suffered a severe gunshot wound to the chest, his organs are in the process of shutting down due to blood loss and the prognosis does not look good.'

A remote camera moved over Lenin's body, pausing at the site of the wound. X-ray images overlaid the video footage as the professor continued.

'As you can see, the bullet entered just below the heart, and pierced one of the lungs. The doctors inform me the patient has less than a ten per cent chance of survival, something that under the Injury Survival Scoring system would be deemed as unsurvivable.'

Fermi moved to Lenin's side, pulled back the bedsheets and picked up a device from the tray beside his bed.

'In any medical emergency, time is always seen as critical

factor. Any battlefield surgeon will tell you that the first hour is the most important and can be the difference between life and death. I believe they call it the "Golden Hour"?'

Fermi activated the device and the lights dimmed momentarily as the light from the quantum field generator flared.

'No need to be alarmed — the energy levels contained within the unit are carefully regulated. Now observe the wound closely.'

He ran the handheld device, which resembled a glowing magnifying lens, over Lenin's wounds. As he focused the light on the edges of the flesh, small flickers of energy glistened over them.

'Time doesn't have to be our enemy. By accelerating it in a localised way, we can encourage the body to heal more rapidly.'

The video feed from the camera focused on the wound as it began to close; the skin and tissue knitted together at an incredible rate. Those in the observation room stared in amazement as the wound healed in a matter of minutes.

Lenin's vital signs improved almost instantaneously; both pulse and blood pressure monitors registered a return to normal levels.

'This is just one of the ways quantum distortion could revolutionise our world — troops healed and back on the front line in under an hour — imagine the effect it would have on morale. They would be virtually invincible!'

There was a round of applause from the observers, although Fermi had already turned away from them. He knew that he had just secured the extra funding to make this project a reality.

He powered down the quantum field generator. Josh's

watch sat floating in the middle of the torus. He carefully plucked it from the magnetic fields that were holding it in place and put it in his pocket.

Lenin groaned as the anaesthetic began to wear off. Fermi motioned to the medics to attend to him. He was still comatose, but his signs were stable. They pulled out the bed from the wall and wheeled it into the corridor and down to a waiting ambulance.

Fermi turned back to his audience. 'Now, I believe drinks are being served in the executive suite. If you would be so kind as to meet me there, we can discuss terms.'

69

RETIREMENT

Josh walked into the kitchen and put the basket of freshly picked vegetables on the worktop. They were still caked in mud. He took each one and washed the dirt off under the tap, scrubbing at their surface until they were shiny.

The colonel had shown him the best years from which to harvest: the farms and allotments of the 11.900s were his particular favourites. There was a different pattern to life back before the First World War. It was hard to describe — there was a sense of innocence back in that era. The people he met there were almost like children. They were kind and trusting, and their doors were never locked — mainly because they had nothing worth stealing. Josh had spent days wandering through the countryside of Kent in 11.902 without any idea of where he was going, and had been overwhelmed by the kindness and hospitality of the people that he met.

They had no comprehension of what was happening beyond their village, no television or internet to show them the terrible things that war could do — nor did they seem to care. It was a simple way of life, slow-paced and stress-free.

There was a shout from the study and Josh walked in to find his mother and the colonel in some kind of deadlock. The colonel was clutching a small stack of newspapers tightly to his chest, while his mother was wearing an apron and a pair of rubber gloves and was wielding a large black rubbish sack.

'Mrs Jones, I must insist that you leave my things as you found them!'

His mum looked well. She'd spent the last two weeks in the room next to his. He'd requisitioned some of Marie Antoinette's bedroom furniture from the Antiquarians. It was good to think of her sleeping in a bed made for a queen.

Once Josh had convinced her that the house came with his new job and that she would never have to go back to the flat or her sister's, her recovery seemed to accelerate — especially after he showed her the garden.

Each morning he would bring her breakfast in bed and find her staring out of the window, planning what she was going to plant and where.

As soon as Dr Crooke had declared her well enough to get out of bed and resume 'light duties', she'd put her plans into action — like a woman possessed.

'Madam, unhand me!' cried the colonel as his mother tried to wrestle something from under his arm.

Josh couldn't help but smile. He'd seen the man fight against the most formidable enemies, go toe-to-toe with Nazi soldiers and Irish bomb-makers, but he'd never seen him look as scared as he did now. His mother was a force to be reckoned with once she got an idea in her head, and the poor man was about to lose any hope of retaining his old bachelor lifestyle.

In his mother's eyes, the house was a tip, an anathema of all things tidy and organised. Josh knew that there was a system to the colonel's storage, but to an outsider it bore all the hallmarks of a kleptomaniac or a compulsive hoarder.

'Now, now, Mr Westinghouse, we both know that these old papers are a playground for mice and beetles. Won't do to have them cluttering up the house now, will it?' his mother said as if talking to a small child.

She wrenched one edition out from his grip, and it tore slightly as it went.

'Look at this one. It's from 1834 - what an earth could you possibly want with something that old?'

The colonel looked pleadingly at Josh for some kind of support, they obviously couldn't tell her the truth, but Josh could see that the old man was having trouble coming up with another reasonable alternative.

'He used to work for the papers, Mum,' intervened Josh, much to the colonel's relief. 'They're like a hobby for Mr Westinghouse. They sell for quite a lot, especially the old ones.'

Josh had gone with a two-pronged approach: giving the colonel a profession in which she would have no real interest, and the vaguest hint that the thing she was trying to throw away might have some value.

'Well they can't stay up here. It's unhygienic,' she replied, 'and they're taking up so much space.' She went back out into the hall and disappeared through the basement door.

The colonel slumped into one of the chairs, which were apparently leather, something Josh had not known until his mother had tidied the study the day before.

'This isn't going to work,' the colonel sighed.

Josh nodded. He knew it was unlikely the two of them were going to get along. They were too set in their ways to change, and they had mutually incompatible lifestyles.

'Give her a minute, she's up to something.'

The colonel smiled. 'While I have you to myself, I've been meaning to speak to you about taking a sabbatical.'

'Do we get holidays? I never checked the small print on the job description.'

The colonel laughed.

'Kind of a holiday — one with no end date. The Order has a policy of allowing old dogs like me to go off-road at the end of their service. Some call it the "long walk". I get to study some of the more remoter parts of time and add to the corpus, while they get rid of an old interfering fart to make way for new blood — it's all part of the cycle.' He pointed at the tattoo on Josh's arm.

'Ah. Cool. Where were you thinking of going?' Josh asked, hoping that it meant he wouldn't need to move his mother out after all.

'More a case of "when" actually. I was thinking more like a sojourn around the Mesolithic. I have always wanted to see the Holocene spring.'

Josh remembered the view from the cave and the smell of Caitlin in the furs beside him. He could relate to the old man's desire to go somewhere uncomplicated, untainted, and just chill out.

'How long for?'

'No idea — until I get bored or something else takes my fancy. Don't worry, you can always come visit. I've been told you're a bit of an expert yourself in that era.'

They could both hear his mother crashing around downstairs. 'Do you think they would let Mum and me stay here for a while?'

'Of course, this is your home now. There are going to be a lot of changes in your life. The Order has been waiting for you for a thousand years. The Determinists will want to disprove your existence; others will see you as some kind of Messiah. Whatever happens next, you must always remember you have a place here, somewhere where you can be yourself, not what they want you to be.

'Are you sure you don't want to hang around and remind me?'

The colonel thought for a moment, as if weighing up the offer, then shook his head. 'No, I'm afraid you have outgrown me. I would just be holding you back. You have to find your own way.'

Josh's mother reappeared with a large crate and began to transfer newspapers from the shelves into it. 'There's plenty of room downstairs for your archive,' she smiled. 'I take it you wish them kept in chronological order?'

'Yes, thank you, Mrs Jones,' the colonel replied.

'So when are you going?' Josh asked.

'Soon, but first I have some things to attend to,' he said, watching Josh's mother carefully out of the corner of one eye. 'The council is still in something of a mess after your inquisition and the founder wants me to assist him with some of the more dissident members. Bring them into line, as it were — bloody politics, I hate it.'

The colonel spent the new few weeks coming and going from the house, appearing at random hours of the night with large, old trunks and packing various mementoes carefully inside them. Josh helped him sometimes, and they would talk about the adventures that had been connected to each of them.

ANDREW HASTIE

It was a time for reflection — as the colonel called it. The accumulated mementoes of more than ten lifetimes had to be sorted, categorised and stored by a team of Antiquarians. Josh's mother was soon organising that, and more than one mentioned to Josh how useful it would be to have her look at the Great Library, but he reminded them she was still a sick woman, even if her MS seemed to be in total remission.

Josh had begun to see another side to the colonel, and considered asking about the woman and the child he'd seen in his timeline, but there was never a right time and the colonel seemed distracted by too many other things. The Council had returned to some semblance of normality, but the colonel still seemed concerned with something that he wouldn't discuss.

The day came too soon when the curiosities room was cleared, and the last of his personal belongings were being wheeled out by a team of Antiquarians disguised as removal men, a typical cover for them apparently. He and the colonel sat in the kitchen while Josh's mother was out weeding in the garden.

'You're not going to the Mesolithic, really, are you?' Josh asked.

The colonel scratched his beard. 'I might do.'

'Caitlin reckons you're going after the fates. Did you ever find out who made the Greek computer?'

'Who made it, yes, but not who gave them the design. I do have a new lead to follow, and, no, I can't take you with me.'

Josh smiled. 'She said you'd say that.'

The colonel stood up and put his cup in the sink, and the cat jumped up on to the worktop to scavenge any last dregs of tea.

'Do you remember the day I broke in?' Josh asked.

'You mean the day I left the door open?' the colonel corrected him, stroking the cat.

'Do you ever wonder what would have happened if I hadn't?'

The colonel laughed. 'There were many times when you didn't.'

Josh looked a little stunned. 'You mean —'

The colonel silenced him with a raised finger. Looking at him with deep, kind eyes he sighed. 'Sometimes fate needs a helping hand.'

He took out the small gear wheel he had removed from the analog computer on the ship.

'I'll miss you, Joshua Jones. Take care of the cat.'

Then, with a wink, he disappeared.

70

PARADOX

The Copernicans spent the next two months investigating every corner of Josh's life. There wasn't a secret moment left that hadn't been documented in triplicate and stored on the punched cards that their strange little typewriters produced. A senior investigator called Xavier Lusive had spent an entire week trying to prove that Josh was some kind of spy or infiltrator from the Fatalists, which was the first time he'd heard a member of the Order talk about them without laughing — he'd gone away empty handed. There was no proof and no amount of interrogation by his seers made any difference.

Josh had met every senior member of the High Council — including the haughty Madame Bullmedrin of the Antiquarians, Paelor Batrass of the Scriptorians and the larger than life character of Master Aqueous of the Draconians. Each of them had taken great pains to explain how they were privileged to make his acquaintance and that they would be truly grateful if he would join their guild — he accepted their offers of dinner and thoroughly enjoyed the extravagant banquets they threw in his honour, but never committed to any of them. He was finding it hard not to enjoy his new celebrity status.

Caitlin and Sim had stayed beside him throughout all of the investigations. Cat was always ready to bring him back down to earth whenever he began to believe his own hype and Sim was on standby when she had one of her moods and stormed off.

They spent many nights in The Flask, talking about their adventures and especially the look on Dalton's face when Kelly had revealed the truth about Josh in the court. No one had seen or heard from the Eckharts since that day — the rumour was that they'd gone back to their family castle back in the Eleventh and that Dalton was at some kind of special seer rehab in Bedlam.

Josh didn't care — he was having far too much fun. As he sat watching Sim re-enacting the court scene for the others, pulling ridiculous faces for their great amusement, he wondered what his life would have been like if he had never broken into the colonel's house that day. There'd been a part of him that wanted to go into his timeline and look at the paths not travelled, but Caitlin had told him that only led to depression, or madness in some extreme cases. She reminded him of the cries they'd heard in Bedlam — the sound of people grieving for lives that they never had.

He thought about his old friends — Shags, Benny, Dennis, and Lilz — they would be totally freaked out if they could see him now. There was a rule about leaving your old life behind and that had made him sad for a while. He knew that they'd all be happy for him — they'd always been able to see the potential in him even when he couldn't.

He spent a lot of time thinking about Gossy, of the life he'd never got to live. The children that never were — it had been a hard choice; if he went back and changed it once more, he wasn't sure what he would have done differently. Caitlin had explained to him how they'd gone back and altered his timeline, that Gossy had originally died in the car crash when they were twelve.

Josh had no memory of that version of events — one of the drawbacks of editing your own life apparently — but she'd told him how much Lenin had used it against him, like a debt that could never be repaid. He'd given Gossy another ten years, not that much in the scheme of things, but the defect in his heart would always have taken him in the end, and he knew that Gossy had at least lived those years to the full.

As for Lenin, he had totally vanished after the fight in the school. The Ghost Squad fragmented into two rival gangs that went back to hustling cars and other small-time stuff. It seemed that without the ambition of their leader there was no real desire to hit the big time. Josh decided not to go looking for him. As far as he was concerned, Lenin may as well be dead. Whatever had bound the two of them together disappeared when Lenin had shot his mother — that chapter of his life was finally over.

Now Josh had a new gang, one that he had chosen to be part of. He had spent his entire life fighting against a system that didn't seem to want to include him. He'd been deemed a misfit, a rebel; he was just trying to understand what his role was in this life, and now finally he had some idea of what it might be. Finally he had part of an answer to the one question that had haunted his life — although he had little more than the slimmest of leads. He wasn't sure how it was going to play out yet, but he knew in his heart that this was the beginning and maybe with the help of the Grand Seer, he would finally be able to find out who his father was.

71

ART OF WAR

[Boju, Chu. Date: 9.494]

T he battle was over a mile away, at the bottom of the
valley that folded into the hills around them. It was a
beautiful spot and would have been an idyllic place for a
picnic if it hadn't been for the carnage that played out across
the fields below them.

The war was between two rival kingdoms Wu and Chu,
the latter had taken heavy casualties, mainly due to the
clever strategies of the Wu Commander in Chief — Sun Tzu
the most celebrated Chinese general of the sixth century
BC. Caitlin was in her element, taking great pleasure in
pointing out every detail of the Wu battle plan while
drinking wine and picking at the food he'd laid out.

Josh had spent the last two weeks planning this day. He
wanted it to be more than perfect. Sim had helped with the
venue — Josh had remembered his very first conversation
with Caitlin about *The Art of War* and how she'd been
studying it at university before he'd crashed into her life.
Sim had found him the relevant co-ordinates and helped

plan out the meal. He was fast becoming one of Josh's favourite people. He'd never had a brother, but Sim had all the qualities he imagined one should have.

As he sat next to Caitlin in the long grass, he searched for the right words to say how beautiful she looked. Her auburn hair was radiant, and her smooth, perfect skin glowed in the sunlight. He watched her lips move, not hearing a word she said, as she commentated on every manoeuvre of the two armies below. She was always so passionate about everything she did; he loved the way she cared so deeply about everything. There'd been so many boring days during the months that followed his investiture, so many questions, so many tests. She had stayed by him throughout every single one, always the first to greet him when he was released, always the last to leave him when he went to bed — leaving that awkward silence where he couldn't find the right way to ask her to stay.

She was the only thing that got him through that incessant and relentless inquisition.

When he'd finally proven to them that he had no idea how to jump into the future they'd lost interest in him. It had been something of a disappointment to many of the upper echelons of the Order. The invitations to dinner dried up and died out as various rumours developed about his lack of success. Even Dalton finally reappeared from obscurity to disseminate spurious nonsense about Josh being a false prophet. But no one really took him seriously, and life finally returned to a kind of normal.

So Josh had decided to thank her, to do something special to show her how much he appreciated her.

How much he loved her.

It was an unspoken thing between them, but he was hoping she felt the same. He'd never really had a long-term girlfriend; there'd never been enough time to develop that kind of relationship. Not with a sick mother and a drug dealer busting his ass — or so he told himself. If he were being really honest, he'd never really put himself out there. Most of the girls he'd been with were nothing more than simple one-night stands with no complications. Josh didn't really want to believe he needed anyone else, it was far easier to keep it simple, but it was also lonely, and no matter how he tried to convince himself he was better off alone, he couldn't imagine his life without her in it.

He touched the wooden box that he'd kept hidden, knowing that she would ask what it was the moment she saw it. This was his surprise.

Caitlin turned back towards him and picked one of the spring rolls from the bowl and ate it whole.

'These are delicious,' she said with a mouth full of beansprouts.

'Best Chinese take-out ever,' he joked.

She smiled at him with her eyes, and he lost himself in the moment.

'What's this all in aid of anyway? Not that I'm not really grateful — I have always been meaning to visit the Battle of Boju. Just doesn't seem your kind of thing?'

Josh took out the slim wooden box and handed it to her. 'I wanted to say thank you.'

Caitlin took the box and turned it over to read the Chinese inscriptions along the sides.

'If you know both yourself and your enemy, you can win numerous battles without jeopardy.' Her eyes widened as she translated aloud.

'*Art of War*, chapter fourteen,' smiled Josh, watching her take out the bamboo book.

'The lost chapter!' gasped Caitlin. She held it like it was

made of crystal, carefully laying the entire book of jointed bamboo slats out on the picnic blanket.

'How did you know?' she asked, without taking her eyes off of the wooden treasure.

'You told me back in the library — don't you remember?'

'Yes, but I didn't think you were paying attention to what I was saying,' she answered with a smile.

Josh grinned. 'I heard every word.'

'Thank you! This is amazing. Where did you get it?'

'I had some help. It wasn't easy.'

She rolled it back up and placed it back in the box.

'You don't do anything by halves, do you,' she murmured, moving a little closer.

'Neither do you. Remember when we were back in the cave?'

'When we were freezing to death, you mean?' she said, flushing a little.

'So in court you said we ended up together — that we had a family?'

'Ah, you want me to tell you what happened?' she asked, moving closer to him so her arm brushed against his.

Josh could smell the sun on her skin as she came nearer — a mixture of exotic scents that set his senses on fire.

'No,' he answered, putting his arm around her, 'I want you to show me.'

Her arms were round his neck.

'About time, Joshua Jones. I was starting to think you'd never ask,' she said breathlessly.

Josh closed his eyes as he felt her lips touch his. He could feel her body pressing against him, the electricity between them as they entwined. Time seemed to stand still as they fell back into the grass.

Then there was nothing.

He was holding thin air.

He could still feel the warmth of where Caitlin had lain on the flattened ground seconds before, but she had simply vanished.

Something had gone very wrong. An icy dread formed in the pit of his stomach as Josh frantically searched for any trace of her existence in the blades of grass. His mind caught vague echoes of Caitlin in the natural fractal structures of their timelines, but there was nothing more than a fleeting glimpse, nothing he could use. He pounded the ground with his fists, tearing out clumps of long grass in frustration. He couldn't explain it, but somehow he could sense that the continuum had just been radically altered; the past had been disrupted, and Caitlin had been swept away in the aftermath.

To be continued...

ALSO BY ANDREW HASTIE

The adventure continues in ...

Buy now on amazon

ABOUT THE AUTHOR

For more information about The Infinity Engines series and other Here Be Dragons books please visit: www. infinityengines.com

Please don't forget to leave a review!
Thank you!
Andy x

ACKNOWLEDGMENTS

Thanks to my wonderful family. Karen, you are truly amazing. Aimée and Ellie, I am so proud of you girls. I am so grateful for your support and encouragement throughout the last two years.

To Sam, who was not only my editor but also someone that believed that I could do it. If this is half as good as you think it is — I will be a very happy man, thank you.

To all those who read it along the way: Aaron, Jez, Andrew, Mark, Mish, Mike, Lesley, and the many others who had to listen to me drone on about it, thanks for putting up with my obsession.

To the 8:34am to Waterloo, without your boring journey this story may never have got told.

Finally, to my parents, Mum and Dad, you gave me everything I could ever wish for, encouragement and belief in my creativity, and a childhood filled with adventure, as well as a generous helping of Blake's 7, Star Trek and Dr Who...